NIGHT LAUNCH

Senator Jake Garn
and Stephen Paul Cohen

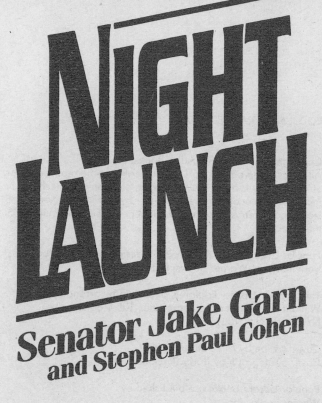

POPULAR LIBRARY

An Imprint of Warner Books, Inc.

A Warner Communications Company

This Popular Library Edition is published by arrangement with
William Morrow and Company, Inc., 105 Madison Ave.,
New York, N.Y. 10016

Cover design by Mike Stromberg
Cover photograph by Barry Blackman

Popular Library books are published by
Warner Books, Inc.
666 Fifth Avenue
New York, N.Y. 10103

W A Warner Communications Company

Printed in the United States of America

First Popular Library Printing: March, 1990

10 9 8 7 6 5 4 3 2 1

SOMEONE ON BOARD
THE *DISCOVERY*
IS A PSYCHOPATHIC CRIMINAL
AND A PROFESSIONAL TERRORIST.

·

JOEY WELLS: the handsome Texas pilot whose reckless exploits earned him the nickname "Cowboy." His unpredictable style and his romantic entanglements have the secret services of two superpowers worried that he's a security risk...

AELITA ZAKHAROV: she acquired her space credentials in the tough Soviet cosmonaut program. But her fighter-pilot husband died in the unpopular Afghanistan war, and her outspoken opposition to certain Soviet policies has made her suspect in certain quarters...

CONRAD WILLIAMS: a top-flight NASA hotshot and air force test pilot. On the surface, he's the most even-tempered crewman on the shuttle. But some say Connie got the job as mission commander for political reasons: he's the mission's only black...

ALEX VONBERGER: the East German payload specialist who's never been in space before. He's hungry to prove himself to his superiors—but his weakness for long-limbed Texas beauties will be the ruin of his professional career...

GEORGE EVANS: the British scientist whose RAF experience made him the perfect political choice to cement international relations. But despite his unflappable good cheer, nobody really seems to know anything about him...

VLADIMIR TURNOV: he holds a world-record total of fifteen months in space. He has more trouble adjusting to gravity than to weightlessness. If anyone is equipped for combat in free-fall, it's Turnov...

▼▼▼▼▼▼▼▼▼

"Night Launch has the feel of reality....
There are many surprises in this story."

—Orlando Sentinel

ALSO BY STEPHEN PAUL COHEN

■

HEARTLESS
ISLAND OF STEEL

This book is dedicated to all of the people who work to make our nation's space program a success. Most of them are unsung heroes, whose efforts are quietly realized in laboratories, offices, control rooms, training centers, machine shops, and specialized assembly facilities throughout the NASA organization. Without all their efforts, no launch would ever take place, no mission would be accomplished, and this nation would be earth-bound.

I also feel a personal sense of dedication to my fellow crew members who flew aboard *Discovery*, Mission 51-D, April 12–19, 1985:

Colonel Karol "Bo" Bobko, Commander
Captain Don Williams, Pilot
Dave Briggs, Mission Specialist
Rhea Seddon, M.D., Mission Specialist
Jeff Hoffman, Ph.D, Mission Specialist
Charlie Walker, Payload Specialist

These are the six wonderful, competent, capable, and dedicated people with whom I shared the most incredible experience of my life. I grew to know and respect and feel as close to them as members of my own family, and they have truly shaped the rest of my life.

—Jake Garn, Payload Specialist
#2, Mission 51-D

Acknowledgments

I have often said that until I began training for my space flight I never really had a true appreciation for how much goes into the preparation for a launch and a shuttle mission, or how many people play such critical roles in that process.

I have now learned that much the same can be said about the preparation of a book for publication. I must express my appreciation to my co-author, Stephen Cohen, whose imagination and writing skills brought together a plot and story line that enabled me to express some deeply held ideas and beliefs about the space program. I know the many hours I spend reviewing manuscripts and making suggested revisions and technical corrections were undoubtedly exceeded by his efforts to produce the first draft. Before he could do that, he spent a great deal of time reading materials I had written about my space-flight experience, reviewing videotapes of the crew training, the flight itself, and speeches and press conferences, and going over notes of our lengthy conversations on the subject. His skill as a wordsmith has made this book one I am proud to have co-authored with him.

My thanks go as well to others who helped assure accuracy and continuity, especially in the technical details of space flight, augmenting my own experience and recollections with their technical expertise. Special thanks go to friends who took their own time to review the manuscript and offer suggestions.

As with any book, the list of names could fill pages. It is my sincere hope that all who assisted feel that the finished product justifies their personal, individual efforts.

PART I

THE PF
FLYERS

There is thus no end to the life, education, and improvement of mankind. Man will progress forever. And if this be so, he must surely achieve immortality.

—Konstantin Tsiolkovsky

1

THE
YELLOW
DOOR

ALEX Vonberger waited, squatting gently in the dark. The rain had stopped and a yellow mist was gathering in eccentric swirls underneath the streetlights. Camino Drive was a long, curving street that served primarily as a driveway for the Camino Village Apartments. At this time of night, an hour could go by without a car, but right now a man was out there walking his dog. It was impossible to make out the man's facial features, but he appeared to be an older man, and smallish. On the other side of the drive from the apartments was a giant field of dead grass. But tonight Vonberger couldn't see the field. He could see Camino Drive, the man and his dog, and the outlines of the far curb, but then his vision ended in a wall of blackness. And from beyond the blackness came the insistent rhythm of the screaming crickets.

The old man and the dog moved under one of the streetlights and Vonberger studied them more carefully. The man was wrapped in a big coat that didn't seem to fit right: One

side was bigger than the other. Vonberger laughed to himself.
It was a classic mistake of not getting the buttons lined up
right. The man had a scarf twisted several times around his
neck, with one end sticking up in the air right behind his left
ear, and the other tucked away somewhere inside the coat.
There was no hat. You could almost hear his wife screaming
after him to wear a hat, but he didn't really need one. After
all, he was just out walking the dog.

But the best part of his outfit was his sneakers. Men reach
a certain age where they feel that it is no longer socially
acceptable to wear sneakers unless they are on the tennis
court. But that doesn't mean they don't *like* sneakers. And
there's something deliciously rebellious and rejuvenating
about making a clandestine use of the comfortable old things
to take the dog out for a late-night walk. Yes, the man's
outfit was perfect for walking a dog.

The dog itself was a medium-sized mutt with short hair
and a long snout. He was making an all-out effort to sniff
everything in sight, and to raise his leg at every tree and bush
he could find. He pulled on his chain energetically.

The man was perfect and the dog was perfect, but together
they were all wrong.

Old men had old dogs. It was a truism that could not be
overlooked. Okay, so maybe his old dog died and he bought
a replacement. A possible explanation. But, the KGB never
liked anything that had to be explained. Either it worked, or
it didn't, and this guy and his dog didn't work. The KGB
would have used an old dog. Vonberger felt sure of it.

He pressed himself up against the side of the building,
making full use of the bushes for cover. Just because the guy
wasn't KGB didn't mean Vonberger's troubles were over.
Dressler had been nailed by a drunk, off-duty Soviet cop.
Who knew what kind of evils could be lurking here in Houston, Texas. This guy could be some kind of off-duty cop. Or
perhaps he was one of those civilian crime watchers that
Vonberger had heard about. Maybe he carried a gun. Or a

walkie-talkie to the police! For all Vonberger knew, the man could be a murderer!

Vonberger felt a drop of cold sweat run down his back between his shoulder blades, and he thought about the night Johann Dressler had been killed at the Iranian border. In the darkness he could practically see Dressler in his government-issued work boots, squatting in the bushes. Had he been listening to crickets? Could he smell the cold salty air of the Caspian Sea? Why had he waited so long? By the time Dressler was found by the Soviets he should have been sixty miles into Iran. And later Vonberger learned from Hans that the drunken Soviet policeman who had found Dressler was off duty and had literally tripped over Dressler in the dark while looking for a place to urinate. Maybe Dressler had lost his cool.

The dog went into his stoop and the man held the chain and looked off into the black void of screaming crickets. Maybe the guy was KGB. Maybe he wasn't. It didn't really matter. Vonberger wasn't supposed to know anything about the KGB. Vonberger was just an adventurous East German cosmonaut sneaking out of his apartment to get a drink, mix with the locals, and maybe find some healthy-looking cowgirl who had a bed that was too big for her. That was the only thing that Vonberger was supposed to have on his mind tonight.

The dog was finished but he had a few other things he felt needed sniffing. The old man pulled on the leash, and just over the roar of the crickets, Vonberger heard the man's voice crack in the darkness. "Come on, Jasper! Let's go!" Vonberger watched them walk back down Camino Drive and around the corner of the building.

The street was empty. There were no cars. It was quiet enough to make anyone who didn't know anything about the KGB think it was all clear. So Vonberger stood up and stepped quickly out from the bushes. Under a streetlight on Camino Drive he inspected his new cowboy boots for mud, and then he checked to see if he had gotten his favorite jeans dirty. At last he checked the burning feeling on the inside of his left forearm, where he had scraped himself on the brick wall, climbing out of his window. It wasn't bleeding, but it was a little scraped up. He rolled down the sleeves of his Ralph Lauren shirt to cover it, and then walked quietly down Camino Drive.

In early December, Alex Vonberger had received official notice from his government that the Soviet Union had selected him to join their team in the Peace Flight Program with the United States. Vonberger had immediately told Hans of his selection, and Hans had arranged for Vonberger to travel to Dresden for a secret meeting with Das Syndikat. They had given Vonberger simple instructions on how he was to make contact with their American branch, but had given him no indication of what they wanted him to do. Vonberger knew that operating within the United States would be risky, but he trusted Das Syndikat, and he followed his instructions to the letter.

For the first three weeks in Houston, Vonberger had played his part as a dutiful and patriotic member of the Soviet team. He eagerly trained with the rest of the Soviet team, intent upon learning everything there was to know. He had participated in all of the social and political events. There had been no snooping about. No secret meetings. No stealing of keys. Nothing.

And then one night he had gone back to his Camino Village apartment after dinner and waited until the rest of the Soviet team had all filed back to their own apartments. By ten-thirty he had put on a fresh shirt, and was quietly backing out of his door, being sure to close it ever so quietly. He stepped lightly as he passed the door of Andrei Kulikov, the Soviet liaison officer, and noticed, for the record, that Kulikov's lights were out. Then he made his way down the stairs and out to Camino Drive. From there it was a ten-minute walk to Jason's, a country and western bar where the cowboys all wore big hats and big belt buckles and everyone danced around in a little circle on the dance floor. Not much happens at Jason's on Tuesday nights, so Vonberger had a few beers, Becks of course, and went back up to his apartment. A harmless little visit to the local watering hole.

Vonberger would never know how Andrei Kulikov had found out about his adventure, though it didn't really matter. At ten o'clock the next morning he was called into Kulikov's office and screamed at for half an hour. Vonberger was a representative of the East German and Soviet peoples. As a representative it was not fitting for him to be seen drinking and womanizing at all hours of the night. The Americans might allow their astronauts to participate in such corruption, but Kulikov would not stand for it from his cosmonauts. And all the time, standing at attention and gritting his teeth and listening to that slimy Soviet bastard, all Vonberger could think about was all the years he had put in to being a pilot and a cosmonaut, and he hoped that whatever Das Syndikat had planned for him would make all this trouble worthwhile. And, for the next week and a half, Vonberger again played the part of the good little East German cosmonaut.

Tonight Vonberger had sneaked out of the window from the living room of his apartment, as if he could outwit Andrei Kulikov, and as if there was no such thing as the KGB. When he got to Jason's, it was crowded, and like the good thirsty and horny cosmonaut he was supposed to be, he drank beer. Lots of beer. Then, as would be expected, he tried to meet American women. Three of them to be exact. Two of them turned him down flat. The third, some flimsy little redhead, actually seemed to take a liking to him and he finally had to resort to vague insults to make her lose interest.

And somewhere in the bar there was a KGB agent, although it would be impossible to pick him out. Vonberger tried anyway, just for the fun of it. Acting was always more fun when you knew who your audience was. Then you could always do little things to mess them up, like sit right next to them and start talking to them. Or spill a beer in their lap. Something graceful. It would have to be one of the cowboys who looked totally at ease and totally in place, like one of the two in the far corner checking out the dance floor. No, too obvious. Maybe the one at the other end of the bar, talking to the bartender like they were old friends. Anyway, whoever he was, he would have seen it all. And based on Vonberger's actions they could draw only one of two conclusions: Either Vonberger was just a lonely and horny cosmonaut, out looking to get laid, or Vonberger was an amateur spy, who had neither an ounce of precaution nor a smidgeon of talent.

And then there was the bonus, the one thing that neither Vonberger nor Das Syndikat could have possibly planned. Joey Wells, the American astronaut whom everyone called "Cowboy," showed up. There he was, at the bar at Jason's drinking a beer and flirting with the women. It was more than Vonberger could have asked for, and it was too good to leave alone.

Joey Wells had a boyish face and big dimples in his cheeks and he let loose one of his crooked laughs when he saw Vonberger. "Hey, Alex Vonberger," he said, in his pathetic imitation of Vonberger's accent. "How is my favorite little commie-naut? Heh?"

"Hello, Cowboy," Vonberger laughed. "It is good to drink a beer again."

"Yeah, I'll bet it is," Joey Wells said, back in his slow Texas drawl. "Hey, Alex, man. Somebody told me that Kulikov chewed you out for coming down here last week."

Vonberger suddenly felt worried. "What does that mean? 'Chewed me out'?"

Joey Wells laughed some more. "You know. Yelled at you. Gave you hell. Read you the damned riot act!"

And Vonberger felt himself relax. "Cowboy, do me a favor, please?" Vonberger leaned closer and spoke softly in Joey Wells's ear. "Don't tell anybody you saw me here tonight. Please? I think if Kulikov finds out about this he will kill me for certain."

Joey Wells's eyes seemed clear and he smiled. "Don't you worry about a thing, old boy. Kulikov isn't Cool Enough."

And they both laughed and Joey Wells bought Vonberger another beer, and Vonberger bought one for Joey Wells, and pretty soon they were comparing notes on the women. Vonberger knew that by noon tomorrow, all of NASA would know that Vonberger had been out at Jason's, drinking beer and trying to meet American women.

Everything was going perfectly. Vonberger knew that he was doing everything just right and, yet, he was worried. He thought of poor Dressler, gunned down at the Iranian border. He had no doubts in Das Syndikat, but he knew that no matter how well things were planned, something could always go wrong. And so Vonberger felt a shudder of relief when he looked up at fifteen minutes to midnight and saw *das Mädchen*, the girl. She came stumbling in the door, wearing a red blouse and a denim skirt, and only after Vonberger had taken another sip of beer and calmed himself down, did he realize how beautiful she was.

He leaned against the bar with his Becks in his hand and watched her and her girlfriend flash some identification at the door, pay the cover charge, and then giggle with each other over something so private and juicy that men could dream about it. They came down the bar in his direction and sat about ten feet away. They hadn't even seen him.

Vonberger swung around to check her out. She had blond hair down to her shoulders, wavy but not curly, and her face was one of those simple pretty American faces, nothing severe or unhealthy, just big blue eyes and a delicious-looking mouth. And the body! Those beautiful shoulders that stayed pinned back. It was all a question of posture. When they kept their shoulders back, they looked taller, and their chests looked better. She had it down. And good long legs sticking out from under her skirt. *Wunderbar!*

The only problem was her girlfriend. Nobody had said anything about a girlfriend. Maybe the girlfriend was a cover. Or maybe she was part of the setup. Hell, what did it matter? At fifteen minutes to midnight she came stumbling into Jason's wearing a red blouse, and Vonberger, all along, had followed a plan that would make him ready for her, and only now did he appreciate the planning. Das Syndikat had done it again! *Das Mädchen* was beautiful!

Vonberger drank more beer and watched some local cowboy move in on the two women. The girlfriend was the same type as the one in the red blouse, only plainer. Somehow she just didn't have the same spark. It didn't look like the local cared which one he got though. His hands rested on the back of each of their chairs, and his shoulders were centered, his head turning easily back and forth, from one to the other. Vonberger couldn't hear the whole conversation. He caught the wave of a hand, and something about "my friend's husband," and suddenly it was all over. Just like that. God, she was good, and now it was Vonberger's turn.

He shuffled down and put his elbows on the bar, and then leaned forward on his elbows. She had her back to him, and was talking to her girlfriend. He leaned forward even more, almost as if he was trying to lie down on the bar.

The girlfriend saw him first and her reaction made the one in red turn around. She looked over at him and then quickly looked away. She'd have been shown pictures of him. She knew it was he. But she wasn't interested. She went back to her conversation with her girlfriend. *Wunderbar!* There was nothing more exciting than a well-played game, when you knew from the start that you were going to win.

"Excuse me," he said, still leaning over on his elbows, trying to smile. A vague feeling came over him that they had stopped the music so everyone could watch, and he became self-conscious of his accent. "Can I buy you two young ladies a drink?"

She turned and looked at him again: checking him out. Anybody could see she was checking him out. What an actress! Vonberger almost thought she was going to turn him down. "Sure. I'd like a vodka and Seven-Up."

Vodka and 7-Up! Das Syndikat, you're so good to me! Keep up the small talk. Smile at her. Check her out. Look at those legs! Oh, how can I be so lucky. Out of the corner of his eye, Vonberger looked for Joey Wells. Come on, Cowboy, look at this. Look what I got. Here's a story for you to spread around NASA. And KGB man, whoever, and wherever you are. Look at me! I got me a real live cowgirl.

Her name was Laura Gold and she worked at the hamburger place down the road, called Fuddruckers. They laughed about the name even though it was already an old joke. Her girlfriend's name was Anita and she worked at Fuddruckers too. Laura seemed drunk, but she didn't drink a lot. She took a strong liking to Vonberger, and soon had her thumb slipped in his belt loop. She was completely natural. Just a drunk horny Texas girl falling in love with an astronaut with a German accent. Vonberger played along, all the time thinking to himself, she's just beautiful. Where did they ever find her?

Laura was slurring her words when she told him that she had to give Anita a ride home, but she pulled Vonberger closer and whispered in his ear. "Come with us."

She slipped her arm around him and they followed Anita toward the door. Vonberger turned and found Joey Wells in the far corner and he waved. Joey Wells was laughing and he lifted his beer in a toast to Vonberger, and then Vonberger led Laura Gold out into the parking lot. So long, Cowboy, he thought. Come on, KGB. She stopped him in the middle of the parking lot and stuck her tongue in his mouth. Right there in the parking lot! Then they went to her car. He managed to pull his six-foot-two hulking frame into the backseat and Anita got in the front. They all laughed a lot as they drove Anita home to some little house in a development. Maybe she did have a husband. Maybe she had no idea what was going on. How brilliant: a completely innocent cover. When Anita got out of the car, Vonberger moved to the front seat. It was a little Pinto with bucket seats and he had to move the seat back to get his legs in. Then he closed the door, and suddenly Laura was attacking him. Right there in Anita's driveway!

Her mouth was warm and wet and she pushed it up against him in a hungry fury. She climbed up out of her seat and slipped onto his lap, her hands grabbing his hair and his neck. He was beginning to wonder if maybe he had made a mistake. Maybe she really was a horny cowgirl. Maybe she had just happened to walk into Jason's at fifteen minutes to midnight wearing a red blouse. Maybe it was a coincidence that she drank vodka and 7-Up. But then she lifted her head so that he could kiss her neck and very softly she began to speak.

"Keep kissing my neck and listen to me. This is the last time we'll ever be able to talk. Okay? Only now in the car. After this we say nothing. Not even in my apartment later."

Vonberger kissed her neck and listened to her voice. It sounded different. A little deeper maybe, or older. No, it was clearer. That's what it was. She was sober. He kept kissing her, and licking her neck.

"I'm going to drive us to my apartment. We'll kiss more in the car there. Then you'll follow me from the car to my apartment. I'll drop my purse, and you'll pick it up for me."

"How come?"

"I'm drunk. I'll give you the keys and you let us in. In the apartment you'll pour us drinks, make some small talk, and then turn out the lights. Then we'll go into the bedroom." Vonberger slowly worked his way down her neck. Her blouse was open slightly and he kissed the broad flat area just under the neck. No complaints. She kept talking. "We have five minutes in the bedroom. I have a clock radio you can use to time it. Then—"

"Time what?"

"Five minutes."

He wasn't paying attention. He knew he wasn't paying attention. But *das Mädchen* was beautiful and she was sitting on his lap and describing every detail of his seduction. How was anybody supposed to concentrate? "After five minutes you'll leave," she was saying. "Go to the living room and close the bedroom door behind you. They can't see into the bedroom if the lights are out, but they'll be able to see the lights from the hall when you open the front door." She brought her head down and started kissing the sides of his neck and his ears. She was whispering. "Remember, the bedroom door must be shut before you go out the front. Once you're out the front, go down the stairs, past the entrance, and down into the basement. You'll come into the laundry room."

She pulled away from Vonberger and sat back down in her own seat, straightening out her blouse and checking her hair in the mirror. "They're behind us," she said.

"If you can see them, it's not them," Vonberger said. "The KGB are only there if you can't see them."

"I thought it was the CIA."

"You can't see them either."

"Then how do you know who it is?"

Vonberger laughed. "You don't."

She pulled out of the driveway with that deliberate slowness of an extra-careful drunk, and headed back out toward NASA Road 1. Before Vonberger could say anything she was talking again. "If you get down to the laundry room without seeing anyone, then take the hall that goes to the left off the laundry room. There are a few fire doors and the hall turns a few times. Just keep following it until you can't go any further. When you get to the end of the hallway there's a yellow door that leads off to the left. Knock on it softly once. Just one short knock. Like this," and she knocked on the dashboard. "Don't wait for an answer. Just knock like that and go in. It will be pitch-black inside. Let the door close behind you."

"*Um Gottes Willen!* For heaven's sake! Will you watch where you're going?"

Laura Gold slowly steered her car back onto the road from the shoulder and she turned to Vonberger and smiled. "I'm drunk, remember?"

"Yes, but please don't kill us."

"If you meet anyone between my room and the yellow door, ask them which is the way out and then leave. Go home. If you go home without getting in the door down in the basement, meet me in Jason's next Tuesday night at eleven. It's a date. You don't have to pick up other girls, show up early, or get drunk. You and I have a date.''

"I can't wait. What happens after I go through the yellow door?"

"I don't know."

"Do I get to come back upstairs?"

"I have instructions to leave the door unlocked."

"Well that's a good sign. Where'd they get you from, anyway?"

"I'm a call girl from Seattle."

"Yeah, right!"

She laughed and the car slipped out onto the shoulder again. "It's the only true thing I'll probably ever tell you about myself," she said, and the car casually fell back into the lane.

She *was* driving like a drunk. Down NASA Road 1, barely stopping at the lights, barely staying in lane. Then down some suburban highway with a divider. Suddenly Vonberger panicked. He had to remember where they were going. What if he had to walk home? And then he realized that it was all part of the plan. What could be more innocent than a drunk cosmonaut asking for directions to his own apartment? Hell, they'd thought of everything. Every beautiful detail.

At last they arrived at her apartment. It was one of those new complexes of attached buildings, like Camino Village. And like Camino Village, the buildings looked out onto the street, and the parking and entrances were in the back. Behind the parking lot was a big empty field. Or at least it looked empty in the dark.

She parked the car and jumped on him again. It wasn't quite as much fun this time. All her talk and instructions had bored him. Still he felt himself begin again to get aroused. He reached his arms down and grabbed her legs. Oh, those legs. She was grinding her body against him. Was this all part of the act or was she into it? What difference did it make if she was a hired call girl from Seattle? You take what you can get. A call girl from Seattle. No way!

She finally slid off him and got out of the car and he followed her up the walk to her building. In the light she dropped her purse, just as she said she would, and he picked it up and handed it to her. There was no one around, but Vonberger knew they were being watched. He could feel the KGB in the air, like the fog. She handed him the keys.

Her apartment was clean and sparse and Vonberger pulled a beer out of her refrigerator and settled into the couch in her living room. She kicked off her shoes and sat next to him. Vonberger sipped slowly from his beer. He knew he had to slow down on his drinking and be ready for whatever awaited him behind the yellow door, but sitting so close to Laura was making him nervous. He couldn't stop wondering if he was going to get to sleep with her.

"So when do you fly the shuttle, Alex?" she asked. Her pretty feet were making designs in the carpet.

"I don't know. They haven't told us a date yet."

"Are you nervous?"

"No." Vonberger felt suddenly irritated by the situation. Was she really interested? Or was she just making small talk? They had to be paying her, and yet her interest seemed genuine. "The shuttle is very safe now," he heard himself say. "There is nothing to be nervous about."

"You have nice eyes," she said, and she leaned over and kissed him.

He wrapped his arms around her and they kissed. It didn't matter what was behind the yellow door. It would all be worth it if he got to sleep with *das Mädchen*.

"I like the way you kiss me," she said. "Do all Germans kiss like that?"

They turned the lights out and Vonberger followed her into the bedroom where they laid down on the bed with all of their clothes on. He leaned over to kiss her but she turned away, and so he placed a peck on her cheek and then rolled onto his back. He wasn't going to get to sleep with her after all. This could turn out to be torture. He listened to her breathing and wondered how much she knew about Das Syndikat. Was she a member? Part of the American branch? Or was she being paid for her services? Maybe she really was a call girl from Seattle.

She squeezed his arm and in the darkness he saw her point to the digital clock radio. The five minutes were up already. It was time to leave *das Mädchen* and find out what his mission would be. It was time to find out what Das Syndikat had planned for him.

Alex Vonberger got up and went out to the living room, closing the bedroom door behind him. He crossed the living room and then stepped out through the apartment door into the hallway. She had instructions to leave her door unlocked. Did that mean he would be allowed to come back? Would he be able to see her again? Or had *das Mädchen*, the beautiful girl, just passed out of his life for good? He pushed these thoughts from his mind and headed down the stairs toward the laundry room. There was no one in the laundry room. And there was no one in the hallway that led off the laundry room. Alex Vonberger followed the empty hallway until he got to the yellow door. He knocked softly and then stepped into the darkness, letting the door close behind him.

He could see nothing.

"Welcome to Houston, Twenty-seven," a voice said softly in English.

"I'm not Twenty-seven. I'm Forty-four," Vonberger replied.

"You've been promoted."

"Thanks."

"Don't thank me. Thank The Organization. There's a chair about three steps to your left. Have a seat." Vonberger shuffled slowly and felt the chair and sat. "You recognize my voice?"

It was a soft American voice, but Vonberger felt certain he had never heard it before. "No."

"Good. There is no reason why you should. Did you sleep with Laura?"

"Was I supposed to?"

"She's being paid enough. You might as well. I've heard she's a lot of fun."

Suddenly Vonberger felt annoyed, and he had to bite his tongue to keep in the obscenity that was rising in his throat.

The voice continued from the darkness. "I will be your instructor. Laura will be your cover, just as you were the cover for Number Eighty-five in Kaliningrad. Each meeting will last forty minutes. There is a lot for you to learn."

"Can I ask you a question? What am I going to be doing?"

"We'll get to that. How is Mr. Kulikov treating you?"

"He is a *linke Kommunist,* a crooked communist."

The Instructor laughed. "Did he reprimand you for last week's little journey into the wild side of Houston?"

"Yeah. He chewed me out."

"Good. And everything else has worked out as planned?"

"Yes."

"Good. Next Tuesday you will meet Laura at Jason's at eleven o'clock. It's a date. You set it up with her tonight. If for some reason either of you doesn't show up, you try again on Wednesday. If that doesn't work, you try Thursday. If that doesn't work you wait to hear from us."

Vonberger felt himself smile. He would see her again. "Okay," he heard himself say.

"Tonight, we will only discuss how we will arrange the meetings and how you will use Laura as your cover. At the next meeting we will begin your instructions. These instructions are part of your training here in Houston. We will need six meetings of forty minutes each. We will try to have one a week. There are ten weeks of training. That means we can abort up to four meetings. Now, let's talk about Laura."

"Fine."

"You met her tonight. She works at Fuddruckers. She has just gotten divorced and has moved here from Seattle."

"I thought she said she was a call girl."

"Forget that. She's divorced."

Again Vonberger felt annoyed. "Listen, they will find out if she was a damned hooker."

"Twenty-seven, keep your voice down please! Of course they will find out. But it is natural for her to lie to you. She's lying to you because she loves you. She's here to make a new life for herself. . . ."

"Working at Fuddruckers?"

"She is going to school to learn to be a hairdresser. Now listen to me. You met her tonight. She was drunk and needed you. You went up to her apartment and slept with her. When we are finished you will go back upstairs to Laura's. If you run into anybody in the hallway or stairs, you ask them which is the way out and you leave. It doesn't matter if they look like KGB or not. You go home. If you get back inside her apartment, wait until five-thirty and then she will drive you home. Otherwise you will walk. Whichever you do is the story you tell. Nothing else. You are to let your story be known without actually telling it, of course."

Vonberger thought about Joey Wells and smiled. "Of course. I've got that under control."

"If you can convince anyone at NASA to take you to dinner at Fuddruckers, Laura works there every night from four until ten except Monday and Tuesday. Try to visit her. Show her off to your friends. Remember, you think you love her. And I am to relieve you now of any of love's ordinary worries. She loves you too, and you are going to be lovers for a few months. You two are, what we might call, a match made in heaven."

Vonberger felt himself smile again. A few months! What could be better than a few months with Laura Gold! Then, suddenly the smile slipped from his face. "You still haven't told me what I'm going to do."

"The Organization will require your participation in a hijacking and hostage situation."

"A hijacking and hostage situation," Vonberger repeated automatically. He suddenly felt dizzy. He wished he could see something. Anything. The Instructor, the floor, his own hand. Anything. "What is it that they're going to hijack?"

"No, Twenty-seven, the question is what is it that *you* are going to hijack?"

"Fine." He gripped the chair seat tightly and he pushed down on the soles of his feet, trying to anchor himself on the floor. "What is it that *I* am going to hijack?"

Vonberger never heard the answer. All he heard was his own voice screaming in the darkness. "Are you crazy? They want me to hijack the space shuttle? They must be out of their minds!"

"Twenty-seven! Your voice!"

Vonberger was standing up. He couldn't help himself. "You're crazy! They want me to hijack the space shuttle?"

"Twenty-seven! Please! Listen to me now. You may bow out of the operation now and it will not be held against you."

"The space shuttle?"

"Yes, the space shuttle. They want you to hijack the first flight of the Soviet-American Peace Flight Program. If you want out, tell me now. Otherwise, it is time for you to go upstairs to Laura. You want out?"

Vonberger felt for his seat and sat down. This was unreal. "The space shuttle?"

"You want out?"

"No, I don't want out. I just can't believe they're serious. What the hell are we going to do with the space shuttle?"

"That is for next week's meeting. Now go up to your Laura. I understand she has some interesting techniques."

Vonberger left the dark room and headed back up the hallway. Das Syndikat wanted him to hijack the space shuttle. It was madness. What were they going to do with the space shuttle once it was hijacked? If you hijack a plane, you take off and you can land in a friendly airport somewhere. But what the hell do you do with a space shuttle?

Vonberger knew that he was a well-placed member of Das Syndikat. In the Soviet Union, he had been instrumental in trying to smuggle Dressler out of the country. Now, as a member of the Soviet Peace Flight Program team, he knew he had access to all kinds of information that could be helpful to Das Syndikat. He knew he was an important man for them now, but Hans had not prepared him for this. The space shuttle! It was fantastic!

Outside Laura Gold's door, Vonberger stopped to catch his breath. He had joined Das Syndikat eleven years ago, while he was training as a pilot in East Germany. His old friend from school, Hans, had already been a member for five years and was high up in The Organization. Hans of the many passports. Vonberger had always believed in Das Syndikat, and he had always hoped there would come a day when they would be able to use him. His assignment in Kaliningrad was important, but hardly satisfying. Vonberger knew that in the big picture, neither he nor Dressler made a difference. Now, he was finally going to make a difference!

Vonberger pushed the door open and stepped into Laura Gold's apartment, and suddenly he panicked. They had not told him whether to lock the door or not. Did it matter? Vonberger tried to think. It didn't matter. But why hadn't they told him? He locked the door and gently crossed the dark living room to the bedroom door.

"I'm back, honey," he said, sticking his head into the bedroom.

Her voice came back to him, soft and sleepy. "No more talking."

"I mean I'm back from the bathroom."

She laughed. "Come in here." And she threw back the covers, and from the dim light from the street he could see that she was naked.

2

DEADLY
BLUE

PAUL Kelly, the center director of the Marshall Space
Flight Center, stood by the door of the conference room
and eagerly directed his guests to the coffee and pastry.
A small table had been set up with a clean white tablecloth
and a delicate set of hand-painted china. Kelly held a cup in
his big stubby hands, and it shook just a little bit each time
he introduced himself to another member of the group. Russell Madlinger guessed that the china was an old wedding
present brought from home just for this occasion. They didn't
get many visitors at Marshall.

Russell Madlinger took his coffee and pastry and sat at the
large oak table in the middle of the room. At forty-seven, he
was still handsome, but the hard-cut lines of his face had
mellowed, and his deep-set eyes were no longer ferocious,
but merely steady and pensive. A few wrinkles had developed on his forehead over the years and Cathy said it made
him look paternal. She still called him "Deadly Blue" or
sometimes just "DB," a nickname inspired by his eyes. It

was his eyes, and his jet-black hair, that had first caught her attention, all those years ago. It was easy to imagine that he had once been an astronaut, but it was not so easy to imagine that now, in 1990, he was part of the NASA administration. Russell Madlinger was still in excellent physical shape. He had been brought up on a horse farm in upstate New York, and the ruggedness he had developed in his early youth could not be concealed by a suit and tie.

Madlinger watched the other members of the Senior Interagency Group gather around the coffee and pastry. In his twenty-three years working for NASA and visiting the Marshall Space Flight Center, he had never seen the white and blue set of china. The only two people of the group who might have been worth trying to impress were Charlie Roland, the NASA administrator, who certainly didn't expect anything but the usual Styrofoam cups, and the sleepy-eyed national security advisor, Dick Higgins, who probably would have drunk his coffee from an ashtray as long as he was getting a strong dose of caffeine.

The pastries were good, but Madlinger would have preferred the usual Dunkin Donuts. It wasn't that Madlinger didn't appreciate good food, but there was a time and a place for everything, and he saw no reason to treat the Senior Interagency Group like a social club. All the little frills just reminded him of how much he hated these meetings in the first place.

Madlinger closed his eyes and once again remembered the few beautiful hours he had spent floating in space, a long time ago. He could almost see the blue-and-silver earth, sometimes above and sometimes below, depending only on where he pointed his feet. It had seemed that his whole life had led up to that space walk. Konstantin Tsiolkovsky, the early Russian scientist, had once discussed "the bliss that would come to pass" through the abolition of gravity. Out in space, free even from the confines of his Apollo spacecraft, Madlinger had remembered Tsiolkovsky's words and had thought to himself, "This is it. This is the bliss that will come to pass."

The spacecraft seen from the outside, up in space, was not much different from a car. It was just another transportation device. Madlinger pulled on his tether and clumsily maneuvered around to the front of the spacecraft and peered in through the windows at his fellow astronauts. They waved and laughed and exchanged insults over the wireless.

What Madlinger saw, though, was not a $65-million spacecraft. He was no longer looking at a scientific and technological masterpiece that represented the glory of NASA and the free world. He didn't see the years of research that went into building the Apollo and sending men into space and to the moon. What he saw was one of those early covered wagons used by the American pioneers who crossed the wilderness on the Oregon Trail in search of a new life. As a child visiting a museum, he had once seen such a covered wagon, and he had been told that families had lived in these primitive wagons for months at a time while they crossed the continent. And little Russell Madlinger had lingered an extra few minutes and stared into the dark and dusty wagon, and had wondered to himself how they had done it.

That was what Madlinger felt looking in the window of his own Apollo spacecraft. It was as if he were looking back on it from the future. It was small and crowded and primitive, and once again he wondered how they had done it.

Then he turned to face the earth, and suddenly he was frozen by the calm chill that would forever haunt him. Suddenly he couldn't move, and yet, he was floating, not just in space, but in time. Somehow, he had escaped all bounds of time, and the earth, now glistening in the sun, was no longer entrapped in the turmoil of 1973. He drifted over the Middle East, a patch of greens and browns, and there were no armies. The Middle East, Watergate, Vietnam, the protests, the Soviet Union, even the United States, were all gone. They were a part of history, just like the Roman Empire and the discovery of America.

There was really nothing different at all. The earth looked exactly like it had a few minutes before. But it also looked like it had ten thousand years before. Or like it would ten thousand years from now. Space knew nothing of time. It knew nothing about the countries of the world, or about the wars and the violence. Space was ignorant. It occurred to Madlinger that it would be only out of the wildest of coincidences if he were to return to earth and find that it was still 1973.

He felt paralyzed by the calm chill and he floated quietly, alone in space. He and the earth were totally disconnected. Nothing he knew of the earth existed here in space. There was no NASA. No ground control. No Cathy, even. Up here, it was just he and space. And in the calmness he understood that space was not ignorant, but, instead, was timelessly forgiving. From space, the earth would always be beautiful.

On his first night back on earth, Madlinger tried to describe to Cathy the calm chill that had frozen him out in space, but words seemed to fail him. There was no way to adequately explain the feelings of timelessness and calm that he had felt. Cathy was pregnant with their first child and Madlinger lay beside her while she slept, frustrated and confused. He wanted her to understand the calm and forgiveness of space. He wanted her to understand the beauty of the earth.

And then Madlinger realized that instead of trying to describe it, he should try to learn from it. Perhaps he could emulate it. Perhaps he could become the calm and forgiving force in other people's lives. Perhaps he could do for them what space had done for him. He could do it for his wife. For his unborn child. For the children of the world.

Madlinger opened his eyes and the group had begun to take their seats around the oak table. The Senior Interagency Group for the Peace Flight Program was referred to as SIG-PFP, and in the inimitable style of acronyms, it was more affectionately known as "SIG-PIFPY." SIG-PIFPY had been organized almost a year ago by the President to set and implement policy for the new Peace Flight Program, called the

PFP. The PFP would be a joint Soviet and American space program with the short-range goals of establishing a complete global network of communication satellites, and then a permanent manned presence in space. The ultimate goal of the PFP was a joint manned mission to Mars by the year 2000. NASA had appointed Madlinger to the position of Peace Flight Program director, and as such he had to attend the SIG-PIFPY meetings, as well as the meetings of the Joint Soviet-American Task Force.

Dick Higgins sat at the head of the table. To Madlinger, Higgins represented both power and the wisdom of the White House. There was no doubt that the national security advisor ran the meetings, and that his role was to see that the meetings and the actions of SIG-PIFPY reflected the goals of the President. And yet, Higgins was always prepared to delegate important decisions. He understood that there were times when others were more qualified to make decisions.

The NASA group all sat on the same side of the table. First Charlie Roland, the NASA administrator, then Paul Kelly, then Madlinger, and finally Leonard Wolff, NASA's chief engineer for shuttle systems integration. No one man could ever be said to have designed the space shuttle, but if there were such a man, it would be Leonard Wolff. Across the table from the NASA team was George Holmes from the State Department, Bill White from the Department of Defense, Marianne Eagle from the CIA, and Elliot Hacker from the FBI.

"Good morning, gentlemen," Higgins started, and then with a slight apologetic nod to Marianne Eagle, he added, "ladies and gentlemen." One of Madlinger's favorite pastimes when the meetings got boring was to try to figure out if Higgins was really always tired, or if that was just the way he looked. "Just a few things before we start. First off, the President has approved our proposed flight date of May twenty-fourth."

The small conference room broke into applause. The President's approval had never really been in doubt, but it was the last step in setting a definite target date for launch. And May 24 was less than three months away.

Higgins continued. "He has also approved the recommendation of the Task Force that all PFP flights be named "PF," followed by the number of the flight, regardless of whether it is a shuttle flight or a Soviet flight. Thus PF-One is now an official designation for the May twenty-fourth flight. Also, as you know, later this afternoon we will get a chance to look at the mock-ups of the Soviet satellites that PF-One will be launching. Len, you have anything to add?"

Leonard Wolff pulled his seat closer to the table, as if trying to hide himself. "Not at the moment. The mock-ups were prepared here at Marshall by members of the Soviet team, and I guess we have to assume that they do not deviate from the actual satellites."

There were a few chuckles. Higgins poured the rest of his coffee down his throat, and then continued. "Okay. This morning we're going to hear from NASA on their final selection of the crew for PF-One. Charlie?"

Charlie Roland was a small man, with white-and-silver hair that always remained perfectly intact. His big tanned forehead and his red puffy cheeks gave him a healthy and down-to-earth look, and he was in excellent physical and mental shape for his seventy-five years.

Roland cleared his throat. "Yes. Before Russ gives you our final selection, I'd just like to mention that our final list calls for six crewmembers, three from the East, and three from the West, in accordance with the policy recommended by the Task Force a few months ago. We have discussed our selection with the director of flight crew operations and with Andrei Kulikov, the Soviet liaison officer here in the United States. I might add that the Soviets have approved our final list. Russ?"

Madlinger sat up and faced Dick Higgins. "Okay. As commander, we've selected Conrad P. Williams the Third. Williams, as some of you may know, has flown three shuttle missions, once as pilot, and twice as commander. He's an

Air Force test pilot, and came to NASA in 1978. He is not presently assigned to a mission and we think he's a first-rate commander and a perfect astronaut for this mission.''

"Russ," Higgins interrupted. "The President and I have discussed this already, and we agree that Williams is a perfect selection for this mission. From a political point of view, the President is eager to show the world that we have black astronauts, and Williams is already well known for his work with youth groups and in the nation's school systems. As far as the President is concerned, Williams was made for the job."

"Well, that's that," Roland said.

"Any objections?" Higgins looked around the table.

No one said anything, so Madlinger continued. "For the pilot, we've selected Joey Wells. Wells is a Navy fighter pilot who came to NASA about four years ago. He has flown one shuttle mission, as pilot, and has demonstrated outstanding capability."

Bill White from the Department of Defense spoke up. "Wells? Isn't that that wild one they call 'Cowboy'?"

"They do call him 'Cowboy,' " Madlinger answered.

"That man's a wild card! He listens to rock and roll and he drives his car too fast. The guy thinks he's Chuck Yeager or someone out of *The Right Stuff*."

"Wells has never been anything but serious when it comes to his training or missions," Madlinger answered.

"Yeah, but he's immature. That shuttle mission that he flew was a Department of Defense flight. I remember him. Now you're going to send him up into space with a bunch of commies? Who knows what he'll do or say up there?"

"Did you have any problems with him on your flight?" Madlinger asked.

"Well, no, but he sure scared the hell out of us."

Roland cleared his voice again and spoke up. "Now, Bill, none of our astronauts are wild cards. They are all serious, well-trained professionals. What they do on their own time is their own business, unless it interferes with their ability to do their job. We wouldn't let somebody fly if we couldn't trust them one hundred percent. And you have to admit, Bill, he did a flawless job on that Defense mission.''

Bill White pushed his chair back and crossed his arms across his chest, but he didn't say anything. He was not going to argue with Charlie Roland. Very few people did. But he was not going to forget his concerns. Dick Higgins smiled and nodded. ''I'll note your objection for the record, Bill. Russ, you want to continue?''

''The rest of the crew will be sent as payload specialists. For those of you not familiar with the terminology, members of NASA's astronaut corps who fly neither as commander or pilot are referred to as mission specialists. The so-called guests on board the shuttle are referred to as payload specialists. Ordinarily a flight would have one or more mission specialists. In this case, however, since none of the other four crewmembers will be NASA astronauts, they will all be flying as payload specialists. If the whole thing seems petty to you, just remember that the NASA astronaut community is very close-knit. They work together and train long years together to earn a commander, pilot or mission specialist designation within their ranks. You can't just drop an outsider on them and give them equal billing, no matter how qualified they may be or whatever their ranking within their own organization. Okay. The first payload specialist will be George Evans, from Britain. He's from the RAF and he's never been in space. He's been training with NASA for over a year, since before the PFP, and he's completely ready for flight.''

''Objections?'' Higgins looked around. ''Continue.''

''For the Soviets we have selected their most experienced cosmonaut, Vladimir Turnov, who has spent a world-record total of four hundred and fifty-two days in space. Apparently the man now has more trouble adjusting to gravity than he does to weightlessness.''

Everyone laughed.

''Can we get a CIA report on him, please?'' Higgins asked. Marianne Eagle from the CIA was a large blonde, who, like Higgins, always appeared a little bit bored. "Turnov? Party line one hundred percent. No deviations either way. He's a fighter pilot. Apparently did a few years as an instructor in Vietnam, and in Syria, but as far as we know never saw any action. He did once make a statement to the Western press that was contradictory to the official position regarding the use of nonpilots as cosmonauts. That was back in '85, I believe, and he publicly retracted the statement two days later. Obviously a case of being misinformed. Otherwise perfectly clear."

"Okay, thank you. Any objections? Russ?"

"We have also selected Aelita Zakharov, because of her EVA experience."

Higgins dropped his palm on the table. "Damn it, I'll never get all these acronyms straight. What the hell is EVA?"

"Extravehicular activity," Paul Kelly responded quickly. "You know, space walks."

"Zakharov's the woman cosmonaut?" Higgins asked.

"Yes," Madlinger answered.

"Why do the Soviets get to fly a woman instead of us?"

"Is that a problem?"

"Yes, it's a big problem."

"The truth of the matter is, Dick, that none of our women astronauts designated as commanders or pilots have completed their training yet, and there's really no opening for an American mission specialist on the flight."

"So why should we allow them to fly a woman?"

"Because Aelita Zakharov is a good cosmonaut, and frankly, we felt that it was better to have one woman than none at all."

"I'm not sure the President will agree with that."

Roland interrupted. "Well now, Dick. Keep in mind that in the history of the space program, we have put many more women into space than the Soviets have. Valentina Tereshkova was the first woman in space, back in '62, I think. And Svetlana Savitskaya flew once in 1982 and again in 1984. But the next woman flown in space by the Russians wasn't until Ms. Zakharov. And since Sally Ride became the first American woman in space in 1983, we've flown women on nearly a dozen flights.''

''Well, I suppose we can point out that we have women astronauts training for commander and pilot spots, and several others are scheduled to fly as mission specialists. I don't know. I'll have to talk to the President about that. Marianne, what do you have on Zakharov?''

''She's clear. She is a physicist who was drafted into the cosmonaut program about seven years ago. She was engaged to a Soviet fighter pilot who was killed in Afghanistan in '86. She's outspoken on the subject of women's rights in the Soviet Union, but it's hard to tell if that's party line or her own thinking. Apparently it hasn't had a negative effect on her career.''

''Thanks. Objections? None? Okay, that's five. You got one more, Russ?''

''Yes. Number six is the East German, Alex Vonberger.''

Higgins leaned forward. ''Marianne?''

''Alex Vonberger was one of the East German pilots chosen to train in the Soviet cosmonaut program back in '86. Of the four chosen, two of them have flown. One was dropped from the program, probably for medical reasons, and Vonberger was to be the next to go, but he returned to Germany about a year and a half ago, without ever flying. The Soviets claimed that they had only intended to fly two of the four, but some of our sources indicated that there may have been some kind of security problem with Vonberger. It was rumored that his return to East Germany might have been connected to the disappearance of Johann Dressler.''

Madlinger interrupted. ''Who's Johann Dressler?''

Marianne Eagle pushed her chair back from the table so that she could speak to the whole group at once. ''Dressler was one of the young German technicians captured by the Russians after the war. It's rumored that he played an instrumental part in the early years of the Soviet space program as part of Korolev's rocket development team. He disappeared a little over a year ago, and our sources indicate that he may have been killed trying to sneak out of the country into Iran.''

''What does he have to do with Alex Vonberger?'' Higgins asked.

''Nothing, so far as we know. Vonberger was at Star City in the Soviet Union with Dressler around the time Dressler disappeared and he and Dressler had been pretty friendly. When Vonberger was sent back to Germany we thought it might have had something to do with Dressler, but apparently the Soviets have never accused Vonberger of anything. I guess I'm a little surprised that he's still on their golden boy list. It's usually guilt by association over there.''

''What the hell was Dressler going to do in Iran?'' George Holmes from the State Department asked.

''The Soviets seem to think that he was going to sell his knowledge to the Islamic Republic of Iran. Who knows? Maybe he wanted to start his own space program. There's no indication that he was trying to defect to the West. We didn't know about any of this until some time after the fact. The other thing to keep in mind is that Dressler was seventy-two years old. The man might have been losing it.''

''Careful when you talk about old men, young lady,'' Roland said, and everyone laughed.

Higgins's voice cut in through the laughter. ''None of this is new, right?''

''No, this was all turned up in our check on Vonberger when the Soviets first disclosed that he would be part of their team. I throw it out now, just because we really thought that the Soviets had brought Vonberger over as a showpiece.''

Higgins slapped his palm down again. ''Well damn it, are you telling us that you let Vonberger in the country thinking he might be a security risk?''

Marianne Eagle laughed. ''I'm sorry if I haven't made myself clear. If Vonberger is a security risk, the risk is to the Soviet Union, not to us. And apparently the KGB has already cleared him. If he's good enough for them, he's certainly good enough for us.''

* * *

Russell Madlinger and Leonard Wolff walked down the steps of the Marshall administrative building and out to the parking lot. It was unusually hot for February in Alabama, and it was a confusing combination of the early darkness of winter and the warmth of summer. Both men carried their coats over their arms. Madlinger watched Wolff throw his briefcase onto the roof of the rented Buick and start rummaging through it for his keys. Wolff was a serious man with a quiet personality and people often wondered why he and Madlinger were friends. Wolff was awkward at meetings and with associates. He had big bushy eyebrows and his nose drooped down too far toward his lip, almost like a beak. And, as if to emphasize his receding hairline, he wore his sideburns long, too long in fact. On the whole he gave the appearance of someone living in his own little world. But maybe that's what engineering was all about.

Madlinger liked Wolff for his professionalism and his quiet wit. They had known each other for a long time and they lived in the same neighborhood in Houston. Their kids were friendly at school. They didn't talk much as they rode through the Marshall Space Flight Center toward Huntsville. With Wolff, there was never any need for small talk, and Madlinger appreciated that.

They left Marshall and entered the Army's Redstone Arsenal. Every time Madlinger rode through Redstone and saw the cows grazing in fields, he remembered the day he met Cathy. It had been a bad time for NASA. A bad time for space flight generally. In January of 1967, a launchpad fire had killed three American astronauts. Then in April, a Russian cosmonaut had been killed on his return to earth. It was as if the whole idea of space exploration was at a standstill.

Cathy had been a second-year medical student working at Marshall for the summer, and Madlinger had been a rookie astronaut, fresh from the ranks of Navy fighter pilots. He was in Hunstville for orientation and for meetings on the effects of weightlessness on the body. After a long day of meetings and lectures, Cathy had offered to drive him back to his hotel.

Driving back to Huntsville, Cathy had suddenly stopped the car, right there on the side of the road in Redstone. Madlinger had followed her out of the car as she went up to the fence around the pasture, and stared at the cows. The red-and-brown dirty cows. Madlinger, the horse farmer, could appreciate cows, but when they turned to go back to the car, he realized that she had been crying. And over a drink at the hotel, she told him that all summer she had been hearing about the death of the three astronauts, about the cosmonaut, about the race to the moon. And then there were the cows, who didn't know a thing about it, even though they lived just outside the Marshall Space Flight Center, the home of the American rocket. There was something about their innocence, she tried to explain. But Madlinger had reached over the table and grabbed her hand. He understood. He understood what she was trying to say. But he also understood that he was going to fall in love with her.

Now this warm winter's day, he and Wolff were passing the cows. In the growing darkness he could just make out their forms, but not their colors or their detail. "You know what these cows think of the Peace Flight Program, Len?"

Wolff was watching the road. He knew the cows were there. He didn't have to look. "No. Tell me, Russ."

"Nothing."

Wolff kept driving.

"They think nothing," Madlinger continued. "Why should they think anything of peace, when they never knew there was war. Look at the dumb animals. They have no idea that they're outside the Marshall Space Flight Center. They have no idea what we're doing here. They have no idea who Wernher von Braun was. Hell, they probably never heard of John Glenn."

"We're getting old, Russ. I'm not sure my kids even know who John Glenn is." Wolff looked over at Madlinger and smiled. "Their heroes are Prince and Madonna."

"Cathy and I stopped here to look at these cows the first day we met. Did you know that?"

"No, I didn't know that."

"You think these are the same cows? How long do they live, cows? I mean, let's see, that was 1967. I guess cows don't live that long. What am I talking about? These are beef cattle. Hell, the cows Cathy and I saw were probably served at McDonald's twenty years ago."

Wolff laughed. "Anybody ever tell you that you were crazy?"

Madlinger laughed. "Yeah, I've been told that." Maybe he was crazy, but the cows reminded him of what Cathy had taught him that first day. Innocence was bliss. Up in space, years later, he remembered the cows, and their innocence. In space he wondered if innocence was another form of weightlessness. Weightlessness of the heart. And ignorance was weightlessness of the mind.

"How're the kids?" Wolff asked suddenly.

Madlinger slowly turned in from the window. "I hardly get to see them these days," he said.

"I know what you mean. Well, listen. We're having a barbeque on Sunday. Why don't you all come by? I think Lisa already asked Nancy."

Madlinger laughed. "Leave it to our kids to arrange our social lives for us. Sure. I'll check with Cathy." Madlinger stared out at the darkening road in front of them and watched the white lines zip by, like the years since he'd met Cathy.

"Chris going out for varsity next year?" Wolff asked.

"I don't know," Madlinger answered honestly.

"Really? I was sure he'd go out. He's an ace."

"Yeah, well, he won this national competition with a short story he wrote and he's been invited out East for a weekend next fall by the college that sponsored it. I guess it interferes with the football schedule. I don't know what he's going to do."

"Must be one heck of a short story," Wolff said.

Madlinger took a deep breath and exhaled slowly. Ever since Chris had won the competition, Madlinger had felt a sadness growing inside him. Madlinger knew that he would respect his son's decision, no matter what he did. The sadness did not come from fear that his son would make the wrong decision. There was no wrong decision. What made Madlinger sad was that Chris had never offered to let him read the short story. The closeness that Madlinger had always felt with his only son, his oldest child, was slowly slipping away, and Madlinger already missed him, as a child, and as a friend.

They pulled into the big parking lot at the Marriott Hotel in Huntsville and Wolff parked the car. They made plans to meet for dinner and then went up to their rooms. Madlinger's message light was on. There had been a call from his wife.

Madlinger pulled his shoes off and loosened his tie. Then he pulled the telephone over to the bed and dialed the number in Houston.

Somebody answered "Cath Lab," which Madlinger always got a kick out of. It meant catheterization laboratory, but of course Madlinger liked to think it meant Cathy's laboratory. It took them a while to find her, but finally she came on, out of breath.

"Hi, DB."

"Hey, babe."

"How's the meeting?"

"Boring. How's the home front?"

"Newton ran away again this morning."

"Did he come back?"

"Chris went looking for him but couldn't find him. He's worried about him."

"The dog can handle himself. Chris worries about him too much."

"That dog is a pain in my neck, DB. I just don't know what you love about that dog."

"He helps me think."

"Well, I just wanted to say hi. I missed you last night."

"Yeah, I missed you too. You going to be home tomorrow night?"

"No. I'm on call."

"Wednesday?"

"Chris has a basketball game. The girls want to watch."

"Good. We'll send them with the Wolffs. How about a bottle of wine in the tub?"

"Oh, Deadly Blue. We haven't done that in a long time."

"Is it a date?"

"You bet."

"Good. Kiss the kids for me. Tell Chris not to worry about Newton. The dog didn't get to be this old by being stupid."

3

THE
PF
FLYERS

THE idea for the Peace Flight Program had grown out of the President's Task Force on American Space Policy while he was still a presidential candidate. It was then only a little over a year since the *Challenger* accident had claimed the lives of seven astronauts and resulted in an extensive examination of NASA's organizational structure and decision-making procedures. The shuttle's solid rocket boosters were being redesigned, and it was still over a year before the shuttle flights were to resume. The international aerospace community did not know how and when they would be able to regain routine access to space. The Congress was unsure about the merits of building a space station, and Americans, generally, were asking themselves questions about the value and the goals of the American space program.

The presidential candidate had seized upon the uncertain state of affairs as a means of demonstrating a sense of hope and vision for the future. He made the nation's space program an important theme of his campaign and announced the formation of the Task Force on American Space Policy.

The Task Force was made up of people from both the public and private sectors, with a wide range of backgrounds in space and space-related fields. Their research and discussions led them to conclude that there was a strong feeling among the American public that space exploration was valuable to mankind. What was needed, however, was a well-defined space policy that would give the American space program a new sense of meaning and direction. Among other things, the Task Force suggested that the American space program be used to promote international peace and cooperation. The Task Force developed the idea of a joint Soviet and American program with a long-range goal of sending a manned mission to Mars. Unofficial discussions with the Soviet Union proved encouraging and the candidate trumpeted the idea as a campaign promise, which eventually won him the presidency. The Peace Flight Program was born.

In January of 1990, the Soviet PFP team arrived in Washington, D.C., and paraded through the snowy streets. They battled a three-day blizzard while they met America's leaders and members of the press. The President declared that he had now delivered on his campaign promise and that the United States and Soviet Union were embarking on a new era of friendship. The endless ceremonies and banquets would not be stopped even though Washington, D.C., was besieged by one of the worst snowstorms in a decade. In a formal greeting at the White House, the President hailed "our brothers in space," and, in full view of the press, told the Soviet team that if they had any problems during their stay, or if they ever just "felt like chatting," they should feel free to call him personally. The President then asked Vladimir Turnov, the lead cosmonaut, what he thought of the weather, and Turnov won the hearts of all Americans when he answered in his accented English, "It's just like home."

The press, for a change, could not find anything negative to say. The members of the Soviet team were compared to the Knights of the Round Table, and the Peace Flight Program was heralded to be one of the most daring ventures for peace in the history of mankind. Ever since the *Challenger* disaster, it was said, the American space program had been plagued with problems and doubt, but now, at last, NASA had renewed purpose and direction. And now America the generous, America the free, America the beautiful, would share its knowledge and expertise with the rest of the world. Worldwide peace was only steps away. If we could go to space with the Russians, then surely we could agree to limit, or even ban, nuclear arms. Surely we could settle all the brushfires of the world. With the Americans and the Soviets working together, there was nothing that could not be accomplished.

Americans watched their television sets and saw a group of smiling cosmonauts and Soviet engineers who no longer seemed haunted by the dark cloud of secrecy and privacy that usually hung over official visitors from the Soviet Union. One cosmonaut told a news reporter that he planned to stay in America "as long as they let me," and an editorial stated that "this simple answer symbolizes 'glasnost,' the openness of the 'new Russians,' who have finally shed their long coats of paranoia and are willing to take the risks necessary in order to work with a free and open society."

To Joey Wells, it was soon obvious that the Soviets who flew into Ellington Field in Houston aboard a NASA jet were not "new Russians." Arrangements had already been made for the entire Soviet team to stay at the Camino Village Apartments, and Andrei Kulikov, the Soviet liaison officer, quickly arranged with the NASA public affairs office for two NASA vans to chauffeur the Soviet team back and forth from JSC, the Johnson Space Center. The Soviets would attend the NASA functions and formalities but would then quietly disappear, driven away as if they might turn into pumpkins if they weren't home on time. The cosmonauts soon began their training with the American astronauts, and the scientists and engineers went to work with their American counterparts, but every day after work the vans would be waiting. The Soviets, it seemed, were all business. They would share American technology but not American beer. It seemed that the Peace Flight Program would not change American and Soviet relations, but would only extend business as usual to a new arena.

To Joey Wells it seemed that Andrei Kulikov's sole responsibility was to plan the van schedule so that no member of the Soviet team would have an extra minute to mingle with the Americans. And things might have continued unchanged had Joey Wells not taken a liking for Aelita Zakharov, the Soviet cosmonaut. She had sat behind him during training flights in the T-38, and he had watched her long brown hair fall from her head when she took her helmet off. They worked together in the crew compartment trainer and simulators, and he had smelled her perfume, or her shampoo, or whatever it was that made her smell like roses. He had heard her mention how she had always wanted to see the Rocky Mountains. And he had seen her head move slowly, in short seductive nods, anytime she wanted to let someone know that she understood what they were saying. Joey "Cowboy" Wells, who had an indefatigable sense of adventure, decided that he was going to get to know her.

It was a wet and cold winter's day in Houston when the crew for PF-1 disembarked from the KC-135 trainer at Ellington Field. The KC-135 is a modified Boeing 707 that flies parabolic trajectories, during which the passengers experience approximately thirty seconds of weightlessness as the aircraft transitions from a steep climb into a steep dive. American astronauts often refer to the KC-135 as the "vomit comet." After each parabola, the airplane pulls up to start its next climb, subjecting the crew to about two positive g's. The cycling between positive and zero g often causes nausea and vomiting. There is no magic to the KC-135. It works on the simple laws of physics and it is one of the few ways to experience brief periods of weightlessness without going into space.

During the flight, Joey Wells, who had long been famous for his inane witticisms, or "Cowboyisms," had come up with the idea of naming the PF-1 crew the PF Flyers, after the old brand of sneakers. The name had stuck instantly. Now, as the PF Flyers happily adjusted to having their feet back on solid ground, Joey Wells scurried off the ramp and found the NASA van waiting for the three cosmonauts. The driver was a NASA employee from public affairs, and he was easily convinced to run into the hangar to buy a few Cokes for the slightly nauseated cosmonauts.

It took Joey Wells exactly seven seconds to open the hood of the van, remove the distributor cable, close the hood, and stuff the cable into a pocket of his flight suit. He made sure he was walking toward his car when cosmonauts came out and piled into the van. He pretended not to notice that the van wouldn't start, until he had pulled his clean white Mustang right up alongside it. He stopped and looked at the driver, and the driver rolled down his window.

"What's the problem?" Joey Wells asked, and he winked.

Once it was settled that Conrad Williams and Joey Wells would give the rest of the crew rides back to JSC, Joey Wells risked a side wink to Williams, and suggested that he and Williams, as pilot and commander, take the PF Flyers to lunch at Pe-te's Cajun BBQ. After all, it *was* Friday. Williams, who could appreciate a little misbehavior at the right time and place, quickly agreed, and he quietly assured the cosmonauts that it would take no longer than their usual lunch at the NASA cafeteria. And so it was that the PF Flyers disappeared from the eyes of Big Brother for a "quick little lunch" at Pe-te's Cajun BBQ.

Pe-te's Cajun BBQ is not a restaurant where diplomats or politicians usually eat. It looks like an old chicken coop that should have been wiped out in the last dust storm. The old wooden walls creak in the wind and several colors show through the peeling paint. An old screen door bangs open and shut every time someone walks in or out. The inside is jammed with long wooden tables and a jukebox plays Cajun music and old country favorites. The walls are plastered with old license plates and pictures of astronauts. You sit where you want, eat what you want, and say what you want. Nobody listens, nobody sees, nobody cares.

The PF Flyers grabbed their trays, their smoked pork and links, or their blackened redfish and peppers, and their beers, and they filed toward a table in the back of the room. Music from the jukebox filled in the awkward silence that had suddenly descended upon them. The silence was like that between a young couple out without a chaperon for the first time. Then Conrad Williams, their commander, raised his beer and said "To Andrei Kulikov, to the public affairs office, and to us, the PF Flyers!" and everyone raised their beers and laughed, and then the silence was gone, forever.

Joey Wells found himself across the table from Alex Vonberger. They talked about Vonberger's new girlfriend. They talked about Jason's and country and western music. Wells heard himself telling Vonberger about the bars in Dallas, in San Antonio, and in El Paso. And out of the corner of his eye, while he spoke, Wells watched Aelita Zakharov. She was talking with Evans and Turnov and Williams. Williams was trying to explain what Cajun food was. They were talking about crayfish and lobster. They were talking about different kinds of seafood. Turnov was trying to explain what kinds of fish they ate in the Soviet Union. Aelita Zakharov was nodding her head.

The PF Flyers ordered more beer and they all switched seats and Joey Wells found himself sitting with George Evans. Evans had a big round face, but he was lanky and thin. They talked about the KC-135 and about weightlessness, and Evans told Joey Wells about how "bloody" nauseous he had been and how he "bloody" well hoped that he wouldn't get sick on the shuttle. Finally, Joey Wells got to sit with Aelita Zakharov and he couldn't help smiling at her while she told him about her love of horses and of nature. Wells told her about his two pet turtles, named French Fries and Onion Rings. And the PF Flyers ordered more beer.

At three o'clock in the afternoon, the PF Flyers strolled out of Pe-te's Cajun BBQ into the pouring rain. The parking lot was an unorganized mess of gravel and potholes filled with muddy water. They ran to their cars, and Joey Wells made sure that Zakharov followed him to his Mustang. His white, hot, fast, ever capable Mustang. At the last moment, Alex Vonberger grabbed for the front seat, and Aelita Zakharov had to climb in the back. Damn Alex Vonberger!

The roads were wet and the traffic was slow, and the noise of the windshield wipers and the defroster made Joey sleepy. This was not the ride he wanted. He wanted to *move*. He needed to feel the speed and the wind. He wanted to be alive. He slipped a tape of the Charlie Daniels Band into the cassette player. Something to keep him up.

Vonberger and Zakharov were talking about Kulikov again. Vonberger was telling Zakharov about his late-night adventures at Jason's, and how Kulikov had given him hell at first, but now seemed not to care. "Maybe somewhere inside, he is an okay guy, this Kulikov, no?" Vonberger asked, twisting in his seat.

Wells looked up into the rearview mirror and saw Zakharov nodding her head. "Yes, he is okay," she said. "He's just doing his job. He is afraid that we will be won over by the Americans. Like ballerinas." And she laughed. "Anybody that protective doesn't trust himself," she continued. "Maybe Kulikov is the real defector." And then they all laughed.

4

THE
MEN WITH
EARS

"MY mother was a horrible cook." Laura Gold pranced, barefooted, around her tiny kitchen, slicing cucumbers, mixing salad dressing, and checking the potatoes. "I mean, I guess she was okay before my father left us, but after that it was canned vegetables, canned fruit, canned soup, canned meat, canned *everything*. It was like my whole life came out of a can."

Alex Vonberger stood in the doorway of the kitchen and watched Laura move about, as she fixed him dinner. She was wearing a tight pair of blue jeans and a Fuddruckers T-shirt, and even though she wore no makeup, her face was shining and bright. *Das Mädchen* was beautiful! The Instructor had told Vonberger that Laura had no connections with Das Syndikat. She was simply being paid by them to act as Vonberger's lover for a few months. If she did as she was told, there would be a lot of money waiting for her somewhere. A *lot* of money. Vonberger had slept with her three times, and yet he still felt anxious when he was with her. He was always afraid that he might never get to be with her again, as if he might reach for her and she would suddenly melt in his hands and disappear forever.

"Then when my sister got old enough to cook," Laura was saying, "she used to make me peanut butter and jelly and spaghetti, and things like that. It was never anything great, but it sure beat the hell out of all that canned stuff."

Alex Vonberger watched Laura refill her glass with beer. She stood at the counter, leaning over slightly in concentration, and she tilted the glass at an angle as she poured, so as to cut down on the foam. Everything about her seemed natural. Vonberger had called her in the morning from JSC and she had invited him over for dinner. She had greeted him at the door with a warm kiss and a cold beer. And now she was laughing and cooking dinner and filling the apartment with lively chatter. She seemed so natural that it made Vonberger nervous. How could he tell what was real and what was an act? The funny stories and all the memories of her childhood and marriage were undoubtedly an act, done for the benefit of the men that listened in on them, the men with ears. But what about the kisses and the flirtations? What about the way she squeezed his rear end every time she got close to him? Could that all be an act too? And what about what happened in the bedroom? Maybe it was *all* an act. After all, she *was* a call girl.

She squatted in front of the stove and pulled the broiler out, and the room was suddenly filled with the sizzling smell of steak and onions. "How do you like your steak, Alex?" She was slicing into the giant slab of meat with a kitchen knife, and Vonberger felt his stomach rumble in anticipation.

"I like it a lot," he said.

She laughed and pulled the steak apart to show him the inside. "No, Alex. I mean, how do you like it cooked? Is it done enough for you?"

"Ah, yes," Vonberger said, laughing too. As hard as he tried, Vonberger could not find any falseness in her. Her face, her voice, and her every move, were light and cheery, and completely natural. Maybe all American girls were like that, but it made Vonberger nervous. How could she be such a good actress? Didn't it ever bother her that they were being constantly watched? Didn't she ever have to think about what she was going to say for the men with ears? How come she never got flustered or frustrated by the game they had to play?

Alex Vonberger followed Laura Gold into her living room where she placed their dinners on the coffee table in front of the couch. It was the only place in the apartment to eat. Laura had explained that she had spent most of her money from the divorce on her plane fare to Houston, and on her deposit for the apartment. It hadn't left her with too much money for furniture. Vonberger knew there had never been a divorce. Any money she had must have been socked away from her days as a call girl. Perhaps her stash had been supplemented by Das Syndikat, but they wouldn't have given her too much. Not yet, anyway. There was nothing more suspicious than somebody living above their means.

Vonberger took a hefty bite of steak and chewed slowly, savoring the flavor and the juices. At last, he swallowed and he turned to see Laura's big eyes staring at him, waiting for a response. *"Wunderbar!"* he said, and they both laughed.

"It was because of my husband that I started to cook, really," Laura said, cutting into her steak. "I guess it was something my mom taught me, that a girl has to cook if she wants to keep a man. Not that it ever did her any good. And not that it did me any good either."

Vonberger wondered if that was why she had made him dinner. Was she trying to "keep" him? Or was dinner all part of the game, something Das Syndikat had told her to do? Vonberger knew that there had been no husband, and yet the way she talked about him now made Vonberger wonder if perhaps there had been somebody, some man.

"How long were you married?" he asked, watching her closely.

"Four years," she answered, pushing another piece of steak into her mouth. She chewed voraciously for a moment, and then continued. "The first few years were pretty nice, but I don't think he ever knew what he wanted. Anyway, he didn't want me. It ended fast enough, I guess. I mean, it didn't drag on forever or anything. What about you, Alex? How come you were never married?"

"Me? No. I don't know. There was a girl I wanted to marry once, but she didn't love me." Vonberger knew that he should continue, but he couldn't lie as well as Laura could. He couldn't make up stories for the benefit of the men with ears. There had been no girl he wanted to marry. The irony of it all overwhelmed him. He would be lying for them, not for her. They would know he was lying, but they would think that he was lying to impress her. It was all too complicated, and Vonberger knew he couldn't lie that well, so he took another bite of steak, and then started in on his salad.

Women had never played an important role in Alex Vonberger's life. Yes, he had chased them, courted them, slept with them, and loved them, but he had always left them. When it came right down to it, women served their purpose, but no woman could ever be a friend. No woman could ever be a friend like Hans.

Little Alex Vonberger and Hans had grown up on the same street in East Berlin in the late fifties and early sixties. Hans was two years older than Alex, and in the beginning, Hans took the role of the mentor, the older brother that Alex Vonberger never had. But as they grew up they became different from each other. Hans was the troublemaker, always getting into fights and being scolded by the teachers. Alex Vonberger was the model student. He joined the right youth organizations and he was well liked by his peers. And each year, as the differences between the two boys grew, so did their bond of friendship. They held on to each other with a kind of frenzied desperation, each dependent on the other to live out his own fantasies.

Alex Vonberger entered the military and began his training. He studied English and Russian and aerodynamics. Hans worked for a factory that made shoes, and slowly Hans

seemed to fade out of Vonberger's life. He seemed to be
fading out of the world. And then Hans began showing up
in the middle of the night, filled with stories of high adventure.
He called himself Hans of the Many Passports. He was working for a neo-Nazi organization, he told Vonberger. They
called themselves Das Deutschland Syndikat, The Germany
Organization. They had many secret members and one day
they would rise up and reunite Germany. The Reich would
live again! Since childhood, Vonberger had always believed
that Germany had been unfairly victimized by the other na-
tions of the world, and he became excited by the promise of
a reunited Germany. Vonberger was inspired by Das Syndikat, but he was too busy to get involved himself. He was
learning to fly.

On a winter's night in 1979, Vonberger was traveling by
train to see his mother. He stepped into the bathroom and
suddenly found himself face to face with Hans. Hans locked
the door behind them, and the two men, now in their twenties,
embraced. They had not seen each other for almost three
years. Vonberger wanted to tell Hans about the jets he had
been flying, and he wanted to hear about Das Deutschland
Syndikat, but Hans cut him short. He had very little time.
Hans wanted Vonberger to join Das Syndikat. He assured
Vonberger that his membership would always be kept a secret, and that Vonberger would never be asked to do anything
that might jeopardize his position with the Communist party.
Vonberger could continue his training as a fighter pilot. Vonberger was overwhelmed by the sight of his old friend, and
by the chance to join Das Syndikat. He was tired of the
Communists and the Soviets and he wanted to do something
for the real Germans. This was his chance to do something
for Germany. This was his chance to make a difference.
Vonberger agreed, and he immediately became a member of
Das Deutschland Syndikat.

Nothing changed for Alex Vonberger. As the years went
by, he saw Hans infrequently. He would always ask Hans
for something to do. He wanted to help Das Syndikat, but

Hans assured him that the best thing for him to do was to continue to build his standing in the military and with the Party. Hans explained that all orders came from the Inner Circle. These top ten members of Das Syndikat were the masterminds behind the organization. Hans said they were all geniuses and were from the higher echelons of German society. Together these ten men had the wisdom and the power to inspire the German people to greatness. It was up to the Inner Circle to decide how and when to use Vonberger's services. Hans promised to encourage them to use Vonberger, but he could not guarantee any results.

In 1986, Alex Vonberger was chosen to participate in the Soviet space program as a guest cosmonaut. Vonberger was excited by the possibility of going into space, but he also knew his position would make him more valuable to Das Syndikat. And, in fact, in 1988 he got his first assignment. He was a cover for Johann Dressler, giving Dressler the opportunity to meet with a Soviet member of Das Syndikat and plan his escape to Iran. Johann Dressler, a member of Das Syndikat, would be instrumental in rebuilding the Nazi military machine. Vonberger learned to trust Das Syndikat. Operating within the Soviet Union was difficult, but at no time did he feel at risk. Everything was perfectly planned. And Vonberger was perfectly prepared for the questions that the Soviets had for him when Dressler disappeared. His friendship with Dressler had been totally innocent, perfectly set up by Das Syndikat. It was only when Vonberger returned to East Germany in the fall of 1988 that he learned that Dressler had been killed at the border.

There was more bad news waiting for Alex Vonberger when he got home. Hans told him that the annual meeting of the Inner Circle, held that year in Vienna, had been raided by the Austrian police, and all ten members had been arrested and imprisoned. Things looked bad for Das Syndikat. Without the Inner Circle to lead the way, the organization was almost crippled. Hans was a member of a temporary leadership, put together to guide the organization through these troubled times. Vonberger had done everything right in his first assignment, and he knew that with Hans at the top, he would be used again.

Vonberger knew that this time Hans would get something big for him to do. His whole life had led up to it. And then he had received notice that he had been selected to go to the United States with the Soviet PFP team. Everything was going his way. Alex Vonberger would make a difference after all.

Vonberger finished his dinner and then fell back into the couch, resting his head against the back. "You are a good cook, Laura," he said, lacing his hands together over his stomach.

Laura scraped up the last bit of potatoes and salad and Vonberger could see she was smiling as she took her last bite and dropped her fork on the empty plate. She ate like a man, Vonberger thought, but he liked that.

"You don't want to tell me about your girlfriend?" she asked, finally.

He smiled and shook his head. "No. There is nothing to tell."

"Most men love to talk about their old girlfriends."

"No. Not me."

"Okay. What do you want to talk about?" She fell back beside him on the couch and he put his arm around her, suddenly feeling her warmth and her energy. She smiled at him and he searched her face, her eyes, her mouth, but could find nothing unnatural about her.

"Alex," she said softly, moving still closer to him on the couch. "Alex, talk to me."

"Yes," he said, but he couldn't think of anything else to say.

"Alex, what will happen after you fly? Will you go back to Germany?"

"Yes, of course," he said, but it was a lie. There was a good chance he would never make it back to earth alive. And even if he did, it would be a long time before he got to go to Germany. He remembered that night in the bathroom on the train, over ten years ago, when Hans had promised that he would never jeopardize Vonberger's position. It didn't matter now, really. Vonberger would gladly give it all up for a chance to be a hero. Only Das Syndikat mattered now.

"We won't see each other then? After the flight?" She leaned up against him, her nose pushing into his temple, her hands resting gently on top of his.

She didn't know about the hijacking. She didn't even know about Das Syndikat. All she knew was that someone was paying her a lot of money to act as Vonberger's lover so that he could conduct midnight rendezvous in her basement. She had no idea whom he was meeting. And she had no idea how impossible it would be for them to see each other after the flight.

"I wish we could see each other afterwards," she said, softly into his ear.

"I wish we could see each other too," Vonberger said softly, and he held her tightly, suddenly more nervous than he had been before. He had not said it for her, or for the men with the ears. He had said it for himself. He had said it because it was true. "I wish we could see each other too," he said again. And then she climbed on top of him and put her mouth over his, and as she pushed her warm tongue into his mouth, he slowly felt his worries slip away. He was falling for her, and he couldn't help wondering if maybe she was falling for him too.

5

THE GRAND SCHEME OF THINGS

THE Houston FBI offices were quiet at nine-thirty at night, and Elliot Hacker had no more work to do, but he could not get himself to go home. He sat alone and smoked a cigarette, and he stared at the black distributor cable that was sprawled like a snake across the white papers on his desk. His men had found the cable among the empty pizza boxes and the junk mail in the trash bins behind Joey Wells's condominium. It seemed obvious that it was the missing cable from the NASA van that had been stranded at Ellington Field, but only that morning had it been positively identified by the forensics department. In the grand scheme of things, the cable had little investigative or political value. It had not started any love affairs, any defections, or any wars. But for Elliot Hacker, the cable symbolized the beginning of the gentle unfolding of the Soviet team, and the increased workload for the FBI.

Andrei Kulikov had been too embarrassed to protest a

simple lunch at a local restaurant. It would not look good if the Soviets could not trust their own cosmonauts, and Kulikov's official position was that the vans were there for his people's convenience, not as a way of imprisoning them in a schedule. As for the PF Flyers, it was just a beginning. Like all shuttle crews, they seemed to take on their own personality as they trained for their mission. In the spirit of friendship and understanding, the PF-1 crew became known for their openness, and their faith in the Peace Flight Program, and when together, they acted as if Andrei Kulikov and the NASA public affairs office were distant dictators who had long ago lost their powers. Lunch at Pe-te's Cajun BBQ soon became a Friday tradition, and Alex Vonberger was always drafting people to take him to Fuddruckers for dinner so that he could see his girlfriend. American and Soviet camaraderie, and what better word was there for it, had soon infiltrated the ranks of the scientists and the engineers. One night some Americans took a group of Soviet engineers to Premier, a discotheque, and Hacker's men were kept busy all night as they followed each of the Soviets back to Camino Village, the last one practically crawling home at four o'clock in the morning.

Elliot Hacker inhaled deeply on his cigarette and then snuffed it out into the ashtray on his desk. His job had been easier when the Soviets had stuck together, when they had all ridden the vans, and when they had all gone home early to Camino Village, but he had no political opposition to Soviet and American camaraderie. If the Soviets were interested in exploring American society, Hacker would not stand in their way.

He looked at his watch and thought about going home. There was nothing for him to do now. The cast of characters that he was responsible for were all being watched. His men were all trustworthy and they would notify him immediately if they found anything. But Elliot Hacker couldn't move.

It had all started with Alex Vonberger. Vonberger's love

affair with Laura Gold had been the first aberration, and the key to understanding it, as far as Hacker was concerned, was to understand Laura Gold.

He picked up the latest report on her and read through it for the fifth time. Born to a poor family in Toppenish, Washington, her father had left when she was six, and she was raised by her sister and her alcoholic mother. At the age of sixteen she followed her sister to Seattle, where her sister died of a drug overdose a year later. Laura Gold lived off her good looks, working first as a cocktail waitress, then as a Playboy bunny, and finally as a call girl. Why would she suddenly pick up and move to Texas? Had she gotten in some kind of trouble? Had she double-crossed her pimp? And why was she going straight all of a sudden? Hacker knew that people didn't go straight without a good reason. Something must have happened in Seattle.

Laura Gold was lying to Vonberger about her background, but that made perfect sense. She wouldn't advertise her past life. The irony was in the fact that she was perfectly set up to spy on Alex Vonberger, and yet she had not been placed by the FBI. Hacker had checked with the CIA, and she was not one of their agents either. That left only the KGB, and that didn't make any sense. It would be easier for them to watch him at Camino Village than to lure him away from the pack with an American agent. And if Laura Gold was not working for the FBI, the CIA, or the KGB, then that meant that she was just a call girl from Seattle, making a new start in Texas.

Elliot Hacker picked up his telephone and dialed a number from memory. It rang twice and then a man's voice answered. "Hello."

"Steve, it's Elliot."

"Boy, can't a guy ever get any sleep?"

Hacker smiled and looked at his watch. "It's only a quarter to ten, Steve. You can't be sleeping!"

"I was up until two-thirty last night."

"Okay, Steve. I'll make it short. Is your phone secure?"

"You bet."

"Okay. What'd you get from Seattle?"

"Still nothing. She just up and left. Apparently she talked about it for a few weeks, but nobody believed she was going to do it. We can't pin it on any specific event or person. It seemed to come out of the blue."

"Can you follow up on it?"

"Seattle has a couple of agents working on it, but I wouldn't bet on anything new. They've already checked with all of her clientele and all of her associates and there just isn't anything to go on."

"All right, go to bed, Steve. I'll see you tomorrow."

Elliot Hacker leaned back in his chair and lit another cigarette. He wished he could go to Seattle himself. He missed doing his own fieldwork, and he was tired of reading other people's reports. A call girl from Seattle resettled in Texas. It just didn't make any sense.

And then there was Andrei Kulikov to consider. Kulikov was an ex-cosmonaut from the early days of Soviet space exploration. Unlike the United States, where many astronauts joined the NASA administration, most cosmonauts were never promoted further into the Soviet space program, but Andrei Kulikov had proved himself to be a valuable administrator and a loyal party member. There was no doubt that the open and free attitude of members of the Soviet team was not inspired by Kulikov, but he was tolerating it. Why was he allowing all of this sneaking around? Everything had been easier in the years before *glasnost*, when the Soviets kept an eye on their own people. Was this all part of *glasnost*, or was something else going on?

And finally, there was Aelita Zakharov. She, like Vladimir Turnov, was a model cosmonaut and a careful Russian. She trained enthusiastically and she was warm and friendly, but she showed no overt interest in participating in American culture. Still, Hacker could not help wondering if she had been the inspiration behind Joey Wells's theft of the distributor cable. He picked up the cable and held it in his hands while he smoked. Joey Wells was definitely the adventurous type, always playing the role of the errant cowboy, and not beyond the practical joke, but such extreme measures as stealing cables from NASA vans would not have been taken without some encouragement. Had she somehow prompted him? Had she flirted with him, or teased him? Someone was going to have to have a talk with Joey Wells.

Elliot Hacker threw the cable back down on his desk and watched the rubbery cord settle in among his papers and his ashtrays. Surveillance was one of the toughest jobs. As long as you found nothing, you always thought you were missing something. He pushed the cigarette into an ashtray and shut his desk light. He had done his work for the day. Now if he could just get himself to go home.

6

BE-BOP-A-LULA

ELITA Zakharov stood outside the hangar at Ellington Field, waiting for Joey Wells. She had changed from her flight suit into a pair of blue jeans and a soft blue blouse. The wind swept her hair gently across her face and she used her left hand to shield her eyes from the warm April sun.

Zakharov knew that Ellington Field was a retired air force base used now by the National Guard and by NASA, and yet, it seemed to her to be like all other air force bases she had ever known. It had that same clean and dry feeling of isolation. The roads were straight and empty and seemed to be there for the sole purpose of getting the pilots to the runway. Their single-mindedness reminded Zakharov of the roads at home. The old ramshackle barracks stood out in the sun with their paint-chipped walls and broken windows swept clean by the Texas wind. These unused wooden shacks would be allowed to stand because they weren't in the way of the jets, and the only thing that really mattered at an air force base was the jets. At least, that was the way it seemed at home.

Then there was always the extra security checkpoint to get to the runway, as if you hadn't gone through enough security checks already. Zakharov had been surprised that the Americans had these too. Sometimes it was like the security checks were only there to make the pilots who went through them feel more important. It was like that discotheque in New York City that she had heard about, where people waited in line for hours just to get in. She had heard that the fun was being important enough to get in the door. She had to hand it to the Americans. They had somehow made it recreational to stand in line. If only the Soviet government could do that.

Still, the worst thing about air force bases, Zakharov thought, was that they all reminded her of Mikhail. She had met Mikhail Petrovsky at the Chkalov Air Force Base while she was training at the Gagarin Cosmonaut Training Center in Starry Town. She used to go to the base for training flights on the Ilyushin-76 cargo planes, and often she would see Mikhail, strutting off the runway in his helmet and flight jacket, with buckles dangling everywhere, and that arrogant look in his dark brown eyes. He had always known he was the best.

Aelita Zakharov watched as a big white convertible drove up to the security checkpoint at the gate. The top was down and rock and roll was blasting from the speakers. Joey Wells could not have possibly looked more American. Zakharov watched him flash his pass at the guards and she could see the guards laugh. He had probably hit them with one of his Cowboyisms.

At home they had made it clear enough that Joey Wells would be a bonus for her. If she successfully won his affections then there might be a nice apartment in Moscow waiting for her upon her return, or perhaps a privileged administrative job like Andrei Kulikov's. She had politely declined their offer, of course, explaining that she was a physicist, not a prostitute, and that she didn't feel capable of "winning" anyone's affections. They seemed to understand. They smiled in that knowing way that only KGB agents could, and they told her the offer would always be open, and then they wished her good luck.

Joey Wells pulled his car up to where she was standing and he turned the music down. "Ready to fly?" he asked, smiling from ear to ear.

In the last few weeks, Joey Wells had become increasingly flirtatious. It was as if he was playing right into their hands and Zakharov found it slightly annoying, for she had deliberately distanced herself from him. She did not want the KGB to think that she was working for them. But Joey Wells seemed oblivious to everything. He joked and teased and carried on as if he were a teenager with a schoolboy crush. How could anyone so smart be so stupid? Never mind her broken heart. Never mind Mikhail Petrovsky, blown to bits over the rugged Afghanistanian hills. How could Joey Wells believe that an American astronaut and a Soviet cosmonaut could become romantically involved? It would be like living in a fishbowl, with the entire international intelligence community looking in at them all the time. That was not the kind of love she wanted.

Zakharov made herself comfortable in the front seat of Joey Wells's car, and they sped past the guards and out past the empty, dilapidated barracks. And then they were flying down a wide highway in his beautiful white car. They didn't build cars like this in Russia. All four wheels were on the ground, but they were flying. Zakharov leaned over and looked at the speedometer. At first she was relieved, they were only going seventy-five, but then she remembered that the speedometer would be in miles per hour, not kilometers. She threw her head back, her face up to the sun, and she let the wind blow her hair. Flying had never been so much fun.

Even the rock and roll was fun. There was something tough and wild about it, like Mikhail's flight jacket. The man singing had a voice that was both warm and strong. He loved his women and he wasn't afraid of his love, even if the women didn't love him back. He could love without giving up any part of himself. Joey Wells was concentrating now on his driving, passing cars on the right, and then on the left, and then on the right again, and Zakharov was free to listen to the music, rolling like the hills, racing like the car, hard like the mountains, smooth like the desert.

"Who is this, singing?" she asked, finally. She had to speak loudly, over the music and the wind.

"Gene Vincent. He's the greatest!"

"And what does Be-bop-a-Lula mean?"

"Be-bop-a-Lula?" Joey Wells shrugged and frowned. "Damned if I know. Maybe it's the girl's name."

Aelita Zakharov laughed. Imagine a girl named Be-bop-a-Lula. *Neptune*, the cosmonaut newspaper at home, would use Be-bop-a-Lula as the name of a female American astronaut in one of their political cartoons. Be-bop-a-Lula. She would have to remember that, and she laughed some more.

Joey Wells smiled at her. "What's so funny?"

"What a name, Be-bop-a-Lula. Do you know any girls with that name?"

"No, not me."

"No? Do you have a lot of girlfriends, Cowboy?"

Joey Wells blushed and busied himself with his driving. "A few," he said, at last.

A few. It had been over four years since Mikhail Petrovsky had been killed. Four years was a long time without a man. Joey Wells could be her number two, if that was what she wanted. But she didn't want a number two. What she wanted was a new number one. And that meant that one day she would have to get over the old number one. One day, maybe. But not today. Not with Cowboy.

There was a small party at Joey Wells's apartment. The plan was to practice making chili as a team, so that they would all be ready for the annual chili cook-off in a few weeks. Joey Wells called it a chili simulation. The team, called the PF Flyers, of course, consisted of the entire PF-1 crew except for Vladimir Turnov. Turnov had somehow been persuaded to join Andrei Kulikov's team, the Comrades.

"How does Kulikov know how to make chili anyway?" George Evans asked. They all sat around the big table in the dining area reading over copies of the recipe that Joey Wells had passed out. Laura Gold was there, sitting next to Alex Vonberger, and Conrad Williams had brought his eight-year-old son, Conrad Junior.

"Hey, let me tell you something," Williams said, grabbing his son and hoisting him up onto his lap. "That's one chili that you're going to want to stay away from."

Joey Wells laughed and sat up in his seat. "Yeah, I'll bet you they could use Kulikov's chili down at the Jet Propulsion Lab in Pasadena."

Zakharov laughed with everyone else and then she took a long slow sip from her beer. She was having fun in spite of herself. She was afraid of Joey Wells, afraid of becoming too comfortable with him, but the party was easy and natural and the beer was making her feel light-headed. She and George Evans were assigned to onion duty, and while they sat and chopped onions, she found herself telling Evans how she was named after a character in a book by Alexei Tolstoy. The fictional Aelita had lived on Mars, and had fallen in love with a man from Earth. Zakharov wanted to tell Evans how her father used to read her the book when she was little, and how much she used to daydream that she was the fictional Aelita, living up on Mars, but she had never been very good at talking about herself, and she didn't think that Evans would understand.

"Hey Aelita," Conrad Williams called down from the other end of the table. "How come you and Alex didn't join Kulikov's team?"

Zakharov looked at Alex Vonberger, who was chopping green peppers with Laura Gold. Vonberger winked at her and said, "Because we have defected," and everyone laughed.

"What is defected?" Conrad Junior asked, pulling lightly on his father's arm.

"That's a good question. It means . . . well . . . If somebody defects it means they leave their country and go to another country."

"You mean, like when we went to Mexico?"

Williams smiled. "No. It's when someone leaves their country for good. Like if we went to Mexico to live forever."

"Why would anyone do that?"

"Oh, lots of reasons. Maybe they were unhappy in their own country, or maybe they liked the country they moved to more."

"Hey, wait a minute, wait a minute!" Joey Wells stood at the head of the table with a butcher's knife in his hand. "These two aren't defectors. I think these two are spies! I think you guys are here to get my recipe so you can bring it back to Andrei Cool Enough!"

Everyone laughed. Everyone except for Zakharov. She knew she should be laughing, but it was too hard. Everything was too hard. She hadn't thought about the Aelita from Mars in a long time, and for some reason it was making her sad. The beer was making her feel dizzy and hot, and the onions were making her eyes tear. She excused herself and stepped out into the courtyard in the back for some fresh air.

The courtyard was a small patio and garden area surrounded by a solid wooden fence for privacy. It had gotten dark already and a few spotlights lit up the area by the sliding glass door. Zakharov left the pavement and the light and walked out to the edge of the courtyard and stood in the grass, looking up at the stars. She wanted to be Aelita, the one that lived on Mars.

Joey Wells had taken her hand to help her out of the car when they had first arrived. And while she was chopping onions, he had come up behind her and looked on, resting his hands comfortably on her shoulders. She couldn't let herself start thinking about him now. He was too much like a kid. It was almost hard to believe that he was a pilot and an astronaut. She liked that he had two pet turtles, and she liked the way he had taken her hand to help her out of the car. He had nice hands, strong and soft at the same time. She wondered if he had been with a lot of women, and then she laughed at herself. She must be drunk to be thinking like that.

She turned to go back in to the party and Joey Wells was standing there. His hand came up to her cheek and wiped away a tear that had been left from the onions, and she suddenly felt embarrassed because he would think she had been crying. His other hand reached for her neck, and she let herself be pulled toward him. She rested her head on his shoulder. It had been a long time and she felt the years of anguish and loneliness well up inside her. She needed to talk, but she didn't know who she could trust. Joey Wells was forcing her to see that she had locked herself away, but she knew that he could never understand her. She was the Aelita from Mars, and he was the man from Earth. He was warm and kind, but he was an alien, and he would never understand. If only he knew how she thought of him.

7

THE
CASE OF THE
RED HANDS

A STATIONARY object two hundred miles from earth will be pulled to the earth's surface by the force of gravity. The only way to accomplish a prolonged stay in space at that distance is to place the object in orbit. Orbit can be maintained by creating the proper acceleration of the object, so that the object's centrifugal force, generated by moving around the earth, equals the force of gravity pulling it toward earth. If this balance is maintained, then the earth's surface will curve away from the moving object at the same rate that the object falls. The object will thus never reach the earth's surface, but instead, will move in a circle around the earth. The force of gravity decreases as one travels farther away from earth, and thus, the key to obtaining a desired orbit is to achieve the proper speed. Too much speed, and the object will leave the desired orbit and continue out into space. Too little speed, and the object will fall back to earth.

This was all secondary knowledge for a cosmonaut, but Alex Vonberger was having trouble concentrating. In fifteen minutes Laura Gold was going to pick him up and they were going to go back to her apartment to celebrate his thirty-fifth birthday. Tonight would be his last instruction, but it would also be a chance to drink champagne with Laura and to have a little extra time to roll around with her in her bed. Still, he knew he had to review for tomorrow's exercises in the shuttle simulator.

Vonberger left the simulator workbook spread out on the coffee table and got up for another beer. Why did they bother teaching him this stuff, when they never let him do anything? The Americans, just like the Soviets, were treating him as if he were an idiot. Surely, he would develop a case of red hands before too long. The case of the red hands was an old joke about the first Czechoslovakian cosmonaut, Vladimir Remek, who, as the story goes, developed a case of red hands while in space with the Soviets. Soviet doctors in Moscow were baffled until Remek explained that every time he reached for a switch or a dial on the Soviet craft, the Soviets would scream, "Don't touch that!" and they would slap his hands, until they turned red. Like the Czechoslovakian cosmonaut, Vonberger knew that his presence on PF-1 was purely political. He was like the monkeys they used to send into space. He was a political monkey. A political monkey with red hands.

Vonberger flopped down on the couch and pulled the workbook onto his lap. Tomorrow's exercise would simulate a deorbit, the reentry of the orbiter into the earth's atmosphere, and the landing. The theory behind the deorbit procedures was that if the speed of the orbiter was reduced sufficiently, then it would descend to an altitude where gravity and aerodynamic drag would cause it to glide to earth. The process of reducing the orbiter's speed was called the deorbit burn.

Vonberger got up again and turned on the television. He flipped through the channels until he found some action, and then sat back and watched. It was one of those American cop shows. Somebody was chasing somebody else in a car and pedestrians were dropping like flies. Vonberger sipped his beer and thought about PF-1, and he wondered if they would ever get to do a deorbit burn.

At nine o'clock, Alex Vonberger went down to Camino Drive to meet Laura Gold. He felt himself smile as he saw her green Pinto, waiting in the usual place. Even though he knew it was bugged, Vonberger had grown fond of her little car. She had bought it with her own money when she had first arrived in Texas, and to Vonberger it symbolized the "realness" in her that he had begun to trust. His early doubts had given way to a warmly felt knowledge that her tendernesses were above and beyond the call of duty. She loved him, and Vonberger could feel it in the gentle way she touched him, when nobody else could possibly be looking.

Laura Gold had a light supper and a bottle of champagne waiting for them when they got to her apartment. They toasted Vonberger on his birthday, and they kissed between bites of their sandwiches, and pretty soon they were in bed and she covered him with champagne-flavored kisses and pushed her warm body hungrily against him.

Nine hours after his final instruction, Alex Vonberger, Number 27, sat in the shuttle simulator with Vladimir Turnov, Conrad Williams, and Joey Wells. NASA liked everyone to know what everyone else was doing on a mission, and so it was Turnov's and Vonberger's turn to sit in the simulator while the commander and pilot did a deorbit, reentry, and landing. Turnov and Vonberger had nothing to do. In fact, if they tried to do anything they risked getting a case of red hands. All Vonberger could do was to watch Williams and Wells, so that when it came time to land he would be able to make sure they were doing everything right.

The inside of the shuttle simulator was identical to the flight deck of the real orbiter, except that the simulator was entered from the back, through a door, while the flight deck of the actual orbiter was entered via an access ladder from the mid-deck. The space was small and crowded. The commander's seat was in the front on the left, just like an automobile, and the pilot sat in the front on the right. In the simulator there were two backseats for additional crewmembers, observers, or instructors. These seats would be used for launch and landing in the real orbiter, but would be stored out of the way for the rest of the mission. There was no need for seats in zero gravity.

As Alex Vonberger buckled himself into one of the backseats he heard a Mission Control Center transmission over his headset. "*Discovery*, Houston. Radio check, over."

Conrad Williams replied, "Houston, *Discovery*, loud and clear."

They waited for the Control Center to announce that they were ready to start the simulation, but nothing happened. "Alex, I heard your girlfriend kept you out pretty late last night," Joey Wells said over the headset, while they waited.

"It was my birthday."

"Must have been some celebration," Williams said. "Happy Birthday."

"It is a good thing that she is not coming on the flight with us," Turnov said. "He would get nothing done."

"Right," Vonberger laughed. "Instead, now, it will be Cowboy who gets nothing done."

Williams and Turnov laughed.

"Hey, listen guys," Joey Wells said, trying to turn around in his seat. His seat belts held him back. "Just once more for the record. My interest in Ms. Zakharov is purely professional. There's nothing else to it. Got it? Nothing."

"What about the night of the chili simulation at your house?" Williams asked.

Joey Wells banged his palm against his forehead in exaggerated astonishment and then started to laugh. "Damn, Connie. You don't forget a thing, do you?"

"What happened?" Turnov asked, nudging Vonberger with his elbow.

"Don't you dare, Connie," Wells warned.

But Williams was already laughing and Turnov and Vonberger egged him on.

"Connie, I'm warning you. I'll crash-land us in the Indian Ocean." And Joey Wells pushed forward on the orbiter hand controller.

"What happened?" Turnov asked again.

"Should I tell them?" Williams was chuckling, the proud owner of a secret.

"Connie!"

But Williams couldn't resist. "Cowboy said he went to kiss her and it was like coming up against the Iron Curtain."

"That's it! You're dead for that! Into the ocean." And Joey Wells pushed forward on the hand controller as if he was taking the orbiter down, and they all laughed.

"Hey, what do you think they'll throw at us today, Connie?" Joey Wells asked, suddenly turning his concentration to his checklist.

But Turnov wasn't finished. "She told you off?" he persisted.

Wells ignored him. "I'll bet you they give us an OMS fuel leak."

"She told you off," Turnov said confidently.

"Hey, Vladdy baby." Wells tried again to turn around in his seat. "What's it to you?"

"Don't feel bad, Cowboy. You are in the good company of about two dozen cosmonauts. You know, if she had gone for you, there would have been a lot of unhappy men back home. It probably could have started a world war."

Suddenly the simulator began to tilt backward. The simulator was capable of tilting back ninety degrees to give the astronauts a realistic feeling of sitting in the orbiter on the launchpad. The backs of the seats would be parallel to the ground and the astronauts would have their faces pointing, appropriately enough, toward the sky. When the simulator had completed its tilt, it was almost as if the crew were lying down on shelves. If they didn't keep their hands and arms up on their chests, they would fall back behind them, down toward the back of the simulator.

The first time in the simulator was always disorienting for

a new crewmember. There was no reference point that let you know the simulator was being tilted back. Suddenly, the little room, which still looked exactly the same, had some weird idiosyncrasies. You felt heavy in your seat. The check-lists that normally hung down on lanyards floated up from the floor, and the lanyards themselves looked like pieces of wire sticking straight out from the walls. If the person sitting in front of you held an unrestrained pencil up and let go, it would fly back into your face. Vonberger had enjoyed the feeling of disorientation when he first experienced it in the Russian simulators, and upon arriving at JSC, he had a slight feeling of satisfaction in observing that gravity obeyed the same rules in the United States that it did in the Soviet Union. Now all of these little details just bored him, and he was confused because the simulator was not supposed to be tilted back for a landing simulation.

Williams spoke over the headset. "Houston, *Discovery*. Are you ready to start simulation?"

"*Discovery*, Houston. We are go for simulation."

"Houston, we've got a little problem up here," Williams said.

There was no answer.

"Houston, we've got a little problem up here. Do you copy?"

"We copy, *Discovery*. What's your problem?"

"There's something strange going on. We're supposed to be doing a deorbit burn. We are two hundred miles above the earth, and yet it feels like we're on the launchpad!"

The sound of laughter from the Control Center came over the headset. "We copy, *Discovery*." There was more laughter and then, "Our nutritional engineers inform us that the reported sensation has a direct correlation to a caffeine shortage here in Mission Control."

"Did you say a brain shortage?" Joey Wells asked.

There was more laughter from the Control Center. "No, Cowboy. We said caffeine shortage. Now if you all will just bear with us, we'll have you straightened out in no time."

"Roger, Houston."

As the simulator leveled out, Williams and Joey Wells began teasing Turnov about Kulikov's chili, but Vonberger wasn't listening. He was thinking about his last instruction. He would never have believed that hijacking the American space shuttle could be so easy. If the commander and the pilot were both restrained, then there was no way for the shuttle to land. They would orbit peacefully, until Vonberger's demands were met, or until they ran out of oxygen. Up in space, there would be no way for the United States or the Soviet Union to attempt a rescue. They would have to give in, or else they would lose their astronauts. It was all that simple.

"*Discovery,* Houston. Are you guys ready yet?"

Williams and Wells were laughing. "Anytime, baby," Williams said.

"Okay, *Discovery,* we are go for simulation."

"Roger."

"Clock's on. L minus one hour, forty minutes and counting."

Vonberger tried to pay attention to the simulation. He had to watch carefully, so he would be able to make sure they did everything right for the real landing. Williams and Joey Wells began preparations for the shuttle's deorbit. First they prepared the RCS, reaction control system, the cluster of small rocket motors in the nose and tail pods, which would be used to turn the orbiter around. Once the orbiter was turned, they would be ready to fire the OMS, orbiter maneuvering system, engines, which would slow the orbiter down and thus begin the descent to earth. Joey Wells went through the checklist for prestart of the auxiliary power units (APUs) needed to control the craft in its descent.

At L minus 1:21, Joey Wells programmed the computer for the deorbit burn. Vonberger watched carefully as the pilot pressed "OPS-3-0-2-PRO." They waited another four minutes, while Mission Control evaluated telemetry of the orbiter systems, to ensure that all preparations were complete.

"*Discovery*, Houston," Mission Control said, at last. "You are go for deorbit burn."

"Roger, go for deorbit burn."

Williams began flying the orbiter with his hand controller, while watching the altitude indicator, directly in front of him. Joey Wells was throwing switches on the overhead panel, preparing the OMS engines for ignition.

Then Williams spoke. "Houston, *Discovery*. Maneuver to burn attitude complete."

"Roger, *Discovery*."

Mission Control Center's transmission was clipped by the sudden buzzing of the master alarm. The master alarm is tied into all of the shuttle's major systems. It's loud enough to wake the crew if they're sleeping, and it's annoying enough to make it impossible to concentrate if they're up and working. The first thing a commander will do when a master alarm sounds is to turn it off, so that he and the pilot can communicate. The alarm itself does not tell the crew anything about the nature of the malfunction, just that a malfunction exists. The crew must look to the cluster of caution and warning lights and the computer screens on the front panels to identify the malfunction. A light in the caution and warning matrix indicated an OMS problem and Joey Wells punched into the computer to find out exactly what was wrong with the OMS system.

"Aha! I told you!" Wells shouted.

"What is it?" Turnov asked.

"A fuel leak in the left OMS. Didn't I tell you that's what they were going to give us?" Wells reached overhead and closed the tank valves.

"Okay, Cowboy," Williams said patiently. "Guessing the disease is one thing. Now let's see you cure it without killing us. You've got about three minutes before we need to do the OMS burn or else we've got to go around again."

"Kill us? Would I do that?"

"You did last week."

"I didn't kill us. We made a perfectly acceptable emergency landing in the Atlantic Ocean."

"And we all would have died."

"There was nothing else to do, Connie. Maybe we would have died, but at least we had something to do on the way down." Wells looked at the OMS fuel pressure gauges above his forward window. "We've got enough fuel in the right OMS to do the deorbit burn."

Williams studied the computer display. "All right, cross-feed and start the APU," he said. "We'll be able to do this without going around again to do an RCS burn."

"What is RCS?" Turnov asked.

"Reaction control system," Williams answered, still working with the computer. "We can use the RCS engines to slow us down, instead of the OMS engines, but it takes a longer burn."

As Williams and Wells continued to work the simulated emergency, Alex Vonberger lost track of what was going on. With the launch date now only two weeks away, Vonberger found that he could think of little else. To go into space in and of itself would be exciting enough, but to hijack the space shuttle added an intensity that was beyond anything Vonberger could have ever imagined. Everything had begun to feel dreamlike and unreal. Vonberger was one of only several people in the whole world who knew what was about to happen. And it was all so simple. His demands would be met. The imprisoned members of Das Syndikat's Inner Circle would be released and flown to Iran, where they would set up their new government-in-exile. Vonberger would allow *Discovery* to do a deorbit burn and return to earth. Of course, they wouldn't land at Cape Canaveral as planned, but instead, they would land on a remote desert runway in Iran. Still, the shuttle and the astronauts would be returned and Alex Vonberger would be free to live in Iran with his fellow exiles from Das Syndikat. And when they were ready, they would march back into Germany and the Nazis would reign again.

The only problem now was Laura Gold. What was he going to do about *das Mädchen?*

"Houston, *Discovery*," Williams said. "We've isolated an OMS fuel leak, and completed a cross-feed."

"Roger, *Discovery*. We like your configuration and confirm you're go for the burn."

"OMS engines armed and ready," Joey Wells said.

"We copy, *Discovery*. OMS engines armed and ready. Standing by for deorbit burn."

When Alex Vonberger had returned to Laura's apartment after his final instruction, Laura had saved him some champagne. She was drunk and she sat on the bed. The sheet was dropped down around her waist, and her shoulders were squared back, so that her breasts were sticking out into the air. She looked so good it was obscene. Vonberger knew then that he would have to figure out a way to be with her after the hijacking. He would never be able to just say good-bye and be done with her. As he sat next to her on the bed, he took her hand, and without saying a word, held it tightly in his own. Then she grabbed him and they rolled over onto the bed. Alex Vonberger and Laura Gold tumbled around in the champagne and the sheets, and then down onto the floor, where she pulled off his pants, and they went at it again, and again, and again.

"Houston, *Discovery*. Countdown to OMS burn ignition: five . . . four . . . three . . . two . . . one . . . ignition."

8

THE
IRON
CURTAIN

I N the darkness of his room, Joey Wells watched the fluorescent blue lights of his digital clock radio. It was 3:52 A.M. Damn. In less than five hours, he had to be out at Ellington Field for landing simulations with Conrad Williams. Joey Wells knew he could fly on four hours of sleep, he had done it many times before, but for three nights now he had been unable to sleep, and it was beginning to get on his nerves. Three nights now, ever since that night in the courtyard.

Joey Wells stuck his head under the pillow and breathed deeply. If he just stayed still and didn't think about anything, maybe he would be able to drift off to sleep. He concentrated on his breathing, taking in deep lungfuls of air and then slowly exhaling. In and out. In and out. All he needed was four hours of sleep. In and out. In and out. The night before he had slept only four hours and he had performed perfectly in the shuttle simulator. In and out. He could handle anything they threw at him, and yet, something about that day in the simulator made his skin crawl. Something had happened that day. In and out. It was Conrad Williams, that's what it was. Williams and his dumb crack about the Iron Curtain. Why had he ever told Williams that? He should have known that Williams didn't have an ounce of discretion. It was bad enough getting the cold shoulder, but now all of NASA had to know about it. In and out. In and out. Joey Wells threw the pillow off his head and looked at the clock. It was 4:08. Damn.

All right. He would give himself until four-thirty. Zero four-thirty, as they'd say in the Navy. If he was still awake at zero four-thirty, he would get up and raid the ice box. There was probably still some left-over chili. What could be better than a middle-of-the-night snack of cold chili and beer? The military had a name for operations in the middle of the night: zero dark thirty. If he was still awake in twenty minutes, he would do a zero dark thirty raid on the ice box.

4:11.

The Iron Curtain. What was wrong with her, anyway? Couldn't she see that they were perfect for each other? There was chemistry there, damn it! Real live chemistry! So what that she was Russian and he was American? What was wrong with a little Romeo and Juliet? There was chemistry. She couldn't ignore that. There's no fighting the forces of nature!

4:16.

Okay, cool it, Cowboy, he told himself. You've been over this a million times. Why don't you just forget her and move on to something new? You've been rejected before. Sure, sometimes it was all part of the game, it made her a better challenge and more desirable, but you always knew when to quit. What was the point if she just wasn't interested? Why bang your head against a wall? Why bang your head against the Iron Curtain? It's a simple matter of self-preservation. Just move on to something else.

4:20.

Ten minutes to ice box time. Why call it an ice box, anyway? All day long it was called a refrigerator, and then suddenly you raid it in the middle of the night and it becomes an ice box.

4:23.

Oh, hell. What was the sense in waiting? It was time to raid the ice box.

Joey Wells got up and turned off the air conditioner. As the sound of the air conditioner died down, he could hear a light scraping sound. He never would have heard it with the air conditioner on, and it never would have woken him if he had been sleeping. It was a distinct sound of metal on metal, but it was very soft. It was like a fan hitting a tiny piece of metal. No, it was slower, more occasional, than that. Like someone tapping a knife randomly against a metal table. He sat on his bed and tried to figure out where it was coming from. Downstairs. Somewhere downstairs. He pulled on a pair of boxer shorts and stepped out into the hallway. The warm humid air stuck to his skin as he stood at the top of the stairs in the darkness. The noise was definitely coming from downstairs. Joey Wells turned and walked quietly back into his bedroom. He walked around to the far side of the bed and reached under the frame and felt for the holster. The gun slid out easily. A Remington .22, six-shooter. He hadn't cleaned it in years, but it would still be loaded.

He thumbed off the safety and rotated the cylinder to set a bullet into place. Then, holding the gun out in front of his naked chest, he walked slowly down the steps, his bare feet making no sound on the soft carpeting.

He stopped when he was four steps from the bottom and he stooped down and looked into the living room. Some light filtered in through the windows from the courtyard and he could see that the living room was empty. He came down another step and looked around the corner into the kitchen. Empty. He let one foot drop to the next step, and then froze. The shadows in the living room and kitchen moved, and suddenly he realized that there was someone out in the courtyard, trying to come in through the sliding glass doors.

There were too many possibilities. He could go back upstairs and call the police. He could wait until they got in and
then blow them away. He could jump down and shoot them
through the glass. He could sneak around the front and surprise them. And then suddenly the lock on the door clicked
and the glass doors slid open: his company was coming in.
Wells reached up and hit the light switch and jumped down
the last few steps. He landed in a squatting position with his
gun pointing at the door.

"Move and you're dead!"

The guy was short but he was well built. His hands shot
up into the air and he stood, frozen, just inside the door. He
had a tough-looking face, with a big forehead and a chiseled
chin, but his skin was pale and pasty. He looked hard and
soft at the same time, like a statue that had just come to life.
He was grinning from ear to ear.

"FBI, son," the man said.

"FBI, my foot. Keep your hands up or I'll blow your head
off."

"Please, let me explain," the man said, still smiling. "My
name is Elliot Hacker and I'm with the FBI. It is extremely
important that we turn the light out. I can't be seen here."

"Are you kidding? Get in here. Sit down at the table. Put
your hands on the table. That's right. Just stay like that. I
almost blew you away, you know that? Now, you just sit
there. I'm gonna call the police."

"No, Joey!" The man stood up.

"Sit down!"

"Joey, please! Don't pick up that phone!"

"How the hell do you know who I am?"

"Please. If you'd just let me explain. Can I show you my
identification?"

"Keep your hands on the table!" Joey Wells moved around
the table, keeping his gun trained on the man's head. The
man was wearing a suit and tie. What kind of a jerk ran
around at four in the morning breaking into people's houses

wearing a suit and tie? ''Okay,'' Wells said to the man. ''Get up. Nice and slow. Put your feet out. Hands on the table. That's good. What the hell are you smiling about?''

''Gun's on the left ankle. Badge is in the inside left coat pocket.''

Wells pulled the gun out from a holster on the man's left ankle, and then checked everywhere else. It would be a nice trick to tell him where one gun was and then carry another. The badge was on the inside pocket. Elliot Hacker. FBI. Damn.

''You're lucky you didn't kill me,'' the man said, reaching his hand out for his gun and badge.

Wells laughed, and dropped them on the table. ''No skin off your back, though, huh?''

''Can we turn the light off now?'' the man asked.

''What for?''

''Nobody can know I'm here.''

Wells turned the light off, and then sat down on the bottom step, facing the table. He flipped the safety switch on the gun. ''That was pretty stupid,'' he said into the dark. ''You could've been dead meat. I almost killed you.''

The man's voice came back at him. ''I couldn't take the chance of anyone finding out about this meeting.''

''So you break into my apartment?''

''I'm sorry. It's a matter of national security.''

''It's pretty stupid. I mean, when the CIA wanted to talk to me about the defense mission, I just met them in Building One. It seemed a lot easier. What is this anyway? What do you want from me?''

''We have reason to suspect that Aelita Zakharov is working for the KGB.''

Joey Wells felt a pang of fear and hurt, but he laughed. ''So what else is new? You guys suspect everybody.''

''That's what we're paid to do.'' The room was suddenly illuminated by a match, and Wells watched as the man brought the tiny flame to the end of a cigarette. Wells could see the reflection of the yellow light in the glass doors to the courtyard, and he laughed to himself. The man couldn't be too worried about being seen. "The Russians are eager to learn about the defense mission you flew last year," the man said. "They would stop at nothing to get information on our spy satellites."

"Oh, come on."

"I need you to tell me everything that has gone on between you and Zakharov."

"Yeah, right."

Wells followed the orange glow of the cigarette as the man sat back down at the table, where Wells had first put him. "Joey, it's not a request. This is a fact-finding mission, and I need you to fill me in on a lot of details."

"What details?"

"All the details. Including the part about how you removed the distributor cable from the van at Ellington Field."

"That was over a month ago!"

"What happened the night you brought her back here to make chili?"

Joey Wells rubbed his face in his hands. This was ridiculous. "The night I brought her back here to make chili?"

"Yeah. Tell me about that."

"I brought her up into my bedroom and we made passionate love for two hours, and then I proceeded to tell her all about my mission last year, and everything I had ever discussed with the CIA, the Department of Defense, and the National Security Agency."

"That's not funny, Joey."

"Look. I gotta fly in three hours. That's not funny either. I don't mean to be unpatriotic or anything, but I'll tell you right now that Aelita has done nothing to get information from me. In fact, right now, she's avoiding me. So why don't you take your badge and your suspicions and go bother someone else?"

"Did you say she was avoiding you?"

"Well, not avoiding me. She's . . . made it clear she's not interested in me."

"She could be playing hard to get."

"Playing hard to get? Oh, I get it. The Russians really want to know about the satellites we launched last year. Is that right?"

"Exactly."

"I see. So they tell us they will participate in the PFP, and they send Aelita over as part of the team, somehow knowing that both she and I will be picked to fly the first mission. They know that I will fall for her on my own initiative, but just to make sure I really fall hard, they tell her to play hard to get. Just to really get me. Then once she's got me, she's gonna squeeze me for everything I know. Is that how it works?"

"Does it sound ridiculous?"

"You bet it does."

The man stood up and Joey Wells watched the orange ash circle in the air as the man gestured wildly. "Well then you better grow up, *Cowboy!* These are Russians we're playing with. This isn't some high school sock hop! These are Russians! And whether you like it or not Zakharov is one of them. Don't believe everything you read in the press about the PFP being the final bridge to peace. That's all a lot of crap. They're Russians and don't you ever forget it!" He slowly walked around the table and stood in front of Joey Wells. Then he lowered his voice and continued. "Now I didn't come here to play games with you. I need all the information you can get me on Zakharov so that we can make a proper determination to see if she is dangerous to the PFP program. Your failure to cooperate would amount to nothing short of treason. Do you understand that? *Cowboy?*"

"It's called the PFP."

"What?"

"It's called the PFP. Not the PFP *program*. Or did they school you at the Department of Redundancy Department?"

"You haven't heard a word I said, have you?"

"Yeah, I heard." Joey Wells sighed and looked at the figure looming up in the dark in front of him. It suddenly dawned on him that he was wearing nothing but his boxer shorts. Why couldn't it have been Aelita at the door? Why did it have to be this stupid FBI man with his talk of spies? Wells remembered his joke the night of the chili simulation, about how Aelita and Vonberger were spies, and he remembered how Aelita was the only one who hadn't laughed. It would have been a dead giveaway not to laugh. A spy would have been sure to laugh.

"She's not a spy," he said finally.

"Then how come you're protecting her?"

"I'm not protecting her!"

"Joey, let me make the conclusions."

"Okay. But there's really nothing to tell you. She's not a spy. It was all my idea. She hasn't come after me, or tried to seduce me or anything like that. It was all my idea. I stole the cable from the van so I could get to know her. What can I say? I fell for her. And she doesn't want me. Okay? What else do I have to tell you?"

The man's figure backed off to the table, and Wells saw the orange glow disappear as he crunched out his cigarette. "How do you know she doesn't want you?"

"That's a little bit personal, isn't it?"

"No, Joey. It's important."

Wells let out another big sigh. "I made a pass at her a few nights ago. Here. Out in the backyard."

"The night of the chili?"

"Yeah."

"How did you get her out to the backyard?"

"She went out there by herself. I followed her. I thought maybe she wanted me to follow her. I thought maybe it was her way of telling me she wanted to be alone with me."

"What happened?"

"I stood at the door for a minute and watched her back. She was just standing there, looking up at the sky. And then she turned around and there were tears in her eyes. She had been crying."

"Are you sure she was crying?"

"There were tears in her eyes."

"She could have been faking."

"Why would she do that?"

"It's the best way to win a man."

"Are you talking from personal experience?"

"What was she crying about?"

"How should I know?"

"You could have asked."

"Look, I'm sorry, but you hadn't given me a script to read."

"Okay. What happened then?"

"I . . . I wiped a tear away from her cheek."

"Go on."

"I pulled her close to me and she put her head on my shoulder. We stood like that for a few minutes not saying anything. I thought she was into it. I wasn't forcing myself on her or anything. I thought she liked it. So I picked her head up to kiss her."

"Yes?"

"She turned away and told me that she didn't think it was right."

"And what did you say?"

"What did you say your name was again?"

"Hacker. Elliot Hacker."

"Hacker, don't you have anything better to do with your time than to get the intimate details of other people's love lives?"

"What happened after she said that she didn't think it was right?"

"Damn. I really wish we didn't have to get into this."

"Come on, Joey. It's important."

"I told her I . . . I told her that I thought I could love her."

"And what did she say?"

"She said that I didn't know what it meant to love. Then I tried to say something but she cut me off. She told me to forget it, and she walked past me back into the party."

"And that was it?"

"That was it."

"And have you forgotten it?"

"I'm sorry?"

"Have you lost interest in her? Do you still want her?"

"Of course I still want her."

"Then it worked."

"What worked?"

"She made you fall for her."

"Come on! You think the Russians have love down to such a science?"

"I know they do. Have you seen her since then?"

"No, not really. I've seen her, but there's always been other people around. She's avoiding me."

"Look, Joey. We're not going to jump to any conclusions. She passed all of our initial investigations and security checks. It really is your interest in her that first raised our suspicions. The Russians can be very subtle."

"I think you're cracked."

"You are not to tell *anybody* about my visit. Do not assume that anybody knows about this, because they don't. You are to continue your pursuit of Zakharov. Do not let her know we suspect anything. Just be very careful, and we will be back in touch in a few days. Remember, do not let her know that we suspect her."

"You mean you want me to work for you guys now?"

"No, Joey. For your country."

"I already work for NASA. Isn't that enough?"

"I'll let you answer that question yourself."

"Hey, Hacker," Wells said to the man's back as he was leaving. "Next time feel free to use the front door."

The man stuck his head back in. "No, thanks. Too many locks."

Wells waited a few minutes and then climbed back up the stairs and got into bed. The room was hot again but he didn't feel like putting the air conditioner on. It was 4:57. Maybe working for NASA was enough. Maybe it wasn't. That wasn't the question that was bothering him. It was the other question. "Do you still want her?" Damn, he still wanted her. And what if she *was* playing hard to get? Maybe that's why he couldn't forget her. Maybe she really did want him. She wasn't a spy. She just wanted him and she was playing hard to get. She couldn't be a spy. It just wasn't possible.

5:03.

If he was still awake at five-thirty he would go down and pull a zero dark thirty raid on the ice box.

9

COOL
ENOUGH

I N the end, it was the softball game that broke Andrei Kulikov.

All space shuttle crews are moved into isolation quarters one week prior to flight in order to maintain their health. The Thirteenth Annual Flight Crew Operations Directorate Chili Cook-Off was held just two days before the PF Flyers were to go into isolation, and thus it served as a sort of send-off party for the PF-1 crew. Chili lovers of all ages roamed from table to table, as each chili team eagerly dished out samples and added last-minute spices. Groups of people picnicked on the lawn, while others warmed up in the field for the softball game. And like any good chili cook-off, there was plenty of beer, and everyone was drinking it. Even Russell Madlinger. Even Andrei Kulikov!

Andrei Kulikov wore a large white chef's hat and a friendly smile as he dished out servings of his chili, and yet, he still seemed distant, not quite a part of what was going on around him. All other barriers of distrust between his people and the

Americans had disappeared, and only curiosity and friendship
remained. Leonard Wolff and Conrad Williams watched in
amusement as little Conrad junior pitched balls to Vladimir
Turnov and yelled out instructions on how to swing the bat.
Alex Vonberger walked hand in hand with Laura Gold, sam-
pling chili and drinking beer, and he could not stop himself
from laughing at Kulikov's chili, for even Vonberger had
learned that real chili was not supposed to have beans. George
Evans dished out the PF Flyers' chili and playfully called
out, "Try the best! Try the bloody best!" Joey Wells, taking
his cue from Conrad junior, volunteered to teach Aelita Zakharov how to swing the bat, and he stood behind her with
his arms around her, showing her how to move the bat slowly
through the air.

Russell Madlinger had been so busy in the last few months
that he enjoyed the opportunity to spend some time with his
family. He and Cathy sat on the grass beneath a large shadowy
tree, and they watched their children playing and mingling
easily with the crowd. Madlinger ran his hand through Cathy's
hair, and enjoyed her warmth and her closeness. Chris sat
with them for a while, and he told his father that he wanted
to show him the short story he had written. Madlinger, of
course, said he would be happy to read the story, and he was
about to tell Chris that he was proud of him, but Chris was
suddenly up and running. He watched his son walking around
the tables of chili and snapping pictures with his new camera.

When it was time for a group shot of the the PF Flyers,
five of them gathered around a picnic table and waited for
Alex Vonberger, who had gone off to a far corner of the lawn
with his girlfriend. Vonberger and Laura Gold came jogging
slowly back to the table, and they arrived blushing and slightly
out of breath, and the PF Flyers teased them. Alex Vonberger
took his place at the table with the crew and he took the
baseball mitt that someone had put on his head, and he put
it on Joey Wells's head, and Wells put it on Zakharov's head,
and Zakharov threw it up in the air. The mitt seemed to float
in the air for a few seconds, as if it were weightless, and

then as it came down, they all tried to catch it, and Chris Madlinger snapped a picture.

Then Russell Madlinger brought out the shoe boxes, six of them, and handed them out, and all crewmembers got their own pair of ankle-high red sneakers. They were not real PF Flyers sneakers, since they had stopped making PF Flyers a long time ago, but the NASA PF Flyers decal was printed on the side. The crew hurried into their new sneakers, and Joey Wells was going crazy. "These are great! I love these!" Then they all lined up with their sneakers on and Chris Madlinger took a picture of them and somebody else took a picture of their feet.

And then it was time for the softball game. The first team, made up of mostly astronauts and cosmonauts, called themselves the Orbiters. The other team, made up mostly of the engineers and managers, called themselves Ground Control. The Soviets had never played softball, but it didn't stop any of them from trying. And even though Turnov and Zakharov had both gotten some instruction, only Alex Vonberger seemed to master the art of swinging a bat.

By three-thirty it was the bottom of the seventh inning and there were three empty kegs of beer, and a fourth on its way out. Ground Control was at bat and they were losing by two runs. Peggy Kellner, the center director for the Johnson Space Center, hit a hard line single to left field. That brought up Andrei Kulikov. He had struck out twice, but was still convinced that he could hit the ball. On the second pitch he actually connected, and this caused such mass confusion in the infield that he made it to first base, and Peggy Kellner swung around to third. Then Cathy Madlinger walloped one over the heads of the outfielders. It could have been an easy home run, but Kulikov was in front of her, and he was so excited by her hit that he forgot to run. After much encouragement and screaming and yelling, Kulikov finally started around the bases.

Chris Madlinger had been pitching, and he ran in toward home plate to catch the throw coming in from the outfield.

The throw was long, but Chris Madlinger went for it, and at the same time, Andrei Kulikov had rounded third and was coming home. Kulikov wasn't looking where he was going. He was looking at the outfield, and at remarkable Cathy Madlinger coming into third.

With all the screaming, only the people standing near home plate could hear the thud when Chris Madlinger and Andrei Kulikov collided. They had both been moving so fast just before the collision that they literally bounced off each other and landed about fifteen feet apart. Chris was a pro. Years of sports training had taught him to roll into his fall, and he came up quickly on his knees, his palms bleeding, his shirt torn, and the ball nowhere in sight. Andrei Kulikov had a harder time of it. The force of the collision had turned him around and thrown him down on his stomach. His face hit the dirt and then he slid for about five feet before coming to a stop.

It was typical that the three Madlingers, Russell, Cathy and Chris, were the first ones there. Russell was always the one to come by when your car was broken down on the side of the road. Cathy was the doctor. And Chris was the responsible son who had far too many adult attributes for a sixteen-year-old.

Andrei Kulikov rolled over onto his back. His hands and arms and face were covered with dirt and blood. He managed to stand up and Chris gave him his torn shirt to clear the blood from his face. Everybody waited, not going too close, not crowding, but waiting to see if he would be all right. Cathy Madlinger was wiping Kulikov's face. She touched it to find out where it hurt and to see if anything was broken. She looked in his mouth. He hadn't lost any teeth. He hadn't broken his jaw, or his nose. The blood was coming from scrapes on his forehead and cheeks. Just a lot of scrapes. He would be all right, she announced. She would fix him up. Everything would be all right. Andrei Kulikov began walking away from the field, slowly, with Russell Madlinger on one side of him and Cathy Madlinger on the other.

And then it happened. Andrei Kulikov began resisting. He was pulling away from Russell Madlinger, and at the same time he was grabbing Cathy Madlinger's arm and pulling her. Nobody understood what was happening. Kulikov, his face still dirty and bloody, was coming back toward the field. Even Russell Madlinger looked confused. Then with a sudden burst of energy that he could no longer contain, Andrei Kulikov began to run, pulling Cathy Madlinger behind him. And just as the Orbiters began to understand, Andrei Kulikov jumped up in the air and landed on home plate, and then swung Cathy Madlinger around behind him. Then, to allay any lasting confusion, he pointed his dirty bloody hand toward the keg of beer, and sure enough, there on the ground, in a puddle of muddy beer, sat the ball, still untouched, uncaught, and unfielded.

Andrei Kulikov laughed like nobody had ever heard a Russian laugh before. It was not a laugh of victory, nor of trickery, but of fun. It was a laugh that knew no boundaries, that cut through the years of hate and mistrust. It was a laugh as big and as deep as space itself.

And when Andrei Kulikov came back with bandages on his face and hands, he was presented with a box of Hamburger Helper, as the prize for the worst chili, and he carried it around proudly, and threatened to bring it back to the Soviet Union for scientific analysis. Everyone laughed, and at last everyone had their answer. Andrei Kulikov was Cool Enough.

10

BANANA
RIVER

THE PF Flyers, of course, had become world heroes. Three days before the launch, they were flown to the Kennedy Space Center where they stayed at the crew quarters in the Operations and Checkout Building. There they continued to prepare for their mission, under the watchful care of Mary Posner, often referred to as the "den mother" of crew quarters. On the morning of launch the crew rose in darkness and they dressed quickly in their flight suits. They had a light breakfast with Mary and joked quietly among themselves. It was still dark outside when Mary wished them luck and gave them each a peck on the cheek, but when they stepped from the crew quarters the floodlights came on and there was a roar of applause from the waiting press corps. Someone cried out, "You guys look great!" and someone else yelled, "The whole world loves you!"

It was a short walk to the van that would take them to the launch pad, and the PF Flyers, all smiling and excited, waved enthusiastically at the press. Joey Wells wished that he could have stopped to throw off some clever responses to the questions being shouted out, but this was no time for a press conference. There were less than three hours until takeoff and the crew had to get out to the shuttle and get buckled into their seats.

The PF Flyers were quiet as the van drove them through the Florida darkness, all of them lost in their own private thoughts and prayers. When they reached the launch area it was bathed in light, and it seemed as though they all gasped at once, overwhelmed by the beauty and the magic of the shuttle and the tower. The giant external tank and the solid rocket boosters seemed bigger than ever, and *Discovery* looked like an old friend, ready to take them for a ride. They rode the elevator up one hundred and ninety-five feet and then crossed the access arm toward the shuttle. The white room was a small chamber just outside the hatch that led into the orbiter. In the white room they were all assisted into helmets and launch harnesses, and then, one at a time, they passed through the open hatch into *Discovery,* their home for the next six days.

In the gray early morning before a launch, the birds along the Banana River get crazy. Russell Madlinger had once mentioned this observation to someone, and he had been told that his sensitivity to the increased noise was due only to the residual hangover from the traditional prelaunch party at the Mousetrap. Madlinger had stopped going to the Mousetrap years ago, but the birds were still going crazy.

The swampy mangrove islands in the river were clustered with gulls, herons, and pelicans, fluttering their wings and shaking their bodies in nervous expectation. Unlike the cows at Redstone, the birds understood. The birds could accept man's flight in airplanes and jets, since this sort of flight was exactly what the birds had been doing all along. But space flight was different, and the birds looked upon man's flight into space the same way that the fish must have looked at the first amphibians who left the water for land. In the cries of the birds, Madlinger could hear a desperate clinging to the status quo, and an unyielding fear of the unknown.

Russell Madlinger could not see or hear the birds from Firing Room 1 at the Launch Control Center, but he could see *Discovery* on Launchpad 39A. Kennedy's Launch Control Center would be in charge of the space shuttle until it cleared the tower, at which time the Mission Control Center in Houston would take over.

Firing Room 1 is a big airy room, at least compared to Mission Control in Houston. The entire east wall is a group of large windows that look out across the marshy area toward the launchpads. The floor is covered with computer consoles that are used by engineers to monitor all major systems of the orbiter. On the elevated section of the firing room, near the windows, is the launch director's console. The launch director is in charge of the launch and the firing room. Near him is the test director, who coordinates communications among the various system engineers, and communicates with the crew during the countdown. The voices of the test director and the crew are broadcast over speakers located throughout the Kennedy Space Center, so that the press and spectators can hear them. Once the shuttle clears the tower, the capsule communicator, or CapCom, in Houston's Mission Control Center, is the voice heard speaking to the crew.

The two corners on the elevated side of the firing room are separated from the rest of the room by glass walls. These areas are for official guests and observers. The proper functioning of the firing room requires a complete absence of extraneous personnel, and so getting onto the firing room floor is almost as difficult as getting into the orbiter itself.

The weather was perfect for a launch, and the countdown had gone smoothly. At T minus nine minutes the clock stopped for a scheduled ten-minute hold. Firing Room 1 was buzzing with activity, as engineers at their consoles ran last-minute checks on the cabin pressure, communication systems, and engine status.

From his console in the guest section of the firing room,

Russell Madlinger watched a lone sea gull fly in frantic circles outside the big windows. Perhaps it was a spy taking a peek at the shuttle's brain center for the troops of birds out on the marshes, or maybe it was a diplomat, making one last effort to stop the launch. The bird kept circling in front of the window, and Russell Madlinger began to think that perhaps the bird was trying to understand why it was that man wanted to go into space in the first place.

"We go because it's there," Madlinger answered in his mind. Yes, there was all the technology and science, and yes, there was even the prospect of world peace, but Madlinger knew that man went into space because it was there. And even so, this was only half an answer, because it really said more about man than it did about space. To accept space's existence as a reason for space travel, was to accept the fact that man was by nature an explorer. Madlinger believed that man's need to explore was a manifestation of a more basic human instinct: man's desire to improve himself and the world around him. Man wanted more than to eat and survive and continue. Man wanted to make the world better. And he couldn't make it better by sitting at home. In the crudest terms, dear bird, Madlinger thought, that was why man was going into space, and why you and cows would forever stay home.

At T minus two minutes the test director's voice came over the communications system. "*Discovery,* external tank pressurization is okay. You are go for launch."

Commander Williams's voice came back, "Roger. Go for launch."

At T minus fifteen seconds, valves were automatically opened for the sound suppression system on the launchpad, and thousands of gallons of water were sprayed onto the mobile launch platform under the shuttle to reduce acoustic noise and reflected sound waves.

At T minus six seconds the shuttle's three main engines ignited, and at T-zero the solid rocket boosters ignited, spewing yellow and orange flames out onto the launchpad, instantly vaporizing the water and turning it to steam. *Discovery,* flight PF-1, lifted off the pad.

Even inside the firing room, Madlinger could feel the vibrations and hear the roar of the solid rocket boosters. He knew that those people watching from outside would be able to feel the pressure on their chests and in their ears. The whole world was shaking.

Within seconds the launchpad was covered with a mass of billowing white smoke and steam that lifted up in clouds and folded into itself, like giant melting marshmallows. The burning orange flames from the solid rocket boosters followed the shuttle up as it cleared the launchpad, and the public affairs announcer's voice was almost lost in the noise as he reported, "We have lift-off! The shuttle has cleared the tower!" And then the firing room team broke into applause. The applause was more quiet and tentative than the applauses during the launches of the early shuttle flights. Too many people in the room still remembered the day when they applauded the lift-off of *Challenger,* only to watch it fall from the sky seconds later. There had not been an accident since then, and they knew that everything humanly possible had been done to prevent one from happening again, but they also knew that the risk of space flight could never be completely removed.

Russell Madlinger joined the others at the window and he watched as *Discovery* slowly climbed into the sky. For the first time in history, American astronauts and Soviet cosmonauts were going up into space in the same spacecraft, and an American spacecraft was flying into space carrying Soviet satellites. PF-1 just might help bring peace to the world, and not even the birds could protest that.

11

WEIGHTLESSNESS

F ROM *Discovery's* mid-deck, where there is only one small window in the hatch, lift-off was exactly like the simulations, except for the gravity forces. Alex Vonberger felt the vibration when the main engines ignited and he felt the shuttle lurch and then recoil, almost as if it was poising to jump. Suddenly the solid rocket boosters ignited and in a fury of thunder and vibration, *Discovery* leaped off the launchpad. The gravity forces were nothing compared to those experienced by Vonberger as a fighter pilot, and Vonberger found himself giving the thumbs-up sign and then leaning over to shake hands with George Evans. Then he settled back into his seat and smiled to himself. He was finally going up into space.

As *Discovery* approached the speed of sound, the main engines were throttled down to about 65-percent power, in order to minimize stress on the shuttle, but the sound and vibration continued. Then the call came to throttle up, and there was a slight increase in the g forces as the main engines went up to 104 percent of rated power. After two minutes the solid rocket boosters burned out and were separated from the external tank. They fell back to earth where they would be recovered from the ocean and used again. At T plus four minutes and twenty seconds, the CapCom from Mission Control Center in Houston came over the headset. "*Discovery,* Houston. Negative return."

"Roger, Houston," Williams replied. "Negative return." A return to the launch site was no longer possible. Any abort at this point would, at the very least, bring the orbiter to Spain or Senegal, which were the two optional transatlantic abort-landing sites.

Main engine cutoff, called MECO, occurred at exactly eight minutes and thirty-nine seconds. The external tank was separated from the orbiter and allowed to tumble back toward earth, where it would burn up in the atmosphere. After MECO, everything suddenly seemed quiet and Vonberger began to feel the first sensations of weightlessness. His helmet felt light on his head and he became more aware of the straps that held him into his seat. There was nothing to do now but wait until Williams and Joey Wells fired the final OMS burns that would insert *Discovery* into orbit.

Once in orbit, there was plenty to do. All of the launch and landing equipment had to be stowed, including the seats. Equipment had to be taken out of the lockers for use in flight. Vonberger stayed strapped into his seat so that he was in a stable position, and could more easily pack away the gear that was handed to him by George Evans and Aelita Zakharov. When that was done, Vonberger unbuckled himself and stowed his own gear, and then he let himself play in the weightless environment.

Vonberger had experienced short periods of weightlessness while training in NASA's KC-135, but he was not ready for the feeling of complete exhilaration that overtook him as he floated about the cabin in a prolonged weightless state. The most surprising thing to Vonberger was his ability to propel himself with very little force. Simply by tapping his finger against a wall he could move himself across the deck, and if he was sitting on the floor and he squeezed his buttocks together, he would slowly drift up toward the ceiling. The trick was to move slowly and carefully, and to Vonberger it seemed as if the whole crew was in slow motion. Vonberger felt clumsy and he kept colliding into walls and into the other members of the crew, almost as if he was drunk.

A less surprising, but no less disorienting, thing about weightlessness was that there was no such thing as "up." If Vonberger strapped himself to the floor, members of the crew "sitting" on the ceiling looked upside down, but if he moved to the ceiling, then they appeared right side up, and someone on the floor would be upside down. Slowly, Vonberger got used to seeing people at different angles, and he stopped trying to figure out who was right side up and who was upside down.

Vonberger and Evans were the only ones who had never experienced weightlessness for a prolonged period of time, but it was Vladimir Turnov who was the first to get sick. Turnov vomited into a shuttle "comfort bag" and then laughed out loud.

"Hell, Vladdy," Joey Wells said. "I thought you'd be used to this by now."

"You never get used to it," Turnov answered, and then he laughed again, and then he got sick again.

But weightlessness hits everyone differently. Turnov was up and about in a few hours, and Vonberger's sickness didn't hit him until just before dinner. He had been fighting it for a few hours, but as soon as Williams announced that it was time for dinner, Alex Vonberger got sick. And he stayed sick for a day and a half.

Alex Vonberger's first night in space was miserable. Everything was wrong. His insides felt like they were being twisted and squeezed into a golf ball. The nausea and pain were so all-encompassing that his feet and hands hurt. If he had been on earth, he would have spent the night tossing and turning, but there was no reason to toss or turn in space. You couldn't lie on your back or your side, because you couldn't lie down at all. All you could do was float. The crew wore black sleep masks, which they called Lone Ranger masks, when they slept. These masks served to keep the bright sunlight out of their eyes, since for half of their "sleep periods" they would be on the day side of earth. Vonberger had slipped into his sleeping sack and turned onto his left side, like he did on earth, but as soon as he covered his eyes with his Lone Ranger mask, he was floating, and this made his stomach feel worse.

The NASA doctors had promised Vonberger that any sickness would disappear in forty-eight hours. Perhaps it was just natural fear of what he was about to do, or perhaps it was his growing affection for the PF Flyers, but part of Alex Vonberger wished that he would never get better. He could never proceed with the hijacking if he was as sick as a dog. It just wouldn't be physically possible. But Vonberger forced himself to stop thinking about his crewmates by thinking about Laura Gold.

Vonberger knew that it had been risky to arrange a special meeting with the Instructor, but he had told Laura that he was homesick, the prearranged code word for the need for a special meeting, and somehow or other Laura had arranged it. At the meeting, Vonberger had bluntly stated his request, that he wanted Laura to meet him in Iran afterward, after the hijacking. They had already planned to smuggle her into Mexico. Certainly it would not be a problem to get her to Iran. The Instructor promised to check with Das Syndikat, and at the chili cook-off, Laura told Vonberger that she had been informed that everything had been arranged. Now, in his sickness, Vonberger could not stop thinking of how she would look when he saw her again, and how it would be when they lived together in some remote speck on the globe, and married, and loved their way into oblivion.

That first night, Vonberger let the pain in his gut roll over him and carry him slowly through the descending stages of consciousness, and somewhere between his hopes that he was dying, and his fantasies of Laura, he drifted off to sleep.

Once in the middle of the night, Vonberger awoke in fright, with the feeling that he was falling. There was nothing to hold on to. Nothing to see, nothing to lean against. It was like he was in a sack, falling in the dark. Then he remembered that he was wearing his Lone Ranger mask and he tore it off his head, and tried to reorient himself. The mid-deck was bathed in soft fluorescent light, and he could see a brighter light coming from the flight deck. He "lay" there as his eyes adjusted and his breathing subsided, and he realized that he was tightly gripping his sleeping sack, as if he might fall out of it. He loosened his grip and he felt the muscles in his hands and arms relax.

From where he was, he could see the silent sleeping forms of Williams and Evans, their arms floating out in front of them, as if in some weird religious ritual. In the last few days before launch, Vonberger had grown fond of George Evans. Evans, though always self-effacing, never lost his sense of humor, and because Vonberger and Evans were the only two who had never been in space before, a friendly bond had formed between them. Vonberger thought about the hijacking, and then he felt the pain in his stomach again. He put his mask back on and closed his eyes and thought about Laura, and slowly he drifted off to sleep.

On Day 2 everyone was feeling sick, but Vonberger and Evans seemed to have it the worst. They spent all of Day 2 strapped into their sleeping sacks in mid-deck, trying to stay out of everyone else's way. Once, Vonberger snuck up to the flight deck to look at the earth. The spectacular blue-and-white sphere loomed out at him, and yet, Vonberger only winced with pain: He was too sick to even appreciate it. He drifted back to the mid-deck where he and Evans tried to cheer each other up by making fun of themselves and watching the clock, waiting for the sickness to subside. The second night was a little better just because Vonberger was more tired, and when he woke up on Day 3, he was better. Completely recovered. Just like the doctors at NASA had promised!

Once Vonberger was over his nausea, he found that he adapted to weightlessness with incredible ease. He also discovered that his body had changed. Because there was no gravity force to pull the body fluids toward the feet, the body fluids were more "evenly" distributed. This made everyone's upper body bigger than it was on earth, and made everyone's legs skinnier. It was a noticeable difference and to Vonberger it looked like everyone was always holding their breath.

The first thing Vonberger did was eat a big breakfast: scrambled eggs and sausages and dried peaches. Everything tasted good, and everything stayed put. Then he began to float about the cabin, and he quickly noticed that he had already gotten better at moving around in weightlessness. While at first he had insisted on using the ladder to get from the mid-deck to the flight deck, he now found that it was easier to "dive" through the access port without using the ladder at all. He also found that he had learned to estimate the proper amount of force to use to propel himself without bumping into everything, and everyone, in sight.

That night it was Vonberger's turn to prepare dinner for the PF Flyers. Food preparation was simple. It was mostly a matter of finding the right trays, marked for each day and meal, mixing some of the foods with water, and sticking the others in the oven. It took Vonberger about twenty minutes to prepare dinner that night for the PF Flyers. He "made" shrimp cocktail, beefsteak, rice pilaf, and broccoli au gratin, with butterscotch pudding for dessert.

And eating was fun. It was a good time for the crew to be together and now that Vonberger was feeling better he could join in the conversation and the fun. The crew strapped themselves to the walls or the ceilings as they ate. There was no need for forks. All of the food would stay in its container, and then would stick to a spoon by virtue of surface tension. Escaped liquid would form spheres and float around the cabin. Vonberger found that he could stick a straw into the sphere and drink it out of the air. Escaped particles of food had to be captured, and this often led to comical chase scenes of crewmembers floating around the cabin, trying to grab an escaped piece of dried fruit, or a biteful of macaroni and cheese.

The heat from the sun in space is intense, since there is no atmosphere to diffuse it. The orbiter's cooling system, large radiators mounted to the insides of the cargo bay doors, serves to disperse excess heat into space. The cargo bay doors therefore remain open at all times, except for launch, deorbit, and landing. Normally, the orbiter is rolled so that the cargo bay faces the earth. From the earth's point of view, it looks as if the orbiter is flying upside down. One of the advantages of this attitude is that the crew can see the earth through the front and overhead windows on the flight deck. Out the back windows they can see the cargo bay and cargo bay doors, and they can see the tail of the orbiter as it traces a line around the edge of the earth.

This was another thing Vonberger came to enjoy as he felt better. Watching earth gave him a feeling of serenity and security. Before he went to bed on Day 3, Vonberger floated up to the flight deck and looked out at the world passing beneath him. Asia passed below in varying shades of green and blue and brown. It seemed to be an indifferent world, and Vonberger felt overwhelmed by all the wrongs and injustices that went unnoticed. Why should two foreign governments be allowed to keep his people apart? Why should the members of the Inner Circle be imprisoned for their beliefs? Why should a man like Hans be forced to travel at night and incognito? It was an unfair world, but Alex Vonberger knew that soon he would be able to do something about it, soon he would be able to make a difference. And as they passed over the Pacific Ocean into night, Vonberger knew that soon they would be passing over Texas, and that by now Laura Gold would probably be meeting her connection, who would be taking her across the border.

12

QUOTA
COVE

DEPUTY Steven Brandt drove slowly on the hard Texas
road that ran along the Rio Grande, outside of El Paso.
It would be another hour before the sun came up, but
there was already a hint of daylight along the edges of the
horizon. The last of the wetbacks from Mexico would have
turned back by now. Last night, anywhere from one thousand
to ten thousand Mexicans had probably illegally crossed
through Brandt's jurisdiction into the United States. Somewhere from one to a thousand pounds of marijuana had probably been smuggled in. Who knew how many jeeploads of
guns had crossed the jagged mountains into Mexico. The
border was a mess, and a poor tired Border Patrol man like
Brandt couldn't do anything about it. He did the best job he
could, and that was all he could do. He could stop a few
killings, confiscate a few kilos of drugs, or send a few people
back across the border, but it didn't really help. All he could
do was try to keep the peace. That was the main thing. You

couldn't stop the flow, but you could try to keep the peace. And you picked up the bodies.

Picking up the bodies was the worst part. At first it really got you, seeing all these women and kids left to die in the desert. After eleven years he had gotten used to it, if you could call laughing about it getting used to it. There was nothing funny about it really, but after you had seen enough of them, you had to laugh. Either that or you killed yourself.

Brandt pulled his car off the road and heard his tires crackle over the rocky dirt road that led down to the river. He and his buddies called this portion of the river "Quota Cove," because you could always catch a few Mexicans crossing here. The river at this part was shallow and dark, and there were bushes all along the American side to use for cover. Brandt wasn't looking to fill a quota. This late at night, they all would have been through already. He was just making sure they hadn't left anybody behind. A few months ago the boys on the next shift had found about a dozen of them left behind, lying in the bushes, and Brandt had caught hell because he had told his superiors that he had checked the cove.

As he pulled down to the river his eye caught a quick red flash, a reflection as his headlights passed over something in the bushes. He drove a little closer and then stopped and turned out his lights. He hadn't been out of his car in a few hours, and he didn't look forward to facing the El Paso heat that he knew awaited him. Across the river, Brandt could see the outlines of the Juarez slums and the rolling desert hills. In less than an hour he would be able to see the small wooden houses with corrugated roofs, and the old American pickup trucks with tarps draped over the backs. The poor Mexicans.

He picked up his big metal flashlight from the seat beside him and banged it like a club into his cupped hand. Then he opened the door and stepped out into the prickly heat. The sound of the door closing behind him seemed to echo in the desert stillness, and with one hand on his gun he approached the bushes where he had seen the reflection. The dry dirt cracked beneath his feet in the sizzling darkness. His eyes followed the beam of his flashlight as it zigzagged back and forth across the bushes.

Then he found the dusty taillights. A car was buried about three feet into the thicket, not quite hidden, but not quite obvious. Deputy Brandt felt his pulse pick up as he approached the car. Why the hell would someone drive a car into the bushes? There was no tag. He shined his light into the dirty back window and could see a figure at the wheel. The bushes were thick on both sides of the car, so Brandt reached for the handle of the hatchback and it popped open in his hands.

He jumped back with his gun in his hand. "Freeze!" he yelled, but the driver didn't move. "What are you doing in there?"

The driver still didn't move and Brandt cursed out loud in the darkness. Another one.

Brandt didn't like the idea of crawling up through the car to a dead body in the front seat, so he slammed the back closed and hacked his way through the bushes. Why me? he thought. Why on my shift? He stopped for a second and thought about pretending he hadn't seen the car, but they would never believe him. Once, maybe, you can get away with that trick, but twice, never. This one was his. There was no way around it. Just don't be too bad, he thought, continuing through the bushes. Just don't be too bad. The window next to the driver was open. Brandt heard the gurgling of the river and he turned his flashlight toward the front of the car. The left front tire was just a few feet away from the river, and buried in mud. Was this guy actually trying to drive across the Rio Grande? Brandt took a deep breath and turned his light into the car. Just don't be too bad.

It was a white woman. There were bloodstains all over the front of her dress, and there was something funny about the way her head was resting over the steering wheel. Brandt figured out what it was, but it was too late. He had already opened the door. Her body toppled out onto the ground, and her head rolled like a bowling ball into the muddy Rio Grande. Deputy Steven Brandt turned his head away from the little green Pinto, and got sick.

PART II

"STEALING THE STARS"

13

BLOODY
THIS, BLOODY
THAT

THINGS have a way of happening overnight in space. Actually, there are about sixteen nights in each twenty-four-hour period, so "overnight" is really an arbitrary eight hours during which the crewmembers sleep. The schedule on a shuttle mission follows a twenty-four-hour day, starting with lift-off. The schedule for the three days prior to launch is modified to reflect the schedule planned in flight, so that the crew avoids any possible adverse reactions during the flight from adjustments to their biological clocks. Human functions follow the twenty-four-hour schedule, and thus crewmembers generally feel rested after eight hours of sleep and are hungry at mealtimes. But some things seem to follow the rotations of the earth rather than the biological clock, so that while the crew sleeps, these functions of rotation speed around the earth five times, and when the crew wakes up it is almost as if it is five days later.

And so it seemed to Alex Vonberger that he woke up on the morning of Day 5 hating the PF Flyers. Suddenly he could not remember what he had liked about them. Every little thing they did just bugged the hell out of him. Cowboy's incessant flirtations with Aelita were juvenile and transparent. How could they behave like that? Did they have no pride? No discretion? Vonberger cringed as he watched them, two adults, two astronauts, giggling together like silly little schoolchildren.

Then there was Conrad Williams, who had somehow been transformed from a benevolent leader to a bossy dictator. George Evans had gone from friendly to pestering. And Vladimir Turnov, that arrogant Russian, was trying to give Vonberger a case of red hands. Who the hell did he think he was?

Throughout the day, Vonberger nurtured his hatred. He didn't let himself think about Laura. He smiled and remained polite, but he let the hate build up inside of himself, like liquid fuel in a rocket. He went out of his way to get his hands slapped. He *wanted* red hands, because it was things like red hands that made him join Das Syndikat in the first place. So he touched things he was not supposed to touch. And he asked Williams if he could do things which he knew he would not be allowed to do. And he forced himself to watch Wells and Zakharov play their little games.

In the afternoon, after they had launched the second satellite, Vonberger was supposed to work on his experiments. He spent an hour pretending to be photographing zero-gravity crystal growth, but most of the time he just watched Evans. That stupid clown was taking his little "bloody" experiments so seriously it was almost funny. Didn't he know his experiments were beside the point? Didn't he realize that he was only in space as a political experiment? A British monkey? There was something so incredibly lame about Evans. It was almost as if he *liked* having red hands. The irony was not lost on Vonberger that with two Americans and two Soviets on board, it was still the Brit he hated the most, with his "bloody experiments," "bloody satellites," and "bloody *Discovery*." Everything was "bloody" this and "bloody" that.

Every night after dinner Conrad Williams went up to the

flight deck to check the status of the orbiter's systems on the shuttle computer. Sometimes Joey Wells, or somebody else would go with Williams just to keep him company or to watch the earth in the overhead windows, but on Day 5 Joey Wells was in fine form, and everyone was lingering over their dinners and desserts and laughing. Alex Vonberger watched carefully as Williams's feet disappeared through the access port to the flight deck, waiting to see if anyone would follow. It wouldn't matter if anyone followed, but it sure would be easier if Williams was alone. It was time to move.

Vonberger excused himself and pulled himself out of the mid-deck, through the access port, and into the flight deck. Williams was already strapped into the pilot's seat and was reading information from the computer screen. The straps were simply to hold him in place, so that he didn't float away every time he hit a button on the computer. Vonberger unzipped the top outer right pocket of his pants, and as he silently floated up behind Williams he felt himself smile. It was all so beautifully simple.

He stuck the little automatic pistol to Williams's temple. "Okay, Connie. Just listen to me."

"Where to, bud?" Williams had not taken his eyes off the computer.

"Just drop your arms and bring your hands down around the back of your seat. Nice and slow."

"Cuba, maybe?"

"Hey, Connie. I'm not kidding around. See this?" and he showed Williams the gun. "I'll blow your brains out. Now put your arms behind your seat."

"Hey, where'd you get that? God, it looks real!"

"Damn it, Connie! It is real!"

"Well, look, Alex. I'm a little busy right now. Can we do this later?"

The one thing Vonberger had not expected was total disbelief. Sure, maybe at first they would not believe him, but he would show them the gun and raise his voice and sooner or later they would have to catch on. But Williams showed no sign of ever catching on. Vonberger felt the blood pumping to his head. He had tried to be nice. He had tried to be polite. And the dumb condescending clown just didn't believe him. Fine.

Vonberger floated back around behind Williams and jammed the nuzzle of the gun hard into the back of Williams's head. "Listen, my friend," he spoke almost in a whisper. "If you don't put your hands behind your seat this instant, I swear I'll blow your brains all over the inside of the cabin."

Williams turned in his seat and Vonberger moved to the side so that their eyes met, and so that Williams could see that Vonberger was not smiling. Vonberger could almost hear it register, and Williams brought his hands down slowly behind his seat. Vonberger pulled a pair of handcuffs from his pants pocket and slipped one end under the seat's safety strap, and then clipped the two rings around Williams's wrists. Without the seat belt fastened, Williams would have been able to let his legs float up, and then he could have pulled his arms up over the top of the seat, but the seat belt held him in place, and he couldn't get his hands free to undo it.

"Now listen to me, Connie. You stay still and keep your mouth shut. Nobody has to get hurt."

"What the hell are you doing, Alex?"

"I'm hijacking us."

"Alex, man, put the gun away. This really isn't funny."

Vonberger floated up over the commander's seat and pointed the gun toward the access port. "Hey, Cowboy," he yelled.

The laughing and talking from the mid-deck stopped, and Joey Wells called back. "Yeah, what?"

"Come up here." Then Vonberger showed the gun again to Williams. "Don't say a word, Connie. Not one word."

"What for?" Wells yelled back from the mid-deck.

"Connie wants you."

Joey Wells cursed and then somebody said something and they all laughed. Then Joey Wells floated into the flight deck. "What's up?"

Vonberger waved his gun in the air to make sure that Wells saw it, and then he moved along the ceiling toward the rear of the cabin. "Sit in the commander's seat," he ordered quietly.

Joey Wells was grinning from ear to ear. "What the hell's going on?"

"We're being hijacked," Williams said.

"I told you to stay quiet. Go on, Cowboy. Get in the commander's seat."

"Hijacked? Have you gone MECO of the brain?"

"Get into that seat!" Vonberger screamed.

Evans's head appeared in the access port. "What's going on?"

"We're being hijacked," Joey Wells answered, still grinning as he floated over the access port. "Look, Alex has a gun!"

Evans laughed and disappeared back into the mid-deck. Vonberger kept his gun on Joey Wells as he listened to Evans telling the others. "Hey guys, we're being bloody hijacked!" Vonberger heard the laughter and commotion from the mid-deck. He watched Joey Wells and he noticed that Wells was staring at the back of the pilot's seat, and at the handcuffs around Williams's wrists. Joey Wells stared back at Vonberger, and his eyes showed that he understood. Suddenly, Evans, Turnov, and Zakharov came pouring into the flight deck, their hands all positioned into the shapes of guns, and their voices making all kinds of sounds, from Evans's "pow, pow, pow," to Turnov's semirealistic imitation of a machine gun.

The moment comes. Things can go wrong in any operation. You spend months in planning and training, but the moment comes and all of a sudden proceeding according to the plan is like being the only actor on stage who is following the script. Alex Vonberger knew that the time had come to improvise. He had seen it in Joey Wells's eyes. This was the crucial moment. This was the moment of danger. For Alex Vonberger, this was the moment when he was the most alive.

Adrenaline pumped into Vonberger's blood, and suddenly he was watching himself from the outside, as if he was the hero on one of those stupid American detective shows. No matter how simple the plan was, this was simpler.

He was practically surrounded by them, so there was no need to aim. For some reason, Vonberger found himself watching the expression on Joey Wells's face. It was an odd mixture of prescient warning and comic disbelief. It was almost as if Joey Wells knew something that Vonberger didn't, and just before he squeezed the trigger, Vonberger realized that he had forgotten to anchor himself. The Instructor had told him to anchor himself before he pulled the trigger. But it was too late.

Firing a gun in a small pressurized cabin was like launching the space shuttle from inside a gymnasium. After five days in space, hearing only beeps and blips and soft speaking voices, the deafening blast of the gun was painful and the echo seemed to roar around the cabin, as if looking for a means of escape. The explosion of the gun sent shock waves throughout the orbiter. Vonberger had not braced himself against the force of the shot, and he found himself pounding up against the front windows of the flight deck. He almost lost the gun when his hand slammed against the glass, and he grabbed the top of the commander's seat with his free hand, and tried to stop himself from bouncing back into the center of the cabin. His feet rebounded from the wall and shot across the overhead of the flight deck. He straightened his legs and his feet hit the ceiling, and using the top of the commander's seat, he pulled himself back into the corner.

He took a deep breath and turned his attention to the rest of the cabin. It all seemed so unreal. The master alarm was buzzing and had somehow broken loose all over the flight deck. Instead of one red light on the console, the alarm was hundreds of little red bubbles, floating aimlessly amid the confusion. Everyone seemed shell-shocked. Vonberger wondered why Williams hadn't turned off the alarm. Damn the sound was irritating! Slowly, over the noise and the confusion, Vonberger remembered that Williams was handcuffed into his seat, and then he realized that the little red bubbles floating all over the cabin had nothing to do with the alarm.

Because nobody had "fallen," it took Vonberger a few seconds to figure out where the blood was coming from. Turnov was in the back of the flight deck with Evans. Joey Wells was still dangling over the access port and Zakharov was right beside him. Vonberger looked again at Turnov and Evans. There was no color in the Brit's face, and only then did Vonberger see the blood spewing from Evans's left shoulder.

"Everybody below!" Vonberger had to shout to make himself heard over the sound of the alarm.

Turnov and Zakharov helped Evans through the access port, but Wells kept floating on the flight deck. "How about the alarm, Alex?" he asked.

"I'll take care of it. Go downstairs and take care of Evans. Patch him up."

"You son of a bitch!"

"Go!" Vonberger surprised himself with the intensity of his own scream. He watched through the bubbles as Joey Wells disappeared through the access port. Then he pulled himself down to the commander's seat, fastened the seat belt, and turned off the master alarm. A blessed quiet filled *Discovery*, and Vonberger suddenly felt a calm sense of optimism. A light in the caution and warning matrix indicated that there was an atmospheric problem and Williams did not say a word as Vonberger leaned over the keyboard and punched number 66 into the computer. A full readout of the atmospheric control system flashed onto the screen. Vonberger and Williams studied it together.

"Oxygen supply is off," Williams said.

"I can see that."

"Check the switch. It's on panel L-two, over there. Top left switch."

Vonberger leaned to his left and found the switch for the primary oxygen supply. Small metal guards, the shape of large staples, bracket each switch on the orbiter to protect against accidental movement. The primary oxygen supply switch was off. Apparently the switch guards couldn't protect against human bodies being thrown about after firing guns. Vonberger flipped the oxygen switch on, and he and Williams studied the computer screen. The word "nominal" came on next to oxygen. That meant normal.

"What happened to Evans?" Williams asked.

"He took a bullet. You fools didn't believe me."

"How is he?"

"I don't know."

"You going to tell me what the hell you think you're doing now, Alex?"

"Relax, Connie. You are no longer in command."

Vonberger unbuckled his seat belt, drifted up out of the commander's seat and faced the mid-deck access port. It was time to get these jokers organized. "Okay, everybody. I want you up here one at a time. Turnov, you're first. Bring up some towels and the vacuum hose to clean up this mess. Let's go. One funny move and your blood will be out here too. I have a bullet here for every damned one of you."

14

THE
BLACKOUT

RUSSELL Madlinger sat in the Viewing Room behind the Flight Control Room at the Mission Control Center in Houston. He was slouched down in his chair, with his legs up on the seat in front of him and a pile of papers on his lap. His left hand held a plastic container of coffee, half empty and almost cold, and his right hand held a pencil, which he tapped casually on the papers in front of him.

He was talking to Senator Paul Ryan, who had come to Houston to observe the flight. Ryan was the chairman of the Joint Committee on the Soviet-American Peace Flight Program, the special congressional committee that had been set up to oversee the program. Madlinger had worked closely with the committee during the early stages of the PFP and had often testified before the committee on the progress of the program. Madlinger and Ryan had grown to respect each other.

Madlinger watched the Flight Control Room while he spoke. The biggest difference between Mission Control in

Houston and the Launch Control Center at Kennedy is that there are no outside windows in Houston. The room is also quite a bit smaller than the Launch Control Center. It has a series of tiers, almost like a theater, that graduate toward the back of the room, and the front wall has several projection screens. A map of the world is usually displayed on the big screen in the center, with sine wave-shaped lines showing three ground tracks of the orbiter. Each line is numbered to indicate which orbit it represents, and a small, blinking orbiter-shaped figure moves along one of the lines, changing its position at two-minute intervals, to indicate the orbiter's approximate location. To the left of the map two screens displayed a series of readings about the orbiter's systems and supplies. The screen to the immediate right of the map was blank at the moment, but usually displayed whatever view was being downlinked from the video cameras or VCRs on board the orbiter. The screen on the far right displayed another series of data readings.

Four rows of consoles fill the floor of the Flight Control Room. The flight controllers work nine-hour shifts. There are three shifts in a twenty-four-hour period, with a half-hour overlap between shifts to ensure a smooth transition. The flight controllers report directly to the flight director, whose console is located in the center of the room, one row in from the back. At 8:00 P.M. on Day 5, Andrew McKenzie was the flight director. McKenzie, like most flight directors, had worked his way up through the ranks of flight controllers. He had started at NASA as a flight dynamics engineer, and became a backroom flight controller during the shuttle flights in the early eighties. From there he became a flight dynamics officer, referred to as FIDO, and two years before PF-1 he had become a flight director. McKenzie was a by-the-book flight director, which was what all successful flight directors had to be. Their job was to follow standard procedures. Although flight directors had total control over the Flight Control Room, their authority to operate outside the original flight plan was limited. Serious problems were referred to the mission operations director, who sat behind the flight director, and who was a member of the Mission Management Team.

Madlinger watched McKenzie at the flight director's console. On Day 3, McKenzie had overseen the launching of PF-1's first satellite, and Madlinger had been impressed with McKenzie's impeccable performance. Now, papers and checklists were spread out all over his console and he was drinking a soda and talking to his assistant. There was not much for him to do on this shift.

Through the soundproof glass between the Viewing Room and the Flight Control Room, Madlinger saw the little red light on the flight director's console start to blink. Because of the soundproof glass, and the small size of the light, most people in the Viewing Room would not notice it. Madlinger quickly brought his feet down and sat up in his chair.

Senator Ryan sat facing Madlinger, resting on the back of a chair in the row in front of them. "Something wrong, Russ?" he asked.

"No," Madlinger answered instinctively. "I don't think so," he added. Madlinger studied the floor of the Flight Control Room, but it was hard to tell what was going on. McKenzie was standing up and seemed to be listening to his headset. Everything else appeared normal. "I'd better check it out," Madlinger said softly, and he excused himself and walked slowly down the steps of the Viewing Room.

There was no direct entrance to the Flight Control Room from the Viewing Room. Madlinger picked up his pace as soon as he heard the door to the Viewing Room close behind him. He turned down the hallway and hurried toward the Flight Control Room. The door had an electronic lock, and Madlinger cursed as he fumbled with his key card and punched in his access code. After getting through the outer door, he flashed his gold pass at the guard in the hallway outside the Flight Control Room, and the guard pushed the button that buzzed the inner door open.

Madlinger checked his pace again as soon as he stepped into the Flight Control Room. He walked slowly across the floor to the flight director's console, where McKenzie was standing as stiff as a board, facing the CapCom. The mission operations director had left his console and was standing behind McKenzie. He moved back a few steps to make room for Madlinger, acknowledging the arrival of a senior manager. He showed no signs of resenting Madlinger's presence. Perhaps he felt more secure, since now if anything went wrong, they would have Madlinger's experience and judgment in calling the shots. Madlinger donned a headset and tuned in to the flight director's loop. He checked the board on McKenzie's console and saw that the audio feed to the internal TV network, known as "NASA Select," had been cut off. He knew that now no one outside the Control Room could hear the air-to-ground communications.

"What's the problem?" Madlinger asked.

"Hard to say," McKenzie answered, without looking at Madlinger. "FIDO reports an unusual vibration. Electric reports oxygen is off. We're trying to raise them."

The CapCom spoke into his headset microphone. "*Discovery,* Houston. Do you copy?"

"Flight, Electric." It was the electrical and environmental control officer. "Oxygen is back to nominal! Computer shows it was turned back on. It reads nominal."

McKenzie and Madlinger exchanged glances, and then McKenzie nodded again at the CapCom.

"*Discovery,* Houston. Do you copy?"

"Did you get a report on the vibration?" Madlinger asked softly. He didn't want to appear to be looking over the shoulder of the flight director, but he couldn't help himself.

"FIDO, Flight. Report, please," McKenzie said into his headset. Like the mission operations director, McKenzie might have felt some relief having Madlinger on hand.

The flight dynamics officer did not face McKenzie and Madlinger, but kept her eyes on her console. "A single vibration with a high reverberation, not longer than a second. Monitoring for further developments. The vibration itself was not of dangerous magnitude but the cause is unknown. It appears to have been internal but I don't have a full report yet. My backroom is trying to isolate it.''

"Internal?'' Madlinger heard himself ask.

"Yes, sir.''

"Like what?''

"Some reaction inside the cabin of the orbiter. Like an explosion.''

"An explosion? Inside the orbiter? What kind of explosion?''

"We don't know yet. We're checking.''

"There's no reported damage,'' McKenzie added quickly.

Madlinger shook his head. "It doesn't make sense. Try to raise them,'' he said.

"*Discovery*, Houston. Do you copy?''

Madlinger checked the map on the front wall. The orbiter was passing over Southeast Asia and into the Pacific. The Soviet satellites launched by PF-1 were intended to be used in conjunction with existing American satellites to form a worldwide communications network, but it would take some time to get the system operational. Until then, orbiting spacecraft would pass through areas where there was no air-to-ground communication. This was called loss of signal, or LOS, and could last anywhere from a few seconds to twenty minutes. "How long until LOS?'' Madlinger asked.

"LOS in five minutes thirty seconds,'' the communications officer reported.

If Russell Madlinger had not been concentrating so hard on the issue at hand, he would have realized that the flight controllers had begun responding directly to his questions. McKenzie was no longer acting as an intermediary. Madlinger had command of the Flight Control Room.

"Did you run a full systems check?'' Madlinger asked McKenzie.

"It's being run, Report Errors Only. We won't hear unless there is a problem.''

"Flight surgeon report?" Madlinger asked.

"Negative, sir," the flight surgeon responded from the back row of consoles. "No data at this time."

"When is the Dynamics report due?"

"Six minutes," McKenzie said.

Madlinger nodded slowly. "Okay. We have to wait. CapCom, thirty-second intervals."

"Yes, sir."

Madlinger sat down in McKenzie's seat. McKenzie stood over his console and drummed his fingers lightly on the top of the computer. The room was absolutely quiet, except for the CapCom's voice repeating his call every thirty seconds.

"*Discovery,* Houston. Do you copy?"

Madlinger realized that he was still carrying the papers that had been on his lap in the Viewing Room. He went through them slowly, trying to distract himself. There was a NASA memorandum from Charlie Roland about future meetings of the Joint Soviet-American Task Force. It was too routine to read right now. There was a hundred-page checklist that contained the crew activity plan (CAP) for PF-1. The CAP outlined, in a series of time charts, exactly what activity was scheduled to take place at any point in the flight. Time was expressed as mission elapsed time, or MET, and was printed in days, hours, and minutes from lift-off. Madlinger checked the MET on the console in front of him. It was 4:11:07 MET and he flipped to that page in the CAP. Nothing was planned that would involve equipment or systems that might cause the unexplained vibration. Madlinger closed the book and looked at the last document on his lap. It was Chris's short story. Chris had finally given him a copy and he had been carrying the story around for two days, but had been either too busy or too tired to read it. He pulled up the story and put it on top of the pile. It was called "Stealing the Stars."

"*Discovery,* Houston. Do you copy?"

Madlinger looked at the neatly typed pages on his lap, and suddenly he was reading.

There's a river that I travel in my dreams. A river where my father has never been. The water is smooth and gray, but it glistens when the sun hits it in the morning. And the great mountains that push in along the edges are like my father, who looks in on me when he thinks I'm sleeping.

Sometimes I am the river. They build along my shores, cross me with their bridges, ride me with their boats. They fish my bays and swim my beaches. But I am the river and they will never understand me.

"*Discovery,* Houston. Do you copy?

I also have nightmares. I dream that I am the ditch on the side of the road. A garbage receptacle for beer cans and bags with names of fast-food chains. I am the forgotten three-foot strip that runs along the tracks, where the trainmen smoke cigarettes and the rats live. I am the forgotten by-product of man's technologies. The junkyard of the twentieth century.

My father was an astronaut, and he stole the stars from me. But there are some things he doesn't know.

"*Discovery,* Houston. Do you copy?"
Suddenly the air-to-ground loop crackled with a reply. "Houston, *Discovery,*" It was Williams. "We copy."
The flight controllers broke into applause, and the CapCom couldn't control his excitement. "Where you been, man? We've been worried about you."
There was no answer.
"Ask him about the alarm," McKenzie ordered, suddenly back in control.
"*Discovery,* we read a master alarm at MET four-eleven oh two."
"Roger, Houston."

"We recorded a highly unusual vibration and a momentary cutoff of oxygen supply. What are you guys doing up there?"

Everyone in the Flight Control Room laughed.

"Houston, we've been hijacked."

More laughter.

"*Discovery,* you want to confirm the vibration and momentary cutoff of oxygen?"

"Roger, Houston. We confirm."

"It's like pulling teeth," McKenzie said quietly, and then to the CapCom, "Would you mind asking him for an explanation?"

"*Discovery,* Houston. Flight director requests an explanation of malfunctions."

There was a brief pause, and then Williams's voice came back, a little shaky. "Houston, *Discovery.* Vibration was secondary to the discharge of a twenty-two caliber automatic pistol. Momentary cutoff of oxygen supply was caused by switch for primary supply accidentally thrown."

A few of the flight controllers laughed quietly.

"LOS in forty-five seconds," the communications officer reported.

"They pick one hell of a time to have a party," Madlinger said. "Tell him we want a report before LOS."

"*Discovery,* Houston," said the CapCom and glanced at Madlinger. "We have the director of PFP in the Control Room at this time, and he appreciates your sense of humor and your good spirits, but he would like a report on the vibrations and the oxygen cutoff prior to LOS, in approximately thirty seconds."

Again, there was a pause, and then "Tell him he's got it. We've been hijacked!"

Madlinger was about to grab the headset out of the CapCom's hands, but the communications officer interrupted, "LOS, sir. Next communications in eighteen minutes, forty-three seconds."

"Damn!" Madlinger flew back into McKenzie's seat, and he stared at his son's short story which he had thrown on the floor with the rest of the papers. It wasn't like Williams to pull a practical joke like this. Everyone made a few wisecracks now and then, but after a master alarm with an upcoming eighteen-minute LOS, you just didn't fool around like that. Madlinger's instincts told him that Williams knew better. And Madlinger, who had long ago grown to trust his instincts, hoped like hell that this time they were wrong.

"Flight, FIDO. We have a report."

Madlinger looked up from the floor.

The flight dynamics officer was now standing in front of her console. "It's impossible to precisely identify the vibration, but it appears to have occurred on the flight deck, approximately two tenths of a second prior to the cutoff of the oxygen supply. My backroom confirms that the cause of the vibration was some kind of explosion. Perhaps a piece of equipment blew up."

Madlinger raised his chin slightly. "Such as?"

"We are coordinating with the operation integration officer to make that determination."

"Could it have been a gun?"

She nodded, as if against her will. "Yes, sir."

Madlinger stood up and looked at McKenzie. "Let's have a complete blackout of the Mission Control Center. Nobody comes or goes until we reestablish communications. Flight controllers will not communicate with anyone other than their backrooms without the flight director's permission. Complete blackout."

"Okay, all controllers, this is the flight director," McKenzie announced. "As of this moment we are imposing a complete MCC blackout. Until further notice, no communications outside the building." And McKenzie leaned forward, raised the red cover, and hit the switch on his console, locking the door to the Flight Control Room from the inside.

15

UNCLE
ANDREI

ANDREI Kulikov sat at the big kitchen table with Nancy Madlinger on his lap. It had been two weeks now since the softball game and most of Kulikov's cuts and scrapes had healed, but a nasty gash on his forehead was still bandaged. He touched it lightly with his finger as he looked at the drawings of spaceships that Nancy had made at school. He was particularly fond of a drawing of a Soviet space capsule that had the name "Sea Gull" written on the side. *Chaika*, or *Sea Gull*, had been the name that Valentina Tereshkova, the first woman in space, had given her ship. In Nancy's drawing, a woman cosmonaut, whose long brown hair resembled Aelita Zakharov's, appeared in the window of the capsule, and Kulikov felt charmed by the innocent confusion.

When the telephone rang, Chris Madlinger had both of his hands deeply immersed in a bowl of chopped beef, mixing up his favorite hamburger recipe, and Suzanne Madlinger was running tomatoes under the faucet, cleaning them for the salad. After the third ring Chris and Suzanne both screamed at Nancy at the same time. "Get the phone!"

"Okay, okay," Nancy said in a singsong voice. She slipped off Kulikov's lap and reluctantly dropped her drawings on the table.

"It's probably my father," Chris Madlinger said over his shoulder to Kulikov, who sat patiently at the table. Russell Madlinger had invited Kulikov for dinner, but so far had failed to show up. Cathy Madlinger was working, so it was just Kulikov and the three Madlinger children. Kulikov didn't mind because he liked the children. Suzanne and Nancy both called him Uncle Andrei, and he and Chris had been good friends ever since the collision at the softball game.

"Hi, Daddy!" Nancy Madlinger said into the telephone.

"See?" Chris said, and smiled at Kulikov.

Kulikov gently pushed aside Nancy's drawings so that he could look again at the photographs that Chris had taken with his new camera. Most of the photos had been taken at the chili cook-off and Kulikov was particularly fond of a shot of the PF Flyers, all sitting together and reaching for a baseball mitt, which seemed suspended in the air above them. There were other shots of the Madlinger family and of Newton, the golden retriever, who now sat by Kulikov's feet, as if Kulikov was the new master of the house.

"Okay," Nancy said, still talking into the telephone. "Good . . . No, he's making the hamburgers . . . Yes, he's here . . . I was showing him pictures of the space shuttle that I made in school today . . . I don't know. Who do you want to talk to? . . . Okay." Nancy handed the telephone to Kulikov. "He wants to talk to you."

"Hello, Russ," Kulikov said into the telephone, still looking down at Chris's photographs.

"I'm not going to make dinner, Andrei." Russell Madlinger's voice sounded tense and rushed.

"Is there a problem?"

"Yeah, we've got some problems, Andrei. Don't say anything to the kids. I'm afraid you're going to have to miss dinner yourself."

Andrei Kulikov looked up and saw Chris Madlinger making the hamburger patties. "What's the matter?"

"They're coming by to pick you up now."

"Who's coming? I have my car."

"Leave it there."

"Russ, what's going on?"

"I can't tell you now. I'll see you later." And Russell Madlinger hung up.

Kulikov felt his insides stir and he knew it was more than hunger. What kind of problems would require him to leave his car at the Madlingers' and be driven to the Space Center? It had to be some sort of diplomatic or security problem. Perhaps one of his people was in trouble. He looked down at the photograph in his hand. It was a picture of Leonard Wolff, from NASA, standing among a crowd of people at the cook-off. His camera hung from his neck and he seemed to be looking off into the distance. "Well, I'm afraid I won't be staying for dinner, kids," Kulikov said, at last.

"Nooooo!" Nancy Madlinger protested, and she jumped back onto Kulikov's lap. "Now I have no one to play with!"

"How come you can't stay?" Chris asked.

"I don't know. Your father said they needed me down at the Space Center. And I was dying to try your hamburgers."

"Well, some other time, Andrei," Chris said.

When the doorbell rang, Newton jumped up from the floor and began to bark. Kulikov sat at the kitchen table and listened as Chris walked through the living room to open the front door.

"Hi, Chris," a man's voice said, over the sounds of Newton's barking. "Is Mr. Kulikov still here?"

"Who are you?" Chris asked.

Kulikov had heard enough to know that it wasn't anyone from the NASA public affairs office. First of all, the man knew who Chris was, even though Chris didn't know who the man was. And it was interesting that the man asked if Kulikov was "still" there. As if there had been some question as to whether Kulikov would wait for the ride or not. As if the man had been worried that Kulikov might try to escape.

"We're from the government, Chris," the voice said. "Your father told us we could find Mr. Kulikov here."

Something bizarre was going on. Kulikov got up from the table and walked out into the living room. He saw Chris Madlinger standing in the door with his arm across the entrance, and Kulikov could not help feeling proud of the boy. Just like his father, Chris was playing the role of the protector. Two men stood on the front step outside the doorway, and in the fading light, Kulikov could see their stern faces eagerly looking in over Chris's shoulder. The situation reminded Kulikov of something that Russell Madlinger had once said. Russell had claimed that the peoples of the Soviet Union and the United States could be good friends, if only their governments would let them.

It struck Kulikov as interesting that he was not afraid. Under ordinary circumstances, being retrieved by two unknown men claiming to be from the government had great potential for an unpleasant ending. But it was Russell Madlinger who had told Kulikov that they would be picking him up, and nowhere in his mind or his heart could Kulikov find a place that believed Madlinger would set him up for trouble.

In fact, standing in the Madlinger living room, with the dog barking and sixteen-year-old Chris in the doorway, Kulikov felt curiosity, more than anything else. The back door of the Madlinger house was probably being watched, but Kulikov would not have made a run for it anyway. He had to find out what was going on.

"Looking for me?" he asked.

Chris turned to look at Kulikov, but did not lower his arm.

"It's all right, Chris," Kulikov assured him.

Then Chris dropped his arm, and one of the men stepped

up and stood next to Chris in the doorway. "Yes, Mr. Kulikov. Would you mind coming with us, please. We'll take you to JSC."

"Is there a reason I can't take my own car?"

The man in the doorway suddenly smiled winningly. "Must be, Mr. Kulikov, but they sure wouldn't tell us what it was. Some security problem, I suppose."

A security problem. It could have been anything from a stolen pencil to a nuclear war. With more concern than fear, Kulikov said good-bye to Newton and the children and left with the two men from the government.

Kulikov tried asking some questions in the car, but the men wouldn't answer, and he began to worry. Madlinger wouldn't have purposely tricked him, but maybe Madlinger himself had been tricked. These imperialist spies were clever that way. Kulikov was reassured only by the fact that they were indeed headed toward JSC, and he felt better as they drove through the security gate. They continued to the far end of the Center, to a group of buildings that Kulikov had seen many times, but had never been inside. Behind the laboratories for life sciences, in Building 37, there was a smaller building off to the side. They pulled into the parking lot and drove around behind the building. There were a few cars and some NASA vans in the back, but it was dark and there were no people. A security guard sat by the entrance and he opened the door for them. Kulikov had seen no flashing of badges. It seemed these men got in on their good looks.

Kulikov was taken down a poorly lit hallway and shown through a door to a small office. The door closed behind him. In the office there was a table and three chairs, and nothing else. The table was made of plain wood and it had been painted white. The chairs were also made of wood and painted, but most of the paint had been worn off. There were no papers or books or supplies. Just the furniture. Kulikov checked the walls and the floors and corners for wires or bugs. He saw none, of course, but knew that he was being watched. He sat in one of the chairs, facing the door, and put his feet up.

A few weeks before he left for the United States, Kulikov had been visited by some men from the Party: undoubtedly KGB agents. For three hours they had warned him of all the imperialist tricks and instructed him how to handle himself. He had been told in great detail about how they worked, how they got information from people against their will, and how they tricked people into defecting. Kulikov tried desperately now to remember what he had been told, but it had already been several months since the briefing. He remembered that he was not supposed to believe anything they told him, and he wasn't supposed to talk, but he could not remember anything else. Perhaps that would be enough.

The door opened and a man came in and sat in a chair across from Kulikov. The man lit a cigarette and then threw the pack on the small wooden table. As the smoke filled the air, the man introduced himself as Elliot Hacker from the FBI, and he offered Kulikov a Marlboro. Kulikov shook his head and they both sat in silence and watched each other.

"We were on to Zakharov from the beginning," Hacker said, finally.

An intriguing opening, Kulikov thought, but he would have to do better than that.

"We didn't do anything about it because we couldn't believe you would actually be stupid enough to try something," Hacker continued. "I have to admit, we're all a little bit baffled. We don't see what you have to gain. Unless, of course, you think we would actually make any concessions to save our shuttle and our astronauts."

Kulikov shrugged and looked at his watch. It was almost nine o'clock. "Russell Madlinger around?"

"He's in Mission Control. Why?"

"Just curious," Kulikov said.

"Andrei, your position with us would be considerably improved if you talked to us. After all, there's nothing your government can do for you now."

It was going to be difficult not to talk, but Kulikov bit his lower lip and kept quiet.

"It's just you and me now, Andrei. You got nobody else but me."

"Can I get some food?" Kulikov suddenly heard himself ask. Then he forced his voice to sound calmer. "I haven't eaten dinner yet," he said.

Hacker shook his head. "No, I don't think so."

Kulikov shrugged, pushed his chair away from the table, crossed his arms and stared at the ceiling. The hell with this guy, he thought, and he bit his lip some more. The silence dragged on. It was almost funny, the two of them sitting in a little room, with a table, a few chairs, and no windows. They sat staring at each other and the floor, and the walls. Kulikov tried not to think about Chris Madlinger's hamburgers. How come he had been pulled away from the hamburgers? They had probably done it on purpose. These imperialists weren't just tricky. They were mean.

Hacker finally broke the silence. "Of course you realize that we've gone to full military alert."

It all suddenly seemed like a tremendous waste of time. A lot of stupid games, and Kulikov was having a hard time controlling his temper. "That's fascinating," he said. "You're a fascinating person. Really. Next time you're in Moscow you will have to come over for a visit. Alert? Isn't that some kind of American soda?"

"It's not a soda, Andrei," Hacker said. "And neither of us are going to be in Moscow. You know what I mean?"

"Obviously, not," Kulikov said, just to say something.

"Perhaps we could work things out," Hacker said.

Kulikov stared at his shoes. Here it comes, he thought. Please let it come now. Let's just get it over with, and then let me get back to the Madlingers' in time for the hamburgers.

"Wouldn't you like to hear the terms of the deal?" Hacker pushed on.

Kulikov kept staring at his feet. Come on, he thought.

"I'll take your silence as a yes. Okay, the deal is simple.

You call it off, and we'll grant you asylum. We'll let all your people return home, and we'll make a nice life for you here. You ever been to California? We'll work out all the details.''

More silence.

''I'm sure I don't have to explain the alternatives to you, Andrei. Do you think I'm kidding about the military alert?''

Kulikov kept looking at his shoes. There were two possibilities. One, it was all a trick to get him to defect. This was exactly how they would set it up. Pretend that they had him and then offer asylum. The military alert was a new twist, but it was the same game.

But there were a lot of problems with this possibility. Why would they risk trying to get him to defect right in the middle of PF-1? Right when public and world opinion of the PFP was at an all-time high? Would the benefit of claiming his defection be even greater than that of simply completing the first flight? Kulikov just couldn't believe he was that important. Something about the timing was all wrong.

And there was another problem too. If they were going to try to make him feel like he was in trouble, why would they mention things that he knew nothing about. Like knowing about Zakharov from the beginning. Kulikov had no idea what the guy was talking about. Then again, it could be part of the strategy. Confuse the poor Russian until he pleads for forgiveness. Or make him feel like his own government is playing behind his back, like he's been left out in the cold.

But there was also the second possibility. Maybe something *was* actually going on. Something about Aelita Zakharov, and about concessions and the crew. Was it possible that PF-1 was somehow being held hostage to Soviet demands? Could PF-1 have been hijacked? Could his government have planned something like that without telling him? It was ridiculous to even think about! But then again, what was more ridiculous, Zakharov hijacking the space shuttle, or the Americans trying to get Andrei Kulikov to defect?

There were too many ways to look at it, and Andrei Kulikov knew that he had no control over what was going on. All he could do was keep his mouth shut and try hard not to believe anything they told him. As soon as he started asking questions, it would sound like he was interested in making a deal. All he could do was wait them out. That's all he could do.

"C'mon, Kulikov," Hacker encouraged. "What do you say?"

Kulikov stared down at his shoes and said nothing. All he could do was wait them out.

16

THE
BOTTOM
LINE

TWO meetings occurred simultaneously. In Washington, D.C., it was midnight, and the President held an emergency meeting of the National Security Council at the White House, and in Houston, SIG-PIFPY gathered in the secured conference room in Building One. SIG-PIFPY had taken over as the acting Mission Management Team for PF-1, giving it direct access to the Mission Control Center. The President had asked Senator Paul Ryan to sit in on the SIG-PIFPY meeting because of Ryan's broad-based experience with American space policy, and because of his intimate knowledge of the Peace Flight Program. Ryan was already in Houston and he was pleased to join the SIG-PIFPY meeting and to help in any way that he could.

Senator Ryan had always been a strong advocate of America's space program. Before being elected to the U.S. Senate, he had been a member of the Board of Regents of the Smithsonian Institution, where he had taken an active and aggressive interest in the Air and Space Museum, pressing for its expansion into a new facility at the Dulles Airport, near Washington, D.C. Ryan was also a long-time friend of the President, and during the 1988 campaign, the then presidential candidate asked Ryan to head up the candidate's Task Force on American Space Policy. Ryan had accepted the challenge eagerly, and the Task Force not only helped the President win the election, but it was also the birthplace of the Peace Flight Program.

Ryan achieved great prominence as the capable and visionary Task Force chairman, and in the summer of 1988, when the party's nominee for the U.S. Senate in Ryan's state was forced to drop out of the race for health reasons, Ryan was drafted to take his place. Ryan's overwhelming victory in November was a surprise to no one, and he enthusiastically took his seat in the Senate, where he was appointed to the Senate Committee on Commerce, Science, and Transportation, and to its Subcommittee on Science, Technology, and Space. It was one of those fortunate occasions when a senator was given a committee assignment that made good use of his or her background and experience.

At exactly eleven o'clock, the SIG-PIFPY meeting was called to order by the national security advisor, Dick Higgins, who had flown in from Washington, D.C. Senator Ryan sat between Russell Madlinger and Charles Roland, who had flown in with Higgins. NASA was also represented by Leonard Wolff, and by Peggy Kellner, the center director of the Johnson Space Center. Also present were Marianne Eagle from the CIA and Elliot Hacker from the FBI. Neither the Department of Defense nor the State Department representatives had arrived yet, but Dick Higgins was eager to get started. He had instructions to call the White House every fifteen minutes with an update.

"Okay, listen up," Higgins said. "I need a quick summation of the history and the current status of the situation so that I can call the President. Russ, can you do that?"

"Sure," Madlinger answered. "At approximately eight P.M. tonight, an alarm in the Flight Control Room was tripped. Our flight controllers reported a highly unusual vibration and a cutoff of the main oxygen supply. It appeared that it was the cutoff of oxygen that set off the alarm, not the vibration. When we talked to *Discovery*, Conrad Williams told us that the vibration had been caused by the shot from a twenty-two automatic pistol, and that the oxygen system switch had been accidentally turned off. He claimed that *Discovery* had been hijacked. The orbiter then went LOS for eighteen minutes, and we sealed the Mission Control Center.''

''Why'd you do that?'' Higgins asked.

''Standard procedure when there's an unknown problem on the shuttle.''

''What's unknown about a hijacking?''

''Quite frankly, Dick, we weren't sure at that time that there had been a hijacking. It could have been some kind of mistake or practical joke.''

''A practical joke? What kind of astronauts do you have flying this thing?''

Ryan sensed Madlinger stiffen beside him, but Madlinger continued without addressing Higgins's comment. ''When we reestablished contact after the LOS, Williams informed us that the shuttle had been hijacked at gunpoint, and that George Evans had been shot. Williams told us that they had bandaged Evans up and that he's alive, but we have no other information. Right now, we have to assume that his condition is critical.

''Williams said the rest of the crew had been handcuffed into their seats and sleep sacks, and that all crew functions, except for those necessary for survival, had been canceled. He informed us that the identity and demands of the hijackers would be communicated to us at four-twenty-two oh oh MET. That's seven o'clock tomorrow morning in Houston. He said there would be no further communication with us until then.''

''Okay, who is our hijacker? Is it one of the crew, or is there somebody else on board?''

''It has to be one of the crew, Dick,'' Madlinger answered.

"There are only two possible ways someone other than the PFP crew could be on board. One is if someone had stowed away prior to lift-off. They would have had to somehow get past all the guards at the launchpad and then go through the white room into the orbiter. Even if they got that far, there is no place to hide in the orbiter, so it would have to have been done with the crew's knowledge, and that's just absurd. The other way for someone to get into the orbiter is while they're in space, and that's equally absurd. The only way to get into the orbiter, while in space, is through the outside entrance to the airlock, which is in the cargo bay. Besides the fact that the airlock hatch can be seen at all times by a television camera mounted at the back of the orbiter, the airlock itself is controlled from inside. Nobody could force their way in, unless they did it during the crew EVA on Day Four. We've reviewed the videotape of Turnov and Zakharov's EVA and found no entrance through the airlock except for their return. The tape was made on the ground from a live feed, so there's no way it could have been doctored. On top of that, a third person would have required an extra depressurization and repressurization of the airlock since three suited people couldn't have all fit inside the airlock at the same time. We would have seen that operation during our monitoring of life support and electrical systems. That leaves us with the conclusion that the hijacker has to be one or more of the crewmembers on board *Discovery*."

"Well, who could have gotten a gun on board?"

"Any one of them," Madlinger answered. "All they would have had to do is carry it on in the pockets of their flight suit. There's no security check. When you think about it, it's a little bit amazing how easy it must have been."

"Damn it! Am I supposed to tell the President that the Russians could have walked right into our shuttle carrying guns and ammunition?"

"I'm afraid so, Dick."

"Do we have any idea which one of the crew we're dealing with?"

"Not really, Dick. When we spoke to Williams, there were long pauses between his sentences, giving us the impression that he was being told what to say and was communicating under duress. That would eliminate him as a suspect. And the fact that Evans was shot would eliminate Evans as well. That leaves Wells, Turnov, Zakharov and Vonberger. We can make guesses, but we really don't know."

"There's no way to see inside the cabin?" Higgins asked.

"No, not now. There is a hand-held television camera, but it depends on a crewmember to operate it."

Higgins pounded his fist on the table. "This is ridiculous! You mean for," and he looked at his watch, "for seven hours, all we can do is sit here and twiddle our thumbs?"

"I think it's probably safe to assume that an American wouldn't hijack his own spacecraft," Marianne Eagle said suddenly. "I think we should stop kidding ourselves, and admit the Russians have hijacked *Discovery*."

"How do we know that?" Higgins responded. "It could be one person. A freak thing. Maybe even one of the Russians acting without authority. Paul, what do you think?"

Senator Ryan nodded slowly. "I don't think we can assume anything right now. It's hard to imagine what the Soviets would gain by hijacking our orbiter. There's not a lot of technology there that they don't already have access to through the PFP. And the damage such a stunt would do to their image in the eyes of the world would far outweigh any benefit they could derive from it. It could be one of the cosmonauts acting without authority, I suppose, but it's just as hard to imagine what any one person could gain by hijacking the shuttle."

"Come on," Eagle said, obviously exasperated. "It's got to be the Russians. Let's not be ridiculous!"

Ryan shot a hard look at her but he did not respond.

Russell Madlinger shook his head. "I agree with Paul, that there's no way to know, and I think it's dangerous to start pointing fingers. Elliot, am I right that all members of the Soviet team have been taken into custody?"

"That's right, Russ. Kulikov was the last one, and we picked him up at your house a few hours ago."

"It's as if they were all sitting around and waiting for us to pick them up," Madlinger continued. "Now they either had no idea what was going on, or they're playing a very clever game. But I'm not sure any of us can call that now."

"Well," Higgins said. "What I hear is a lot of 'I don't knows.' Nobody's telling me that it's not the Russians, and as far as I'm concerned, that means that we have to act as if it might be the Russians."

"Dick, how come the President hasn't called Moscow?" Senator Ryan asked.

"He has, Paul. And although I can't go into the specifics of his conversations, the long and short of it is that they deny having any knowledge of the hijacking."

"Have we gone to military alert?" Ryan asked.

"No, we haven't, Paul. We've got a very sensitive situation here, and I'm afraid I can't really go into it. What I can tell you is that there's no military threat from the Soviets at the present time, and we don't want to be trigger-happy here, because we can't be sure that it's the Russians that we're fighting. You can imagine our embarrassment if we went to military alert and then it turned out to be one of our own people. All we can do right now is keep an eye on the Russians to see what they do. Okay, Charlie, is the press in line?"

"Peggy can probably answer that better than I."

Peggy Kellner sat at the head of the table, opposite Higgins. As the center director at JSC, it was Kellner's job to oversee and ensure the proper functioning of the Center and its personnel. Having come up through the Office of Public Affairs, Kellner constantly demonstrated an ability to run a tight ship, and to remain flexible and resourceful during crisis situations. "We're playing it as a communications problem right now. Fortunately, McKenzie had turned off the audio to NASA Select. A lot of people saw Russell in the Flight Control Room, and they saw McKenzie's reaction when contact was reestablished and he found out that the hijacking was real. They caught wind of your and Charlie's arrival, so they think something is up. We've told them that you're both here simply to observe the mission and that your arrival was coincidental with the development of a communications problem. We'll keep to that story until further notice.''

"Good. What's the clearance procedure for NASA personnel?"

"Well, we're working on that," Kellner continued. "The flight controllers who were in Mission Control have been put on a double shift. They were supposed to be relieved at midnight, but they will work until eight tomorrow morning. It buys us some time. Extending the shift meant we had to cancel the usual change-of-shift press briefing. That has intensified the questions from the press, but we're sticking with the communications problem story and insisting that McKenzie's team is extending its shift to review events prior to the communications problem in order to troubleshoot it. We said we'd let them know when he'll be available. We've put up an announcement slide on NASA Select that cuts off the view of Mission Control and indicates that the next event will be a change-of-shift briefing by McKenzie at a time to be announced. There are some rumblings, but I think we're covered for now.''

"Okay, I've got to call the President now. Let's take five." Higgins walked to the secure phone in the far corner of the room to call the President, and the rest of the group gathered around a pot of fresh coffee that had just been brought into the room.

Senator Ryan remained seated and watched the sudden activity in the room. Everything had begun to feel unreal. How was it possible that *Discovery* had been hijacked? How could it be that PF-1, the first flight of the Peace Flight Program, born of Ryan's very own Task Force, could end up in tragedy? Ryan didn't blame himself, but his anger overwhelmed him. It just wasn't fair that some maniac could manipulate them all like this. It was not a time to think about politics, but Ryan couldn't help but feel the very real pressure that the President would be under. After all, the President had practically based his campaign on the idea of cooperation in space. This sudden violence would have a devastating effect on the PFP and on the President's political health, but more importantly, the hijacking had suddenly shattered the dream that they had all worked for. A dream of international cooperation and peace. A dream that through space exploration, the world would be made a better place.

Higgins returned to the head of the table and the rest of the group settled back into their seats. "Okay, the President wants to know what we can do between now and seven o'clock tomorrow morning. And I need some information about what kind of deadline we'll be working under. How long can they stay up there?"

"Less than three days," Leonard Wolff answered quickly. "The scheduled return was for tomorrow afternoon at approximately five o'clock, Houston time. We equip all of our missions with two extra days of supplies, in case of emergencies. Most of the supplies and life-support systems will start running dry after that, but oxygen will be the critical factor. If they're not on the ground by five P.M. on Day Eight, they'll all be dead."

An intense silence filled the room as the reality of Wolff's words sank in.

"And there's no way for us to force them down?" Higgins asked finally. His voice seemed softer than before.

"Not without a pilot and a commander," Wolff said. "Somebody's got to fly the thing."

The silence lingered another few seconds and then Higgins continued. "Okay. Elliot, what've you guys got?"

"We've isolated the entire Soviet team in Houston, as well as the two engineers at the Cape, and all of them are being interrogated," Hacker said. "So far they have all pleaded ignorant, except for Andrei Kulikov, who refuses to talk. We can't tell if he knows something or is just being uncooperative. I have a couple of hotshots working on him now in our safe building. Meanwhile, we're following up on all our other leads, and so far, the only problem we're having is locating Laura Gold.''

"Who's that?" Ryan asked.

"Gold is the woman that Vonberger had become romantically involved with. She hasn't been at work for two days, nor has she been home, but we've got a search under way. We'll find her."

"I want constant updates on the girl and on Kulikov. Now, Charlie. What have you guys got?''

"Well, Len and Russ here have put together what we call a tiger team. It's a group of our top engineers together with engineers from some of our contractors. These people know the orbiter inside out and they're monitoring every system and every detail to help us to try to find out what is going on up there. They're developing strategies to protect the orbiter and crew against contingencies and difficulties that may arise, since the crew may not be in a position to help us. We've got to do as much as we can from the ground. We're also working on some possible strategies to save the orbiter, in case that becomes necessary.''

"What kind of strategies?''

"Well, I'm afraid we've got nothing concrete to offer at the present, but we're hoping to devise possible ways to facilitate some kind of rescue operation from the ground.''

"Well, tell me what you've got so far. The President is going to want to know what his options are.''

Russell Madlinger interrupted. "It's really premature for us to report anything, Dick. The last thing you want to hear is a lot of half-baked ideas and way-out possibilities, and those are the kind of things we're working with right now. Our team will work through the night, and I hope we'll have a few concrete options to present by tomorrow morning, but frankly, I wouldn't get my hopes up. There's not much we can do from the ground without the help of the crew.''

"Well, Russ, I need you to come up with something. Chances are the President is going to have to take some action sooner or later, and that means I've got to present him with some options. The State Department and the FBI can help us out, but the bottom line is that we've got a terrorist up in our space shuttle and the way things look right now, it's going to be up to NASA to do something about it.''

A new silence filled the conference room, and Senator Ryan knew that the national security advisor had just let out the naked truth. A lot of things could happen between now and Day 8, but one thing was not going to happen. The President was not going to stand by and watch a terrorist make a mockery of the Peace Flight Program.

17

COWBOY'S
PLAN

THERE had to be a way to get the gun.

Joey Wells was strapped into the commander's seat with his hands cuffed behind him and a Lone Ranger mask over his face. He could not figure out how much time had passed, but his shoulders and arms had begun to ache from sitting in the same position for so long. If it were not for the Lone Ranger mask, he might have been able to see the clock, or at least he would have been able to count rotations around the earth. Instead, he sat blindly in his seat, and all he could think was that there had to be a way to get the gun.

Alex Vonberger was a sick individual. He seemed decisive in his actions and in his instructions to the crew, as if he knew exactly what he was doing, but Joey Wells could tell that Alex Vonberger was slowly coming apart. The air inside the cabin was cool, and yet Vonberger was sweating as if it was a hundred degrees. His eyes darted back and forth with pathetic nervousness, and his upper lip seemed to quiver when he spoke. His voice was filled with panic and terror, as if he was the victim instead of the villain.

Vonberger was a sick man, but he was also a careful man. Now that he had taken command of *Discovery,* he took deliberate steps to isolate and incapacitate the PF Flyers. Williams and Turnov were handcuffed together and put into the airlock, where they couldn't see or talk to the rest of the crew. George Evans was strapped into his sleeping sack on the mid-deck wall. Joey Wells and Aelita Zakharov were handcuffed and strapped into the seats on the flight deck. Only Alex Vonberger had the run of the cabin.

Vonberger was also careful to let only one person at a time move about unrestrained, and he always kept enough distance between himself and that person to make it impossible for the person to get near him. The best way to get the gun would be to have someone distract Vonberger while Wells was unrestrained, but that meant the distraction would have to be planned. The Lone Ranger mask made it difficult to know where Vonberger was, and so it was too risky to propose a plan now to Zakharov, because Vonberger could be right behind them. Wells would just have to wait for the right opportunity, and that took patience. Sooner or later he was going to have to make a move.

Joey Wells tried stretching the muscles in his arms and shoulders, but the pain only got worse. He was worried about George Evans. Vonberger had given Wells the job of trying to patch up the bullet wound, and Wells had done the best he could, but he wasn't a doctor. He had asked Vonberger to let him talk to someone on the ground. The flight surgeon would have been able to tell him exactly what to do, but Vonberger had refused the request. The bullet had entered just below the left collarbone, and Evans had quickly become short-winded and winced with pain each time he took a breath. Joey Wells put his ear near the wound and could hear the air passing in and out through the hole. Joey Wells was no doctor, but he knew a punctured lung when he saw one. He wrapped the bandages around Evans's chest, pulling them tight so as to seal the wound. Then he gave Evans a shot of morphine for the pain, and made him wear an oxygen helmet. The helmet supplied pure oxygen and was usually used by crewmembers before EVAs. Wells knew it was important to keep the oxygen level in Evans's blood from falling. There was nothing else that Wells could do but wait and see if George Evans would be all right.

Even if Evans was all right, how much time did they have? Vonberger had not stated his intentions, but Joey Wells could figure out the obvious. There would be no reason for Vonberger to go through the trouble of hijacking the orbiter unless he planned to hold it hostage to some kind of demand. Vonberger would not have to make any threats to the crew. The mission was to have ended on Day 6, and that meant there was less than three days' oxygen left. Time was on Vonberger's side.

Joey Wells pulled his arms up against the handcuffs and tried to rotate his shoulders. There were worse ways to die than by hypoxia. Wells had experienced hypoxia many times during his years of training. The first symptoms are insidiously pleasant. As the supply of oxygen in the blood is reduced, the brain quickly ceases to function properly, and you are overcome with warm feelings of giddiness and tranquility. Your judgment becomes impaired and you lose all sense of self-awareness. You feel like everything is wonderful. The danger of hypoxia, in most cases, is that you don't realize that it is happening, and this makes you incapable of taking measures to protect yourself. If the lack of oxygen persists your heart rate increases, your skin starts to turn blue, and your vision gets fuzzy. Eventually, the lack of oxygen in your blood causes you to go into shock or convulsions, or to pass out. There were worse ways to die, but that didn't make Joey Wells feel any better.

Wells found himself wondering what they were doing back in Houston. He knew the way NASA worked, and he knew that they wouldn't be sitting around waiting for Vonberger to give himself up. Russell Madlinger would have put together a tiger team to try to come up with some solutions. Wells tried to imagine what NASA could do. They couldn't bring the orbiter down without a pilot and a commander. There was no way they could get up into space to make a rescue. At best, they could try to talk Vonberger into giving up, but Wells didn't have much hope for that. It was going to be up to him to save *Discovery*.

Joey Wells took a deep breath and tried to relax. The crazy thing through all of this was that he still could not stop thinking about Aelita. She was strapped into the pilot's seat only a few feet away, and yet she remained completely out of his reach. As insane as it seemed, Joey Wells was in love with her. The FBI man had suspected her of working for the KGB, but Joey Wells would not believe it. He loved her, and in spite of all of her disclaimers and rejections, he still believed that she loved him too. In fact, the more she rejected him, the more sure he was that she wanted him.

It was horrible to be thinking of love at a time like this. *Discovery* had been hijacked and the entire Peace Flight Program was in jeopardy. George Evans was struggling for his life. All of them were in danger. How could he think of love? How could he be thinking of his own desires? And suddenly, all of the games that he and Aelita played seemed silly, and Joey Wells decided that it was time to come right out and confess his love. But he was not going to do it in front of Alex Vonberger. He would have to wait until he could be sure that he and Aelita were alone.

18

THE
POINTING
FINGER

IT was four o'clock in the morning when Elliot Hacker pulled into the parking lot behind the Calhoun Terrace Apartments and parked his car in an empty spot near one of the Bureau's vans. It was a warm night in Houston, and Hacker stood by his car and puffed at the remains of his cigarette. Over the past few months, he had spent many hours studying the layout of Calhoun Terrace as he and his men devised surveillance strategies, but this was the first time Hacker had seen the apartment complex with his own eyes. From the layout, Hacker knew that Calhoun Terrace was a series of two- and three-story apartment buildings strung together in an angular fashion that vaguely resembled the letter W. Hacker faced the inside of the W, but in the dim lights from the parking lot he could only see some of the terraces and big picture windows of the nearby apartments. The inner buildings were all lost in darkness.

Even if he had not known where to look, Hacker could have easily spotted Laura Gold's apartment in the middle section of the complex. It was the only apartment with a light on, and there was a small group of people gathered outside the entrance to the section. Hacker dropped his cigarette and stamped it out and then he slowly crossed the parking lot toward his men.

Steve Erickson broke away from the group at the doorway and walked out to meet Hacker by the edge of the parking lot. Erickson was the perfect assistant for a man like Elliot Hacker, and had been Hacker's right-hand man for almost ten years. Hacker spent most of his time focusing on the big picture, and thus he needed someone like Erickson who could mind the details. Erickson chased down clues like a bloodhound, and left no stone unturned in his investigations. Hacker had learned to depend on him for his thoroughness.

The two men did not greet each other, but automatically turned and began walking away from the complex, into the dark and unused portion of the parking lot. "What've you got?" Hacker asked.

"The Border Patrol picked her up two days ago along the Rio Grande in the El Paso," Erickson said. Hacker couldn't help but notice the unusual heaviness in Erickson's voice. "They can't make an ID on her until the autopsy's in," Erickson continued, "but we've confirmed it was her car, and everything we've gotten so far seems to fit."

"How come you can't make an ID?"

Erickson stopped and pushed his hands into his pants pockets. It was almost as if he didn't want to answer. "They lost the head," he said quietly.

"They *what?*"

"They lost the head."

"Oh, hell," Hacker said into the darkness.

"Seems when they opened the door it rolled out of the car, and fell into the river."

"Oh, hell, I don't believe this!" The headless corpse felt like the ultimate intrusion, and Hacker realized that it symbolized the sudden violence that had descended upon the

Peace Flight Program. Hacker pulled out a cigarette, and the two men continued walking. "Any suspects?" he asked.

"Not really. Border Patrol seems to think she was hit by banditos. They say there's groups of them that work the border areas, preying on Mexicans trying to sneak across. She had an overnight bag and a purse, and they were both emptied and there was no money or credit cards or anything of value left. Border Patrol thinks she was just in the wrong place at the wrong time."

"That's because they don't know who she was," Hacker said, half to himself. "You think she was trying to sneak across the border?"

"The place where they found her is a favorite crossing spot. I don't know why else she'd be down there."

"She could have been put there to make it look like she was trying to cross."

"It's not likely. Our El Paso team says that she wasn't moved after she was killed. We're trying to work with the deputy who found her, but he's all shook up over the thing with the head. Our guess is that the assailant was in the car with her, in the passenger seat. We got a team going through the car now in hopes that he left something behind, but so far the only thing they've found is hair and prints belonging to Gold and Vonberger. We may come up with something yet."

"Witnesses?"

"No. Even if anyone had seen the car they wouldn't talk. Any witnesses would be illegal aliens, and they're not about to come forward to cooperate with the FBI."

"What've they found upstairs?"

"Nothing yet. A bunch of personal belongings seem to be missing, but we assume that's what she had with her in the car. Nothing else to indicate that she had left, or where she was going. And so far, it doesn't seem like anyone's been in the apartment except her and Vonberger."

"Any other leads here in Houston?"

"No. We had people placed in Fuddruckers and at the hairdressing school, and now we're talking to all of the people that she had contact with at those places, but I don't think we're going to find anything new."

The two men had reached the far corner of the parking lot, and they turned and stood facing Calhoun Terrace. "The frustrating thing, Elliot, is that for the life of me I can't figure out how she and Vonberger communicated without us knowing. Everything we have on the two of them, every tape, every picture, is just as clean as a whistle. I don't see where there was any room for hanky-panky."

Hacker shared Erickson's frustration. "Well, it's hard to get a fix on what role she played," he admitted. "Someone could have hired her to befriend Vonberger in order to keep an eye on him, or blackmail him. Or maybe she was working with Vonberger, as a go-between for him and the KGB, or whoever he was working for. It's also possible that she was just a cover, or a decoy. In any case, chances are she could have led us to whoever is behind this hijacking, and my bet is that's why she was killed. I don't buy the bandito story."

Hacker and Erickson faced each other in the darkness, and Hacker suddenly became aware of the sound of the crickets coming from the nearby field.

"I should go back and keep an eye on things," Erickson said.

"Go ahead," Hacker said. "I'll be with you in a minute." He watched Erickson cross the parking lot and then stood alone in the dark and smoked his cigarette. He had to try to get things straight in his head. Laura Gold's death had changed everything.

At first, Andrei Kulikov had seemed like the best lead. Kulikov was the only Soviet who had not denied having any knowledge of the hijacking. Hacker had good men working on him, but Kulikov still had not budged. Everything about Kulikov's manner and the way he refused to talk had made Hacker feel certain that Kulikov held all of the answers, and somewhere in his mind, Hacker had been convinced that

Kulikov's answers would ultimately point the finger at Aelita Zakharov.

Hacker stamped out his cigarette and began walking back toward the complex. He had long ago learned to go with the best lead, and to be willing to change his course. Marianne Eagle seemed to be sure that the Russians were behind the hijacking, but Elliot Hacker knew that there was no use trying to play that game. If you made your conclusions first, then they got in the way of clear thinking. All you could do was follow all of your leads and keep an open mind, even if it did get overwhelming. For a while, Kulikov had been the best lead, and the finger seemed to be pointing at Aelita Zakharov. Now, suddenly Laura Gold was dead, and that pointed a very big finger at Alex Vonberger.

Hacker reached the apartment complex and met Erickson and another agent in the lobby, just inside the door. He could see the excitement on Erickson's face.

"What is it?" Hacker asked.

"I had them check all of the doors in this area of the complex for prints. They think they've found a set of Vonberger's prints on this door, going down into the basement. We can't be sure until we get the prints verified, and it'll take some time to explore downstairs to see if there are more."

"What's down there?"

The other agent in the lobby answered. "The laundry room, the boiler room—"

"And an underground hallway that connects the entire complex," Erickson interrupted.

"She was a decoy," Hacker said, suddenly sure of himself. "I want a full check on every tenant in this complex since the day it opened its doors. Better check the management and owners, and anyone else who might have a key. Steve, I want you on this personally."

"You bet." And Steve Erickson ran up the stairs to Laura Gold's apartment.

Hacker considered going up to the apartment just to have

a look around, but there was really no reason to. Instead, he nodded at the agent by the basement door, and then stepped out into the Houston night. He lit another cigarette and remembered the saying of one of his early mentors. Follow the leads, and the fingers will point themselves.

19

THE POSSIBILITIES

RUSSELL Madlinger sat in his Oldsmobile station wagon near the edge of the NASA ramp at Ellington Field. The window by the driver's seat was open, but there was no wind and he felt tired and sweaty. He did not allow himself to think about sleep, but he did indulge in a quick fantasy about a shower and a clean shirt. A hint of dawn lay along the edges of the trees to the east, and Madlinger knew that in a few minutes the birds would fill the silence of the empty runway.

The NASA jet from the Cape was not due for another five minutes, so, for the first time since he had seen the alarm blinking in the Flight Control Room, Russell Madlinger had a few minutes to himself. He rested his hands on the lower part of the steering wheel, and let his head fall back against the seat. His thoughts were all crowded into his brain and they screamed for his attention like noisy schoolchildren. If only he had not seen the blinking alarm and there had been no hijacking of PF-1. If only *Discovery* would deorbit and land tomorrow as scheduled. He let these thoughts slip from his mind, like the shower and the clean shirt, and he sat up and looked at his watch. There were four minutes left. He had to get organized.

First there were the unknowns. Who was hijacking the space shuttle, and why? What did they want? What would they say when they communicated in the morning? Were the Soviets behind it? Was Kulikov in on it? Would they be able to negotiate for the return of *Discovery* and the crew? Or would it be up to NASA to save the orbiter?

Then there were the emotions. Madlinger felt consumed by anger and by an overwhelming sense of helplessness. He felt betrayed by Andrei Kulikov, and by whoever it was who had shot George Evans and taken over PF-1. On a deeper level, Madlinger felt a growing sadness over the disruption of the PFP, and he feared the ultimate consequences of the hijacking. He felt a need to protect his children.

And then there were the anxieties. Leonard Wolff had taken over much of the management of the tiger team, but Madlinger worried that it was too much work for one man. There were dozens of engineers reviewing data from the flight, and trying to gather as much information as possible. There were others developing contingency plans in case of emergencies that threatened the crew or the orbiter. Still others were doing feasibility studies of possible rescue operations. There were almost a hundred engineers working all over JSC, and someone had to make sure that the team stayed focused, that no time was lost, and that all possibilities were being pursued. How could Leonard Wolff handle all of that by himself?

So far, so good. There were unknowns, emotions, and anxieties, all brewing inside Madlinger's head, and yet he knew that for now, they could all be left alone. The unknowns would be answered, the emotions would change with the circumstances, and the anxieties would be resolved. But there was one more category of thoughts still swimming around in his mind. The possibilities.

Madlinger looked at his watch. He had two and half minutes. In order to properly consider the possibilities, Madlinger knew he had to think big. He had to go beyond the anxieties and the emotions. He had to go beyond the tiger team, and the seven o'clock communication. He had to go beyond the politics and the science and the meetings. He had to assume there would be no miracles. Somewhere along the line he must have thought about this, for he had made that telephone call to the Cape, and he was sitting on the ramp, waiting for the plane to come in. Now it was time to focus on it. Now it was time to consider the possibilities.

Possibility: Negotiate with the hijackers for a peaceful return of the orbiter and crew. Madlinger knew any form of negotiation would be a job for the FBI, the Department of Defense, or the State Department. They all had their work cut out for them. But Madlinger also knew that he could not depend on peaceful negotiations to end the tragedy. Dick Higgins had made it clear that in the end it could be up to NASA to rescue the orbiter.

Possibility: Orchestrate a rescue of the orbiter from the ground. The tiger team was already working on this. So far, the best idea had been to try to trick the hijackers into believing that one of the critical life-support systems was malfunctioning. If it was a system that only the American astronauts knew how to fix, then they would have to be given the freedom and the tools to fix it. The plan assumed that the Americans were the hostages and not the hijackers. It also assumed that once the Americans determined that the system was working naturally, they might be able to take some action against the hijackers. It was a long shot, but it was worth pursuing.

Possibility: . . .

Madlinger looked out his windshield into the sky and saw the lights of a plane approaching, right on time. He got out of the car and walked further out onto the ramp. The air felt good and he felt rejuvenated. His thoughts were organized, his mind was clear. He could see the plane starting to make its approach, and he watched it without thinking about anything. He just stood on the ramp with his hands in his pockets, a slight breeze now blowing his uncombed hair. Watching the jet come in for a landing, he could have been anyone, anywhere.

When the wheels of the jet hit the pavement, Madlinger felt the impact in his gut, and he was snapped out of his daze by a sudden sense of responsibility. He watched the jet slow to taxi speed and he remembered the thirty-second telephone call he had made earlier in the evening to the Cape. He had awakened Benjamin King, the shuttle operations manager, and without explanation or apology, had asked one very specific question. Was there any possibility that the new orbiter, sitting on Launchpad 39B, awaiting a main engine test firing, could launch within forty-eight hours? And King, half asleep, had mumbled back, "Anything's possible, Russ."

Madlinger waited for the pilot and copilot to disembark from the jet before he bounded up the steps, two at a time, to see Benjamin King. King sat alone in the passenger cabin. His briefcase was open on the seat beside him, but there were no papers in front of him, just a mug of coffee, and an ashtray full of cigarette butts. When he saw Madlinger, he waved at the seat across the cabin. King was an intense and nervous little man, with big horn-rimmed glasses, and a constant worried look. He had been a backroom man at NASA for many years, until the *Challenger* accident. Suddenly he was discovered as the kind of careful thinker that NASA needed.

Madlinger sat in the seat across the cabin from King, and bent down to look out the window. In the growing light, he could see the pilot and copilot crossing the ramp to a NASA van that waited for them next to the NASA hangar. Madlinger and King were alone.

"PF-One has been hijacked," Madlinger said.

"Hijacked?"

"We don't have much information yet, Ben. We're really short on answers at this point. And short on time. What I need are some details on the new orbiter."

"What are you going to do? Go up there after them?"

"Can we do it?"

King took a deep breath and slouched back into his seat. His glasses had the effect of magnifying his eyes, and they looked sad and tired. Madlinger didn't push him. King was a worrier. In a sense, that was what he was paid to do. King's worrying came not out of carelessness, but out of wisdom, and so it wasn't a waste of time to sit for half a minute and let King worry. King sat up and lit a cigarette, and then blew out a cloud of smoke.

"Russ, I know they put me in charge of operations after the *Challenger* accident because they knew I was careful. They liked me because I was slow and deliberate, everything NASA needed to prove they could be. We learned a lot from *Challenger* and the Rogers Commission. It was good for us. We made mistakes, we identified them, and we got ourselves moving again. We're smarter now, and we're more careful. That's what I do for NASA, Russ. I'm NASA's way of being careful. In light of that, you would have to lock me up before I would let that thing fly. We haven't completed the final safety review and operational sign-off. When she left the Orbiter Processing Facility for stacking two weeks ago, we had completed about eighty percent of the systems verification tests. Most of the critical systems check out, and the others could probably be handled with change-outs of components or using alternative modes or work-arounds for those systems. But, Russ, we haven't test-fired the main engines yet."

"Can you change them out with already tested engines?"

"Not in forty-eight hours."

"They've been fired in the test stands, haven't they?"

"Of course, and they looked good, but a lot can happen in transit and installation."

Madlinger nodded. "Okay. Now, Ben, talk to me like you don't work for NASA. Talk to me like a friend."

King nodded, showing that he had anticipated Madlinger's question. "Our testing techniques have improved tremendously in the last five years. We've devised new means of testing, new tests, new programs for analyzing data. Our previous orbiters have never undergone such extensive testing. I feel good about this. This orbiter passes every test we give it, and NASA has flown spacecraft based on what we have done so far. But remember, Russ, we've also killed astronauts.''

''What about the main engines?''

''On paper everything looks good. We've reviewed the documentation on every part in all three engines, and found nothing to raise a red flag. We've examined every connector, every valve, every control, and it all looks good, but there's simply no substitute for a test firing.''

''What's your gut feeling?''

''Oh, come on, Russ. You're not going to launch based on my gut feeling.''

''Of course not, but I trust you.''

''Yeah, but Russ, I'm not the one who makes these decisions. I just run the tests. You know that. I'm good at my job because I'm careful and I know what to look for, and how to verify it, but I wasn't chosen to make decisions like that. It's not fair to ask me, Russ.''

''Come on, Ben. If I can't ask you, then I can't ask anyone.''

''Don't push me on it, Russ. As good as we are at it, testing is still a hit-and-miss proposition. You could test from now until forever, get perfect results, and then lose it. Or you could do no testing at all and have a flawless flight. You're playing with odds, Russ, that's all it is. The more you test, the better the odds. But odds don't mean anything when they fall against you. What good is knowing you had a ninety-nine-in-one-hundred chance if you fall within the one percent? And what difference does it really make if we send up a vehicle with only a seventy-percent chance, if it makes it? It's all a big crap shoot, Russ.''

Madlinger nodded his head, slowly beginning to understand his own position. Okay, Ben. What are the odds?''

''Are you asking me as an employee, or as a friend?''

''Both.''

"Employee says fifty-fifty. *At best.*"

"And friend?"

King inhaled on his cigarette and blew the smoke out slowly, watching it drift up toward the air vents. "Friend says, that with some change-outs and work-arounds, she's got a ninety-percent chance of getting off the ground and coming back in one piece."

"Ninety percent," Madlinger said softly.

"We don't fly with those kinds of odds," King said.

Madlinger nodded again and then looked at his watch. It was time to go. "I got you booked into the Hilton. I don't want you going to the Center. The press is already going wild. Keep a low profile and wait to hear from me. Come on. I'll drop you off. And don't get too comfortable, because you might be going back to the Cape."

As they crossed the ramp to Madlinger's car, Madlinger noticed the brightening sky. Since his early days as a pilot, dawn had been his favorite time of day. The new orbiter, OV-105, did not even have a name yet. The President had asked the Young Astronauts to conduct a nationwide essay contest where the students were asked to suggest a name and explain its significance. The deadline for submissions was still a month away.

Madlinger listened for the birds, but could not hear them over the wind, which had quickly picked up from the west. Ninety percent. Ben King was right that NASA didn't fly with those kinds of odds, but Madlinger couldn't think about that now. It was not Madlinger's job to decide whether to fly or not. It was only his job to come up with possibilities.

20

THE
LONE
RANGER

ALEX Vonberger squatted by the open door of the cargo plane and stared out at the darkness, wondering if he would make a difference. There was no wind and no noise. It was almost as if the plane was sitting still on a dark runway, but Alex Vonberger knew that they were in the air, high over *Deutschland*. He was vaguely aware of the people behind him, milling about the interior of the plane. They were the Inner Circle, and they had all come to see him jump. He was going to be their savior. He was going to be their hero. For some reason he went out back first, and just before the plane disappeared into the darkness, he saw the Instructor, sitting in the door with a wicked grin. Vonberger panicked and reached for his ripcord, but there was no ripcord. There was no parachute. He was falling in the dark.

Vonberger reached out desperately, trying to grab hold of something, and his left hand slammed against the storage lockers on the mid-deck wall. He woke up with a start and grabbed wildly at the Lone Ranger mask covering his face.

It slipped out of his hand and the elastic snapped it back against his eyes. He tried again, this time pulling it over the top of his head and practically ripping off his ear with the elastic. Then he held the mask tightly with both hands, wringing it like a wet washcloth. He breathed deeply, sucking air into his lungs with exaggerated forcefulness, as if the supply had been cut off. He was shaking uncontrollably.

Vonberger had never actually seen the Instructor, and he realized with terror that the Instructor could have been wearing that wicked grin throughout all of their meetings. It was as if the Instructor knew something that Vonberger didn't. Vonberger had been told that somewhere inside NASA there was a man who would program a deorbit burn and arrange for the orbiter to land in Iran. The man at NASA was a member of the American branch of Das Syndikat, who had worked his way up through the NASA ranks, all the time keeping his membership a secret. He was the American counterpart to Alex Vonberger: a fellow neo-Nazi who had kept his political beliefs to himself, quietly waiting for a chance to be of service to Das Syndikat. This inside man would be Vonberger's parachute. But what if it had all been lies? What it there was no man at NASA?

The orbiter was on the night side of the earth, and the mid-deck was mostly dark, except for a stream of light from the flight deck. Vonberger could see the outline of George Evans, strapped into his sleeping sack on the mid-deck wall. Williams and Turnov would be in the airlock, and Zakharov and Wells would be strapped into the seats on the flight deck. Everything was as it should have been, and Vonberger unclipped the restraint strap he had attached to a wall bracket to keep himself from floating across the cabin.

George Evans was still having trouble breathing but he was alive. Vonberger looked at him through the glass visor of the oxygen helmet and wondered if he would make it. He wished that he could have let Joey Wells talk to the flight surgeon, but allowing any kind of communication would have been too risky. Evans suddenly opened his eyes, and in the dim light, he gave Vonberger a pathetic and helpless look. Neither of them said anything, but Vonberger felt himself smile. Somehow the look emboldened him. He *had* actually hijacked the space shuttle.

Vonberger left Evans and pulled himself toward the waste management compartment. He closed the privacy curtain and maneuvered himself onto the toilet seat using the handholds and foot restraints. Then he secured himself, and hit the button that started the airflow through the system. It wasn't quite like going to the bathroom on earth, but once you got used to it, it was easy. You just had to get yourself firmly anchored.

The personal hygiene station was directly across from the toilet. There was a clear plastic handwashing enclosure which Vonberger used to wash his hands. He put some cold water on his washcloth and washed the sweat from his face. He stopped in front of the galley on his way out, but he was too nervous to eat. The Instructor had made it clear that he was supposed to force himself to eat every meal, even if he wasn't hungry, but somehow breakfast just didn't seem that important.

Vonberger pulled himself through the access port into the flight deck. It was impossible to tell if Zakharov or Wells was awake. Their heads were up, but that meant nothing in weightlessness. They were both wearing the Lone Ranger masks that Vonberger had put on them before the sleep period. They could not remove the masks by themselves because of the handcuffs, and thus, the masks served to further isolate them from the rest of the crew. Vonberger decided that he would leave them on throughout the day.

Vonberger floated with his feet toward the ceiling as he lowered his head in front of Wells and slowly lifted the Lone Ranger mask over the top of Wells's head. Wells's eyes were open but blurry, and he stretched his shoulders and yawned. "You sure are an ugly sight first thing in the morning," Wells said, pulling his arms up against the back of the seat and moving his hands around inside the handcuffs.

"You don't look very good yourself," Vonberger replied.

"I am going to give you fifteen minutes to go to the bathroom, and to have some breakfast. Fifteen minutes is all you will get, Cowboy. Understand?"

"Hey, Alex," Zakharov called out from behind her Lone Ranger mask. It was part of human nature that people always spoke louder when they couldn't see. "Take this mask off my head."

"What is the matter?"

"Nothing is the matter. I just want to see. Take this thing off my head."

"You will have to wait your turn, Aelita. Now, come on, Cowboy. Show me how you can cooperate when there is a gun at your head." Vonberger reached out, unlocked the handcuffs, and then quickly backed away, holding the gun out in front of him. He knew that if any of them would cause trouble, it would be Joey Wells, and thus, he had to be extra careful. Vonberger anchored himself against the ceiling, and watched carefully as Wells slipped his hands out of the cuffs, and then opened his seat belt so that he could float out of his seat. He turned around and faced Vonberger. "You look horrible, Alex. Did you get any sleep at all?"

"Never mind how I look. You have fifteen minutes, and I am going to be watching you."

Wells linked his hands together and did some stretches and isometrics, as if he had all the time in the world. He talked while he stretched, "Man, you don't have any idea how uncomfortable that is. I don't mind you hijacking the orbiter, Alex, but do you have to make me sleep with my hands tied behind my back? I'm putting in a request right now for the airlock tonight."

"Me too!" Zakharov called out.

"Come on. Let's go," Vonberger said.

Wells let out a big yawn. "Hey, Aelita." He brought his head down closer to Zakharov's ear. "Don't worry about not being able to see. You're not missing a thing. Alex looks like hell." Wells laughed and pushed himself toward the access port.

Vonberger allowed each of the crew fifteen minutes and then spent some time helping Evans to the waste management compartment and then back into his sleeping sack. Then Vonberger spent half an hour performing orbiter maintenance. He cleaned up the trash from breakfast, and closed up the galley. He dumped the waste water overboard, and changed the lithium hydroxide canisters. These canisters were used to absorb excess carbon dioxide and odors from the cabin atmosphere. Failure to change them at regular intervals would eventually result in the buildup of dangerous levels of carbon dioxide. There were two canisters installed in the cabin air ducts under the floor of the mid-deck. Ordinarily, one canister would be replaced every twelve hours, but Vonberger replaced both canisters, just in case the day got busy.

At 4:21:55 MET the orbiter entered darkness over the North Atlantic, and Alex Vonberger strapped himself into the pilot's seat. Joey Wells was handcuffed into the commander's seat, and he sat silently behind his Lone Ranger mask. Vonberger ran a systems check on the computer and was relieved to find that everything was nominal. The last thing he needed right now was a technical problem.

Vonberger leaned over and typed number 917 into the computer keyboard, calling up the uplink text pages. This system allowed Mission Control to input text into the computer's memory for use by the orbiter's crew. A technical description appeared on the screen, and at the bottom of the page the word "green" appeared. It looked innocuous enough, but Vonberger felt a wave of panic. It seemed too obvious, sitting there by itself, two lines below the rest of the text. Vonberger felt an irrational fear that someone else was looking at it. He quickly hit the clear button, which returned the computer display to the operations program. Green. It meant Das Syndikat really did have a man at NASA. It meant there was a parachute after all. It meant Alex Vonberger had a fellow neo-Nazi looking out for him. It meant, "Proceed according to plan."

Vonberger plugged in his headset. He switched the controls to external communication, set it for voice-activated microphone, and turned up the volume. Normally one audio unit would be left in the receive mode, with the volume up, so that emergency communications could be received from Mission Control, but Vonberger had turned off all the communications during the night. Any real emergencies would show up on the master alarm, which had remained silent. Since Vonberger was wearing the only headset, none of the crew would be able to hear Mission Control's transmissions. It was important to keep the crew in the dark.

Vonberger cleared his throat. This was the moment he had been waiting for. This was the part of the operation that he had fantasized about over and over. He had repeated this communication to himself so many times that the words had lost their meaning, and what he said became a sort of chant, a ritualistic prayer that signified his own ability to change the world. To make a difference.

He spoke into the headset microphone. "Houston, *Discovery*. Do you copy?"

The CapCom's voice came back quickly. "*Discovery*, Houston. We copy."

Vonberger thought he recognized the voice of the CapCom from the night before, and that meant they had not allowed the Mission Control Center to change shifts. He could almost see them, gathered around the CapCom's console, their eyes bloodshot and tired, their hands shaky. Vonberger waited a few extra seconds, just to let the suspense build. They had waited up all night for this.

He started his chant, slowly and calmly, aware that Joey Wells would be hearing every word. "Houston, this is Alex Vonberger. PF-One is in my command. You will listen carefully to my instructions. They must be followed exactly or you will lose your orbiter and the crew. Do you copy?"

"We copy, *Discovery*."

No comments or questions. That was good. It meant that they were prepared to cooperate. Vonberger continued, "My instructions are simple. Ten members of Das Deutschland Syndikat are being held as prisoners in Vienna. They are to be transported alive and unharmed to Tehran, Iran. Upon their arrival there and their release to the people of Iran, you will be contacted by an official of the Iranian government. This official will request that he be put in touch with me directly by telephone hookup. When this official communicates with me, identifies himself, and informs me in prearranged code that the prisoners have all been delivered to his country, I will allow you to make arrangements for the orbiter's return. Do you copy?"

"We copy, *Discovery*. We have some questions."

"Yes, of course. I am not finished. You will want to know what happens if you do not comply. *Discovery* will not be allowed to land unless the prisoners are freed and I am contacted by the Iranian official. Attempting to arrange a deorbit from Mission Control would be useless, as no one will be available to maneuver the orbiter once it reenters the earth's atmosphere. I will warn you only once, Houston. Do not think that I can be fooled by tricks or games. I have anticipated all of your moves, and I am prepared. You must comply with my instructions, or you will lose *Discovery* and the crew. It is that simple. Do you copy?"

"We copy, *Discovery*. We have to talk to Commander Williams."

"Negative, Houston."

The CapCom's voice came back louder. "It's not a request, Vonberger. We have to talk to him!"

Vonberger gently turned down the volume on his audio system and then pulled the headset cord out of the audio terminal unit. He had a strong mental image of the NASA executives gathered around the CapCom's console, waiting for a reply, and exchanging worried looks. The orbiter was surrounded by darkness, and the windows acted like mirrors, reflecting images of the flight deck at different angles. Vonberger looked up at an overhead window and saw his own reflection looking back at him. He just had to sit still for a few minutes and enjoy his power. He was in absolute control.

Slowly, Vonberger became aware of a soft hissing sound, like the sound of air passing through a vent. He concentrated carefully, without looking, trying to figure out what it was. He was about to punch in a systems check on the computer, when suddenly he realized that the sound was coming from Joey Wells. Wells was hunched over in his seat and his head was moving up and down.

The feeling of power grew within Alex Vonberger. Joey Wells was crying. Vonberger knew that if he could make Joey Wells cry, then he could make the world cry. And if he could make the world cry, then he knew he was making a difference. At last, people would listen to him. At last, Das Syndikat would have to be reckoned with. *Deutschland* would be born again!

The short stuttered breathing sounds coming from Joey Wells grew louder, and then, with one large ugly blast, Wells broke out in hysterical laughter. Laughter! He was laughing! Alex Vonberger had hijacked the space shuttle, and this idiot was laughing!

"Okay, wise guy," Vonberger said at last. "What's so funny?"

Wells chuckled a little to himself. "You, man. You're funny."

Vonberger stowed the headset that he had used to talk to Mission Control. He knew that he should not talk to Joey Wells, but he felt afraid of the silence. "What is funny about me?" he asked.

"You really think they're gonna let ten criminals go free just because some clown has hijacked the PF Flyers?"

"You should hope that they do, Cowboy. Because otherwise you are dead."

"Oh, I'm dead all right. We're all dead. But, you know what I think, Alex?"

"I don't really care what you think, Cowboy."

"I don't think there is any official in Iran who is going to contact you."

"Think what you want."

"I think you're up here all by your lonesome. Yes, sir, I think . . . . I think you're just another Lone Ranger."

"We'll see about that." Vonberger undid the straps and floated slowly out of his seat.

"There's one thing I gotta ask you." Wells spoke louder. "Who's gonna be making it with Laura after you're dead?"

Until that moment Alex Vonberger had not thought about Laura going on without him. Sure, something could go wrong and he could be killed. He was prepared for that. What he hadn't thought about was Laura still being alive without him. Being alive and with someone else. And suddenly Vonberger felt trapped. Suddenly the orbiter was small and crowded and hot, and Vonberger felt as much a hostage as the rest of the crew. "Go to hell, Cowboy," he said.

"Yeah, I'll go to hell, but you'll get there first, Mr. Lone Ranger."

21

THE
FOUR
STAGES

A YOUNG man with sandy brown hair stood in the doorway, and Russell Madlinger blinked at him stupidly, trying to figure out who he was and what he wanted. The man pushed the door all the way open and stepped back, letting Madlinger see Senator Paul Ryan, who stood in the hallway. Madlinger propped himself up on his elbows, with his long legs stretched out in front of him on his office couch, and suddenly he remembered that the young man with the sandy brown hair was one of the support staff for SIG-PIFPY. Senator Ryan stepped into the doorway, beside the young man, and gingerly leaned his head inside the office, as if spying on an endangered species.

"Russ, are you up?" the senator asked.

Russell Madlinger swung his feet around onto the floor, and checked his watch. It was almost ten o'clock in the morning. The SIG-PIFPY meeting, which had convened in Building One immediately after Alex Vonberger had made his demands, had been adjourned at nine by National Security

Advisor Dick Higgins. Higgins was needed by the White House, and he was patched in by telephone to a meeting of the President, various advisors, and several Cabinet members. Russell Madlinger had used the opportunity to sneak back to his office for a quick nap. Madlinger knew the lack of sleep would eventually threaten his ability to think clearly, and so, for the next few days, he would have to get his sleep any way that he could. He sat up now and scratched his head, as if it might help his brain work. "Any coffee?" he asked.

"Sure," the young man said. "How do you like it?"

"Just black."

"Would you like coffee, Senator?" the young man asked.

"Please. Cream and one sugar," Senator Ryan said.

The young support staff member disappeared down the hallway and Senator Ryan stepped through the door into Madlinger's office. "Sorry to wake you, Russ," he said, and he closed the door.

"That's all right, Paul. I just thought I'd steal some sleep while I could," and he waved the senator into a seat. Senator Ryan had joined Dick Higgins in the conference call to the White House, and Madlinger knew that Ryan would have some new information. Madlinger rubbed his eyes and scratched his head some more. "What's the latest?"

"Not good." Ryan plopped himself down in a chair facing Madlinger. "The President is between a rock and a hard place, Russ. Loss of *Discovery* and the crew right now would undoubtedly spell disaster for the Peace Flight Program, not to mention the President's own political health. It was hard enough to get NASA back on its feet after *Challenger*. The President's afraid that something like this will completely sour the public on the entire space program, and could have devastating effects on America's prominence in space. We're talking about the future of the country here, Russ."

"He's not thinking of giving in to Vonberger's demands, is he?"

"No, of course not. He's not even considering it. Austria might even release the prisoners if we asked them to, but we're not going to, and neither are the British or the Soviets. Nobody wants to appear weak on terrorism. We've all been down that road before, and it's a no-win situation.''

There was a brief knock on the door and the young staff member entered and handed them their coffees. Madlinger watched Ryan sip his coffee, and for the first time he noticed the strain in Ryan's eyes. It wasn't that they looked tired. It was that they looked empty.

Madlinger thanked the young man and took his first, ever-needed taste. He found it somehow reassuring to be able to sip a cup of hot, black coffee. Madlinger waited until the young man had left and the door was closed before he spoke. ''What have they found out about this Deutschland organization?'' he asked.

''Not much. Apparently it's been around for quite a while, but nobody's taken it very seriously. It started as sort of an underground grass-roots group in West Germany about fifteen years ago, and somewhere along the way it merged with a group of neo-Nazis from East Germany. Its primary targets have been the East German government and the Soviet Union, and I'm afraid the KGB knows a lot more about them than we do. They've hit a couple of Western targets, but never American, and so the CIA isn't really up on them. A couple of years ago Interpol stumbled on the annual meeting of the organization's leadership. It was a complete accident. They thought they were raiding a smuggling operation. It turned out they had enough evidence to lock them all up for various terrorist charges, and things got quiet after that. I guess they figured that they had crushed whatever there was of the organization.''

''And Vonberger's a member of this organization?''

''Probably. One of the reasons that nobody knows anything about them is that their membership is completely secretive. The KGB says that there are less than one hundred members worldwide, but Interpol says there could be as many as twenty thousand in East Germany alone. Nobody really knows, Russ.''

"Ultimately, what does this organization want?"

Senator Ryan shook his head and looked down at the floor. "Nothing short of the reunification of Nazi Germany."

Madlinger heard himself laugh, even though he knew it was not funny. He just couldn't believe that in 1990 the world was still fighting Nazis. It had been over forty years since World War II, and yet Nazis were still around, like a bad disease for which there was no cure. "How'd they hook up with Iran?" Madlinger asked.

"Seems it's the only country in the world that hates both the United States and the Soviet Union as much as they do, and Iran has no problem associating itself with terrorists. They would like nothing more than to see us get our noses bloodied. Seems like Das Syndikat is looking to set up shop in Tehran. They want to build a government-in-exile. They want to build their own army. The problem is that Iran seems to be the only country that has any contact with the organization at all, and so we've got to do our negotiating through them. The State Department is looking for a middleman, but we're having a hard time. Neither of the Germanys wants to go near it. The Soviet Union, Britain, France, Austria, nobody can do anything. Standard middlemen like the PLO or Saudi Arabia can't get near Iran. The only two possibilities we have are Red China and Syria. Both countries have decent connections to Iran, but we don't even know who the hell we're supposed to be talking to over there. We've got less than three days now, and I don't think we can depend on the Iranians to be very cooperative."

Ryan sipped his coffee and then continued. "The only good news is that I think we've managed to patch things up with the Soviets pretty well. Everybody's thankful that we didn't do anything rash. We're leaning over backwards to be nice to them, and to be apologetic for taking their team into custody, and they're doing the best they can to be cooperative. They're supplying us with a lot of information on the organization. The high level of cooperation is really good to see, Russ. I'd like to think it's a sign of the times."

"How's Andrei Kulikov?"

Ryan smiled. "As soon as he found out what was going on, he changed his tune completely. Apparently, he thought we were trying to trick him into defecting, and that's why he wouldn't talk. He's being given the royal treatment now, and we may even let him sit in on a few of the SIG-PIFPY meetings."

Madlinger let out a slow sigh of relief. He felt outraged by the hijacking and the violence, but somehow he could still find hope in the fact that he had trusted Andrei Kulikov and that Kulikov had not betrayed his trust.

"At any rate, Russ," Ryan continued, "the President has come up with a four-stage plan for dealing with the crisis."

"Let's hear it."

"Okay. Stage one: The State Department continues trying to make contact with the organization through Iran, in hopes of being able to negotiate a peaceful solution. The hope is that we can persuade them to allow *Discovery* to land, and then to continue negotiations through a third party. Hopefully, we could do this without having to let the crew be held hostage to these negotiations, but so far we haven't been able to get a line through to the organization."

"Stage one continues until we make progress, and meanwhile, we move ahead on the other stages. Stage two is to try to negotiate directly with Vonberger. The deputy assistant secretary for low-intensity conflicts from the Department of Defense is working with the CIA, the FBI, and various advisors to put together a plan for the best approach. There's some legal problems over which agency has jurisdiction in space, but everybody seems to be working together. Right now, it looks like they're going to use Laura Gold's death to try to turn Vonberger against the organization."

"How would they do that?"

"Well, a staff of FBI psychiatrists believe that Vonberger became strongly involved with Gold on an emotional level, even though they had been set up. From listening to tapes of their conversations, the psychiatrists feel pretty certain that the relationship developed into a real romance. They also feel certain that Vonberger did not know that she would be killed. The FBI thinks that if we tell him about her death at the hands of the organization, then he might lose his resolve. He may no longer be willing to risk his neck for the organization, if he believes that they killed Laura Gold.''

''But, Paul, why would Vonberger believe us when we tell him that Laura Gold has been killed? Wouldn't he think we made it up just to try to make him surrender?''

''Well, they're working on that, and they think they can present it in a way that will leave no doubt in Vonberger's mind. The danger, of course, is that he might take his anger out on the crew. They're going over the pros and cons of it all now, but I think the ultimate decision will be to inform him of her death, and make a simultaneous offer of his freedom in return for *Discovery* and the crew.''

The two men stared at each other and sipped their coffees in silence. Madlinger understood the sudden silence to mean that stages three and four would involve NASA in a more direct way. He and Leonard Wolff had put forth two proposals at the SIG-PIFPY meeting in the morning, and he knew now that he was about to hear the President's response. Senator Ryan looked at his watch, and then stood up. ''Russ, we've got to get upstairs. They're reconvening.''

Madlinger didn't move. ''What about stages three and four, Paul?'' he asked.

''I'll tell you about them on the way up.''

The two men left Madlinger's office and headed toward the elevators in the middle of the building. The halls were relatively quiet and they could speak softly without risk of being overheard.

''Stage three is your ground-based rescue attempt using the fire detection system,'' Senator Ryan said.

''I was afraid of that.''

''And stage four is your rescue operation using the new orbiter.''

''I was afraid of that too. They're both very risky, Paul.''

"The President knows that, Russ, but he needs to take some action. If the negotiations with Vonberger don't produce results by tonight, then we are to move ahead with stage three."

"And if that doesn't produce results?"

"He wants a launch."

"Paul, are you sure that he understands the risks involved?"

"We explained them to him, just as you explained them to us."

"And he's willing to waive all requirements for a safety-review signoff?"

"He wants a management-level flight-readiness review, but he's authorizing us to bypass all other preflight requirements."

"Well, I hope it doesn't come to that. For everyone's sake."

"I know what you mean, Russ."

The two men entered the elevator and rode upstairs to the secured conference room where SIG-PIFPY had gathered. Upon entering the room, Madlinger walked to the secure telephone. He called Ben King and instructed King to get back to the Cape immediately and to begin preparations for a launch. Madlinger then talked with Charles Roland and Dick Higgins and it was agreed to excuse Leonard Wolff and Peggy Kellner from the meeting. Wolff was to work with the tiger team to make final preparations for a ground-based rescue attempt. Kellner was instructed to organize the JSC mission planning staff and to start gearing up for the rescue mission on a contingency basis. Launch would have to be in less than forty-eight hours.

22

A GESTURE
OF
FRIENDSHIP

ANDREI Kulikov squinted his eyes against the early afternoon sun, and walked down the steps from his apartment into the Camino Village parking lot. He caught himself looking for his car, and then remembered that he had left it at Russell Madlinger's house. Across the lot he saw the large, dark blue sedan that belonged to Robert Colbert from the State Department. Kulikov crossed the lot to the sedan and found Colbert in the driver's seat, reading the paper. Kulikov tapped lightly on the glass.

Robert Colbert looked up in surprise and then jumped out of the car. "I'm sorry, Mr. Kulikov. I didn't see you coming."

"That's all right."

Colbert stepped back and pulled open the rear door of the car. "Did you have a good nap, Mr. Kulikov?"

"Yes, it was fine," Kulikov answered, and he slid into the backseat of the air-conditioned car, where he was immediately welcomed by the cool air and by the gentle sounds of classical music.

Colbert closed the door and then slid into the front seat. "Where to, sir?" he asked, his eyes focused on Kulikov in the rearview mirror.

"JSC. Building One."

"Yes, sir."

Colbert shifted into gear and the car seemed to drift out of the parking lot, and onto Camino Drive. It had been a long and grueling night for Andrei Kulikov. The FBI agents had not let him sleep or eat. When Robert Colbert from the State Department had shown up in the morning, Kulikov was prepared for another imperialist trick, but he was quickly allowed to confirm through his own people that Alex Vonberger had hijacked the orbiter, and he soon realized that Colbert's apologies and overtures were sincere. Colbert insisted on becoming Kulikov's personal chauffeur and assistant for the next few days. "Consider my services a friendly gesture from my country, as an apology for the inconvenience that you have suffered," Colbert had said, by which time Kulikov had been too tired to refuse. Colbert had driven Kulikov back to his apartment, where he immediately fell asleep. Now suddenly, he realized how hungry he was, and he knew that he would have to eat a good meal before he would be ready to go to work.

"Robert?"

"Yes, sir?" Colbert's eyes again appeared in the rearview mirror.

"I'd like to get some lunch. Do you know where I can get a hamburger?"

"Yes, sir."

"Don't call me sir."

"Yes, Mr. Kulikov."

"And don't call me Mr. Kulikov. You can call me Andrei."

"Yes, Andrei."

Kulikov rested back into the fine upholstery of the dark blue sedan, and wondered if this was what it was like to be a capitalist. "Robert?"

"Yes, Andrei?"

"Robert, step on it. I'm starving to death."

And both men laughed.

23

THE
SIMPLE
EMPTINESS

ALEX Vonberger drifted aimlessly about the flight deck, fantasizing about his new life in Iran. They had prepared a beach house for him by the Arabian Sea, and he and Laura would live with their Arab servants in luxury and abundance. There would be nothing to do but walk on the beach and make love by the sea. He kept his eyes closed and thought about how he would be honored as the savior of Das Syndikat. Perhaps he would be asked to join the Inner Circle. He would have to stay in Iran for several years, but after that he could travel incognito, like Hans. And Laura would always be there, waiting for him when he got back, just like she was waiting for him now. Yes, Alex Vonberger would be a hero.

"*Discovery,* Houston. Do you copy?" The booming voice of the CapCom suddenly filled the flight deck.

Vonberger had left one of the audio units in the receive mode with the volume up, in anticipation of a communication. This was it! He was burning with excitement, but he forced himself to breathe deeply. He had to stay calm. Zakharov and Wells were masked and strapped into the seats on the flight deck, so Vonberger plugged his headset into the audio unit. He did not want them to be able to hear the transmission.

It was 5:05:43 MET, almost eight hours since Vonberger had communicated his demands. They had had plenty of time to consider their position. Vonberger switched his headset to voice-activated microphone and took another deep breath. "Houston, *Discovery*. We copy," he said.

The voice of the CapCom was clearer over the headset. "*Discovery*, you've got a communication coming in on your TAGS hard-copier."

The text and graphics (TAGS) hard-copier replaced the teleprinters used on earlier flights. It was an uplink system that allowed the ground to send pages of text and graphics to the crew. Vonberger caught his breath and considered the situation. Why were they sending him a hard-copy message? The TAGS hard-copier was activated from the ground, so he could not cut off the communication even if he wanted to. How come Das Syndikat had not thought of that? Curiosity pulled at him. What could they possibly be sending him? Vonberger checked the uplink text pages on the computer, but there were no messages from Das Syndikat. His curiosity got the better of him, and he spoke into his headset microphone. "Roger, Houston. Standing by to accept TAGS communication."

Vonberger instantly realized that he had made a mistake. It didn't matter what they were sending him. They had decided on the means of communication, and he had accepted it, and thus, they had manipulated him. He should have refused the communication. He could have disconnected the TAGS terminal. It was too late now. It was a small mistake, but he could not let it happen again. He had to remain in absolute control.

Vonberger unplugged his headset and moved into the mid-deck. The TAGS terminal, located on the aft wall between the airlock and the waste management compartment, did not look much different from an ordinary copying machine, except that it was smaller. The transmission was already complete by the time Vonberger got to the terminal, and he reached into the paper tray and pulled out a two-page communication.

He read the first page twice before its meaning sunk in.

Laura Gold found dead at Mexican border three days ago. Decapitated. We believe Das Deutschland Syndikat responsible. The deal: Release of the crew, return of *Discovery* and disclosure of all you know about Das Deutschland Syndikat, in return for your freedom. This is a final communication. The United States Department of Defense.

Vonberger felt the blood pump to his head as he separated the pages and looked at page two of the communication. It was a photograph of a naked body stretched out on a clean white table, and there was no head. But Alex Vonberger recognized the body.

Suddenly weightlessness felt just as it had the first few days of flight. He needed something to hold on to. Everything was falling apart. Everything was spinning. Vonberger tried to reach for a comfort bag from one of the mid-deck lockers, but it was too late. His vomit spewed out into the cabin in big shapeless globs. He pushed himself away from the free-floating vomit, but his eyes remained focused on the word "decapitated." More than the photograph, it was that word that bothered him. Something about it. Something about the simple emptiness of it.

He crumpled up the communication and threw it as hard as he could against the mid-deck floor. He was only vaguely aware of how the ball of paper collided in space with a spherical glob of vomit. Vonberger pushed himself into the flight deck and pulled the gun from his pants pocket.

"You ready to die, Cowboy?" He stuck the gun into the back of Joey Wells's head.

"What's the matter, Alex?" Wells spoke from behind his Lone Ranger mask. "Didn't you get what you wanted for Christmas?"

"You're going to die!" Vonberger screamed.

"Alex . . ."

"They think I am a fool!" Vonberger continued screaming. "They think I will give up that easy, just because they killed *das Mädchen!* They think it will scare me?! They can't trick me like this!"

"Alex, man, what are you talking about?"

"I know how your CIA works! They are the same as the KGB! They are all murderers!"

"Alex, man, calm down."

Vonberger pushed the gun harder against Wells's head. "I didn't start the killing, Cowboy! I didn't start it!"

"Alex, don't do it!" Zakharov screamed suddenly.

"Shut up! You will die too!"

"Alex, if you kill all of us, how are you going to land this thing?" Wells asked.

"Your government does not care if I land this thing or not! How does that make you feel? Your life is worth nothing to them. Good-bye, Cowboy."

"Alex! Don't!" Zakharov screamed.

"Shut up!"

"Alex!"

Vonberger did not pull the trigger. He floated for a few seconds with the gun at Wells's head, and then he slowly backed off. Laura was dead. Shooting Joey Wells now would not be a just revenge. It was better to let him die slowly. Better to let everyone sweat for a couple of days. Why make it easy for them? Vonberger pulled the mask up over Wells's head, and then pulled the mask up over Zakharov's head. "Killing you now would not be fair," he said. "I want you both to be able to count the hours. We have until seven-oh-eight oh oh. Isn't that right, Cowboy?"

Wells did not answer.

"I said, isn't that right, Cowboy?"

"So what?"

"So you have fifty hours to live. I think I'll let you watch the clock."

"And what are you going to watch?"

"I'm going to watch you."

"You're not a healthy individual, Alex."

"Fifty hours. I think I'll let you two lovebirds sit here and think about that."

24

FOR
A DIFFERENT
REASON

JOEY Wells did not watch the clock. Instead, he kept his head back and stared at the white-and-blue earth, as *Discovery* passed over the northern coast of Africa. Scattered white cloud puffs sprinkled the sparkling Mediterranean Sea, and out to the east there was the solid gray swirl of storm clouds. Wells tried to remember the different kinds of clouds: altostratus, nimbostratus, cumulus, stratocumulus. Then he tested himself on his geography, naming the bodies of water as they passed below: the Nile, the Gulf of Suez, the Red Sea, the Arabian Sea, and finally the Indian Ocean. When they passed into darkness, and he could no longer see the earth's surface, he tried naming the capitals of the fifty states. Austin, Santa Fe, Phoenix, Sacramento, Reno? No, it wasn't Reno. He could not remember the capital of Nevada. He would have to come back to it. Denver, Cheyenne, Salt Lake City . . .

At 5:09:00 MET, Alex Vonberger began releasing the

crew, one at a time, to use the waste management compartment. He did not let them eat dinner. Vonberger had grown silent and withdrawn, but beneath the quiet there was violence, waiting to be unleashed. Joey Wells knew that it would not take much to provoke him, and when it was his turn to be released, Wells kept his mouth shut and he moved slowly and carefully. When he got to the mid-deck, he found George Evans's condition had stabilized. His breathing was still short and uneven but Evans said that the pain had subsided. If only they could get him to a doctor.

Conrad Williams and Vladimir Turnov were handcuffed into sleeping sacks next to Evans, and they all exchanged solemn looks. "You're going to be all right, George," Wells said.

"How do you know?" Vonberger suddenly asked, his voice tense and angry.

Wells was handcuffed and put into the airlock with Aelita Zakharov. As he pushed himself through the hatch, Joey Wells had two things on his mind. First, he knew this was the opportunity he had been waiting for to devise a plan to get the gun. Second, he knew that this was his chance to tell Aelita how he felt about her. With the two spacesuits hanging on the walls, the airlock was more crowded than Wells had expected and it took some maneuvering to get comfortable. His hands were cuffed behind his back and so he grabbed the spacesuit and pulled himself up against it. Zakharov adjusted her position, so that her eyes were at the same level as his, and he felt her body brush against him, filling him with a stinging desire. He held on to the spacesuit to keep himself in place.

"This is cozy," she said, smiling.

Wells heard the airlock hatch shut as Vonberger locked them in, and he felt Zakharov's breath against his cheek. Suddenly he felt inhibited by her smile and her nearness.

"What are we going to do in here?" she asked.

It was ridiculous how little space they had. There was very

little that they *could* do. "Let's see," Wells said, trying to hide his sudden nervousness. "We could play hide-and-go-seek."

"Or softball," she suggested.

"Or have a treasure hunt."

"We could put on the spacesuits and go for a walk."

"Wait a minute . . ."

"No, Cowboy." Zakharov shook her head. "I thought of that already. Most of the equipment is out on the mid-deck. And there's no way we could get suited up with these hand-cuffs on."

"Yeah, I guess Alex is smart enough for that," Wells said. "Besides, where would we go?"

Zakharov tossed her head back to try to get the hair out of her eyes. "We need to get the gun," she said softly.

"I know, I've thought of that. The problem is he's always so damned careful that I can't get near him."

"I have a plan," she said.

Joey Wells laughed softly. "So do I."

"If you distract him the next time I get my hands free, maybe I can get to him."

Joey Wells laughed again, a little louder this time. "That was *my* plan, only I think you should distract him, and I should try to get the gun."

"No, Cowboy. That would be too obvious. If your hands were free and I made a distraction, he would know it was a trick and he would watch you. But if my hands were free and you distracted him, he might forget about me."

"How can anyone forget about you?"

Zakharov laughed and nodded her head.

"I love the way you nod your head," Wells said. It just popped out and he suddenly felt embarrassed and self-conscious. Yes, he wanted to tell her how he felt, but not now. Not like this.

Her smile disappeared and she looked at him closely. Her look made him even more nervous and he started to talk again just to avoid the silence. "Look, I don't mean to be a hero or anything, but I think you should let *me* try to get the gun. If it comes to a struggle, I would have a better chance. After all, I'm built bigger than you.''

Zakharov's expression had not changed. It was as if she had not heard anything he had said. It was as if she was studying him.

''Unless of course you know some kind of zero-gravity karate, or something . . .'' But Wells stopped. She was not listening to him, and there was no running away from her eyes. No talking around them. Why did she have to look at him like that? Why wasn't she saying anything? He tried to stare back at her, but it was too hard. ''What's the matter?'' he asked at last.

''You love me, don't you, Cowboy?''

He looked back into her eyes. First she had the same idea of getting the gun, and now she knew that he loved her. It was as if she had been reading his mind. He nodded his head slowly, and answered, ''Yeah. Yeah, I do.''

''I have to tell you something.''

Oh, no. Could she be about to say what he had waited for all these months? Was he about to hear what he had wished for? Hoped for? Wanted more than anything else in the world? And how come suddenly he didn't want to hear it? Not here. Not now. Not when they were packed in so close, with their hands cuffed behind their backs and no place to look but at each other.

Her eyes seemed to turn a darker shade of brown and she spoke more softly. ''Before I left my country, some men from the government came to talk to me. I will spare you the details, but they wanted this to happen to us.''

The government? Wells felt his heart sink into his boots. Not this! Not what Hacker had said. How could that fool have been right? It wasn't fair! It couldn't be!

''I refused, of course,'' she continued, still staring into his eyes. ''I am a cosmonaut, not a spy. When I came over here and I met you, I knew right away why they wanted me to do it. There was something vulnerable about you. I never changed my mind about my decision, but as I got to know you, I began to realize that I wanted the same thing they did.''

Wells swallowed hard and he felt dizzy and confused. What was she getting at? Was she a spy or wasn't she? Or perhaps it wasn't that simple. Wells felt heavy despite his weightlessness. This was unreal, and yet, he believed it all. He believed it all, because now everything was starting to make sense.

"I wanted the same thing they did, Cowboy," she said her mouth moving closer to him. "Only I wanted it for a different reason.''

And then she pressed her lips against his cheek and they felt like fire. "I couldn't let it happen, Cowboy.'' They were cheek to cheek now, and she was whispering. "They would have seen it as if I was doing it for them. They would have started to ask me questions and tell me what to do. I didn't want that for us. I didn't want us to be used like that. I just wanted . . . I just wanted you . . . I just wanted you for myself.''

Joey Wells closed his eyes and felt himself soaring in weightlessness and confusion. He was soaring beyond the airlock and the orbiter. He was soaring beyond the hijacking, and beyond Alex Vonberger and the gun. He was soaring beyond anything he had ever known before. Suddenly, their mouths came together and he felt her burning lips on his. Her tongue was hot and strong, and he gently bit her lower lip to keep them from floating apart. She *did* love him! He had known it all along! And then Joey Wells pulled his head back, their mouths separating, and for the first time in his life, Joey Wells was frightened of death.

25

THE
FLIGHT CONTROL
ROOM

B Y nine o'clock, a somber and quiet mood had descended upon the Flight Control Room, and the silence hung thick and still over the flight controllers. Neat rows and columns of information and data flashed across the console computer screens. Red, amber, and green indicator lights blinked on the panels. Human hands reached for coffee cups and fingers tapped lightly on the console desks. Some of the controllers whispered quietly among themselves, but everything was covered by the stillness and the silence.

This was the shift of flight controllers that had been on duty when Vonberger had first hijacked the orbiter. For security reasons, the Mission Control Center had switched to thirteen-hour shifts, and the first shift, who had worked through the night and had been given an eleven-hour break, were now back on duty. They had been briefed by the off-going second shift on the status of the hijacking situation. At 2:45 P.M., Houston time, NASA had sent a communication to the orbiter on the TAGS hard-copier, offering Vonberger his freedom in return for the release of *Discovery* and the crew. At 5:00 P.M., Houston time, there had been a brief communication with Vonberger, and Vonberger had made it clear that he was not going to give himself up. His demands stood. He would return the orbiter and the crew only upon the release of the ten prisoners from Austria.

A Mission Control Center blackout was still in effect, and the Viewing Room remained empty. Leonard Wolff and his tiger team had taken over two consoles in the back of the Flight Control Room. Not much else had changed since the first shift had been in the Flight Control Room, and yet they took their positions with a new sense of optimism.

Flight Director Andrew McKenzie continued to control flight operations, but the flight controllers made reports of data and information to Wolff's tiger team. They reported temperature changes, atmospheric changes, equipment use, electrical loads, and water quantities. Wolff and his engineers diligently processed all of the information and data they received. They quickly established whatever facts they could, and worked to make their assumptions. A large diagram of the orbiter's crew compartment took up one of the screens on the front wall, and six cardboard cutouts were positioned to show the assumed location of the crewmembers. From time to time, one of Wolff's engineers would make an adjustment based on new facts or new assumptions. The flight controllers did not stop to think about how their data would be used by Wolff's team, nor did Wolff's team stop to think about the usefulness of their own conclusions. The tiger team was doing everything they could, as NASA's top engineers, to extrapolate as much information as possible from the orbiter. It was up to the NASA management to make use of the information.

As the evening wore on, the stillness became oppressive, and frustration replaced optimism. Everyone had secretly been hoping that their dedication and attention to detail would somehow save the orbiter. Somewhere along the line there was supposed to have been a breakthrough. As it became obvious that nothing was going to happen, the controllers began to lose faith, and they found themselves hoping that new instructions would come from Building One. There had to be something that NASA could do besides sit and watch.

Their wishes came true at 5:12:15 MET, and the stillness broke suddenly when Russell Madlinger entered the Flight Control Room, accompanied by a young engineer. The controllers watched with curiosity and concern. The engineer, a woman named Julie Larsen, was a design and maintenance engineer, not a flight controller. She belonged in a backroom, with the support personnel. Why had Madlinger brought her into the Flight Control Room?

Still, it was as if Madlinger had freed the controllers after years of imprisonment. They stretched and yawned. They smiled and refilled their coffee cups. Even Andrew McKenzie had a giddy grin across his face. And the controllers were quick to notice that the Viewing Room had suddenly filled up with NASA executives, members of the planning group from Building One, and more engineers from the tiger team. At last, something was going to happen.

The flight controllers waited patiently while Madlinger focused his attention on the flight director's console. Madlinger read through several computer screens of data, and studied the screens on the front wall. When at last he spoke, his voice was quiet.

"The plan is open for the next half hour," Madlinger said to McKenzie, referring to the crew activity plan.

It had not been a question, but McKenzie answered anyway. "Yes."

"Good." Madlinger donned a headset and plugged into the flight directors' loop at McKenzie's console. "Flight controllers, listen up." Madlinger's voice came over the headsets full of confidence and calm reassurance. "We are about to attempt to orchestrate a rescue of the orbiter from the ground. Members of our tiger team have worked throughout the day to devise the plan, but its chances of success are still rated as poor, on top of which it may expose members of the crew to further danger. Nonetheless, the plan has been endorsed by the President and by the Soviet premier, and we're going to do the best we can to pull it off.''

Madlinger's words were not taken lightly. The flight controllers immediately understood that this was a high-risk operation with only a poor chance of success. It meant that they would have to pursue it with the utmost care and attention.

The operation itself would be relatively simple to perform, Madlinger explained. Julie Larsen would bias the computer monitoring program to make it appear that the fire detection system was malfunctioning. Joey Wells was the only member of the crew who could fix a malfunction in the fire detection system, and so Vonberger would be forced to release Wells to fix it. The plan would not work if Vonberger was so reckless as to allow a malfunction in the system to go unattended. However, there were still two days' worth of life-support systems and supplies on *Discovery,* and thus it was safe to assume that Vonberger would still try to protect himself and the crew from the dangers of fire.

The limits on the computer monitoring program would be revised in a way that would cause the orbiter's warning system to indicate a malfunction, and the computer would show that Fixed Fire Extinguisher Number 3 was nonoperational. Number 3 was located in one of the avionics compartments on the mid-deck. In order to access that area, a number of the lockers in the mid-deck would have to be removed, and thus Vonberger would require assistance. Ordinarily, if an extinguisher was found to be malfunctional, and could not be fixed, then a portable fire extinguisher would be brought out as a backup. Wells would quickly determine that the extinguisher was not malfunctioning, but he could easily use the opportunity as an excuse to bring out a portable fire extinguisher. It was hoped that Wells would be able to use the portable extinguisher as a weapon to subdue Vonberger.

Madlinger stood with his hands in his pockets staring out over the Flight Control Room. The flight controllers did not watch him, but kept their eyes on their consoles. "The primary goal of this plan is to give Joey Wells an opportunity to subdue Alex Vonberger." Madlinger's voice suddenly sounded softer and older. "As you all know, there is no way we can communicate with Wells prior to uplinking the bias. Once the limits are changed, the operation is out of our hands. It's a desperate and dangerous plan. We could be placing the crew in further jeopardy than they are already. But as I told you, this plan has been endorsed by the President. We must do everything we can, and we must hope for the best."

A silence hung in the room as Madlinger turned toward Julie Larsen and nodded slightly. Larsen made her way to the electrical and environmental control systems console. The flight controller stood up and stepped away from his position, and she nodded to him apologetically as she took his seat. The other controllers looked on skeptically as she pulled herself up to the console, and only the clicking sound of her fingers on the computer keyboard challenged the silence of the Flight Control Room. Her keystrokes were quick and determined, indicating that she needed no time to plan or to think. She knew exactly what she was doing, and when she was finished she pushed her chair away from the console and faced Madlinger. She said nothing.

Madlinger spoke into the flight director's loop. "Okay. When Ms. Larsen uplinks the new limits for the fire detection system, the warning siren will sound on board *Discovery*. Flight controllers are to react as you would to any system malfunction. All of you are to continue complete and full monitoring of your systems. Any questions?"

There were none.

Madlinger sat down and put his hands behind his head. "Okay, Ms. Larsen. Uplink."

Changing sensor limits in the orbiter's computer program is as easy as changing a flat tire, if you know what you're doing. Larsen leaned forward in her seat and punched a few buttons on the console keyboard. She sat back and opened her mouth but her words were cut off by an immediate report by the systems controller.

"We have a fire detection system alert," he shouted into his mike.

Everyone was expecting it. Everyone was waiting for it, and yet the loud announcement jarred their senses, and brought them back with renewed diligence to their consoles and their computer displays. A warning light was flashing on the systems console, and Flight Director McKenzie ran a full systems check. On page three, the words "Fire Detection System" were blinking. Vonberger could easily call up a similar display on board *Discovery*. A detailed check of the fire detection system was part of another display on the computer, and McKenzie called it up. Chances were that Vonberger would have to look in one of the checklists, or ask Joey Wells to direct him to the proper display.

Calling up the detailed display brought more data on the fire detection system. The first page contained a list of detectors and extinguishers. Next to the words "Fixed Fire Extinguisher Number 3," a down arrow was displayed. On data page 38 for the fire detection system, a diagram of Fixed Fire Extinguisher Number 3 appeared on the screen, with all the parts numbered. By entering a search code, the computer automatically displayed the number of the part that was malfunctioning. When McKenzie ran the search code, number 54 appeared, indicating that a part called the sensor connector was nonoperational.

Vonberger would probably be able to get this far on his own, but he would not know how to proceed. He would not know where to find Fixed Fire Extinguisher Number 3, nor would he know how to check the sensor connector. He would have to contact Houston, or use Joey Wells.

When enough time had passed to allow Vonberger to find the malfunction, Madlinger nodded at the CapCom. "Establish communication," he said.

The CapCom had been standing by. "*Discovery*, Houston. Do you copy?"

There was no response.

The Flight Control Room remained perfectly still, but nobody was quite sure what they were waiting for. Nobody really expected a transmission. Most of the flight controllers were staring at the diagram of the crew compartment, as if the cutout representing Joey Wells might magically be set free and start moving toward the broken fire extinguisher. They watched their computer displays for any indication of movement or change.

It was Andrew McKenzie who broke the silence. "He's gonna let it go," he said to Madlinger quietly.

Madlinger stared up at the crew compartment diagram and nodded his head slowly. "Maybe. CapCom?"

"*Discovery,* Houston. Do you copy?"

Again there was no response.

Madlinger spoke into his headset. "Len, is there any movement up there at all?"

"Nothing we can track," Wolff replied. "He could be anywhere in the compartment, but he hasn't done anything that we can monitor. He could be reviewing the data on the fire detection system, or checking the computer. He could be talking to Wells. He could be sleeping for all we can tell."

"He's not going to do anything," McKenzie said.

Madlinger looked at the flight director with curiosity. "How do you know?"

"He would have acted already. He would have contacted us."

Madlinger slouched down further into his seat. "Let's give him more time."

Nothing happened, and it happened for a long time. Fifteen minutes of eerie silence passed in the Flight Control Room. If the flight controllers began growing restless, they didn't show it. They took their cue from Russell Madlinger, who sat, slouched down in his seat, eyes half closed, waiting as if he had all the time in the world.

Suddenly, Vonberger's voice cracked through the silence. "Houston, *Discovery.* Do you copy?"

"*Discovery*, Houston. We copy."

The flight controllers sat up in their seats, but their eyes stayed glued to their consoles. Vonberger's voice continued, "You have uplinked a change of limits in the computer monitoring program for the fire detection system. I have warned you that I am prepared for your tricks. One more like that and Joey Wells will do an EVA without a spacesuit! Do you copy?"

Vonberger's voice was filled with an ominous power, and cries of frustration and horror filled the Flight Control Room. How had Vonberger figured out that they had changed the limits? A new sense of helplessness suddenly descended upon the flight controllers. It could be seen in the dropped jaw of Andrew McKenzie. It could be seen in the distraught face of the CapCom, who stood waiting for instructions. But it could be seen best of all in the eyes of Russell Madlinger.

Madlinger took a deep breath of resignation. "We copy," he instructed softly.

"*Discovery*, Houston," the CapCom said. "We copy."

Russell Madlinger stood up slowly and faced the Viewing Room. Members of SIG-PIFPY, and other NASA executives and engineers, were all visibly angry. Everyone was getting out of their seats and moving toward the door. Everyone except Senator Paul Ryan. The senator was sitting in the front row of the Viewing Room, staring out into the Flight Control Room, and only Russell Madlinger seemed to notice that Ryan's eyes were burning holes through the glass.

26

THE
MISSION
SPECIALIST

SENATOR Paul Ryan and Russell Madlinger walked quietly along the lighted pathway, across the broad, landscaped area that separated the Mission Control Center from Building One. The early night air had turned humid and Ryan found himself wondering if the humidity was in Houston to stay for the summer. The rescue attempt from the Mission Control Center had failed, and the two men were now headed to the SIG-PIFPY meeting, where the final stage of the President's plan would be discussed. Ryan and Madlinger reached a large pond and they stopped and stood by themselves, looking out across the water. "Well, it looks like we're going to be sending up a rescue mission," Madlinger said.

"I'm afraid so," the senator replied.

"It's hard to believe that there's nothing else we can do, but I guess we've tried everything."

"We *have* tried everything, Russ. We've tried negotiating with Vonberger, we've considered negotiating with Iran, and now we've tried tricking Vonberger into releasing the crew.

Hell, we've even tried seeing if the Soviets had a spacecraft available for the rescue. This is our only hope, Russ, and you and I both know it.''

They stood in silence, and Ryan watched the lights from Building One reflect off the surface of the pond. ''Have you a got a crew in mind?'' Ryan asked.

Madlinger laughed softly to himself. ''Yeah, I've got a crew in mind, but it's not going to go over very big.''

''What do you mean?''

Madlinger looked down at his feet and then looked out over the water. ''Well, on a mission like this, even more so than on a usual mission, the astronauts are all anxious to be selected. They all want to be able to help their compatriots.'' Madlinger paused and then faced the senator. ''Picking the commander and the pilot was pretty easy, because we had two backups for the PF-One flight. They're obvious choices and nobody can really object.''

''So, what's the problem?''

''Well, the rescue mission also calls for one mission specialist, and because we didn't have any mission specialists on PF-One, there is no obvious choice. In addition, whoever flies as mission specialist is going to have to undertake some pretty risky operations. It's a difficult slot to fill.''

''Who'd you pick?''

An odd expression suddenly appeared on Madlinger's face, and then he broke into a sheepish grin. ''Me.''

Ryan stared, open-mouthed. Madlinger couldn't be serious. He was the director of the Peace Flight Program. He selected crews and planned missions. He didn't fly them! And why would Madlinger go into space when he would be needed on the ground to oversee the rescue operation? Ryan finally found his voice. ''Russ, you've got to be kidding!''

Madlinger still wore the remains of a grin, but he shook his head. ''No, I'm not kidding.''

''Russ, there's no way you can justify going as the mission specialist!''

"Look, Paul, I've got to do it! I put those people up there. Yes, PFP was your idea, and was supported by the President, but I'm the one who put it into action. I selected the crew. I planned the mission. Paul, those are my people up there! I put them there! I couldn't live with myself if anything happened to them!"

Ryan studied Madlinger in the dim light from a nearby lamppost. "Russ, I understand your feelings, but I think you're exaggerating your own responsibility for the PF-One crew. The Peace Flight Program is an international effort. Thousands of people have helped with its planning and organization. You can't take all the credit for that, nor all the blame. Besides, you're going to be needed here to supervise the mission."

"Paul, nobody here is indispensable. That's one of the beauties of NASA. We've got redundancy on the ground with our personnel, as well as in the spacecraft's critical systems. Everyone's got a backup. There are people here who can handle anything that needs to be done on the ground. You've been around NASA long enough to know that."

"All right, I can't deny that. And I'm also not going to try to argue that you should leave it to someone younger and in better shape, because you're disgustingly physically fit. But what about the actual rescue attempt? Isn't it going to involve an EVA?"

"I've done an EVA, Paul. Okay, it's been a long time, and it was not from an orbiter, but I've been out in space on my own. I know what to expect. And I'm sure I can handle the MMU with a little fast training on the controls."

"What's the MMU?"

"The manned maneuvering unit. It lets you maneuver yourself out in space without being tethered to your vehicle. Look, Paul, getting suited up and getting in and out of the airlock is easy enough. I'm comfortable in space, and I'm one of the fortunate ones who doesn't experience space sickness, so that's not going to slow me down. Hell, Paul,

I may be an old guy, but I'm still an astronaut, and that's something that never leaves you. I know I can get the job done.''

"So send someone else with flight experience and no previous symptoms."

"I've already taken that into consideration in picking the commander and the pilot. Paul, I've got to go. That's all there is to it. The rescue mission is my idea. I suggested it as soon as I found out that it was feasible. Since then we've done a lot of work and preparation, and we're going to be as prepared as we possibly can, but it's still going to be a risky operation. I wish we didn't have to go through with it. It would have been better if one of our other plans had worked, but they didn't. We've tried everything, and this is the only thing left. It's a risky operation, but it was my idea. I'm going!''

Ryan turned and stared into Madlinger's eyes, as if he were seeing him for the first time. He had always admired and respected Madlinger, but it was because of the competence Madlinger had displayed in his current position and because of what Ryan knew about his past accomplishments as an Apollo astronaut. Now suddenly, Ryan was seeing deeper into Madlinger's soul, and he saw a new kind of determination and strength. Here was a man who could get the job done. Here was a man with the ultimate kind of strength. Not the strength that comes from courage, although there was plenty of that, but the strength that comes from having a sense of humanity. It was the kind of strength that no computer, robot, or spacecraft could ever have. It was a strength as solid as mankind.

"It's your choice, Russ," Ryan said at last, "but you're right that it's not going to go over big."

"Can I count on you to support me?"

Ryan nodded slowly. "Yeah, you can count on me."

The two men turned away from the pond and continued their walk toward Building One. Ryan had not mentioned the nebulous suspicion that he had developed while sitting in the Viewing Room, but he was not sure how to broach the subject.

It was Madlinger who spoke. "Paul, there's something bothering you. I saw it in your eyes from the Flight Control Room."

Ryan smiled to himself, appreciating Madlinger's perceptivity. "Something is bothering me, Russ. It was that rescue attempt we just tried in Mission Control. How did Vonberger know you had changed the limits?"

"He must have checked the program."

"Does he have the sophistication to do that?"

"I guess so. He's pretty good on the shuttle computers."

"How did he know to check it?"

Madlinger shook his head. "I guess he was suspicious."

"How come we didn't consider that he might figure it out? How come we didn't think of it?"

Madlinger stopped suddenly. "Paul! What are you driving at? We did the best we could—"

Ryan held up his hand to stop Madlinger. "I'm not blaming anyone, Russ, I'm trying to make a point."

"Which is?"

"Isn't it possible that Vonberger was warned?"

"Warned by whom?"

"By someone on the ground."

Madlinger laughed suddenly. "How could he have been warned? You were there, Paul. Nobody warned him."

"Couldn't somebody have sent up a warning on the computer or something?"

"Paul, the only way to get to the computer is through the Mission Control Center. Unless you're suggesting that Vonberger has someone at NASA looking out for him?"

"Isn't it possible?"

"Frankly, I find the idea rather absurd."

"Listen, Russ. I don't mean to get paranoid, but just think about it for a minute. This organization we're up against is highly sophisticated and has a completely secret membership.

Who knows who could belong to the organization? All they would have to do is have one well-placed person inside NASA and they'd be able to protect Vonberger from any of our rescue attempts. Nobody wants to be the one to point fingers, Russ, but it could be disastrous to your rescue mission. I just think we should look into it as a possibility."

Once again the two men continued their walk. "Well, it's an interesting theory," Madlinger said, finally, "but we've really got nothing to base it on. Maybe you should talk to Elliot Hacker about it."

Ryan nodded his head. "Yeah, I think I will. But first I've got to talk to the President."

"What for?"

"Well, if you're serious about trying to land this job as a mission specialist, you're going to need all the help you can get."

27

THE
DARK
ROOM

WILSON'S Camera Shop was the sole occupant of a small white stucco building on Galveston Road. Elliot Hacker squeezed his car into the tiny parking lot in the front, between an old Dodge pickup truck and Steve Erickson's Ford. He looked out his front windshield at the bright orange neon sign that announced FILM DEVELOPED—24 HOURS. A cardboard sign in the door said SORRY, WE'RE CLOSED—PLEASE CALL AGAIN. From the dim lights inside the shop, Elliot Hacker could see the glass counters and the neatly arranged display cases filled with cameras and equipment. The empty store gave him a quiet and lonely feeling, and he got out to join his men in the parking lot.

Erickson briefed Hacker while one of the agents worked the lock on the front door. "We've tracked down almost four hundred leads today, Elliot, and only three haven't checked out. One tenant moved out about two years ago and hasn't been heard from since. One family moved to Dallas, and the husband disappeared about four months ago, but it seems to be a domestic problem. This guy here"—and he nodded casually at the camera store—"he's still a resident at Calhoun Terrace. He hasn't been home all day, and the shop's been closed."

"Family?"

"You bet. He's got a sister in St. Paul who hasn't heard hide nor hair from him. There's a kid who works here who says Wilson would have told him if he was going anywhere. The kid showed up for work this morning and the door was locked. The kid hung around for a while because Wilson's truck was parked out in front, but Wilson never showed up. That's his truck, over there."

Elliot Hacker stared at the old Dodge pickup he had parked next to, and suddenly everything seemed to fall into place. It was easy to imagine how it must have worked. Alex Vonberger would go home with Laura Gold, and in the middle of the night he would sneak downstairs and cut through the underground hallway to meet Roger Wilson. Wilson did not have the background of a big man in the organization, and his role was probably that of an intermediary. Perhaps he carried information back and forth between Vonberger and the organization. After the meeting, they would both go back to their apartments, and in the morning, Vonberger would go to JSC and brag about his love life. Wilson was free as a bird, and could easily make contact with The Organization without fear of being watched. Hacker suddenly felt nervous. The whole plan with Gold and Wilson was a perfect setup for a local connection with Das Deutschland Syndikat, and the camera shop was only a few miles from the Johnson Space Center.

The front door popped open, and Hacker followed his men inside. The store was immaculately well kept. The display cases and glass counters were polished and clean, and the tiled floor was spotless. Cameras, lenses, and tripods were neatly locked away behind glass cabinets. Everything seemed to be in perfect order. Erickson pushed open a door that led into the back room, and then Hacker knew they were too late.

The bookcases and filing cabinets had all been emptied into a giant pile in the middle of the floor. The top of the desk had been swiped clean and the desk drawers were turned upside down on top of everything else. Hacker felt his stomach quiver and he stepped aside and let his men through to check the closets, the windows, and the doors. The floor was a foot deep in refuse, and Hacker waded through the mess, looking carefully, and touching nothing. He leaned over and used a handkerchief to pick up a photograph that caught his eye.

"Elliot, in here." Steve Erickson's voice was calm.

Hacker slipped the photograph into his pocket and plodded across the floor to join his assistant. Erickson stood in the doorway of a fairly sizable darkroom and Hacker had to wait for his eyes to adjust to the darkness. A dim red light hung over a large table in the middle of floor, and slowly the outlines and forms of the rest of the room began to take shape. Sinks, enlargers, equipment, and chemicals cluttered the outer walls, and rolls of film hung from the ceiling.

Roger Wilson was in the corner.

His hands were tied behind his back and he was in a kneeling position, bent over so that his head was on the floor, or at least, what was left of his head. He lay in a puddle of blood, and pieces of his skin and hair were splattered on the nearby wall.

Hacker stepped out of the darkroom and lit a cigarette. Perhaps he had already spent too many years behind a desk. This sort of thing never used to bother him. He inhaled deeply on his cigarette and was only vaguely aware now of his assistant giving orders to the men. He leaned against the wall and tried to calm himself, but time was running out. First Laura Gold and now Roger Wilson. The FBI was working fast, but someone else was working faster.

28

THE
PERFECT
BALANCE

THERE were no clouds to the east, but the sky was pink and orange. Russell Madlinger stared out the window of the NASA jet at the brightly colored and perfectly still Atlantic Ocean. Below him he could see the long runway at KSC, the Kennedy Space Center, and he knew he would be on the ground before the sun came up. This was the same runway the orbiters used. *Discovery* had been scheduled to land the evening before, but PF-1 was now into Day 7, with less than forty-eight hours' worth of oxygen left on board. The world had been told there were communication difficulties that would delay the orbiter's return. It wasn't far from the truth, Madlinger thought, if you could consider an incapacitated crew a communication difficulty.

The NASA jet made a smooth landing, and Madlinger gathered his belongings and waited patiently while the jet taxied back to the ramp. He had managed to get a few hours of sleep during the flight, and now he looked forward to that first cup of coffee. At the ramp, he thanked the pilots, and quickly crossed the runway to the NASA van that waited just outside the gate. He climbed into the backseat of the van and pulled the door shut behind him.

It had been a long night. After their talk by the pond, Madlinger and Senator Ryan had joined the SIG-PIFPY meeting in Building One. Senator Ryan's suspicion that Das Deutschland Syndikat might have a member placed within the ranks of NASA was met with skepticism from the SIG-PIFPY members. Ryan had no real proof that Vonberger had been warned, and it was generally agreed that Vonberger could have checked the computer program for the fire detection system on his own initiative. At any time during flight, there was an almost endless number of transmissions being relayed back and forth from the ground to the orbiter. Attempting to monitor and review these transmissions in search of a warning would be an overwhelmingly burdensome task. Instead, it was decided that as a safety precaution, the FBI would investigate the backgrounds of all personnel on duty at the time the revised program was uplinked. Any warning would have had to come from the Mission Control Center, and thus, there was a limited number of people to investigate.

"Headquarters, sir?"

Madlinger looked up and realized that the van had not moved. "No. The Auditorium Building, please."

"Er . . . yes, sir."

There was something odd about the driver. He busied himself putting the van in gear and releasing the parking brake, but he seemed nervous. Madlinger took a deep breath and gazed out the window as they rolled out of the runway parking area. The problem with Senator Ryan's suspicion was that there was no end to paranoia once it began.

They turned right on the Kennedy Parkway and drove past the OPF, Orbiter Processing Facility, the twin buildings where the orbiters are replenished and prepared for flight. They passed the 525-foot-tall VAB, Vehicle Assembly Building, where the orbiters are mated to the external tanks and solid booster rockets. Next to the VAB is the smaller Launch

Control Center, which houses the firing rooms where the shuttle launches are controlled. Madlinger recalled the morning of the PF-1 launch, and he remembered the lone sea gull that had circled outside the firing room windows. It made Madlinger sad to think how only a week ago, PF-1 had been so filled with hope.

The van continued down the long road toward the "industrial area," where KSC Headquarters and other buildings were located. Madlinger stared out the window at the scrubs and mangrove bushes and watched for the tree with the eagle's nest. Naturalists had installed a video camera in the tree in order to study the eagle's habits, and Madlinger found it somehow satisfying to see the nest and the video camera, sitting on opposite branches of the same tree. He marveled at the eagle, who had meticulously chewed through the cable of the camera several times before the naturalists learned to hide it. Now the bird and the video camera shared the tree in peace, demonstrating the perfect balance of nature and science.

Madlinger's thoughts returned again to the SIG-PIFPY meeting. His choice of the mission specialist had been greeted with the same skepticism as Ryan's suspicion that Vonberger had been warned. Everyone, from Higgins and Roland to Elliot Hacker had argued with Madlinger, and in the end, it was only the President's vote in Madlinger's favor that had turned the tide. At one o'clock in the morning, Houston time, Madlinger had left the meeting and was driven out to Ellington Field, where a NASA jet was waiting to take him to KSC.

The NASA van now turned left onto NASA Parkway and pulled up to the gates outside the KSC industrial area. Madlinger noticed an increased number of guards at the gate, and inside the streets were busy for this time in the morning. As they passed through the security check, Madlinger studied the driver's face in the rearview mirror. It was only natural for the driver to react strangely. It was not often that the industrial area was so heavily guarded and patrolled. And it was not often that a senior NASA official flew into Kennedy so early in the morning, and asked to be taken to the Auditorium Building. The small Auditorium Building is located between the main Headquarters Building and the Operations and Checkout Building. Another NASA van was parked out in front, and a security guard looked on while two NASA maintenance men unloaded supplies from the back of the van.

In the lobby of the Auditorium Building, Madlinger found a table with a thirty-gallon urn of fresh, hot coffee. He eagerly poured himself a cup of black, steaming fortification, and then walked through the doors into the auditorium. A few maintenance men were setting up tables and microphones, but otherwise the large room was empty. Sections of the auditorium had been identified with signs on poles, indicating which groups were to be seated in which sections. In the aisle next to each section was a floor microphone, from which any group representative or member could address the room. On the stage, there was a long table with several telephones and a microphone in front of each chair. Except for the lack of flags, balloons, and bands, the auditorium almost looked like it had been set up for a convention, with the various delegate sections on the convention floor and the leadership on the rostrum. But instead of carrying the names of voting districts, the signs all had names like CREW EQUIPMENT, VEHICLE STATUS, and WEATHER. The auditorium was being set up for the final review and sign-off meeting of the rescue mission. The planning team of the rescue mission had been given the official designation Rescue Operation Team, or ROT, and members of the team would soon be arriving from NASA centers across the country, together with advisors from the CIA, the FBI, and the Department of Defense. The mission itself was being called RM-105.

Madlinger walked down the long aisle to the stage, and he climbed up to the table and faced the empty auditorium. He had not been able to tell Cathy about the rescue mission, and he wondered now if she would understand why he had to go as mission specialist. He had argued his case to Senator Ryan, then to SIG-PIFPY, and then to the President himself, and he had won the debate each and every time, and yet he still churned their arguments inside his head. Why not send a young fresh astronaut who didn't have a family? Why not send someone who had already done an EVA from the orbiter? Why not send someone who had experience with the manned maneuvering unit? Why not send someone who wouldn't be needed on the ground to supervise the mission?

Their arguments were all valid, and Cathy would be able to see that. But she would also be able to understand that Madlinger couldn't ask anyone else to go. She would understand that if he sent someone else, and something went wrong, he would have to live with the thought that he should have gone himself. Perhaps it was not fair to his family that he should put his own life in jeopardy, but it also wasn't fair that they should live in a world where terrorists could sabotage the chances for world peace. Madlinger would give it his best shot, and he knew his family deserved that.

Madlinger sat at the big table on the stage and sipped his coffee. He had half an hour before Gerald Bingham, the RM-105 commander, and Brad Parker, the RM-105 pilot, showed up. Together, they would have an hour to go over the preliminary plans for the rescue operation, but Madlinger knew he would also have to take the time to sell himself to the astronauts as the mission specialist. He was prepared for them to be initially cool to the idea, but he was also confident that he would be able to persuade them that he was the right man for the job. He had already had his practice persuading SIG-PIFPY and the President.

Still, he had half an hour to review his files and get ready for the day's meetings. Madlinger's watch said that it was five-thirty, but it was still set on Houston time. If he called his family, he would not be able to tell them about the hijacking, or about the rescue mission. He could say hello, and he could tell them that he was at the Cape for a few days. They would know better than to ask questions. He could tell the kids that he missed them. He could tell Cathy that he loved her. Russell Madlinger picked up the telephone from the table in front of him and dialed his number in Houston.

29

BEING
THE
HERO

JOEY Wells awoke to the clanking sound of the airlock hatch being opened from the outside. Aelita Zakharov's head was by his shoulder and their legs were twisted together. It was about as intimate as they could get, floating in weightlessness with their hands tied behind their backs. They had only their legs to keep them from floating apart. Wells yawned and stretched and Zakharov opened her eyes and pushed her face into his neck. They kissed and Wells soaked up the feeling of her skin and her hair, enjoying her scent and her warmth. Then he remembered their plan, and suddenly his stomach felt hollow and queasy. He was nervous, but not for himself. In the end, Joey Wells had been forced to concede that Aelita's plan was better than his own. Vonberger trusted Wells the least, and thus it was Wells who received the most attention. Aelita was not so carefully watched, and so she had a better chance of getting the gun.

The plan was simple. Joey Wells was to wait until he was sure that Zakharov's hands were free. It was possible that

Wells would not be on the mid-deck when her handcuffs were removed, and so they had arranged a signal. Once her hands were free, Zakharov would be allowed to go to the waste management compartment. She would be able to make enough noise closing the privacy curtain so that Wells could hear it, regardless of where he was. That would be his sign, and Wells would then make his move.

"Cowboy first!" Vonberger's voice came in through the hatch. "Nice and slow, Cowboy. I feel like shooting someone this morning."

Joey winked at Aelita Zakharov and then he slowly worked his way through the airlock hatch. He pushed his way out, feet first, and found Vonberger floating near the access port to the flight deck. He was relieved that Williams and Turnov were not on the mid-deck, and he assumed that they were tied into the commander and pilot seats. It was two fewer people who could get hurt. Wells looked over at Evans, who was sleeping soundly against the wall. His breathing seemed calmer and Wells felt optimistic. Now if he could only get the gun, and bring this thing home.

"What time is it?" Wells asked, looking at Vonberger for the first time.

Vonberger's demeanor had not changed. He held himself in the corner of the mid-deck, with the gun pointing at Wells's gut. He appeared calm, but in the same way a volcano appears calm when it's getting ready to blow. "It is Day Seven," Vonberger said.

"I said what *time* is it, not what *day* is it."

"It is Day Seven. Never mind the time!"

"Easy for you to say. You haven't been cooped up in the airlock all night. Am I gonna get to eat something?"

"No."

"Oh, well. At least I know you're gonna let me take a leak, because otherwise I'm gonna have to go in my flight suit."

"Face the locker and I will open the handcuffs."

"Still stalemated with the folks downstairs, huh?"

"Turn around!" Vonberger's voice suddenly flashed with anger, and Joey Wells felt the butterflies in his stomach.

If only he could save Aelita from having to go up against this madman. Wells turned around so that Vonberger could release the handcuffs. All he had to do was wait until Vonberger was behind him and then he could spin around and kick. He could use the lockers to brace himself, and maybe if he turned fast enough and kicked hard enough, he could throw Vonberger against the opposite wall.

Vonberger grabbed his wrists and Wells heard the key in the handcuffs. He felt the cuffs pop open, but he could not move. Joey Wells cursed himself for his paralysis, but he knew that it was useless. It was not fear that kept him from attacking Alex Vonberger. It was love. Wells knew that Aelita's plan was the best opportunity they would have to get the gun, and he knew that if he did something stupid now, he would ruin that opportunity. It wouldn't help her or the crew if he was shot. The only way for him to be a hero right now was to be practical, and that meant doing nothing.

Wells waited until Vonberger backed away, and then he moved slowly into the waste management compartment. It felt good to urinate, and Wells didn't want to stop, because he didn't want to go back out there. He was scared for Aelita and angry that she had to do the most dangerous part. Objectively, he knew that letting her go for the gun was the smartest thing, but in his heart he wished that there was something else they could do. He didn't want to be her decoy, and as long as he sat, anchored to the toilet, he knew she was safe.

When there was no more delaying the inevitable, Joey Wells pulled back on the operating handle to turn off the airflow through the toilet. Then he pulled up the pants of his flight suit and opened the privacy curtain. Vonberger was waiting with the gun, and the handcuffs were floating near the lockers where Wells had left them. Vonberger nodded at the handcuffs and told Wells to put them on—Wells would not be allowed to eat or wash. Wells felt rising panic as he floated to the lockers and grabbed the handcuffs.

He spun around slowly with the cuffs in his hands and faced Vonberger. What would Vonberger do if he refused to put them on? What if he just let the handcuffs float, and then stretched out in one of the sleeping sacks? Would Vonberger have the nerve to shoot him in cold blood? Shooting Evans was one thing, because everyone had been moving in on him, but what if instead of going for the gun, Wells just smiled and floated up to the flight deck? Would Vonberger dare shoot him in the back? Joey Wells looked into Vonberger's eyes, and suddenly he saw the lava of hate and violence waiting to erupt. There was no human being there. Only evil. Joey Wells swallowed hard as he reached behind his back and slipped the handcuffs on his wrists. It was all going to be up to Aelita Zakharov now.

Wells could barely breathe as he slipped back up into the airlock and pulled his body up against Zakharov's. It was the best he could do for a hug, and then he winked at her again. He was too scared to talk. She nodded her head once, the way he liked, and then he felt her slowly slipping past him, through the hatch and into the mid-deck. He couldn't help wondering if she had just slipped from his life forever.

Joey Wells was hyperventilating. He listened carefully as Vonberger instructed her to face the lockers, and he thought he could hear the click of the handcuffs opening, and the rattle as Zakharov shook them off her wrists. He heard Vonberger grunt, and then he listened and waited. Finally he heard the release of the straps on the privacy curtain, and he heard it flap as Zakharov pulled it closed. It was time to move.

Joey Wells took one more deep breath, and then pushed himself out of the hatch, screaming as he went. "The airlock's losing pressure! We're losing pressure!" His feet plowed out into the mid-deck. "Alex, we're losing pressure!"

As his head came out into the mid-deck, he saw Alex

Vonberger waiting for him, the gun aimed at the hatch where he emerged. "Get back in there!" Vonberger screamed.

"Alex—"

"Get in there or I'll kill her!" And Vonberger suddenly turned the gun toward the waste management compartment.

"Alex, no!" Wells didn't waste an instant. He pushed his feet as hard as he could against the outer wall of the airlock and propelled himself toward Vonberger. As he soared across the mid-deck he saw Zakharov come flying out from behind the privacy curtain, and he screamed. "No!"

The gun fired and Joey Wells felt himself stop midway across the cabin, as if by magic, and then he slowly started floating backward toward the airlock. He was aware of a few things. Aelita had grabbed the galley with her free hands to stop her motion, and she and Vonberger seemed to be frozen in their positions. They were both staring at Wells, as if he had just said something outrageous. Then Joey Wells saw the red bubbles, and knew that he had been hit.

Alex Vonberger began screaming. "Damn you! I warned you! Why wouldn't you listen to me? What the hell is the matter with you!"

Zakharov let go of the galley and came floating over to Wells. She put her hands on his cheeks. "Okay, Cowboy. You're going to be okay." Her voice was smooth and calming and her eyes were like brown pools of warmth.

Maybe she said something else, or maybe it was Vonberger talking. Joey Wells closed his eyes. Yes, that felt better. Maybe he would just float and sleep. That was all he wanted. He thought he should open his eyes to see where he had been hit, but it was too much work. All he wanted to do was sleep. Float and sleep. Everything else would be all right.

30

A
SHOT IN THE
DARK

THE morning sun was already scorching the runway pavement at the Kennedy Space Center when the first of the jets arrived. The jets came from Houston, from Huntsville, and from Washington, D.C. The passengers were NASA engineers and NASA program managers, with a sprinkling of advisors from other agencies. They collected their briefcases and overnight bags and lined up patiently at the gate, where security guards checked their identification badges. Then they filed through the fence to the two double-decker tour buses waiting in the parking lot. The Rescue Operation Team had been working under tight security for the last twenty-four hours, and so they were not surprised by the use of commercial tour buses to disguise their arrival.

They had already put together the essential components of the RM-105 mission. The flight would closely follow the orbital insertion sequence of PF-1, and thus a great deal of the normal planning work had already been done. The flight would last less than twenty-four hours and would carry no deployable payloads. There was a crew complement of only three. Still, the task of planning a mission on such short notice was overwhelming, especially given the extraordinary care and the expanded testing and safety procedures which NASA had instituted since the loss of *Challenger*. The brand-new orbiter, still nameless, had never been flown, and the team was working against an expedited launch preparation schedule. In light of all of this, RM-105 seemed like a daring proposition.

At precisely seven-thirty the two tour buses left the runway parking lot and sped along the empty roads toward the KSC industrial area. The passengers had not slept much in the last day. Some reviewed papers from their briefcases, while others engaged in quiet debate over issues regarding the RM-105 flight plan or the readiness of their respective systems. The buses were waved through the security checkpoint into the industrial area, and they pulled up and parked in front of the Auditorium Building. The weary ROT representatives shuffled off the buses and into the lobby, where they congregated around the large urn of coffee.

Inside the auditorium, the table on the stage was already full. From left to right sat Ben King, KSC shuttle operations manager; Russell Madlinger, director of PFP; Gerald Bingham and Brad Parker, NASA astronauts; Pete Fletcher, the KSC launch director, and Major George Hoffman, the deputy assistant secretary of low-intensity conflicts, from the Department of Defense. The new arrivals quickly found their designated sections on the auditorium floor and took their seats.

Pete Fletcher cleared his throat and pulled his mike closer to the edge of the table. He spoke with a deep southern drawl and his voice boomed out over the auditorium's PA system. "All right, ladies and gentlemen, we can begin. I see I have your undivided attention. Houston and Marshall, are you still with us?" He looked up at the television monitors, which established secure teleconference links with the Johnson Space Center and the Marshall Space Flight Center.

Metallic voices responded. "We're prepared to proceed here at Marshall."

"Roger that at Houston."

A brief smile crossed Fletcher's face. Perhaps he appreciated the appropriately distinct responses from the two NASA centers. Marshall, a center of engineers and flight hardware designers, was more formal than Houston, where the astronauts and flight controllers frequently fell into their own vernacular.

Fletcher cleared his throat again and continued. "Okay, folks, we've got a lot to accomplish here this morning. I don't think I need to remind you all, but I will, that this is a highly classified conversation we're about to have here. This ROT meeting will serve as a combination of the management-level flight-readiness review and the L-minus-one briefing for the flight crew. Now, I know as well as you do, that we usually don't hold these two events at the same time, but Alex Vonberger has broken all the rules and it's a different ball game now. You can bet that we're gonna be playing by a whole new set of rules. I want to start by congratulating you all for your work in the last twenty-four hours. Because of your diligence and expertise, we have managed to plan and prepare a mission in less than a day and I think you all deserve a round of applause for that."

The auditorium broke into sudden applause, but it stopped as quickly as it began.

"Yes, I wanted you all to clap while you could, because I'm afraid you just heard the only good news you're gonna be hearing today. We have just received word from Houston that Mission Control has monitored another vibration on board *Discovery* and they believe there has been another discharge of firearms. They have not been able to establish contact with the orbiter, and so we don't know what the heck is going on up there. For all we know, another member of the crew may have been shot. Now I see that anger in all of your eyes, and I'm gonna tell you right now to push it aside, because we got a lot of work to do.

''I don't think it's necessary to introduce the crew up here with me, but I might point out that Russ is not up here in his capacity as director of PFP, but as the RM-One-oh-five mission specialist!''

A loud murmur passed through the crowd in the auditorium, as people exchanged surprised looks and comments.

''That's right. Some of us older folks had the chance to kick him out into orbit a few years ago and watch him dance around in space at the end of a tether. Well, you younger folks will now have your chance. We all know that the big unanswered question is still sitting out on Launchpad Thirty-nine-B, and I'm gonna let Ben King here talk about that in just a minute. But first I'd like to point out a few things to our crew.

''There is no way that a forced entry can be made upon *Discovery,* and therefore, the success of RM-One-oh-five depends on, among other things, our ability to induce an EVA. Now we've got a couple of ideas along that line that Major Hoffman here will be talking about, but I want you all to recognize that even if we get you up there, we can't guarantee a PF-One EVA. I'm afraid nothing can be forced on our little bad apple up there if he isn't prepared to take precautions to save his own life and the lives of the crew. Now, even if Vonberger decides to allow an EVA, there is no way for us to know who he will send out. The two Russians would be the most likely candidates, since they were completely trained for EVAs, but Joey Wells might have a better chance of making the necessary repairs. It is also possible that Vonberger might not trust *anyone* and will volunteer to do the walk himself. Now, we've tried to take all these variables and unknowns into consideration but given the time restraints, I'm afraid there may have to be some improvisation on your part, particularly for the mission specialist, Russ, and I just want you all to be prepared for that.

''Okay. I'm gonna shut up now. We've got a brand-new bird out there on Pad Thirty-nine-B, and we've got less than twenty-four hours to get it up into orbit. Ben, what have we got?''

Ben King pulled his seat up closer to the mike, and began talking. His voice was soft, almost meek, compared to the booming sounds of Fletcher's southern drawl. "As you know, Pete, OV-One-oh-five was rolled out to the pad last week to get ready for a main engine test firing. When she left the OPF two weeks ago for stacking, we had completed about eighty percent of the systems verification tests. There were two problems with critical systems, and we've been able to complete change-outs to fix those during the last twelve hours. Th :re are two other problems listed in the preliminary data file for this mission. One is a hydrogen tank heater anomaly and the other is a flow transducer bias in the fuel cell/power reactants storage and distribution system. We can fly using alternate modes or work-arounds for these systems, and we expect no mission impact from them.

"The data processing system, and the environmental control and life-support systems look good. We'll look at the flight software when all of our plans are finalized, and then we will load the mass memory units. Hydraulic systems, auxiliary power units, and flight instrumentation all appear ready to support a launch. The solid rocket boosters have undergone all mandatory and optional testing prior to mating with the external tank. The tank itself looks good and we will begin tanking in . . . let's see . . . about four hours from now.''

King pushed his chair away from the table so that he could face the three crewmembers. His face looked tired, and through the thick lenses of his glasses his eyes showed the deep emotional and intellectual strain from the last few days. "I'm afraid that's all the good news I've got,'' he said. His voice was only barely audible through the PA system. "As I explained to you, Russ, it would be breaking all the old rules, let alone the new ones, to send you up on untested engines. They've been fired in the test stands and everything has been inspected and reviewed and everything looks good. But the bottom line is, I have no solid basis for validating those engines as flight-ready. I cannot give a final okay.''

A stark silence filled the auditorium. Everyone had known that the main engines had not been test-fired, but somehow they had not been prepared for King's blanket refusal to give an okay. It was Fletcher's voice that broke the silence. ''Marshall, you want to add anything regarding the main engines?''

''Only this,'' came back the metallic voice. ''We have every confidence in those engines. You all know that we could not make that statement lightly after what we've been through in the past five years. Every resource we have and every capability we possess has gone into perfecting as much as is humanly possible the design, engineering, and production quality control of the shuttle propulsion systems. Our intention has been to develop a product that would challenge and withstand *any* testing system conceivable. We are convinced that we have done that. And we believe that the performance of the shuttle's main engines in the past five years backs us up on that.''

There were general nods of agreement among the people in the auditorium. NASA's sense of pride and confidence had slowly been restored since the *Challenger* accident, and yet everyone was still painfully aware of the dangers of overconfidence. Whether or not overconfidence had contributed to the *Challenger* accident, it was still regarded as something that had no place in the space program. Humanity, being imperfect and therefore prone to failure, had to be constantly on its guard, for when it came to failure, space was unforgiving.

Ben King responded. ''There is no doubt about your record, Marshall. My purpose in life is to try to prove you wrong, or at least to challenge you every step of the way, and I have to admit that your record is excellent. But I can't make my decisions based on your record. It's not my job to play the odds.''

There was a brief silence in the room, and then Russell

Madlinger grabbed his microphone. "Ben, we appreciate your honesty, and your position is noted. The question here really is do the objectives of this mission justify the risk? For what it's worth, I wouldn't be up here if I didn't believe that they did. However, the ultimate decision for launch will not be made by me, by you, or by Marshall, but by our President."

"That's right," Fletcher piped in. "My understanding is that the President will review the results of this meeting and will make his final decision by two o'clock this afternoon. In the meantime, we are to proceed with preparations for launch. So let's get to work."

The meeting continued for three more hours. The flight dynamics engineers described the orbital mechanics of the rescue operation, and the rendezvous and station-keeping procedures necessary to bring the orbiter into position in *Discovery*'s "blind spot." Weather conditions were discussed. The forecast looked good for the launch site, the two transatlantic abort sites, and the alternate landing sites. Propellant and consumable loads were discussed, and it was agreed that full loads of each should be on board, even though the mission was expected to take less than a day. This would ensure maximum flexibility to handle any contingencies. The crew would be able to dump any unused propellant in order to get down to nominal landing weight. A team of engineers discussed the checklist for the EVA and instructed Madlinger on the procedures for disabling *Discovery*'s cargo bay cameras and the latching mechanism for the cargo bay doors.

At eleven-thirty Fletcher turned the meeting over to Major Hoffman from the Department of Defense. Hoffman was older than most of the people in the auditorium, in the same way that his department was older than NASA. He cleared his throat, but his voice was still deep and gravelly. "Thank you, Pete. We understand that the success of this mission depends on our ability to lure Vonberger into allowing an EVA. We have consulted with some of your engineers, with members of our own staff, and with advisors from the FBI, and our conclusion was that the best bait for an unscheduled EVA would be a life-threatening situation that required repairs to be made on the outside of the orbiter. We chose the idea of disabling the cargo bay doors, because that does not put the crew in any immediate danger, but would certainly be life-threatening if the orbiter was to attempt to land. Now this still presumes that Alex Vonberger will be interested in saving his own life, and that of the crew, and in order to best ensure this, we have concluded that Vonberger should be informed of our willingness to cooperate with his demands.''

There was a brief hush in the auditorium. ''Now, I didn't say that we were *going* to cooperate. I only said that we would inform Vonberger of our *intentions* to cooperate. We have worked out an arrangement with Mission Control whereby my department will send Vonberger a hard-copy communication indicating that his prisoners are en route to Tehran. It is hoped that this will be sufficient to prompt him into taking all necessary measures to save the crew. He will understand that failure to do so on his part would be an indication to us that he has no intention of returning the crew. Therefore, he will be forced to take appropriate action in order to convince us that he plans to stick to his end of the deal.''

''Now, I think it's only fair that I discuss with the crew here one very important aspect of our decision. Informing Alex Vonberger that we intend to, and are in the process of, meeting his demands, cuts off all other means of obtaining the release of the orbiter. It cuts short our ability to try to bluff him out or to negotiate with him in any way. Thus, we are hesitant to transmit such a message until we are sure that it is necessary for the successful completion of the rescue operation.''

Major Hoffman stopped and Fletcher leaned forward and spoke into his mike. ''At what point would that be, Major?''

Major Hoffman hesitated and then said, ''Well, with all due respect to members of the crew, my department would like to postpone the communication until after the successful launch of RM-One-oh-five.''

There was more silence in the auditorium as the meaning of the major's words sunk in.

It was Russell Madlinger who broke the silence. ''Major, on my own behalf, and I think I speak for the crew, I see no reason that the Department of Defense should jeopardize any other means of obtaining the release of *Discovery* and the crew until you are sure that the main engines have safely lifted us into orbit.''

The other crewmembers nodded in agreement, and suddenly the auditorium broke into a spontaneous round of applause.

By the end of the day, the final mission plan was complete, the President had given his final approval, and the launch countdown was in progress. Russell Madlinger had returned to the Operations and Checkout Building where a mock-up of the MMU, manned maneuvering unit, had been hastily assembled. The MMU is a self-contained backpack that latches onto the spacesuit and allows an astronaut to move about in space independently. It is propelled by nitrogen gas and controlled by hand controls at the end of the MMU armrests. Madlinger and various engineers and advisors went over the operation of the MMU and through the sequence of events that he would follow out in space. All of the possible scenarios had been considered and Madlinger and his team went over them in great detail. Still, Madlinger knew that RM-105, like the launch itself, would be a shot in the dark.

That evening, as the sun was setting over the mangroves and the swamps of Florida, Madlinger took a long walk on the beach with a man named Peter D'Angelo, weapons specialist from the CIA. D'Angelo explained how the bullets would be specially sealed in order to ensure that the oxygen inside them did not escape into the vacuum of space. Normal bullets could work, he explained, but it was better to be safe.

He showed Madlinger how they had redesigned the trigger mechanism of the gun so that the finger of a spacesuit glove could fit inside. Whoever Madlinger handed the gun to might not have the time to take their gloves off before they used it on Vonberger, and there was always the possibility that Madlinger might have to use the gun himself, if Vonberger did the EVA.

Madlinger held the gun in his hand and looked out over the pounding surf of the Atlantic Ocean. For some reason he thought of his son's short story. "I never meant to steal the stars," he thought. "I only wanted to bring them closer."

PART III

ZERO DARK THIRTY

31

PANDORA'S BOX

SOMEWHERE between the darkness of the earth's night and the dense blackness of space, a thin light appeared, and Conrad Williams felt the first crevice of despair slip into his gut. A few dim lights in *Discovery*'s cabin turned the windows into mirrors, and Williams watched the reflection of Alex Vonberger floating in the back of the flight deck. Out in the darkness, the white thread of light grew in length and began to widen, like the opening pit in Williams's stomach. The edges of the white line turned red and blue and curved in an arc that followed the earth's horizon. Suddenly the layers broke, spreading out into bands of colors, like a peacock spreading its tail. The reds and pinks and yellows spread quickly over the surface of the earth. The blues were light, dark, and purple, and they layered the horizon like a winter's quilt, each color more brilliant than the next.

Conrad Williams had always understood that the beauty of space was matched evenly by its danger. Space would always be a hostile environment for mankind, and thus, space travel could never be without risk. Williams knew that he was the kind of person who got a thrill from risky living, from challenging the elements, and exploring the unknown. That was why he was an astronaut. But the hostile forces had always come from outside the spacecraft, and it seemed so wrong now that the danger came from within. Vonberger's hostilities had violated the delicate balance between the deadly vacuum of space and the controlled safety of the orbiter. As the rays of the sun pierced through the spectrum of the earth's atmosphere, Williams felt angry and helpless. It was Vonberger's challenge to the sacred unity of the crew that had planted the seed of despair.

The sun popped over the horizon and the orbiter exploded in brilliant whiteness. The earth directly below was still dark, but the cargo bay and cabin of *Discovery* were bathed in light. Williams was in the commander's seat and Vladimir Turnov was handcuffed into the pilot's seat. Beneath them the red and pink earth silently turned a golden blue. The sun had risen for the 119th time for PF-1, and they had less than twenty-four hours' oxygen left.

Joey Wells had been shot in the head. Williams had been given the job of taking care of him, and he had found Wells floating and unconscious on the mid-deck. Wells's forehead was a bloody mess of skin and bone, but he was still alive. There was no way to know how serious the wound was. If the bullet had entered the brain, Williams knew, it could be fatal, but if the bullet had lodged in the skull, or only scraped the surface of the brain, Wells could be saved.

Williams cleaned the wound as best as he could and wrapped a bandage around Wells's head. He put a small plastic airway into Wells's mouth, to keep his lips open and his tongue down. Then he moved Wells into a sleeping sack, next to Evans. Two down, Williams had thought, but then he stopped himself. No, they weren't down. They were both alive. And as long as they were alive, there was hope.

The orbiter was somewhere over the brown and white

mountains of central Asia when Turnov broke the long silence. "The beauty never ends," he said. He spoke softly, his words intended, perhaps, for himself, but Williams listened. "I've spent almost a year and a half of my life in space, and I never get tired of watching the earth." Turnov was gazing out the window, and then turned his head quickly toward Williams, as if it had been Williams who had broken the silence.

"That's my country down there, Connie," Turnov said, turning back to the windows. "I wish you could see it. I'm sure they've told you lies about it, the same way they told me lies about your country. Your country is not as evil as I was led to believe. But I have not seen the beauty that I have seen in my country. There is nothing like the great steppes, and the old cities. There is nothing like the royal winters with the fresh snow and the open sky. I wish you could see it, Connie. I wish everyone could see it."

Williams felt the emptiness swell up inside him and he felt his despair slowly creep up his spine and the back of his neck. He knew they could all be dead in twenty-four hours, but he had to hold on to his hope, for it was only his hope that would keep him going now. "It will always be there," he heard himself say.

"Yes, I know."

Asia was slipping slowly beneath them. A wide band of clouds covered the coast, and the Pacific Ocean stretched out in infinite blue beyond that to the horizon. A thin line of color separated the curves of the earth from the darkness of space. Williams found it hard to breathe. His skull began to tingle and his eyes felt like they were going to burn. Watching the earth sharpened his pain, as if the beauty itself was wedging its way into his soul, but he wouldn't let himself close his eyes. He knew he could not give in to his despair, and somehow, watching the earth helped him hold on to his hope.

"The beauty never ends," Turnov said, his voice even

softer than before. "There is land and water, but it's not a map. I know what I am looking at because I have looked at maps, but up here there is only land and water. No borders. No countries. From here there is only beauty. How can there be wars when there is so much beauty?"

There was nothing new or profound in what Turnov was saying, nothing that every space traveler hadn't thought of a hundred times. But, still, his words were soothing in their finality and their clarity. "Beauty" was a word that Williams had used his whole life, but only now did he understand what it meant.

"The tragedy is that there are fools who are too greedy and blind to understand the beauty," Turnov continued. "Fools who are determined to impose their own views of how the world should be on the rest of the planet, rather than accepting the world's beauty for what it is. There is enough beauty to go around."

"No amount of violence can kill the beauty," Williams said.

"Do you feel that?" Turnov asked.

"Right now," Williams admitted, "all I feel is a giant pit in my gut."

There was nothing left to say. They watched the clouds give way to a view of water and land, familiar shapes they had been taught to call Japan and Korea. A body of water they called the Pacific Ocean was almost too rich, and too blue. All Williams could do was sit and wait. All he could do was wrestle with his emotions and try to bury the feelings of doom and despair. He had to hold on to his hope.

Williams did not fall asleep, but his eyes were only half open. The beauty and the tragedy held his thoughts, like the handcuffs on his wrists. He had no idea how much time passed, floating and dreaming and silently struggling. As he stared at the deep blue Pacific Ocean and all that beauty, a flood of pictures suddenly flashed through his mind, pictures of Conrad Junior. And in his son he found hope. Williams suddenly felt the despair evaporate from his heart and he started to breathe freely again. The difference between doom and risk was hope, and hope was going to keep him going. PF-1 Commander Conrad P. Williams III sat in the commander's seat on the flight deck of *Discovery*, and felt his eyes moisten with tears.

32

THE
SLEEPING
GIANT

RUSSELL Madlinger had slept six hours in the last three days and he stared out the window of the NASA van at the Florida darkness and rode the rolling waves of his sleepless fog. There were no more plans to be made. There were no more decisions to be confronted. Stage four, a last and desperate effort to rescue PF-1, had received the President's final green light. Despite the risks, RM-105 was go. The final preparations were under way or already completed, and there was nothing left for Russell Madlinger to do but get out to the launchpad and get buckled into his seat. He had lost all track of time. RM-105 would be launched zero dark thirty, and nothing else mattered now.

For the last twelve hours, while the crew completed their final mission preparations, Madlinger had struggled to keep some control over the sleepless fog that had been brewing inside him. Now that all of his work had been done, he let the fog roll over him, and a dizzying confusion of words and images clamored for his attention. All of the thoughts he had relegated to the back of his mind for the past three days suddenly came bursting forward, and he sat back and watched the carnival in his mind.

It was like a slide show of NASA personnel. Faces and voices of the eager engineers and worried managers merged in Madlinger's mind, as if they were having a giant conference in his head. Gerald Bingham outlined the times allotted for Madlinger to sleep. "Once you're in the orbiter, you'll have two hours between the communications check and launch. You'll have three hours after launch before you have to start preparations for your EVA. That's a total of five hours." It would make all the difference, Madlinger thought. He would still be tired, but five hours of sleep would at least clear the fog from his mind.

Madlinger closed his eyes and more pictures swirled into focus. A young engineer explained how Mission Control would uplink a flow limit change for *Discovery*'s nitrogen supply. This would trigger *Discovery*'s master alarm and would distract Alex Vonberger long enough for Madlinger to disconnect the rear cameras in the cargo bay.

Then it was Peggy Kellner calling from Houston. Senator Ryan may have been right. Elliot Hacker now suspected that Das Deutschland Syndikat might have someone placed inside NASA. For security reasons, the flight controllers for PF-1 would not be told about the rescue mission. RM-105 would be announced as an unrelated Department of Defense mission and would be controlled from the secured Flight Control Room in the Mission Control Center, usually used for sensitive Department of Defense missions. Running two flights at once without overlapping personnel required careful planning and organization, but Madlinger knew that Peggy Kellner could handle the job.

The slide changed and Madlinger saw Peter D'Angelo walking on the beach. Just in case something went wrong with the gun, Madlinger would also have a knife, as backup. Redundancy of all critical systems, Madlinger thought. D'Angelo explained, "Both the gun and the knife will be strapped onto the left side of your MMU, just below the armrest. The gun will be here and the knife will be around here." And D'Angelo grabbed Madlinger's wrist and showed him how far he would have to reach. Reaching for the imaginary weapon, Madlinger once again confronted the harsh reality of the mission. It was a mission with only one purpose. "Remember," D'Angelo continued, "the knife will catch the reflection of the sun like a magnet, so don't pull it out until you're ready to use it."

Madlinger opened his eyes and could make out the profiles of Gerald Bingham and Brad Parker in the seat in front of him, and of the driver in front of them. The van used only its parking lights, and it proceeded through the darkness, down the access road to the launchpad. We are riding through the dark to the end, Madlinger thought.

He closed his eyes again and the slide show flashed the famous picture of the earth, rising over the horizon of the moon. Madlinger had always found it inspiring, perhaps because it had been taken by one of the astronauts who had walked on the moon. A man had held the camera that took the picture. Looking at the picture, there was no way to know if it had been taken by a man or a robot. And yet, the picture was famous because it had been taken by a man, standing on the moon.

Why should it suddenly make a difference to him how the picture was taken? The picture was taken by a man standing on the moon.

The picture could have been taken by a robot.

The picture expressed the essence of space exploration, because it was taken by a man. . . .

Russell Madlinger felt a hand on his leg and he opened his eyes and saw Gerald Bingham's figure turned around in his seat.

"You all right, Russ?"

"I think so."

"Twenty minutes. You'll be sleeping in twenty minutes."

Five minutes to get onto the launchpad. Ten minutes in

the white room, where the close-out crew would help them get suited up for launch and assist them to their seats. Five minutes for the communications check. Then he would be able to sleep.

The slide show continued. The red and brown cows at Redstone were eating grass and being ignorant. They didn't care if Madlinger slept or not. They didn't care who took the picture of the moon. They didn't care if a man named Alex Vonberger had broken all the rules and had violated the peaceful calm of space. They cared if it rained or if it was cold. They cared if they had enough grass to eat.

The slide changed again and now Madlinger saw himself, floating outside his Apollo spacecraft. He was frozen by the calm chill of space. There was no gravity and no time. The bliss that would come to pass. His fellow astronauts, like pioneers on the Oregon Trail, had only a limited perception of their own place in history. Man was prehistoric. A picture of the earth from the moon was famous, just because it had been taken by a man, but this was all just the beginning for man. There was no such thing as time.

Soon Madlinger would be out in space again, but this time there would be no calm, because Madlinger was bringing the violence of the earth with him. He hated that thought. The gun and the knife would be strapped to the side of his MMU. Would space ever be able to forgive him? He knew that it was Alex Vonberger who had brought violence into space, and that he was only going up to end it, but he wondered if space could understand the difference.

The launchpad was dark and the van passed through the gate without stopping. The usual array of floodlights was missing, but dim lights sparkled on different levels of the fixed service structure. The service structure, steel blue against the night sky, was dwarfed by the large, gray shadow of the space shuttle. The van stopped at the base of the service structure, and Madlinger felt his legs tremble as he followed Bingham and Parker out into the warm, salty air. Parker grabbed his arm as he stepped out, and Madlinger felt his eyes swell. It was not his nature to let people take care of him, but he knew he had no choice. The sleepless fog had taken over.

From a distance, the launchpad had looked exactly as it must have the night before, but up close Madlinger could see the wisps of vapor from the vent system at the top of the huge external tank and from the bottom of the orbiter. The external tank was now filled with liquid hydrogen and oxygen. To avoid suspicion, the public affairs office had announced that a tanking test would be taking place. There was no way to keep a space-shuttle launch a secret, and so after the launch, NASA would announce that a top-secret, emergency Department of Defense flight had been launched. There would be a lot of skeptics among the media who covered the Cape, and there would be a storm of protest about a military flight during the first PFP mission, but the public affairs office would maintain that the mission required a very specific launch window, and that the launch had not been publicized for security reasons and so as not to conflict with PF-1. It was the best they could do under the circumstances to keep the press in line.

To Russell Madlinger it felt like the morning that he had boarded the Saturn rocket for his Apollo flight, except that there were no people. Only two escorts met them at the elevators. Madlinger was only vaguely aware that Parker was still holding on to his arm when the elevator doors shut, and he wondered if the others could see his fog. This is all a dream, Madlinger thought. Nothing is going to happen. It was a dream without people and without detail. There was just the steel blue service structure, and the giant shuttle. Don't let me go to sleep now, he thought. Let me make it to my seat.

The slide changed, and now the crowds of birds along the banks of the Banana River were going crazy. They were jealous of man's flights into space. Maybe they could see into the future. Maybe they knew that they were being left behind.

The elevator stopped at the 195-foot level, and when the doors opened, Madlinger instinctively looked for the big Saturn rocket. Instead he saw the huge brown external tank and the left booster rocket, and the brand-new orbiter attached piggyback, ready to go for a ride.

The sounds overtook his senses. There was a hissing from the tanks venting as the liquid propellants boiled off, along with a background hum from the circulation systems. Madlinger knew that these were the sounds of science and technology, and yet he felt sure that nothing inanimate could make these noises. It was as if the space shuttle were alive. These were the sounds of a sleeping giant, soon to be awakened. Madlinger listened to his feet as he walked. He heard all of their feet, five pairs of boots, clattering on the metal grated floor as they crossed the access arm toward the white room, toward the shuttle, toward the sleeping giant.

They were led into the white room and Madlinger felt as though he were slipping into the cave of a sleeping giant. Suddenly he thought of Cathy and he thought of slipping into bed next to her warm body. He couldn't let himself think of her now, and yet she came to him. He felt her warmth and her love. Cathy knew all about sleep. In their early years, Madlinger would run himself wild, working, playing, and falling in love. Sleep was a waste of time to the young Russell Madlinger. And then Cathy had taught him all about sleep. The way it healed and soothed. The way it brought center to things that seemed unbalanced. His legs felt weak, as he thought of Cathy. Cathy, who knew all about sleep.

Time was playing tricks on him now. It seemed to take forever to get into the white room. Once inside, he could see the open, inviting hatch of the new orbiter. Standing this close, she seemed even more alive. She was warm. She breathed. She hissed and vibrated. Soon the sleeping giant would wake up and be set free from the confines of the launchpad and the surrounding darkness.

There were three people from the close-out crew waiting in the white room. They helped Madlinger into his launch

harness and his helmet. There were handshakes and words
of encouragement, and then Gerald Bingham led the crew
through the hatch, into the orbiter. The hatch led into the
mid-deck, and because of the upright position of the orbiter,
the lockers on the aft wall were the floor. Madlinger let his
close-out crewmember assist him through the hatch to the
flight deck, and then into his seat. It seemed strange to Madlinger to be climbing into a seat that was suspended from the
wall, even though he had done it in the simulator. He let his
close-out crewmember assist him with the safety buckles and
communications headset. Then he lay back on his seat and
watched the slide show. Newton the dog was running on the
beach. He was a puppy, still frisky and full of energy, and
he was playing his favorite game: putting coconuts on the
ledge of the boardwalk and slowly nudging them into the
water with his nose. It was the dog's apparent fascination
with gravity that had earned him his name.

Now that he was inside the sleeping giant Madlinger felt
a sudden flash of calm. He managed to stay awake for the
communications check, but he barely heard his own reply to
the Launch Control Center. Through the fog he heard the
close-out crewmember wish him luck, give him a pat on the
shoulder and leave the flight deck. Madlinger heard the hatch
close. Two more hours until launch, he thought.

The calmness grew. It was a deep and satisfying calm. He
looked above him and saw Bingham and Parker running
through their checklists. He thought about getting their attention and wishing them luck, but the calmness overtook
him and he let his head fall back against the headrest. Funny
that no matter how you tilted a chair, gravity always pulled
from the same direction. Newton would appreciate that.

Man went to space because it was there. It didn't make
any difference what the birds or the cows thought. It didn't
matter if the picture could have been taken by a robot. Alex
Vonberger had ruined everything, and only the sleeping giant
mattered now. Madlinger vaguely heard communications
coming through his headset, but he didn't pay attention. Take

care of me, you sleeping giant, Madlinger thought. Take care of all of us.

Russell Madlinger woke up to the thunder of the main engines. The noise seemed too loud and too intense, and he thought at first that something was wrong. Then the solid rocket boosters ignited and suddenly the shuttle sprang from the launchpad. The whole cabin shook and Madlinger watched Bingham and Parker jiggling around in their seats from the vibrations. The gravity forces were only about twice the normal force of gravity on earth. They were considerably less than Madlinger remembered from his Apollo flight, but they would have been more than enough to cause some serious new dynamics to Newton's coconut game.

Madlinger suddenly remembered that they were riding the untested main engines that Ben King had refused to validate. This was their crucial moment, and yet Madlinger would not give in to fear. The engines had to work. It was that simple. As the worry slipped from his mind, Madlinger was overcome with the feeling of excitement and fascination. He was riding on millions of pounds of fuel and high explosives, speeding through the earth's atmosphere. The sleeping giant was awake and free. For the second time in his life, Russell Madlinger was going into space!

Madlinger forgot about the main engines. He forgot about Alex Vonberger and the seriousness of the RM-105 mission. He forgot about the danger they were all about to face. He felt himself get pulled down into his seat by the gravity forces, his mind experiencing everything without thought. So many times he had talked about his Apollo lift-off, and yet it was only now, experiencing it again, that he could actually remember what it was like.

The solid rocket boosters separated, and suddenly the ride was smoother. Without the roar of the solid propellants burning off, the noise was more like that of a high-powered jet. The main engines were at full throttle up, and the pull of gravity was now about three times its normal force on earth.

Still, Madlinger did not think about the engines. He merely felt the speed of the shuttle as the g forces pulled him further into his seat. The engines had to work.

At eight minutes and twenty-three seconds, Madlinger heard the CapCom's voice over the headset. "RM-One-oh-five, Houston. You are go for main engine cutoff."

"Roger, Houston," Bingham answered. "Go for MECO."

There was a brief pause and then an unofficial communication from the CapCom. 'Congratulations, RM-One-oh-five!"

The main engines were cut off and the external tank separated from the orbiter. The engines had performed! Madlinger felt himself smile, but he knew that the sudden lightness he felt was not relief, but weightlessness. It felt like going over the big hill on a roller-coaster, but instead of dropping, the feeling just continued. Madlinger had described it many times in his life, but now, feeling it again took his breath away, as his mind and body adjusted to the sensation. His arms and legs floated freely and he knew that all he had to do was unbuckle his harness and he would float out of his seat. Madlinger began to understand that no memories, no words, not even dreams could fully convey this experience. It was something that had to be lived. It was the bliss that would come to pass.

The main engines had worked. The Department of Defense would now be arranging to send Alex Vonberger a communication informing him that the ten prisoners were being released and transported to Iran. Meanwhile, RM-105 would follow an accelerated orbit that would bring it into a rendezvous with *Discovery*. Madlinger felt his eyes close, and before Parker and Bingham fired the final OMS burns that would propel them into their orbit, Russell Madlinger was fast asleep.

33

THE
NINTH
FLOOR

ELLIOT Hacker and his team had taken over Peggy Kellner's large conference room on the ninth floor of Building One to use as the command center for their investigations. Even though he was escorted by Robert Colbert from the State Department, Andrei Kulikov felt uneasy entering the room and seeing Elliot Hacker again. His last meeting with Hacker had been the beginning of a long and tortuous interrogation that had lasted through the night. Now, Hacker sat at the head of the big conference room table and talked on the telephone. The table was littered with files, half-eaten sandwiches, and loose papers, and the whole room seemed to be in a state of confusion. A constant stream of field agents came and went, slipping through the cigarette smoke and the scattered coffee cups.

"Okay, I'll hold," Hacker said, and he put the mouthpiece of the telephone against the palm of his hand. "Come on in, Andrei. Have a seat. I'll be with you in a minute. Bob, would you mind waiting outside?"

Kulikov felt Robert Colbert hovering close by, as if he was afraid he might lose Kulikov in the confusion of the room. "I'd rather wait here," Colbert said.

Hacker shook his head. "Sorry, you'll have to wait outside."

"Mr. Kulikov is not to be further interrogated."

"Look, I'm not going to interrogate him. He's working with us now, and I just need to ask him some questions."

"My instructions are to—"

"I know what your instructions are!" Hacker roared. The room fell quiet, and Kulikov noticed that Hacker seemed embarrassed by his own sudden loss of temper. "Just wait outside," Hacker said softly, and then he turned away and spoke into the telephone.

Andrei Kulikov nodded at Robert Colbert. "I think I'll be okay, Robert. Thank you. You can wait outside," he said. Kulikov was on his guard, but he derived some pleasure from being allowed in a room that even his State Department escort was barred from. He pulled a large chair away from the table and made himself comfortable, and he watched the agents around the room as they sat reading documents or stood quietly conferring. How quickly things changed, Kulikov thought. Yesterday he was a suspect, stripped of all diplomatic and legal rights. Today, even as a Soviet official, he was allowed to sit in the command center of a major FBI investigation. Or was this all a setup? Could they still be playing some kind of game? No, it wasn't likely. This had to be real. But what did Hacker want now?

At last Elliot Hacker got off the telephone, and without looking up, he began digging through the papers and files in front of him. He found a small plastic bag that had a little white identification tag on it. Inside the bag there was a small colored photograph, and Hacker looked at it quickly and then handed the bag to Kulikov.

Kulikov looked through the plastic at the photograph and heard himself laugh. It was a picture of himself, his face covered with Band-Aids and gauze pads. His head was thrown back and his mouth was partly open, caught in the midst of his big Russian laugh, and he was holding a box of Hamburger Helper. As the surprise from the immediate recognition wore off, Kulikov began to feel saddened by the picture. It had been taken only a few weeks ago, but it had been before all the trouble, back when "peace" was still a part of the Peace Flight Program.

"Recognize him, Andrei?" Hacker asked.

"Of course."

"You know who took it?"

"Who took what?"

"The picture. Do you know who took the picture?"

"No. Who took it?"

"I don't know. I'm asking you."

Kulikov shrugged. "I don't know. It could have been anyone. There were a lot of people there with cameras, I think."

"A lot of people where?"

"At the cook-off. The chili cook-off."

"But you don't know who took it?"

"No. Where did you you get it?"

"I found it in the same store with a dead man this morning. A guy by the name of Roger Wilson. Know him?"

"No."

"Think hard, maybe you'll remember him."

"I don't think so. What did he look like?"

"Are you sure you don't know who took this picture?"

Kulikov suddenly felt angered. "This is not supposed to be an interrogation," he said.

Hacker smiled and held up his hands in retreat. "I'm sorry, Andrei. I'm sorry. I can't help myself sometimes." He fell back into his seat and lit a cigarette. "It's not an interrogation. I need your help, that's all. Roger Wilson was a tenant in the building where Laura Gold lived. We figured out that he was the connection to Das Deutschland Syndikat, but we figured it out too late, because when we got to the photo store where he works, Wilson was dead. He'd been shot four times in the head, execution-style. We don't know if his attacker was looking for something, or was just trying to confuse us, but the shop was a wreck. Anyway, we found that photo on the floor. There were a lot of photos around, but you can appreciate my interest in this one.''

Kulikov felt nervous and confused. ''My picture was in the store where this man was killed. What does that mean?''

''Well, Andrei, chances are this guy Wilson was just another link in the chain. The way these things usually work is that the photo store would have been used as a drop-off. Someone from the organization would bring in a role of film that would contain Wilson's instructions. Wilson would study the film in his darkroom, destroy it, and then pass on the information to Vonberger. Pretty hard stuff to trace.''

''He passed it to Vonberger through the girl?''

''No. He passed it directly. We think Vonberger had meetings with Wilson in the basement of the building.''

Kulikov laughed nervously. ''I still do not understand what the picture means.''

Hacker inhaled on his cigarette and then spoke through a cloud of smoke. ''Well, we need to look at everyone who has been in and out of the store in the last few months. Obviously, all the people who brought film in to be developed would be prime suspects.''

''So this picture was developed in the shop, and whoever took it might be the person you are looking for?''

The two men studied each other through the smoke of Hacker's cigarette. Kulikov felt relieved that he was not personally suspected of anything, and yet he knew that there was still something that had not been said. ''Mr. Hacker, I am sure you know what you are doing.''

''Yes?''

''Well, if the photo was taken at the chili cook-off, then it was probably taken by someone who works at NASA.''

Hacker inhaled again on his cigarette. ''I know. That's a possibility that I can't rule out.''

And suddenly Kulikov understood. It was more than a possibility. What Hacker wasn't saying was that it was specifically because the photographer might be a NASA employee that Hacker was interested.

"Look, Andrei," Hacker said, sitting up in his seat. "I've got a million and one leads to follow up, and this is only one of them. I just wanted to show you the picture, and see if you could help me. Hold on to it for a while if you like, and think about it. I'll be here."

Andrei Kulikov left the command center with the plastic bag in his hand. Robert Colbert was standing just outside the door, and he blushed slightly as Kulikov emerged.

"Andrei, I'm sorry. I didn't know—"

"It's okay, Robert. He was very friendly. Come on, we need to get the car."

"Where are we going?"

"To find Chris Madlinger."

34

THE TIP
OF THE
ICEBERG

Ten members of Das Deutschland Syndikat have been released from Austrian prison and are presently en route to Tehran. Estimated Time of Arrival is 7:05:15 MET. Stand by for confirmation of the prisoners' arrival. Entry and Landing instructions to follow. The United States Department of Defense.

It was almost unbelievable. Alex Vonberger clutched the hard-copy message in his hands and felt a deep feeling of power grow inside him. The United States of America had been brought to its knees! The printed communication felt like gold in Vonberger's hands, and each time he read it the feelings of satisfaction and relief grew stronger, until the triumph was flowing through his veins like blood. This was his passport to success. This was his passport to life. The United States of America and the Soviet Union had given in, and the Inner Circle would soon be free! The whole world was at his feet. Alex Vonberger had made a difference! Alex Vonberger was a hero!

And yet, even as he reveled in the glory of his success, Vonberger felt a nagging pull from the back of his mind. Somewhere there was a question that remained unanswered. He floated aimlessly about the mid-deck, studying the message, with its straight margins and solid black print. Why had they changed their minds?

Perhaps their first message had merely been a bluff. Perhaps they had been waiting for him to give up, or had been waiting to see if he was really willing to let himself and the crew die in space. Or perhaps it had been his rejection of their initial offer, and his conviction, even after learning of Laura's death, that had convinced them that he meant business. Yes, it must have been his own conviction that had made them understand that they had no other choice. Still, something nagged at him. It had been a game of nerves, and he had won. Why should that make him feel uneasy?

And suddenly he remembered the photograph they had sent him of the naked body on the clean white table. He had tried his hardest to bury the memories of Laura in the back of his mind so that he could concentrate on what he had to do. But the devastation of her death was too strong, and the horror pulled at his consciousness with unnerving persistence. Some part of him had died with her, and he knew that he was a man without a heart.

Now, somewhere, a thought was forming that he didn't want to have, but as hard as he tried, he could not stop it. He had seen the photograph of her body. He had believed with absolute certainty that the CIA, or one of those organizations, had killed her. Her death had been so definite. But now suddenly, against his will, a seed of doubt had been planted.

Was it possible that the photograph had been faked? What if the entire first communication had been a bluff to get him to surrender? What if Laura Gold was still alive? Surely they could have doctored a photograph to make it look like Laura's body without a head.

Alex Vonberger reached into his storage locker where he had stashed the photograph and looked at it again. The headless corpse was gruesome and it sickened him to look, but he forced himself to study the body. It definitely looked like Laura's body, but how could he really tell? And where was the head? If they really wanted to prove to him that she was dead, wouldn't they have shown him her head instead of her body? Why hadn't they shown him the head? The answer came to him in a flash. They didn't show him the head because the head was still attached to her body! Laura Gold was alive!

The questions were unending. If she was alive, where was she? Had they captured her? Had she made it across the border? Could she be in Iran right now, waiting for him to bring the orbiter down in victory? It was almost too much to think about. How could he go on, not knowing if she was alive or not? And if she was alive, how come the man at NASA from Das Syndikat had not used the computer to tell him that Houston's first communication was a bluff? Hadn't they warned Vonberger about the uplink of the changed limits in the fire detection system? Why wouldn't they tell him that Laura was still alive? Or had they not realized that his involvement with her was real. Perhaps the man at NASA had no idea that her death would really affect him. Otherwise they would have told him. He was sure of it.

Vonberger stuffed the printed message into the pocket of his flight suit and pushed himself across the cabin to where George Evans and Joey Wells were strapped into their sleeping sacks. Both men had their eyes closed. George Evans seemed to be getting better, and Vonberger felt sure that he would be fine if they could get him to a doctor soon. Joey Wells was a different story. If the bullet had hit the brain, Vonberger knew, it would be very serious. So far, Wells remained unconscious, but Williams had said that as long as he was alive, there was hope. If they got him to a doctor, there was still a chance that he might make it. Who knew what kind of doctors they had in Iran, but there would have to be someone there who could help him. Joey Wells would not have to die.

Vonberger found it amusing that he could now feel sorry for George Evans and Joey Wells. They were merely pawns who had been caught up in the bigger game. Both of them were victims, not of Vonberger's violence, but of their own stupidity. He had given them ample warning. He didn't hate them now, but felt sorry for them, and hoped that they would live. Vonberger found that he could easily imagine a happy ending for everyone. Even for himself and Laura Gold.

Vonberger pushed himself up into the flight deck, where Conrad Williams was handcuffed into the pilot's seat. Turnov and Zakharov were in the airlock. He slipped a Lone Ranger mask over Williams's head so that Williams couldn't see the computer screen.

"What's going on, Alex?" Williams called out.

Vonberger was eager to share the good news with someone, but he knew it would be imprudent to discuss it with his hostages. "Nothing is going on," he said, and he buckled himself into the commander's seat.

Vonberger typed number 917 into the computer and accessed the uplink text pages, and found a message from Das Syndikat, two lines beneath the text. It read: "Prepare for OMS burn. $+23.5:0:-5.7$. TIG at 7:00:00 MET."

Vonberger quickly cleared the computer screen, and then instinctively checked to make sure that Williams had not seen it. Then he stared out the overhead windows at the white swirls of a storm forming over the Indian Ocean. He had to evaluate this communication. OMS burns were used to maneuver the orbiter from one orbit to another, or to deorbit and reenter the earth's atmosphere. There was no way for Vonberger to know, based on the program data, where the OMS burn would take them, although it did not appear to be a deorbit burn. It all depended on the attitude of the orbiter and the duration of the burn. The data for the OMS burn must have been calculated by the man at NASA. Typing in the data on the computer keyboard would set up the OMS burn, controlled by the computer program. All Vonberger had to do was execute the burn at the proper time. There was no way for him to know where it would take them, and the TIG, time of ignition, was less than thirty minutes away.

Why did The Organization want him to do an OMS burn? The data did not seem right for a deorbit burn, and he would need more information if it was a deorbit burn. He would need to reorient the orbiter so the OMS burn would slow it down for reentry, and he would have to untie Williams's hands so he could fly the orbiter once it entered the earth's atmosphere. They couldn't cause a reentry without giving him ample time to prepare.

If they weren't going to deorbit, then that meant they were going to change orbits, but that didn't make any sense. What was the point of changing orbits? They couldn't "hide" from NASA. NASA would see that they had moved and would know exactly where they were. It just didn't make any sense. Why did Das Syndikat want him to move *Discovery* just when everything seemed to be going right? The prisoners were freed, and were due in Iran in just a little over seven hours. Why move now, and aggravate the situation? Why complicate things, just when they seemed to be falling into place?

As the orbiter passed into night over the Indian Ocean, Vonberger considered his options. He could execute the burn as instructed, and find out what Das Syndikat had in mind. Or he could ignore the burn instructions. Suddenly he felt like he had lost all control of the situation. Somewhere, there was a battle going on, perhaps between NASA and Das Syndikat, and he felt like he was only seeing the tip of the iceberg. What was really going on? Was Laura alive or not? Were the prisoners really en route to Iran? Why did Das Syndikat want him to change orbits?

Vonberger had approximately ten minutes before he had to start preparing for the OMS burns. Normally the burns would be done by the pilot and the commander, but Vonberger had seen enough simulations to know how to do it himself.

Still, what if he refused? What if he just stayed where he was? If the prisoners were freed and on their way, why should he move the orbiter? Maybe Das Syndikat didn't know that the prisoners had been freed. Maybe they weren't as on top of things as Vonberger had thought.

Maybe. But nowhere could Vonberger find the courage to doubt them. Hans was his leader, and had never led him wrong. If Das Syndikat wanted him to move, there was a reason. They knew what they were doing. And Vonberger would not question them.

35

ANOTHER WORLD

I N his dream, Russell Madlinger was running through the forest. He came to a river and he leapt into the air. As he soared over the water he looked down at his legs stretched out beneath him. He was afraid that he might crash, but he glided effortlessly over the river, and he didn't even land when he reached the other side. This is the kind of dream you have when you're in space, he thought.

Russell Madlinger opened his eyes and was immediately blinded by the brilliant sun, beating through the windows of the orbiter's flight deck. He felt dizzy and disoriented and worried for an instant that something had gone wrong. But then he felt the seat against his back, light and distant, and he felt his helmet floating around his head. He looked at Bingham and Parker and noticed that they had removed their helmets. Then he looked out the window and saw the earth, blue and white and beautiful, looming outside like an old friend. Suddenly he remembered the launch and Madlinger felt himself smile. They had made it into space. The main engines had worked and they were in orbit around the earth. He moved about in his seat and his smile broadened. He was weightless. All he had to do was unbuckle his seat belt and the bliss would come to pass.

He felt tired and weak, but the fog had lifted. There was no more carnival and no more slide show. Russell Madlinger was back in control, and he breathed deeply and enjoyed the peace. He vaguely remembered a sleeping giant, and he recalled the sensations of the launch, the noise and vibrations, and that first feeling of weightlessness just before he had fallen back to sleep. It was like it had all been a dream from another world, and he had to look again at the earth outside the window, to convince himself that it had really happened.

Madlinger watched Gerald Bingham unbuckle himself and slowly float out of his seat. "Well, look who's up," Bingham said with a smile.

"Maybe," Madlinger heard himself say. His voice cracked and he had to swallow to keep from coughing.

Brad Parker also floated out of his seat, but his feet went up to the ceiling, and his head came down to the same level as Madlinger's. It looked like he was upside down. "You missed a couple of beautiful OMS burns, Russ," Parker said. "You would have loved them."

"Sorry I couldn't cheer you on," Madlinger said. He pulled off his helmet, and watched it float up over his head. "How long have I been out?"

"A little more than three hours," Bingham answered. "We're in a catch-up orbit with *Discovery* and should rendezvous in about three hours from now. You've got enough time for breakfast, but I'm afraid you're going to have to have oxygen for dessert."

The cabin atmosphere inside the orbiter was 79 percent nitrogen, but the spacesuit would be pressurized with pure oxygen. Madlinger would have to begin breathing pure oxygen two and half hours before his EVA, in order to purge the nitrogen from his blood. Otherwise, the nitrogen might bubble out of solution while he was inside the spacesuit. This would cause the bends, which could be very painful, and even deadly.

"Any word from Houston?" Madlinger asked, releasing his safety buckles.

"Everything is go," Bingham answered.

Madlinger pushed himself lightly away from the seat and smiled again as he floated out into the middle of the flight deck. "I almost forgot how great this can be!"

He followed Bingham and Parker into the mid-deck and floated around the cabin, enjoying his weightlessness, while they prepared breakfast. His mind was beginning to work. Rendezvous was in three hours. Normally, the crew would rendezvous before they began preparations for an EVA, but now time was precious and it was necessary to have Madlinger ready for his EVA as soon as they reached *Discovery*. Madlinger's EVA had been planned as much as possible, but there were many contingencies that had to be considered. One step at a time, he told himself. They had made it into space, and now it was time for breakfast. The EVA would come later.

Breakfast was a lot different from the kind of meals he had eaten in the Apollo days. This was real food! They ate eggs and muffins and drank coffee, and Madlinger couldn't help enjoying the delights of eating in weightlessness. The eggs did not have good surface tension, and so they would drift off the spoon, and Madlinger would have to capture them with his mouth. He had to suck his coffee out of a carton with a straw, and it didn't spill, no matter which way he turned it. The crew talked about the launch and about the new orbiter, but they didn't talk about the purpose of their mission. They were just another shuttle crew, getting ready to do a day's work.

After breakfast, Bingham and Parker went back up to the flight deck, and Madlinger prepared to start prebreathing oxygen. He retrieved his helmet and plugged the hose into the the orbiter's oxygen supply. Then he donned the helmet, turned on the switch, and began breathing pure oxygen. Madlinger used the prebreathe time to review the crew activity plan that had come out of the ROT meeting the day before. There was still a lot to learn and a lot to remember.

About two hours passed before Brad Parker came down from the flight deck to help Madlinger prepare for his EVA. Madlinger removed his coveralls and donned the liquid-cooling-and-ventilation garment. This was a one-piece garment made of Spandex mesh with plastic tubing woven into the mesh. The garment fit like a pair of long-john underwear, and once it was connected to the spacesuit, cool water would circulate through the tubing to remove excess body heat. Air ducts were attached to the garment to provide ventilation to the limbs, and Madlinger attached the urine-collection device and the in-suit drink bag.

Parker floated into the airlock to inspect the spacesuits that were mounted on the inside wall. The shuttle spacesuits were a vast improvement over the old Apollo suits. They did not have to be tailor-made for each astronaut, and they were lighter and more flexible. Parker brought out the trousers portion of the spacesuit and held Madlinger steady as he pulled them on. Then Madlinger floated into the airlock and slid into the upper torso section of the suit, which was still mounted to the airlock wall. The life-support system was built into the back of the upper torso section, and Madlinger connected the tubes from the system into the cooling-and-ventilation garment. The upper and lower sections were held together by a simple hard waist ring. Madlinger donned a communications cap and plugged it in, and then pulled on the gloves and locked them into the wrist rings. Parker helped Madlinger set the portable life-support system controls, and then slipped the helmet over Madlinger's head and locked it into place.

In less than twenty minutes Madlinger was fully suited. Parker wished him luck and went back up to the flight deck to help Bingham complete the rendezvous with *Discovery*. Once *Discovery* was in sight, Parker would come back and close the door of the airlock. Madlinger controlled the airlock pressure from inside, and when the airlock was fully depressurized, he would begin his EVA. For now, all he could do was wait for Parker to come back. As he floated inside the airlock, a single image flashed across his mind. It was a picture of Alex Vonberger and Laura Gold at the chili cook-off, holding hands and laughing together. It was a picture from another world.

36

THE
ANOMALY

DISCOVERY had less than ten hours of oxygen remaining and Andrew McKenzie's flight controllers began their shift knowing that they would see PF-1 through to its conclusion, one way or the other. They were surprised when Peggy Kellner and the man from the Department of Defense came in to send Vonberger a message on the TAGS hard-copier, but they were even more surprised by the content of the message. Since when did the United States give in to terrorism? The Mission Control Center was preparing for a reentry at 7:05:10 MET, and the flight controllers were relieved that *Discovery* would soon be released and allowed to land, but it seemed odd that the President had given in to Vonberger's demands.

How could they be sure that Alex Vonberger would keep his end of the bargain? How could they have allowed a release of prisoners before *Discovery* was safely returned? Would Vonberger allow *Discovery* to land at the Kennedy Space Center? Or did he have some other destination in mind? And where was Russell Madlinger? He had not been around for almost two days. Throughout the earlier shifts, Madlinger had constantly been appearing to check on the status of the orbiter, to confer with Wolff, or to check on some piece of information. Now his presence was missed.

By nine o'clock Houston time, the Mission Control Center had settled into its morning routine. The flight controllers watched their screens and carefully made notations of data. Leonard Wolff's team had expanded and a makeshift row of consoles was set up along one side of the Flight Control Room. The additional noise and confusion created by the added personnel was a minor annoyance, and Flight Director McKenzie seemed somewhat on edge. It had been a trying few days for everyone, and they had all been working under a great deal of pressure. Nobody was at their best. The morning was threatening to be an exercise in patience, but it would all be worth it to see *Discovery*'s safe return. The quiet was now somehow comforting, and some of the flight controllers allowed themselves to think of the end, of bringing *Discovery* home in safety, and even of a good night's sleep.

The silence was broken by the propulsion systems officer. "Flight, Prop. We see the OMS helium valves open."

This was followed almost immediately by the flight dynamics officer. "Flight, FIDO. We see an attitude maneuver in progress."

"He's setting up for an OMS burn!" Wolff said frantically.

But Flight Director McKenzie remained calm. "Monitor for further developments," he said from his seat, barely looking up.

An OMS burn could mean anything. They could be changing orbits, or they could be preparing for reentry. Any attempted reentry would have to be coordinated with Mission Control. The map on the front wall indicated that the orbiter was passing over the Pacific Ocean, and a deorbit burn now would bring them down somewhere in the Indian Ocean.

"CapCom, make contact," Wolff ordered.

But the CapCom was cut off by Andrew McKenzie. "No

communication!'' McKenzie said harshly, turning in his seat to face the CapCom.

The room suddenly filled with tension, and the flight controllers exchanged looks of concern and confusion. Leonard Wolff, despite his senior position, should have respected McKenzie's authority in the Flight Control Room. Wolff was there as an observer, to obtain data and try to figure out what was going on inside the orbiter, but it was not his place to give orders. Still, it seemed natural to attempt to communicate.

"I want to see what he's up to," McKenzie said, turning to face Leonard Wolff.

"He's doing an OMS burn!" Wolff said in exasperation.

"Well, we don't know where he's going, and there is to be no extraneous contact. That's an order from the center director."

"LOS is in five minutes," Wolff persisted.

"I damn well know when LOS is!" McKenzie snapped back. He turned back to his console but the flight controllers felt the tension build. Since Vonberger had not initiated a communication, it was not likely that he would respond to one, and it was true that Peggy Kellner had ordered a block of all extraneous contact. Still, if Vonberger was attempting to deorbit, there would have to be some communication. It was McKenzie's decision to make, and that decision had to be respected.

"Maneuver complete," the flight dynamics officer announced.

McKenzie kept his eyes focused on his console. "FIDO, what targets does he have?" he asked.

"None. We haven't calculated the deorbit targets yet."

"OMS engines armed," the propulsion systems officer announced.

"I don't believe this," Wolff said.

"Attitude is wrong for reentry," the flight dynamics officer reported.

"Good," McKenzie said, suddenly sitting up in his seat. It was fairly easy to tell from the attitude of the orbiter whether an OMS burn would slow it down for reentry, or speed it up into a higher orbit. If the attitude was wrong for reentry, then that meant an OMS burn would merely change *Discovery*'s orbit. While still mysterious, a change of orbit seemed a lot less dangerous than a reentry.

"Burn enabled. Countdown to OMS burn, fifteen seconds."

"Monitor duration," McKenzie said, calmly.

"Ten, nine, eight, seven . . ."

The Flight Control Room waited silently as the propulsion systems officer counted down. McKenzie sat frowning at his console, with his arms folded across his chest. Wolff held on to the arms of his chair, as if he were prepared for the entire Flight Control Room to take off.

". . . four, three, two, one. Ignition."

Everyone held their breath as *Discovery* fired its OMS engines, and the same question lingered in everyone's mind. Where was Alex Vonberger going?

"Cutoff," the propulsion systems officer announced.

There was a brief silence, broken by Leonard Wolff. "Flight, I suggest you have FIDO calculate a new state vector based on the orbiter's attitude and the duration of the OMS burn. Then we can calculate *Discovery*'s new orbit."

McKenzie stared back at Wolff with fire in his eyes. There was no ignoring the tension between the two men, but where had it come from? Everyone had been working under a tremendous amount of stress, but this sudden power struggle was unprecedented in the Mission Control Center.

"I'll calculate it myself," McKenzie said, pulling his seat up to his console and checking his computer screen.

They would be able to pinpoint *Discovery* with ground tracking data, but they would also be able to get the data of the new orbit by using the attitude of the orbiter and the length of the OMS burn. McKenzie was busy at his console, and Leonard Wolff watched the front wall, as if the blinking orbiter might suddenly move across the room. The flight controllers returned their attention to their consoles, all of them feeling like they had just missed something, some anomaly beyond the surface of things.

37

A
SENSE OF
URGENCY

ANDREI Kulikov rode in the front seat of Robert Colbert's sedan, hoping with all his might that Colbert knew where he was going. They had stopped twice already to ask directions, and now Colbert weaved the car in and out of the westbound traffic on NASA Road 1. Kulikov stared out the windows and watched the strip shopping centers and the fast food restaurants roll by. It was like all of NASA Road 1 was the same block that just repeated over and over again. A gas station. A McDonald's. A hotel. A shopping mall. A gas station.

Colbert stopped the car at a red light and Kulikov tried to calm himself down. Why did he feel such a sense of urgency? The FBI had found a picture of him in the store where a man had been killed, and Elliot Hacker thought that whoever had taken the picture might be Alex Vonberger's connection to Das Deutschland Syndikat. Kulikov tried again to remember the events at the chili cook-off. He remembered being handed the box of Hamburger Helper, and he remembered Cathy

Madlinger standing with him and laughing. But there had been so many other people there. The entire Soviet team had been there, and all of the PF Flyers. How could he remember who had taken his picture? Kulikov reached into his jacket pocket and felt the plastic bag. There had to be a way to figure this out. There just had to be.

The light changed and Colbert hit the gas. "The turn has to be coming up soon," Colbert said.

"I hope so," Kulikov answered quietly.

Kulikov kept one hand on the plastic bag, as if it might slip away if he let go. He could not ignore his sense of urgency. What if the person who had taken the picture *did* work for NASA? What if that person *was* Vonberger's connection to Das Deutschland Syndikat? If Hacker's suspicions were right, and Vonberger was working together with somebody at NASA, then the entire rescue mission could be in jeopardy. Finding Vonberger's connection was no longer a matter of capturing a terrorist. It was a question of saving lives.

"Aha!" Colbert called in triumph, and he swung the car into the right lane and then took a sharp turn off NASA Road 1. The road they turned onto was another wide and straight highway, but there was no traffic, and instead of malls and gas stations, the road was lined with houses. Kulikov felt relieved as the car began to accelerate. They were almost there. The highway quickly ended in a T, and Colbert turned left onto a narrow tree-lined street. Kulikov saw a road sign with a picture of children crossing a street, and then the school appeared on the left.

It was a low, sprawling red-brick building with a large playground on one side and a flagpole in the front. Andrei Kulikov did not let Colbert park the car in the lot behind the school, but insisted on being dropped off near the school entrance in the front. He bounded from the car, not bothering to close the door behind him. He sprinted across the freshly cut grass, and climbed the small set of steps in one leap. The air inside the building was cool and quiet, and

Kulikov was conscious of his shoe heels clicking on the tiled floor. He followed a sign that directed him to the office and noticed a bulletin board filled with drawings of the space shuttle. He stopped abruptly at the door to the office, and pushed it open with deliberate patience.

A woman sat behind a small desk, leaning over her typewriter with a bottle of white-out, and for some reason, Kulikov felt as if he was back in Moscow. The woman looked up at Kulikov, who was trying to catch his breath. "Yes?"

"I need to see Chris Madlinger," Kulikov said, in short gasps, suddenly very self-conscious of his accent.

"Who?"

"Chris Madlinger. He is one of your children."

"He's a student here?"

"Yes, that is what I mean. He is a student here. I need to see him. It is very important."

"And who are you?"

"My name is Andrei Kulikov. I work with NASA. It is urgent that I talk with Chris Madlinger. Can you tell me where he is?"

"Sir, I'm sorry, but we can't pull the students out of class. Can you tell me what this is about?"

Kulikov banged his palms down on her desk and leaned over her typewriter. "It is a matter of your national security! I do not have the time to give you details, but I can promise you that it is urgent. Now, can you please tell me where I can find him?"

"Perhaps you should talk with the principal."

"Yes. That is fine. Where is he?"

The woman looked nervously at her watch and then at the telephone. "Well, he's on the telephone right now, but let me see if he can see you. Would you care to have a seat?"

Kulikov remained standing while the woman disappeared behind the principal's door, and she emerged a few seconds later with a man who seemed to Kulikov too young to be a school principal. The secretary made the introductions. "Mr.

Kulikov, this is Mr. Mitchell, our principal. This is Mr. Kulikov. He would like to see one of our students.''

Mitchell took another step out of his office and looked at Kulikov. ''Are you a parent?''

Kulikov breathed slowly, trying to control himself. ''No. I work with NASA.''

''Who is it you want to see?''

''Chris Madlinger.''

''And what is it about?''

''I am sorry but I am not at liberty to give you the details. It is a question of national security.''

Mitchell raised his eyebrows. ''National security, huh?''

''That's right.''

Mitchell raised his eyebrows some more and frowned. Then he looked at his watch. ''When are the Kellys coming in?''

''At nine-thirty,'' the secretary answered.

Mitchell turned back to Kulikov. ''Okay, Mr. Kulikov. Why don't we step into my office.''

They walked into the inner office and Mitchell closed the door behind them. He sat down at his desk and waved at a seat for Kulikov. Kulikov did not want to sit, but he forced himself. Play the man's game, Kulikov told himself. Let him think he's important.

''Now, Mr. Kulikov,'' Mitchell said at last. ''What's going on with the space shuttle, anyway? I heard a report that there's some communication problem. Weren't they supposed to have landed by now?''

The smirk on Mitchell's face made Kulikov want to hit him, but he just nodded his head calmly. Play the man's game. ''Yes, there is a communication problem. I am sure that NASA will clarify it as soon as they can, and I am also sure that any help you can give me now will be duly recognized by the appropriate government officials. Now, may I see Chris Madlinger, please?''

But Mitchell hadn't finished having his fun yet. ''What is your relationship with Chris Madlinger?''

"I have no relationship with Chris Madlinger. I work with Chris's father at NASA. Perhaps you could—"

"Where is Chris's father?"

Kulikov swallowed hard, suddenly realizing that Chris's father was two hundred miles out into space. "Russell Madlinger is at the Kennedy Space Center in Florida."

"Does he know you're here?"

"Mr. Mitchell. I can assure you that Russell Madlinger would want me to talk to his son."

"How can you assure me of that?"

Kulikov gripped the arms of his chair in frustration, and was trying very hard not to scream when he heard the door open behind him. Robert Colbert stepped in. The secretary was a few feet behind him, trying to explain, "I'm sorry, Mr. Mitchell, but this man says he's—"

Colbert closed the door, cutting off the secretary's words and stepped boldly into the room. "Mr. Mitchell, I'm Robert Colbert from the U.S. State Department." He flashed his identification and moved closer to Mitchell's desk. "Is there a problem?"

Mitchell smiled and leaned further back into his seat. "No, Mr. Colbert, no problem. Are you here with Mr. Kulikov?"

"Yes, I am."

"Well, have a seat. I was just about to explain to Mr. Kulikov that we have a policy against letting the students out of class unless there is parental consent. I'm sure you can understand our position—"

Colbert cut in with a wave of his hand. "Where is Chris Madlinger?"

Mitchell smiled again and shrugged. "If he is where he is supposed to be, then he's in class somewhere. Now, if you two could just get me some kind of parental—"

Colbert suddenly leaned over the desk and grabbed the receiver off the telephone, and stuck it in Mitchell's face. "Mitchell, if you don't get Chris Madlinger out of class this instant, and bring him in here, I'm going to have you arrested for treason. Now do you want to use this to call your secretary, or should I just go ahead and call the FBI?''

Mitchell turned white and he sat staring at the receiver as if it were a gun. At last, he reached up and took the telephone from Colbert's hand. He pushed an intercom button and then spoke into the receiver. ''Mary, will you please send Chris Madlinger in here. Right away. Thank you.''

By the time Chris Madlinger arrived, Mitchell had agreed to wait outside so that Chris and Kulikov could meet in private. Chris was surprised to see Andrei Kulikov and he greeted him with a manly handshake, but his surprise quickly turned to concern and his face turned bright red. ''Is everything all right?''

''There are some problems with PF-One, Chris,'' Kulikov said, pulling the bag from his pocket. ''I'm sure you've heard as much as I can tell you. Right now, I need your help.''

Chris took the plastic bag and turned it over in his hands to study the picture. ''That's you all right. What do you want?''

''I need to know who took the picture.''

''It's not mine,'' Chris said.

''How do you know?''

''I already got back my pictures from the cook-off. You saw them. I would recognize it if I had taken it. Besides, this is in color and I always shoot in black and white.''

''Can you tell me who took it?''

Chris Madlinger stood quietly for a few seconds, studying the photograph in the plastic bag. ''Does this have to do with the problems with the space shuttle?''

Kulikov nodded his head.

''Are they all right?''

''I think so, but I can't really talk about it.''

Chris Madlinger looked into Kulikov's eyes. ''Is my father all right?''

''Yes,'' Kulikov answered. ''He's all right.''

Chris looked back at the picture and then nodded slowly. ''It's really important that you know who took this?''

"Yes. Really important."

"I think I might be able to figure it out, but I need to look at my pictures. Can we go back to my house?"

Kulikov stood up, suddenly nervous and excited. "Of course. I'm sure Mr. Colbert can arrange it."

38

THE
PHANTOM

NO one had slept much in the last three days. Senator Paul Ryan studied the bloodshot eyes and tired-looking faces of the SIG-PIFPY team scattered around the conference room table, and decided they all looked like ghosts more than human beings. National Security Advisor Dick Higgins had sunk so far into his seat that his head barely showed over the top of the table, and even from the far end of the room, Ryan could tell that his eyes were glassy and unfocused. They all listened quietly as Elliot Hacker brought the group up to date on the FBI's investigations. Hacker explained his theory that Das Deutschland Syndikat used Wilson's Camera Shop as a drop-off to get information and instructions to Alex Vonberger. He nodded gently toward Ryan, and acknowledged the possibility that someone from NASA could be involved in the organization. Then he stared at the ceiling, as if the solution to all of their problems were floating somewhere in the room.

Elliot Hacker slowly brought his head down, but he did

not look at anyone when he spoke. "What we're looking at is the possibility that someone from Das Deutschland Syndikat may be in the position to compromise the RM-One-oh-five mission."

"You mean sabotage?" Higgins asked from the depths of his chair.

"Possibly, but I would be more concerned about someone trying to warn *Discovery*."

"Like they did with the fire detection system?" Higgins asked.

Peggy Kellner broke in. "Dick, so far we've been unable to determine if Vonberger was warned of the changed limits in the fire detection system or not. We've got people reviewing all transmission data from the time we uplinked the change of limits in the fire detection system to the time Vonberger communicated with us, but I'm afraid it's going to take a while. I might add that at Elliot's suggestion, we have not told the PF-One flight controllers about the RM-One-oh-five mission."

"I don't get it," Higgins said, still slumped into his seat. "If someone wanted to warn Alex Vonberger about the RM-One-oh-five mission, wouldn't they have done it already?"

It was Charlie Roland who answered. Despite his age, Roland looked more awake and refreshed than the rest of the group. "I'm not sure about that, Dick. It seems to me that anyone who wanted to warn *Discovery* might wait as long as possible, so as to cut short the possibility of RM-One-oh-five changing its tactics. The most critical aspects of the mission are coming up now, with rendezvous in about forty minutes, Russ's EVA in about fifty minutes, and our coordinated uplink distraction in about an hour and twenty minutes. It seems to me that we're in a pretty crucial period right now."

"Well, what can we do?" Higgins asked.

"My men are working as fast as they can," Hacker answered, "but I'm afraid we can't expect any miracles in the next few hours."

"So all we can do is twiddle our thumbs?"

A stark silence descended upon the room, as the group considered the situation. Senator Ryan rubbed his eyes and tried to think. Somewhere inside the ranks of NASA there was a phantom, a secret member of Das Deutschland Syndikat. He could be anyone and anywhere. He had already warned Alex Vonberger of the uplinked changes in the fire detection system, and now he was probably plotting to warn him of the RM-105 mission. Whoever he was, he had to be stopped. But how?

The silence was broken by the loud beeping of the hotline from the Mission Control Center. Peggy Kellner answered it, and then turned to the rest of the group. "It's Leonard Wolff. I'm going to put him on the speaker phone." She replaced the receiver and leaned over the conference table to turn on the speaker system. "Go ahead, Len," she said. "We have you on the speakers."

"Who am I talking to?" Wolff's voice crackled.

Kellner looked around the room. "We've got members of the SIG-PIFPY team here and Senator Ryan. Everyone has clearance."

"Okay," Wolff's voice came back. "*Discovery* has changed orbits. We monitored an unauthorized OMS burn approximately seven minutes ago."

"He's been warned," Ryan said, quietly.

Wolff continued. "We recorded the duration of the OMS burn and with that and the orbiter's attitude, we were able to calculate the new orbital parameters. RM-One-oh-five will have to do an adjustment burn, but they can still accomplish a rendezvous."

"What kind of delay are we talking about?" Higgins asked, sitting up straight in his seat for the first time in hours.

"It's hard to say before we do the calculations, but I'd estimate roughly an hour. I think they should still have plenty of time for the EVA."

Senator Ryan interrupted. "Dick, if Vonberger was warned

of the RM-One-oh-five mission, then even if we do adjustment burns and accomplish a rendezvous, why would he allow an EVA?''

Higgins looked around the room. "Suggestions?"

There was a brief silence, and then Wolff's voice came through the speakers. "I think we have to proceed as planned and hope for the best. I don't see any other choice.''

There were nods of agreement around the room. "Okay,'' Higgins said. He was standing now, pacing around behind his chair. "Can we get *Discovery*'s new orbital parameters up to the RM-One-oh-five Flight Control Room?''

"Yes," Wolff answered. "I can send them through on the computer.''

"Okay, do it. We'll contact them directly and have them calculate the adjustment burn for RM-One-oh-five. Len, was there any indication from Vonberger as to why he changed orbits?''

There was a short pause, and then Wolff's voice continued. "No. Our flight director did not attempt to communicate.''

"Okay, Len. Get that data over to the other Flight Control Room. We'll deal with the rest of it from here.''

Peggy Kellner turned the speakers off and the silence came back over the meeting. Senator Ryan sat with his chin in his hands, and watched Higgins pacing on the other side of the room. The phantom had resurfaced and had warned Alex Vonberger of the RM-105 mission. But what good had it done to move *Discovery* to another orbit, when it could be tracked and followed? Or did they plan to move again? If they moved again, they would be followed again. *Discovery* would not have enough fuel for more than a couple of moves. Something else had to be going on. The phantom had to have another game in mind, and Ryan knew they had to solve it before . . . before what? And then it hit him. They had to solve it before RM-105 did its adjustment burn. Ryan bolted to his feet. "Peggy, who calculated *Discovery*'s new orbit?''

Kellner looked at the senator and shrugged. "It depends.

Probably the flight dynamics officer, but the flight director might have done it himself.''

"What would happen if the wrong orbital data was given to the RM-One-oh-five Flight Control Room?"

Higgins stopped pacing and faced Kellner as she answered. "Then the adjustment burn would be wrong. They'd miss the rendezvous.''

Higgins suddenly caught on. "Can we get someone to check the new orbital parameters? Someone who hasn't worked on this mission at all?"

"Sure, but I'm not sure what you're getting at."

Higgins answered. ''We've got to make sure the new parameters are right. Call the RM-One-oh-five Flight Control Room and tell them *Discovery*'s new orbital parameters are on the way, but they are not to calculate the adjustment burn until we know if the parameters are correct. I don't want RM-One-oh-five to do any burns until they hear from me personally.'' Then he turned to Hacker and gave his order. ''Get the flight director and the flight dynamics officer in here right away. I want to get to the bottom of this."

And Senator Ryan suddenly felt his whole body relax. The phantom was out there but he was close. Very close.

39

CRAZY

ALEX Vonberger watched nervously as Conrad Williams studied the three floating pieces of paper. Vonberger's feet were toward the ceiling of the flight deck, and so to him, the messages appeared as though they were upside down, but he had already read them enough to be able to recite them by memory. Vonberger anxiously wiped his sweaty palms on the pants of his flight suit and suddenly he could no longer conceal his excitement. "Well, what do you think?"

Williams looked at Vonberger. "I think you're crazy."

Vonberger laughed and collected the papers. He folded them and stuffed them back into his pocket. "Really, Connie. Tell me what you think."

"Really. I think you're crazy. They'll never do it."

"Never do what?"

"They'll never release the prisoners."

Vonberger laughed again. "You know what your problem is, Connie? You never believe anything. I showed you a message that says they are going to release the prisoners. It is your ticket to freedom, written in black and white, and you still do not believe it!''

''Alex, let me ask you something.''

''Okay.''

''How come you changed orbits?''

''Oh, I don't know. I felt like it.''

''No, I'm serious, Alex. You must have had a reason. You have somebody out there you want to meet? You have some outer-space cab company coming to pick you up?''

''Connie, you make me laugh.''

''Or are you trying to hide from NASA? Do you think they have some kind of SWAT team that's going to come up here and get you?''

Vonberger laughed some more. He had been floating near the commander's seat, and now he pushed himself over so that he could face Williams directly. ''Connie, you see what I mean about Laura?''

''No.''

''She's alive, Connie. It's obvious. The whole first message was a bluff to get me to surrender. And did you see that picture? It did not even look like Laura's body!''

''I wouldn't know.''

''Believe me, Connie. Laura's got a better body than that.'' Vonberger wiped his forehead with the sleeve of his shirt. ''She's waiting for me, Connie.''

''Where? In prison?''

Vonberger pushed himself back toward the commander's seat. ''No! In Iran!''

''Iran?''

''We're all going to Iran! Did you think I was stupid enough to land at Cape Canaveral? See, I have this all worked out. The prisoners are going to get to Tehran in about four hours. That leaves us another three hours of oxygen. Plenty of time for a deorbit burn, and a landing in Iran.''

''Who's going to fly us?''

''You are!'' Vonberger said, laughing.

"Why should I?"

"Oh, come on, Connie. You want to live, don't you?"

"Not in Iran."

Vonberger was still laughing. "I'm going to miss you, Connie. Don't worry, you'll get to go home. You and Cowboy and everyone else."

"If they're alive."

"You do not have to worry about Cowboy. He is going to be all right. It was just a minor wound."

Williams shook his head. "You're nuts."

Vonberger laughed and pulled himself down into the seat. Connie was a good person. He was a little too serious sometimes, but maybe that came with the territory of being a commander. Cowboy always got the credit for being the funny one, but Connie could be funny in his own way, and he was not as stupid as Cowboy. "I'm glad I did not have to shoot you, Connie."

"That makes two of us."

"I think Cowboy's problem was that he made too big a deal over all of this. If everyone had just done as I had said, nobody would have gotten shot. We could have been back on the ground by now. I think he took it all too seriously." Vonberger pulled the seat belt around his body and fastened the buckles. "Well, at least everything will be all right now," he said.

Williams was staring out the overhead windows at the earth. He looked worried and sad, and Vonberger felt sorry for him. "Hey, Connie," Vonberger said softly, leaning over the center console. "Do you think Cowboy and Aelita had sex in the airlock?"

Williams did not move and Vonberger laughed. "Come on, Connie. What do you think?"

"I think you're crazy," Williams said, staring out at the earth.

40

MEASUREMENTS
AND
ANGLES

THEY made an unlikely threesome. Andrei Kulikov and Robert Colbert wore suits with ties. Chris Madlinger wore blue jeans and sneakers, with a T-shirt. As they rode the elevator up to the ninth floor of Building One, it occurred to Andrei Kulikov that sooner or later Chris Madlinger would have be told what this was all about, but for now, Kulikov thought, it might be better if Chris did not know that he was fingering a suspect. After all, this was not supposed to be a test of his loyalty to NASA.

The door opened on the ninth floor and Elliot Hacker stood in the hallway, waiting to get into the elevator. He reached his hand out to hold the doors while the three disembarked. He appeared distracted and hardly seemed to recognize them.

"I've got an answer for you," Kulikov said proudly, as he stepped into the hall.

"I've got no time," Hacker said, slipping into the elevator. "Wait for me."

Kulikov called out through the closing doors, "Don't you want to know who it is?"

Suddenly the doors stopped and then slowly they began to open again. Hacker stood with his arm outstretched and his hand on the button that controlled the doors. "Who is it?" he asked.

Kulikov looked around to make sure no one else could hear. "Leonard Wolff," he said quietly.

Hacker stood perfectly still inside the elevator, as if debating whether or not to let the door go. At last, he looked down at his watch, swore softly, and stepped out into the hall. He watched the doors close and then turned to Kulikov. "How do you know?" he asked. Then he nodded at Chris Madlinger. "Who is this?"

"This is Chris Madlinger," Kulikov answered. "Russell's son. He can show you that it had to be Leonard Wolff."

Hacker looked at his watch again. "I've got about thirty seconds. Let's go." He led the way back down the hallway to the FBI command center in Peggy Kellner's conference room. The room was buzzing with activity, and Hacker led them over to the far end of the table where Steve Erickson was working. "Steve, I want you to listen to this. Go ahead, Chris."

Andrei Kulikov noticed that Chris Madlinger's hands were shaking slightly as he laid the photographs out on the table. Even though Chris could not know the meaning of his discovery, he obviously understood its importance. "I took all of these at the chili cook-off," Chris said. Despite his shaky hands, his voice was steady. "They were taken in sequence. This one first." He pointed to a picture of a large group of people crowding around Andrei Kulikov. "This one next," and he pointed to a picture of Kulikov being handed the box of Hamburger Helper. "Then this one." The third photograph caught only Kulikov's side as he turned away laughing. "And finally this one." In the last photograph, Kulikov was in the foreground and slightly out of focus, and there was a large group of people behind him.

"I see Leonard Wolff here," Hacker said, pointing to the last photograph. Wolff was among the group, holding a camera in his hands and staring off toward Andrei Kulikov.

"He's also here," Chris said, pointing to the first photograph, where Wolff could be seen lifting the camera from around his neck and fiddling with the lenses. Then Chris brought out the photograph in the plastic bag. "If you look at this picture, you can see the tree behind Andrei's left ear. I was standing just to the right of that tree, right about here," and he pointed to a place on the table about six inches from the photograph. "So I'm here, Andrei's here, and Leonard Wolff is here, with a camera. These pictures had to be taken at just about the same time. It had to be him."

Hacker lit a cigarette and studied the photographs. "Seem right to you, Steve?" he asked finally.

"You bet. I'll get someone to check the measurements and angles."

Hacker held up his hand. "We don't have time for that. Get downstairs to where they brought in that flight director and tell them to wait for me. We're going to have to change our tactics."

41

McKENZIE'S MISTAKE

THE late morning air was hot and humid. Flight Director Andrew McKenzie and his flight dynamics officer walked silently along the path to Building One. They were followed by two escorts, men in suits with no names. McKenzie had laughed when the two men had met them outside the Flight Control Room. Why did they need escorts to bring them to Building One? It was only a few blocks away. Were they afraid they were going to get lost? It was bad enough being replaced by another flight director during a crucial point in the shift, but why did they have to treat him like a prisoner?

McKenzie looked at his flight dynamics officer, but she kept her eyes on the ground in front of them. They had both been working extended shifts for the last three days, and there was no doubt that exhaustion was setting in, but McKenzie knew there was something else going on. It just didn't make sense for Peggy Kellner to call him out of the Flight Control

Room now, not right after an unplanned OMS burn. The whole day had been a series of crazy events. First NASA had launched a top-secret Department of Defense mission right in the middle of the PFP flight, as if there wasn't enough going on already. Then the President had decided to give in to Vonberger's demands. Then Vonberger did an OMS burn for no apparent reason. Then Leonard Wolff started giving orders as if he was the flight director. And now Peggy Kellner ordered McKenzie and his flight dynamics officer to report to Building One, right in the middle of the shift. Nothing was making sense anymore. Where was Russell Madlinger when you needed him?

The escorts led them to the fifth floor of Building One, where they were taken separate ways. McKenzie was directed into a small office with a table and a few chairs. Charles Roland and Peggy Kellner were waiting for him, and McKenzie swallowed hard as the door closed behind him. Whatever was going on had to be pretty serious.

"Sit down, Andrew," Kellner said.

McKenzie sat at the table, across from her and Charles Roland. He had always wanted to meet Roland, but not like this.

"You've been working extended shifts," Kellner said. "You must be pretty tired."

"I've worked long shifts before."

"How long have you been on?" Roland asked.

"Since six this morning."

Roland kept asking the questions. "How long was your last shift?"

"Thirteen hours."

"When was that?"

"Yesterday."

"You *have* been working hard."

McKenzie just could not understand it. There was a hijacking going on and they were concerned with his work schedule! "I guess," he said.

"How are you feeling?"

McKenzie clasped his hands on the table and sighed. "To tell you the truth, I'm feeling a little confused."

"About what?"

"About this," and he gestured around the room. "About why I'm here."

Roland took a deep breath and pulled his chair closer to the table. "Andrew, tell me about the OMS burn."

"What about it?"

"How did you first pick up on it?"

"My propulsion systems officer reported that the OMS helium valves were open, and then my flight dynamics officer reported an attitude maneuver."

"Did you try to make contact?"

"No. My orders were that we were not to attempt to communicate without consent from Building One."

"Didn't you think it was a little strange that he was doing an OMS burn without contacting you?"

"It was very strange. We quickly established from the orbiter's attitude that it wasn't a deorbit burn, and so at least I knew we were not dealing with a reentry."

"Who monitored the burns?"

"It was on the computer. The propulsion systems officer recorded it, but I watched it on my console too."

"Who calculated the new orbital parameters?"

"I did."

"How come?"

"I preferred to do it myself rather than tie up my flight dynamics officer."

"You felt confident in your ability to do the calculations?"

"As Peggy can tell you, I used to be a flight dynamics officer before I became a flight director. I knew how to do it. Is there a problem?"

Roland pushed his seat back, but it was Peggy Kellner who answered. "There is a problem, Andrew. You made a mistake."

"I did?"

"I'm afraid so."

"What kind of mistake?"

"Well, we'd like you to find it." Kellner pointed to a computer terminal in the corner of the room. "The program is ready to run. Take a minute and review it."

McKenzie looked at Roland and then walked to the corner of the room and sat down at the computer. How could he have made a mistake? He recognized the data as soon as he looked at the computer screen. It had only been thirty minutes since he had run the calculations. Had he overlooked something? Had he used the wrong formulas? How did they know he was wrong? Why had they been checking up on him? He tried to put these questions from his mind and focused on the program.

The formulas were correct. He reviewed the sequences and saw no mistakes in the procedure. He was sure about that. Then he looked at the data inputs and they were exactly as he remembered them. He looked down at the solution and caught his breath. It was wrong! The orbital parameters were all wrong. McKenzie turned around to look at Kellner and Roland.

"Find it?" Kellner asked.

McKenzie pointed to the screen but could not get his mouth to work.

"What is it, Andrew?" Roland asked.

"The orbital parameters are wrong," McKenzie said at last.

"How could you make a mistake like that?" Roland asked.

McKenzie looked back at the computer, and suddenly understood what had happened. The data were right, the sequences were right, and the formulas were right. Everything was right, but the solution was wrong. "The result has been changed," McKenzie said.

"Come on, Andrew," Roland said. "It's your calculation. You can see the mistake."

McKenzie shook his head. "No, I swear. This isn't my result. The data and the formula are right, but the result is wrong. There is no way *Discovery* could be in this orbit after the OMS burns they performed."

Roland smiled, but it was not a nice smile. "Are you suggesting that someone altered the orbital parameters after you completed your calculation?"

"I don't know. It's crazy! But I swear these aren't my figures!"

"How do you know?" Kellner asked.

"Look, I'll show you," McKenzie said, pointing to the screen. "These are the correct inputs here, because I remember them. And this is the correct formula. If you run these inputs through this formula . . ." He turned toward the computer and typed into the keyboard. The screen went blank for a second and then the data reappeared. A new set of figures was shown at the bottom of the screen. "You get this result. This is the one I calculated, not the one that was on there."

"What was the orbit that was on there?" Roland asked.

"I have no idea, but it isn't the orbit that *Discovery* is in now."

"How do you know?"

"They would have had to do a completely different set of OMS burns to get into that orbit. Not only that, but this is the orbit that we're tracking them in now."

Roland took another deep breath. "Andrew, you've been working extremely hard and under difficult circumstances. Peggy tells me that you have an excellent record and I'm sure you would like to keep it that way. I'm going to give you a chance to admit that under the strain of the situation, you made a mistake, and I will personally guarantee that it never appears in your file."

McKenzie could not believe his ears. They were still trying to blame it on him! He wanted to jump out of his seat and scream at them, but he forced himself to remain calm. "Mr. Roland, the orbital parameters that were on here were wrong. I'll admit that. But I won't take the blame for it because it is not my mistake. Somebody changed my result."

"Andrew, who would have changed your result?"

McKenzie sat stone-faced and looked at Roland and Kellner. There was something going on here that they weren't telling him. Why were the NASA administrator and the center director getting involved in the calculation of orbital parameters when there was a hijacking going on? Didn't they have more important things to worry about?

Peggy Kellner broke the silence. "Andrew, these were the orbital parameters we pulled out of the Flight Control Room. Now either you calculated them this way, or someone changed them. Right?"

McKenzie slowly began to understand. They knew it was not his mistake. They knew it had been changed. And suddenly he knew who had changed it. Andrew McKenzie looked at Charles Roland and Peggy Kellner with a feeling of confusion. "Leonard Wolff," he said.

"Leonard Wolff?" Roland asked in surprise. "Come on, Andrew. Why would he alter your solution?"

"I don't know. But he . . . he had been acting strangely. He asked me to have my flight dynamics officer calculate the new orbital parameters. I told him I would do it myself. He was the only one in the Flight Control Room who knew what sector of the computer I was working in. If someone in the Flight Control Room altered my result, it had to be Leonard Wolff."

"Are you sure you don't want to admit to the mistake, and have it wiped from your file?"

McKenzie shook his head. "Forget it. It wasn't my mistake."

Roland nodded his head. "Okay, good. You can come in now."

McKenzie spun around in his seat and suddenly the door opened and the room was filled with people. He didn't recognize any of them, but he guessed they were members of the SIG-PIFPY group.

"How'd we do?" Roland asked.

"Not bad," a man answered. "We'll make FBI agents out of you yet."

Another man with big tired eyes nodded at Roland and Kellner. "Good work. McKenzie, good job." Then suddenly he was snapping orders. "Peggy, get *Discovery*'s correct orbital data to the Mission Control Center and tell them to calculate the adjustment burns. I'll have to call them to give them the final go. Elliot, go nail the son of a bitch."

The room emptied as quickly as it had filled up, and McKenzie found himself standing alone in the room with Charles Roland. "Mr. Roland?"

"Yes?"

"Why are they calculating adjustment burns?"

Roland gave McKenzie a sly smile. "So our rescue mission can make the rendezvous."

McKenzie finally understood. That was why the orbital parameters were so important. The new shuttle was up there, trying to catch *Discovery*. The Department of Defense mission was a rescue operation! Wolff must have changed the orbital parameters so that the adjustment burns would be wrong. Wolff had been trying to send the rescue mission on a wild-goose chase. And he had tried to frame McKenzie for it! And then McKenzie smiled, because suddenly he thought he knew where Russell Madlinger was.

"Take the rest of the day off, Andrew," Roland said, as he headed for the door.

"Mr. Roland?" McKenzie caught up to the Administrator. "If it's okay with you, I'd rather go back to the Flight Control Room."

"Well, I'm afraid that might be a little complicated right now, since they will probably be going in there after Wolff. Maybe you'd like to direct the rescue mission."

"I'd like that, sir."

"Okay, go catch Peggy and tell her I want you in there."

"Thank you, sir," McKenzie said over his shoulder, and he ran down the hall after Peggy Kellner.

42

ON
THE
RUN

ELLIOT Hacker bolted from the rear entrance of Building One into the blinding sun, his shoes slapping time on the paved walkway that led away from the building. His jacket and tie flapped wildly as he left the sidewalk and took off across the landscaped lawn on a beeline for the Mission Control Center. He was only vaguely aware of the startled reactions from the people as he leapt over hedges and sprinted across the grass. By the time he reached the Mission Control Center, he had worked up a good sweat, and the air conditioning felt cool against his skin. Steve Erickson was inside the main door at the security booth, and one of their agents was screaming instructions into a red telephone, as two NASA security guards looked on.

"What happened?" Hacker asked, trying to catch his breath.

Erickson turned away from the man on the telephone and shook his head. "We missed him."

"What do you mean we missed him? Where did he go?"
Hacker was surprised by the anger in his own voice.

"He was gone before we got here. He must have suspected
something when we called McKenzie out of the Flight Control
Room. The flight controllers say he left about five minutes
after McKenzie."

"Did you secure the building?"

"It's secured, but he's got twenty minutes on us. I'm afraid
he's out of the building by now. We're securing the entire
Johnson Space Center. We've got an APB out on his car,
we've got his house staked out, and we're watching the air-
ports and all roads going south. We'll get him."

"Damn it, Steve! I don't want him getting away from us!"

"I'm taking care of it, Elliot."

"Don't worry too much about the gates. If he's still on
the grounds he's going to try to leave by foot. Check the
fences and the outer areas."

"I'm taking care of it, Elliot."

Hacker turned away to hide his anger. How could they
have missed him? For days he was sitting right in their hands!
How could they come so close and then lose him? He lit a
cigarette and tried to calm himself down. He couldn't take
his anger out on his men. It wasn't anyone's fault, and he
needed them now. He needed Erickson.

The agent on the security telephone slammed it down.
"Okay, Steve," he said. "We've got a chopper on the
way."

"Good," Erickson said. "Elliot, where will you be?"

"I'll be in the command center. I've got my beeper if you
need me."

"Okay. Don't worry. We'll get him," Erickson said.

Elliot Hacker turned away from the security booth and
headed back out into the Houston sun. He walked slowly,
making his way along the path now, back toward Building
One. He knew he had to stop worrying about the details.
Erickson would take care of the roadblocks and the security

checks and the stakeouts. If Leonard Wolff could be caught, Steve Erickson would catch him. Elliot Hacker knew he had to step back and think. He had to focus on the big picture. After all, there was nothing left for him to do.

43

SEVENTEEN
YEARS

RUSSELL Madlinger waited inside the airlock. The final
adjustment burns had been fired but there would be a
seventy-minute delay before they rendezvoused with
Discovery in its new orbit. Madlinger could not remove his
spacesuit without breaking the prebreathe, and so there was
nothing for him to do but wait, and all he could think about
was Leonard Wolff.

It would take a long time for Madlinger to sort through the
levels of betrayal. Wolff had betrayed the United States and
the Soviet Union. He had betrayed NASA and the Peace
Flight Program, and he had betrayed the crew of RM-105,
who were risking their lives to bring the hijacking to an end.
But to Russell Madlinger, the most devastating betrayal was
that of mankind, for he felt betrayed by the fact that he could
know a man for twenty years and never know the evil he was
capable of. It was hard to imagine the double life that Wolff
must have led: playing the role of the dutiful NASA engineer,

and all the time plotting his revenge on the world. Madlinger knew it was something he might never understand.

The final adjustment burns brought RM-105 within several hundred yards of *Discovery,* and a few minutes later, Brad Parker floated into the mid-deck and told Madlinger that they had made their final approach and were station-keeping in *Discovery*'s blind spot. Parker wished Madlinger luck and closed the door to the airlock, and Russell Madlinger began the depressurization. He reversed his position, putting his feet into the footholds at the top of the small chamber, and waited. It took less than three minutes for the airlock to fully depressurize. Madlinger opened the hatch to the cargo bay, and smiling slightly, he pulled himself out into space.

Seventeen years had changed nothing. Children had been born. Corporations had grown, and merged, and gone bankrupt. New technologies had shrunk the world, and new diseases threatened it. Pollution had destroyed vast stretches of the earth, and nature had reclaimed crumbling seaside towns and abandoned cities. Terrorists had robbed lives and refugees had starved to death. Dictators had fallen. Armies had revolted. All of this, and yet the calm chill of space had not changed.

Madlinger held on to the handholds in the cargo bay, and looked down past his feet at the earth, a giant sphere of blues and browns, floating out in space on its own. From where he was he could not see *Discovery,* but he knew where she would be. As soon as he came up out of the payload bay, he would be able to see her, about two hundred feet away, between himself and the earth. He pulled himself along the bulkhead of the empty cargo bay, toward the MMU, remembering how he had stood in this cargo bay on earth, when the new orbiter had first arrived at the Kennedy Space Center.

The MMU was mounted to the cargo bay wall, and Madlinger pulled out the control arms and backed himself into the unit. It fit like a large backpack and Madlinger fastened the restraining belts and attached the MMU latches onto his life-support system. He settled his elbows and hands onto the MMU control arms and then checked the display module on his chest. Propellant pressure and battery power were nominal, and his life-support systems were working. Madlinger reached back with his right arm and felt the bag of tools attached to the side of the MMU. He reached back with his left arm and felt the handle of the knife, and the handle of the gun. Everything was ready. It was time to learn how to fly.

Madlinger unlatched the MMU from the cargo bay mounts and pushed the translational hand control gently foward. Suddenly he was flying across the cargo bay, and he had to pull back on the control to slow himself down. Then he pushed forward on the rotational hand control and his feet went out from under him as he went in a headfirst somersault, spinning slowly inside the cargo bay. He pulled back on the control, trying to steady himself, and after a few moments of panic, he was able to control his spin. With the rotational control, he changed his pitch so that he was facing out of the cargo bay, and then he moved forward out into space. The dark tiles of the belly of *Discovery* quickly came into view, looking like a black hole compared to the white swirls of clouds around the earth.

Madlinger experimented with the MMU controls some more, now in the freedom of space. He practiced going forward and backward, pitching up and down, and rotating left and right. After a few minutes he felt more comfortable with the controls and he passed by the front windows of the orbiter and gave a thumbs-up sign to Bingham and Parker. They waved back and smiled, and Madlinger briefly remembered the effect that looking into the Apollo command module had had on him seventeen years ago, but this was no time for reflection. He adjusted the controls and began his trip toward *Discovery*.

Madlinger felt an increasing sense of isolation as more distance separated him from the safety of his ship. He was alone, out in space. He was orbiting the earth at five miles a second, a satellite with a heartbeat. If he got into trouble now, nobody could come to his rescue. Madlinger reached back and felt the handle of the gun, and suddenly he was gripped with a horrible realization. For the first time in history, the wars of the earth were about to be fought in space.

Near him were two spaceships and billions of dollars' worth of technology. There had been decades of research, planning, building, testing, and launching. There had been thirty-three years of space travel. All of this sophistication, and he carried a gun and a knife as his only weapons. In the end, men were reduced to guns and knives. It was as if there had been no progress at all.

Madlinger came closer to *Discovery,* and he could make out the individual tiles of her underbelly, but he could not stop thinking about the violent nature of his mission. He was spreading the violence of the earth to space, and space, the great forgiver, would see firsthand what happened on earth every day. Madlinger knew that he had not instigated the violence. It hadn't been Russell Madlinger who had brought the first gun into space and used it to hijack a peaceful mission. Madlinger was in space to put things right. But he still carried a knife and a gun, and there was something almost sacrilegious about that. In the eyes of space, he had merely descended to Vonberger's level.

It was a dichotomy he had wrestled with many times before. Violence to stop violence. Could a pacifist commit violence to save the lives of others? Who was Russell Madlinger to decide that Vonberger was evil and should die for his acts? Who was Russell Madlinger to decide that the lives of *Discovery*'s crew were worth more than the life of Alex Vonberger? Maybe he *was* saving the crew. Maybe he was saving the Peace Flight Program, and the world's hopes for what it might ultimately contribute to world peace. But he would also be killing another human being.

Madlinger approached the underbelly of *Discovery* from above and behind. He flew around the main engines and then maneuvered the MMU around the left OMS pod and down near the port wing. He slowed the MMU and grasped the edge of the cargo bay door, positioning himself between the edge of the door and the wing, just out of sight of the rear windows on *Discovery*'s flight deck. He checked the time on his chest display. It had taken less time than they had planned. With the delay caused by *Discovery*'s move, it had been necessary to resynchronize with Houston the uplink of the changed flow limits in *Discovery*'s main nitrogen supply. Madlinger still had ten minutes.

He looked out at the earth, and realized with a profound sadness that there would always be evil in the world. It didn't mean that man had made no progress. It only meant that no amount of progress could totally rid the world of evil. He was in space to kill a man. It was not a deed that he looked forward to, but one that he had to do. For more than anything, Madlinger knew he believed in space and in man's need to explore, and he would not let one man, filled with evil, stand in the way.

44

ONE
STEP
BEHIND

I T had been two hours since Leonard Wolff had disappeared, and Elliot Hacker returned to the Mission Control Center, frustrated and exhausted. He made his way to the Viewing Room, and finding it empty and quiet, he collapsed into a seat and pulled a cigarette from his jacket pocket. It was unbelievable that they had not been able to find Leonard Wolff. How could he have slipped through their fingers? Hacker puffed quietly on his cigarette and sat back to watch the final coordination with the RM-105 mission. There was nothing else for him to do.

Elliot Hacker felt perplexed by his need to be in the Viewing Room. It was almost as if he was waiting for something to happen. The Flight Control Room, Hacker knew, was about to uplink limit changes that would trigger *Discovery*'s master alarm, and give Russell Madlinger time to disconnect the rear cameras in the cargo bay. Later, Madlinger would disconnect the cargo bay door latches, and the Flight Control

299

Room would have to confirm the broken latches and authorize an EVA. But there was something else Hacker was waiting for, and he stared up at the ceiling and smoked his cigarette, trying to think.

And then he brought his head down and looked into the Flight Control Room, and suddenly he knew what it was. Leonard Wolff. Leonard Wolff had come back into the Flight Control Room and was making his way toward his console in the back. The FBI had been searching all of Houston for him, and here he was, still in the Mission Control Center. In their desperation to keep him from *leaving,* they had forgotten to guard the entrance to the Flight Control Room, to keep him from *coming back,* and Hacker knew that Leonard Wolff had come back, right at this crucial moment, to warn Alex Vonberger once and for all.

There was no time to get from the Viewing Room, out into the hall, and into the Flight Control Room. There was no time to get help. Leonard Wolff had reached his console and he had to be stopped. Hacker jumped over two rows of seats and pounded the butt of his gun on the window between the two rooms. The window did not break, but Wolff turned around and saw Hacker with his gun. Wolf turned back to the console and began typing into the computer keyboard. He had to be stopped!

Hacker calmly stepped back from the window, giving himself plenty of room. He planted his legs firmly and held the gun out in front of him. The first shot was deflected as the window collapsed in a thundering splash of glass and noise. The flight controllers jumped out of their seats in alarm, but Hacker was only vaguely aware of the commotion. He fired a second shot, as Wolff moved away, and the bullet hit Wolff in the arm, spewing blood on the console and the floor. Hacker fired a third shot, and the bullet slammed into the computer screen, shorting out the entire console.

Hacker shifted his position to take another shot as Wolff

ran toward the door, but there were too many flight controllers in the way. He dropped his arms and leapt through the shattered glass. "Call security," he yelled out to the flight director. "Tell them Leonard Wolff is in the building!" And he took off toward the door.

45

THE MAN WHO CHANGED THE WORLD

ALEX Vonberger was smiling as he stared out at the earth below and he thought about the difference he had made. He had successfully hijacked the space shuttle and had single-handedly brought the United States and the Soviet Union to their knees. Now that the superpowers had been beaten, the political dynamics of the whole world would change. The Inner Circle would be free to follow through on their plan to reunite Germany, and the United States and the Soviet Union would be dwarfed by their power. Alex Vonberger had changed history and now everyone would know his name! He would be in all of the history books, as the man who changed the world! He would be remembered, like Alexander the Great, like Napoleon, like Adolf Hitler himself! Vonberger laughed out loud, high on the feelings of power and triumph. He was unbeatable now, and there was nothing anyone could do that would bring him down.

Vonberger looked over at Conrad Williams to make sure Williams could not see from behind his Lone Ranger mask, and then he typed number 917 into the computer and accessed the uplink text pages. The message jumped out at him, stark and bold at the bottom of the screen. "Rescue mission in pursuit. Do not allow . . ."

A single cold drop of sweat tickled Vonberger's back. What kind of crazy message had they sent him? He studied it word by word and tried to figure out what it meant. Could there really be a rescue mission in pursuit? Was that why they had told him to change orbits? What was it that he was not supposed to allow? How could they leave him hanging like that? He cleared the screen and felt himself shaking, suddenly terrorized by the unknown.

Vonberger unbuckled his seat belt and pushed himself up to the overhead windows. On the earth below, the snow-capped Alps appeared, like big white snowflakes sprinkled on the ground. There was nothing else out there. He strained to look in all directions and then pushed himself back to the rear windows and looked out into the cargo bay. He checked the television monitor, in the aft, port station, adjusting the controls and looking through all four cameras. There was nothing there. Vonberger floated back to the commander's seat and accessed the uplink text pages again. The message was still there. "Rescue mission in pursuit. Do not allow . . ." Why had they cut the message off in the middle? He wiped the sweat from his forehead and swallowed hard. He wasn't smiling now, as he stared out the window. There was somebody out there.

46

THE
NATURE OF
THE TASK

RUSSELL Madlinger had thirty seconds left to wait. He switched the controls on his chest display so that his headset would pick up all communications between Houston and *Discovery*. He would not be able to hear the master alarm inside *Discovery*, but he knew that Mission Control would do the uplink on time, and it would be safe to assume that Vonberger was distracted. He reached into his tool bag and pulled out the connector wrench, and then rested his hands on the controls of the MMU. He checked the time on his chest display. Five seconds. Four, three, two, one.

Madlinger maneuvered away from the orbiter, readjusted his pitch and his yaw, and then pushed down on the translational control, propelling himself over the cargo bay door. Inside the cargo bay he reached for the port camera, grabbing it with both hands, and then, working quickly, used the connector wrench to detach the power cable from the back of the camera. As the cord came free in his hands, he suddenly felt like the eagle at the Kennedy Space Center, chewing through the cord of the video camera. Nature takes care of itself, he thought. He pushed off and floated to the starboard camera and disconnected the power cable. Then, using the MMU controls, he maneuvered over the wall of the cargo bay, and down below the starboard wing, out of sight of the rearview windows.

There had been no communication between Alex Vonberger and Houston, but Madlinger could not be sure that he had completed his task undetected. Still, he wasted no time. He moved forward along *Discovery*'s belly until he was past the cargo bay doors. Then he maneuvered himself slowly up the side of the crew compartment, staying between the cargo bay and the forward windows. It was a tricky maneuver, to keep close enough to the orbiter so as not to be seen from the flight deck windows, and yet to be careful not to bump into the forward fuselage. Sound would not carry in the vacuum of space, but vibration was easily transmitted through the orbiter's structure. The slightest bump might draw Vonberger to the windows.

Madlinger maneuvered himself into position so that he could reach out and grab the front port camera and he disconnected the cable. The overhead observation windows made it too risky to fly over the top of the crew compartment, so he maneuvered back under *Discovery*'s belly and around the other side, to get the starboard camera. From there he snuck down into the cargo bay, hugging the forward bulkhead wall. Now that the video cameras had been disabled, Madlinger was not in danger of being spotted by the onboard television, but with the MMU attached to his back, there was no way he could get close enough to the bulkhead to avoid detection if Vonberger looked down from the top of the rear windows. He had to work quickly and quietly.

He easily located the panel he was looking for on the cargo bay wall and he pulled the allen wrench from his tool bag. He held on to the handholds on the bulkhead with one hand, to keep himself stationary, while he worked the wrench with his other hand. His movements were careful and deliberate, as he worked each of the four fasteners. When he removed the last one, the cover came off easily, and he secured it to a handhold with a piece of tape from his tool bag, so that it would not float away. The cluster of wires inside the panel looked exactly like the photographs he had been shown at the ROT meeting. He had been perfectly prepared. He quickly found the correctly numbered wire that ran from the top of the panel into a wire bundle running fore and aft, and he used the special pliers from his tool bag to detach the wire from a connector. One wire was all it took. Now his worry about noise would be less of a problem, since the master alarm would be sounding again.

Madlinger reinstalled the panel cover and stowed his tools back in the bag. Then he propelled himself back over the edge of the cargo bay and under *Discovery*'s belly. Hovering there, he positioned himself so he could see OV-105, and he raised an arm and waved three times, giving the prearranged signal that his tasks had been completed.

Then he settled back to wait for his next move. He wished that he could see the earth from where he was positioned, but he could tell by looking at OV-105 that they were entering darkness. He had completed his tasks right on time. Soon enough they would know if their plan to lure Vonberger into allowing an EVA would work. If it did work, Madlinger would have a two-hour wait before the *Discovery* crew would emerge. If it didn't work, then the RM-105 mission would fail. It had to work, Madlinger thought, suddenly feeling sleepy. After all, nature takes care of itself.

47

TO
WALK IN
SPACE

A LEX Vonberger knew that *Discovery*'s crew compartment could not be accessed from the outside without endangering the crew. Even if someone could open the mid-deck crew hatch, or the emergency, removable, overhead window, the orbiter's atmosphere, and possibly the crew, would be sucked out into the vacuum of space. The only other entrance was the airlock, but the airlock pressure was controlled from the inside. Vonberger tried to reassure himself that there was nothing a rescue mission could do to foil his success, but his thoughts were suddenly interrupted by the buzzing of the master alarm.

He turned off the alarm and looked at Conrad Williams, who was still blindfolded in the pilot's seat. Vonberger knew he had to try to solve the problem on his own, but he was glad that Williams was nearby. A warning light indicated that there was an atmospheric problem and Vonberger typed the access code into the computer for an atmospheric checkout. He studied the data that appeared on the screen. Nitrogen was flowing in system 1 of the pressure control system. Vonberger knew that the only time nitrogen was supposed to flow was to make up the cabin atmosphere. He checked the uplink text pages but there were no messages from Das Syndikat.

"N-two flow is high in system one," Vonberger said. "What do I do?"

Williams answered quickly, speaking for the first time in hours. "There could be something wrong with the pressure control system. Switch over to the alternate. On panel L-two, close N-two system one supply. Right below that there's a switch for N-two system two. Push it up into open position."

Vonberger followed Williams's instructions. "N-two system one supply closed. N-two system two supply open. Okay, now what?"

"Check the computer."

Vonberger looked back at the computer screen. "N-two system two reads nominal," he said. "Are we okay?"

"We've got to figure out what's wrong with system one. How about taking this mask off my face?"

Vonberger suddenly burst out laughing. "I like you, Connie, you know that? I like the way you look with that mask on. I think it keeps you honest."

"Alex, we're existing without a backup nitrogen supply right now, and I think we ought to check it out."

"Okay, Connie," Vonberger said calmly. "Whatever you say. Tell me what to do."

"Take the mask off my face."

"Shut up!" Vonberger suddenly screamed. "I am the one in charge here! I will give the orders! You just shut up!" There was a long silence, and then Vonberger laughed again. "See how mad you make me? Now, tell me how to troubleshoot the pressure control system."

But then the master alarm sounded again.

"Damn!" Vonberger said, as he turned off the alarm. He reached over and called up the Fault Summary on the computer and found a blinking cursor indicating a malfunction of the cargo bay doors. "What the hell is going on? We've got a malfunction of the cargo bay doors."

"Access code is two oh two," Williams said.

Vonberger called up 202 on the computer and studied the data. "It's a latch on the starboard door."

"Go to page seventeen," Williams instructed.

Vonberger paged forward to seventeen and a full readout of the cargo bay door latches appeared on the screen. He studied the data carefully. "Looks like an electrical failure," he said at last.

"Electrical system checkout is sixty-seven."

Vonberger called up 67 and found the break in the electrical system that powered the latches for the starboard door. The computer located the break outside the cabin only a few feet from the latches, but did not indicate the exact nature of the problem.

"What is it?" Williams asked.

Vonberger wiped his forehead on the sleeve of his flight suit. "There's a break in the electric outside the cabin." Vonberger checked the uplink text pages again, but there was still no message. Das Syndikat had warned him of the changed limits in the fire detection system. The fact that there was no message meant that the problems with the pressure control system and the cargo bay door latches were real. But why was everything suddenly going wrong?

"It's got to be fixed, Alex," Williams said.

"How do we fix it?"

"Alex, this is serious. Take this thing off my head."

"How do we fix it?" Vonberger asked, louder this time.

"We've got to do an EVA," Williams said softly.

"We can't do an EVA!" Vonberger screamed. "We're deorbiting in a few hours! We're not doing an EVA!"

Williams remained calm. "Alex, you can't deorbit without cargo bay door latches."

"Why not? We've still got latches on the port side."

"No way, Alex. The air loads will rip that door right off without the latches. We'll fry. You better contact Houston."

"Shut up!" Vonberger screamed. "Just shut up! I can't think with you trying to give out orders. I am in command here!" He pulled on his headset and switched it to voice activate. "Houston! Houston! This is *Discovery*. Do you copy?"

"We copy, *Discovery*."

"We have indications of an electrical problem with the starboard cargo bay door latches. Can you confirm?"

"We confirm, *Discovery*. Power is out on your starboard cargo bay door latches. We think you may have a broken wire between points sixty-two and sixty-four on line three nine five."

"Great."

"Say again, *Discovery?*"

"Are you going to tell us what to do?"

"Roger, *Discovery*. We're trying to verify the problem. Please stand by."

This was unbelievable! Just when everything seemed to be going right, the cargo bay door latches malfunctioned. Vonberger knew that he could not allow an EVA. If there was a rescue mission out there, they would take advantage of the EVA to gain access to the crew compartment through the airlock.

"*Discovery*, Houston. We have verified a break in the electrical system between points sixty-two and sixty-four on line three nine five. Your starboard cargo bay door latches are nonoperational. Repeat. Starboard cargo bay door latches are nonoperational. EVA approval to follow. Please stand by."

Maybe the whole thing was a setup. Maybe the rescue mission had somehow rigged the problem with the latches in order to induce an EVA. Maybe they had cut the wire. There were no messages from Das Syndikat indicating that this was a trick, but they had told him there was a rescue mission in pursuit. And there was something he was not supposed to allow. Was it an EVA? Had the end of the message been mistakenly cut off somehow?

Houston came back on the line. "*Discovery*, Houston. You have EVA approval for Aelita Zakharov and Vladimir Turnov. Please start prebreathe procedures."

Somewhere along the line Vonberger had lost control of the situation, and he knew he had to regain it now, or else it would be lost forever. He could not allow an EVA. "Houston, *Discovery*. Negative on EVA, until you confirm release of prisoners."

"Say again, *Discovery*."

Vonberger screamed into his headset microphone. "I said negative on EVA until you confirm release of prisoners!"

There was a long pause. "*Discovery*, prisoners are presently enroute to Tehran and we should be able to confirm their release in about three hours. If you wait until then to begin your EVA, we will have an oxygen supply problem prior to reentry. Do you copy?"

Vonberger knew they were right. If he waited until the prisoners were released and then allowed an EVA, *Discovery* would run out of oxygen before they landed. Or was it all a trick? Was there a rescue mission up there somewhere, waiting to come storming into *Discovery* as soon as they opened the hatch to the airlock? Vonberger floated back to the aft station and turned on the television monitor. The screen was blank. He tried all four cameras, but he could not get anything on the monitor. Something was going on out there! Vonberger floated to the forward windows and looked out, but he could see nothing. Why were the cameras out? Who was out there?

"*Discovery*, Houston. Do you copy?"

Suddenly Vonberger got an idea. If there was a rescue mission out there, they were probably above *Discovery*, where they could not be seen. All Vonberger had to do was roll *Discovery* over and he would be able to see them in the overhead windows. Vonberger pulled himself back into the commander's seat and buckled himself in. Then he stopped. Maybe it was better if he didn't see them. Then he could pretend that he didn't know they were there. He could allow an EVA and be ready for them. He could send Aelita and

Vladimir out, but not let them come back in. Or maybe he could go out himself. That was it! He would beat them at their own game! He was not expert at EVAs but he had certainly had some training in simulation. Besides, it would be fun to walk in space!

And then he got another idea and he smiled, and he spoke into his headset. "Houston, *Discovery*. We copy. Zakharov and Turnov will EVA. Prebreathing will begin now."

Vonberger disconnected his headset and then burst into laughter. He would have two hours to prebreathe oxygen. That would be plenty of time for him to rig up something so he could bring his gun along.

48

NO
BLOOD

THERE was no blood. The security guard was facedown on the floor in the small hallway between the inner and outer doors to the Flight Control Room. Elliot Hacker held the inner door open with his foot and he snapped his fingers once to get the flight director's attention. He pointed to the body at his feet, noticing for the first time that the gun had been removed from the guard's holster. Then he let the door close, and he headed out after Leonard Wolff.

The long, quiet hallway beyond the outer door was used primarily as an access to the Flight Control Room, and between shifts it was empty. Hacker stood perfectly still with his gun in his hand. There was an exit sign at each end of the hall, but Wolff could not have made it that far. He had to have gone through one of the doors nearby. Hacker needed more men, but there was no time to wait. He had to do it himself. The first door led to an empty office. The next door was locked. He knew it could be locked from the inside, but he went on.

JANITORIAL was written in big black letters across the outside of the next door, and Hacker suddenly knew he was in the right place. He took a deep breath and yanked the door open, jumping back quickly into firing stance. He was hit with a wall of white foam, as Leonard Wolff came flying out of the closet aiming the spray of a fire extinguisher into Hacker's face. Hacker got one shot off, but he had to turn his face away from the spray. When the sound of the spray stopped, he turned around to fire, but Wolff had thrown the extinguisher at him, and he raised his arms to block it. The full weight of the fire extinguisher knocked him to the floor, and by the time he got up, Wolff was headed down the hall. Hacker fired once, but Wolff disappeared through the exit, leaving a trail of blood. Elliot Hacker cursed and ran after him.

The door opened into a stairwell, and Hacker heard Wolff's steps above him. The Mission Control Center was only three stories, and so he knew Wolff could not go far. He took the steps, two at a time, and followed Wolff past the door to the third floor and up onto the roof.

The air was hot and Hacker squinted in the blinding sun. Wolff was running toward the edge of the building, his dark trousers outlined clearly against the white pebbled roof. There was no escape up here. Hacker walked slowly, following Wolff to the edge of the building. When Wolff reached the end he looked back at Hacker and then looked down, as if preparing to jump. Hacker planted his feet firmly and squatted into shooting position. "Don't move, Wolff!" he yelled across the roof.

Wolff was facing out, away from the building. Suddenly he began to turn, and Hacker saw the dark blur of the gun, and knew there was nothing left to do. He squeezed the trigger.

The first shot hit Wolff in the shoulder and spun him around so he was facing in. The second shot knocked him clear off the roof. Hacker ran to the side of the building, and looked down over the edge. Wolff was on the grass, slowly crawling away.

Elliot Hacker lit a cigarette, only vaguely aware of the sound of an approaching helicopter. The world would go on. People would live and die. Hacker knew he had to focus on the big picture, but right now, all he could see was a man shot full of holes, dragging his shattered body across the lawn.

49

A NEW
NUMBER
ONE

AELITA Zakharov floated gently in *Discovery*'s mid-deck with her hands cuffed behind her back and a helmet on her head. For some reason, she thought not of Cowboy, but of Mikhail. She remembered his strength and his warmth. He was gone now, and somehow that made it easier to think of him. She could remember how she had loved him and cherished him, and she remembered the day she was told that he had been killed. She remembered how often he came to her in her dreams. She remembered the picture she kept by her bed. He was gone now, and he was no longer her number one. It did not mean she had never loved him. It just meant that he was gone.

It was harder to think of Cowboy. He had opened his eyes once for about ten minutes, and even though he had not said a word, Aelita knew it was a good sign. Still, she could not look at him now. He floated mummylike inside his sleeping sack, his skin as white as the cabin walls. His face seemed to be set in stone, with his mouth partially opened and his bleached eyelids now shut tight.

Vonberger had let her and Turnov out of the airlock and had told her she would be doing an EVA with him to fix an electrical problem with the latches on the cargo bay doors. There was some reason for hope. Vonberger would not be concerned with fixing the cargo bay door latches unless he was planning to deorbit. Maybe Houston had given in to his demands, or maybe he was giving up. But why was Vonberger going on the EVA himself? Why not send her with Turnov? And why had Vonberger fired those OMS burns? There were still too many unanswered questions, and there was still Joey Wells, strapped into his sleeping sack and fighting for his life.

When the prebreathe was complete, Vonberger removed her handcuffs and made her suit up first. She donned the suit quickly, and just before slipping into the airlock, she took one last look at Joey Wells. As if he knew he was being watched, Wells opened his eyes. His glassy and painful look was almost too much to bear, and then he closed his left eye once in a wink, before both of his eyes closed.

Aelita waited for Vonberger in the airlock. He did not allow her to wear a communications cap, obviously afraid of letting her talk directly to Houston. It was dangerous to do an EVA without communication ability. She and Vonberger would have to use hand signals to communicate with each other. But what if she had to communicate with Houston in order to fix the latches? And what if something went wrong out there? What if there was an emergency?

Vonberger came into the airlock with his gun, and she watched him carefully, his face and neck drenched with sweat, as he attached the gun onto the sleeve of his spacesuit with a strap of restraining tether. The muzzle of the gun pointed slightly away from the arm, and a wire was attached to the trigger. He took hold of the sleeve of the spacesuit and aimed the gun at Aelita and laughed. All he had to do was pull the handle at the end of the wire. Aelita Zakharov knew he needed this kind of device because he would not be able to get the fingers of his gloves into the trigger mechanism of the gun. It was a clever solution, except that he would need both hands to shoot.

Vonberger let the sleeve go and pulled himself up into the torso section. Then he aimed the gun at Zakharov again, this time the trigger wire taut, and ordered her to make the suit connections and lock the midriff ring. When his helmet and gloves were in place, he closed the airlock hatch and began depressurization.

Aelita missed Cowboy. She wondered if she would ever see his smile or hear his laugh again. She wondered if she would ever hear another one of his "Cowboyisms." If Vonberger let them deorbit, then they could get Joey to a doctor and maybe he would be all right. It was only a few hours away now. But how could she be sure that Vonberger would allow them to land? And suddenly she knew it was all up to her. She had not given up Mikhail only to lose someone new. Losing one love was enough for a lifetime.

When the airlock was depressurized, Vonberger and Zakharov reversed their positions, and Vonberger opened the hatch to the cargo bay. He waved Aelita out first, and as she pulled herself through the hatch and moved into the cargo bay, she thought of Joey, and everything they could have. She was the Aelita from Mars, and he was the man from Earth. She wasn't going to lose another love. There was nothing she could have done about Mikhail, but there was something she could do, now, for Cowboy.

50

THE
FINAL
CALM

A ROCKET was shot up into the sky. It lifted over the rivers and the mountains and soared beyond the clouds. It flew over the oceans and jungles, penetrating deeper and deeper into space, until it escaped all bounds of place and time. Somewhere below, the cows were grazing in the hills and sleeping on the muddy banks of the rivers. Somewhere below, the birds were soaring in the wind. There were no computers. There were no machines and no bombs. The human race had killed itself off, or perhaps was still a thing of the future. Dinosaurs were roaming the plains. Russell Madlinger's mind was like the rocket, soaring out into space, and then slowly losing momentum and falling back to earth. Sleep pulled at him like gravity, but it curved away as he fell. He was in orbit, alone in the universe.

Madlinger opened his eyes and checked the time on his chest display. He had heard Vonberger's communications with Houston, and he knew that Turnov and Zakharov would be egressing from the airlock in less than five minutes. This was the preferred scenario. Madlinger would simply hand the weapons to the two Russians, and they could use them to subdue Vonberger once they got back inside the orbiter. It was less risky than a shootout with Vonberger in space, and Madlinger knew it had a better chance of success, but he could not help feeling deprived.

Russell Madlinger knew in his heart that Alex Vonberger had to die, and he had no doubt that, given the opportunity, he would kill the man who had brought evil into space. And yet, the unanswered questions still lingered in his mind. Who was Russell Madlinger to take another man's life? Who was he to decide who got to live and who got to die? Madlinger knew that only by looking into Vonberger's eyes and seeing the evil for himself could he confront the lingering doubts once and for all. He trusted himself to do the right thing, and so his own actions would be the final test of his morality. Now, he would never get that chance, but he knew it was the success of RM-105 and the safe return of *Discovery* that were important.

It was time to move. Madlinger reached down and checked his weapons, and then, using the MMU controls, he did a roll maneuver and adjusted his pitch. Then he pushed forward on the translational control, moving slowly away from *Discovery*'s belly, and up around the starboard side of the crew compartment. As he had done before, he carefully kept himself in line between the forward windows and the cargo bay, so as not to be seen. He stopped before he reached the overhead windows and checked his position. His boots seemed precariously close to the forward windows, but he knew he was in the right position. He eased his head slowly past the edge of the crew module, and looked into the cargo bay. He could have been a barbarian approaching the castle of a hated king. He could have been a caveman, peering over a rock into the enemy's cave.

The blue earth with its rivers and mountains loomed behind him, but he could not look at it now. He watched as Aelita Zakharov came into view, her suit marked with red rings around the arms and legs. She attached her tether and moved along the bulkhead wall toward the starboard longeron. She was agile and quick, and she reached the wall before Turnov had made it out of the airlock.

Madlinger watched as she turned and spotted him hovering over the crew compartment, and he waved gently and smiled to himself. Zakharov waved frantically, as if trying to communicate something, and Madlinger worried that her actions might draw Vonberger's attention. He lifted a finger and put it to the front of his helmet, as a signal to be quiet and still, but Aelita Zakharov had slipped her feet into a foothold and was waving Madlinger back with both hands. Why was she being so obvious?

Suddenly she stopped, and Madlinger looked down to see Vladimir Turnov coming through the hatch. Turnov seemed clumsy as he struggled with his tether belt, and when, at last, he was tethered, he began moving along the wall toward Zakharov. Madlinger reached over the edge of the crew compartment, and pulled himself along the bulkhead wall into the cargo bay, his head coming down near Turnov's. He pulled the gun from his MMU and held it out, and as Turnov grabbed it out of his hand, Madlinger suddenly saw the other gun, attached to Turnov's sleeve. Why did Turnov have a gun? Suddenly, Madlinger looked through the glass of Turnov's helmet, and realized that he was face to face with Alex Vonberger.

Madlinger had already given away his gun. He pulled back on the MMU controls, to try to get away, but he slammed into the bulkhead wall. Vonberger raised Madlinger's gun to fire, his gloved fingers easily slipping into the trigger mechanism. There was no time to get away. Madlinger pulled out his knife and adjusted his controls, but he was already looking into the barrel of his own gun. Suddenly, Zakharov moved in and yanked at Vonberger's tether, pulling him away from the bulkhead wall. Vonberger crashed into the cargo bay floor and Madlinger's gun flew from his hand.

Zahkarov wasted no time. She threw herself at Vonberger

and grabbed his wrists, but Vonberger was too big for her. He twisted loose and kicked her, sending her out of the cargo bay, held back by only her tether. Madlinger adjusted the controls of the MMU and descended upon Vonberger, with the knife in his hands. Vonberger did not have time to aim his gun, but he grabbed the handle of the knife and tried to turn it toward Madlinger. They struggled with the knife, slowly drifting away from the cargo bay floor. The knife came down between their bodies, and Madlinger felt it slowly twist toward Vonberger's chest. Suddenly Vonberger reached out and slammed the controls of the MMU, flipping Madlinger into a spin inside the cargo bay. Madlinger held on to the knife and felt Vonberger's hands slip away.

Madlinger worked the controls of the MMU, trying to pull out of the spin, but he tumbled into the port wall of the cargo bay. By the time he straightened himself out, Vonberger had scaled the starboard longeron, and was trying to lock his boots into a foothold near the top of the wall. Aelita Zakharov was working her way back into the cargo bay, pulling herself in by her own tether. Vonberger got his feet locked into position and he raised his left arm and aimed the gun at Madlinger. Then he reached out with his free hand and grabbed for the wire handle.

Madlinger knew he was out of time. There was only one thing left to do. Maybe another man would do it differently. Maybe someone, somewhere, had all the answers. But right now it was Russell Madlinger with the knife in his hands, and the chance to set Alex Vonberger free. Madlinger readjusted his pitch and slammed down on the translational control, propelling himself up out of the cargo bay. He held the knife firmly in his hands, and as he sped past Vonberger's tether, his thoughts were not of the consequences of his actions, but of his wife and his children, and the children of the world.

Madlinger felt the resistance of the tether as it pulled tight around the knife, and then suddenly it snapped and gave way. He did not hear the gunshot, but he felt the vibration when the bullet slammed into the side of the MMU. The force of the bullet sent him into another spin, moving slowly out into space. Madlinger calmly readjusted the controls and steadied himself. Then he looked for Alex Vonberger.

The recoil of the gun had sent Vonberger over the edge of the cargo bay, and he was spinning wildly as he moved over *Discovery*'s wing, and out into space. He tried firing again, to move himself back toward *Discovery*, but he was spinning too fast to get off an accurate shot. He changed directions several times as he fired, but the last shot left him spinning head over heels out into the vastness of space.

Aelita Zakharov had made it back into the cargo bay, and she waved to Madlinger triumphantly. Madlinger slipped the knife back into the sheath on the side of his MMU and waved back. He looked out at the earth and suddenly felt the burden of his task slip away. There would always be men like Alex Vonberger and Leonard Wolff. Mankind was not perfect. But space was timelessly forgiving, and even the endless evil of the world could never ruin its beauty. Madlinger listened to the infinite quiet, and for the second time in his life, he felt the calm chill of space.

EPILOGUE

JOEY Wells was transferred to an extra-large room to accommodate the impending crowd, and the whole wing of the hospital had been secured for the President's arrival. Russell and Cathy Madlinger joined the PF Flyers around Joey's bed, as they waited for the President. Everyone but Joey Wells had met the President at the White House the week before, but Joey asked them all to be with him at the hospital in Houston when the President came to visit.

The President had been at the Cape to watch the two orbiters come in. *Discovery* had landed first, two hours earlier than OV-105, to allow for the immediate evacuation of the crew, particularly Joey Wells and George Evans, to the medical complex. *Discovery* was quickly moved off the Shuttle Landing Facility to make room for OV-105. By now the wraps had been taken off the rescue mission and a general announcement made about what had happened to PF-1, so the two perfect landings were observed with enthusiastic cheers by a huge crowd of spectators and press people.

And yet, despite the glorious success of the rescue mission, it had not been a time of celebration for the crew members. They were deeply worried about Joey Wells and George Evans, who had been carried off *Discovery* on stretchers, both in serious condition. The rest of the crewmembers of both orbiters were immediately quarantined and spent the next two days in intensive debriefing on their ordeal. After that, the two crews—minus Joey Wells and George Evans—conducted a series of extensive press briefings on the entire experience. And so, a few weeks later, it seemed appropriate for the President to invite the crewmembers to a private lunch at the White House and a public ceremony in the Rose Garden to give them the hero's welcome they deserved.

The rescue mission had been a success and the lives of the astronauts and cosmonauts had been saved. The President chose the occasion to announce that the Peace Flight Program would continue and he reaffirmed his commitment to the exploration of space. It was, he had said, ironic that the near-tragic events of the first Peace Flight served to dramatically underscore the need to combine the best and most positive attributes of mankind in the efforts to explore our next and Greatest Frontier.

As Madlinger recalled the profound feelings they had all felt at the White House the week before, he was especially touched by the President's decision to come to Houston to visit Joey Wells in the hospital. Joey deserved, perhaps as much as anyone, to feel a part of that hero's welcome. He had put his life on the line, as they all had, but had come closer than any of them to losing it.

Joey looked good for the occasion. He still had the bandage wrapped around his head, but the color had returned to his skin and his eyes were bright. Most of all, Madlinger noticed, Joey's sense of humor had been revived, and he was tossing it around the room like a volleyball.

"So my first thought when I came to was 'How come I'm stuck to this bed?' " Joey was saying. "See, and I sort of wiggled around a little, you know, like you do up there in orbit, and, for the life of me, I couldn't figure out why I wasn't going anywhere. And then suddenly it dawned on me that I wasn't in the orbiter, and I wasn't weightless anymore!''

"I'll bet it felt like you weighed a thousand pounds," Conrad Williams said, laughing. "The rest of us had the reentry to get a little used to the weight again, but since your lights were out, you went straight from zero-G to one-G."

"Yeah, I saw the nurse and I said, 'Who turned on the gravity?' "

His visitors all chuckled at Joey's description of his initial confusion, feeling very happy that he was finally able to wake up at all.

"We were worried about you, Cowboy," George Evans said. He sat smiling by the bed. His entire left arm was in a cast and the cast was strapped to his chest.

"Worried about *me*? Look at you, George! You're the one with half your body in a cast!"

"A shot in the shoulder isn't too bad," Evans said. "Besides, you were unconscious for a week!"

"Well, I'm lucky I got a thick skull," Joey continued in his Texas drawl. "The doctors say the bullet missed a critical part of my brain by about an eighth of an inch. Can you believe it? If my brain had been this much bigger, I would've been dead." He laughed. "But I'll tell you one thing, I'd take a bullet in the head any day to having to put up with what you all had to go through with all the press!"

Madlinger interruped. "But I heard that you didn't really get off scot-free from the press. Didn't someone get hold of your room number here and give you a call?"

"Oh, yeah, could you believe that!" Joey rolled his eyes. "I'm lying here eating through tubes and full of needles and this guy calls my room and wants to know if there was any truth to the rumor that me and Ms. Zakharov over here had become romantically involved."

Aelita sat on the bed, gently holding Joey's hand. "They asked me too," she said. "I felt a little like a Hollywood movie star, being asked such personal questions."

"What did you tell them?" Turnov asked.

Joey lowered his voice to mimic a spokesman's tone. "We said that we had no comment to make to the press at this time other than that we were just good friends."

A short silence hung in the room, as if they were all waiting for the punch line. Madlinger watched Aelita's face turn a slight shade of red, and he saw a quick look of confusion pass through Joey's eyes, as he looked at Aelita and then scanned the faces in the room.

"Hell, didn't she tell you?" Joey finally blurted out. "We're getting married!"

The room suddenly broke into pandemonium, everyone clapping and screaming. Aelita leaned over the bed to hug Joey, and both of them seemed to be floating in their happiness, as the PF Flyers surrounded them to offer their congratulations. Amid the sudden confusion and celebration, Russell Madlinger felt Cathy's hand slip into his, and suddenly he understood that the weightless bliss that came in space did have its earthly equivalent. Madlinger felt lifted by the joy and he congratulated Joey and hugged his wife.

There would always be unanswered questions. Questions about good and evil, about life and death. In space the calm chill was bigger than man and bigger than life. But on earth there was love and warmth, and humans could celebrate and laugh and fall in love. Maybe love was like gravity, holding everything together. Maybe it was love that kept everyone from floating away. Maybe Joey and Aelita, falling in love in space, demonstrated more of the promise of space for mankind than anything else that had been accomplished up there so far. Madlinger squeezed Cathy's hand, feeling almost weightless and unbelievably alive.

With all of the noise and excitement, nobody saw Senator Ryan slip in through the door, and when things finally started to calm down, Turnov was the first to notice him. "Cowboy and Aelita are getting married!" Turnov said.

Senator Ryan broke into an enthusiastic smile. "Well,

congratulations to both of you! I have an announcement to make, too.''

The room fell quiet, but the senator kept his smile. ''The President and the Soviet Premier have agreed on the new head of the Joint Soviet-American Task Force on Space Exploration.''

''Well,'' Madlinger prompted, ''who is it?''

Senator Ryan's smile broadened, and then he pushed the door open behind him and stepped out of the way. It looked like a man, but nobody could see behind the big bouquet of flowers held in front of his head. Then slowly the flowers dropped and Andrei Kulikov stood laughing outside the door.

''It is true,'' Kulikov said, coming into the room. ''Agreed upon by the Premier and the President this morning. It looks like I'll be working with NASA for a long time.''

''Cool Enough, Kulikov!'' Joey shouted from his bed. ''Does this mean you're going to learn to play softball, Andrei?''

''No,'' Kulikov came back quickly. ''But next year I am going to win the chili cook-off!''

The room exploded with laughter.

As the laughter subsided, they heard some commotion out in the hall; the sounds of shuffling and pushing, the clicking of heels, and the murmur of authoritative voices. There was no doubt about it. The President had arrived.

The room fell quiet and Senator Ryan and Kulikov moved away from the door. The President and his Chief of Staff came into the room. He looked around the room at the beaming faces, and then he found Joey Wells and he broke into a gigantic grin.

''This is truly an honor for me,'' the President said, approaching the bed. ''You're a brave man, Joey, and your country appreciates men like you. I'm sorry you couldn't be with us in the White House last week. As I told your colleagues who were there, you are all a very large part of the reason I am proud to be a strong supporter of the most exciting venture mankind has ever embarked upon. I wanted to come here and tell you that personally.''

The President talked for a few minutes about courage and bravery and about the expertise and professionalism of NASA, and the unbelievable benefits that come from the space program that improve the lives of everyone on this planet. Then he took a medal from his Chief of Staff.

"I could have just sent you this, after I awarded them to your entire crew last week, but I pinned theirs on, and I wanted to pin yours on, too," the President said, leaning over and attaching the medal neatly to Joey's hospital gown. He stood back and saluted a very embarrassed and obviously very touched Joey Wells.

"Thank you for everything, Joey. I hope you feel as proud of yourself as your country does. Get well soon and get back up there! Good luck to you."

The President turned to go, but Joey Wells stopped him. "Mr. President? Mr. President, Aelita and I would like to know if we can count on you to come to our wedding."

The President beamed. "So, there *was* some truth to what I'd heard about you taking some personal steps to improve relations between our two space programs! Congratulations!" he said, and shook Joey's hand and gave Aelita a hug.

"Believe me, if I can get there, I will, and maybe I can get the Soviet Premier to come along, too," he said. "But I'll tell you what you ought to do. You ought to go back up there and get married in space! *That's* where you ought to be. *That's* where we *all* ought to be, because *that's* where our future is!"